Passion

Passion

P. F. KOZAK

APHRODISIA

APHRODISIA
KENSINGTON BOOKS
http://www.kensingtonbooks.com

KENSINGTON BOOKS are published by

Kensington Publishing Corp.
850 Third Avenue
New York, NY 10022

All Kensington Titles, Imprints, and Distributed Lines are available at special quantity discounts for bulk purchases for sales promotions, premiums, fund-raising, and educational or institutional use.

Special book excerpts or customized printings can also be created to fit specific needs. For details, write or phone the office of the Kensington special sales manager: Kensington Publishing Corp., 850 Third Avenue, New York, NY, 10022, attn: Special Sales Department, Phone: 1-800-221-2647.

ISBN 0-7582-1417-0

First Kensington Trade Paperback Printing: May 2006

10 9 8 7 6 5 4 3 2 1

Printed in the United States of America

For Ivan

Don't presume the satiation of the feeling is the goal.
Think of the passion as an end in itself.
Savor it and enjoy it.
Think of it as balancing on the edge of a cliff without falling over the side.
Stay on the crest of the arousal without pursuing its climax.
Be in it.
Immerse yourself in the fire.
Then be the phoenix and rise from the ashes.

Acknowledgments

I would like to thank my husband, my friends and my family who believe in me and support my writing. In particular, I want to thank MCL, DR and IK for love above and beyond. And to our extended family, a heartfelt *a la famiglia. Ti amo!*

Chapter One

A poem called "The Highwayman" made me cry. That's why I started to write. In the poem, the Highwayman and the innkeeper's daughter, Bess, die trying to save each other. The thought of them being separated upset me so much, I changed the story.

In my version, the Highwayman would kidnap me and gallop away on his black stallion, taking me to his hideaway. Or maybe he would stay at the inn and lure me to his room. Once, I found him wounded. In order to care for him, I hid him in a secret room at the inn.

I started to write down my stories so I wouldn't forget them. I recently unearthed several stories about my Highwayman in a box of old papers. For well over a month now, I have fallen asleep, thinking of him, my Highwayman.

Just last night, I stayed awake until after three in the morning, the story I had woven feeling more real than my life. Even though some of the details changed from night to night, the core story remained the same.

I looked up as the door opened. A large man stood there, tall, muscular and powerfully built. His thick beard framed a rigid jaw. He wore a heavy black coat, made of coarse wool. Both it and the cape he had on over it smelled like wet horse hair, being damp from the melted snow. The cape barely hid the hilt of a sword.

He looked directly at me, with an intense, penetrating stare. He seemed so big and so totally unaware of how fiercely intimidating he looked. His swagger and his comfort with his size sent a shiver down my arms. Even though he frightened me, I still felt drawn to him.

I raised the bottle I had in my hand and beckoned to an empty table in a secluded corner. He took the bottle I offered to him in one hand and my arm in the other. He pulled me toward a table, drinking as he walked. I knew the bottle would relieve the chill in his bones from the cold.

I started to undo his cape, but he pushed me away. Untying it himself, it fell to the floor. He removed his sword and then his coat, being careful to position his sword within easy reach.

He sat with his back to the wall, staring both at me and over me. I watched his eyes, sensing his tension as he surveyed the room for possible threats. It was not uncommon for two men to lay claim to the same woman. He positioned himself to watch for anyone who would challenge his right to me. No one did.

We drank together for a time. He pushed the bottle at me and I drank from it as he did. He kept staring at me with those eyes. I could not look away. He asked, "Do you belong to a man?"

I answered him, "No, not until you walked in."

He touched me. I did not pull away. His hands were large and very strong. He put his hand behind my neck and pulled me to him with a squeeze of his hand. I did not know if he intended to love me or to kill me—and I did not care. I felt his fingers on my neck. It made me feel lost in his power. He nuzzled my long, red hair. He sniffed at me, smelling both my skin and my hair.

I could feel how he wanted the pleasure only a woman could give him. Keeping his hand on my neck, he drank again. I felt his fingers sliding up into my hair and felt the ends pull as he closed his fist. I did not flinch. He looked at me as if not understanding why I did not push him away. I asked, "How long since you've had a woman?"

He answered, "Long enough."

He pulled his sword out of his waistband and threw it on top of his cape. Then he did the same with his belt. After taking another long drink from the bottle, he threw his coat in the corner along the wall.

Grabbing my arm, he yanked me down on top of his coat. He put both hands on my ankles and shoved my long skirt up by moving his hands up my legs. Then he knelt to open his breeches. I started to pull down my loose-fitting pantaloons to ready myself for him. He had just exposed himself when he saw me reaching under my skirt. He grabbed my hand and stopped me. He said, "What are you doing?"

"Baring myself for you," I replied angrily. I tried to free myself from his grip, but could not loosen his hold. He shoved my hand away and pulled off my pantaloons. Before dropping them, he crumbled the garment in his hands, to make sure I had not hidden a blade in them. Pushing my legs farther apart, he lowered himself on top of me. He entered me with one long stroke and I met him with an upward push.

I put my arms around his back and ground myself against him, pushing the length of him as deeply into myself as I could. I hissed, "Fuck!" at him, wanting him to move inside of me. He looked startled and then a sound came from him as if someone had knifed him in the back.

He pounded me with his body, his thick organ stretching me almost beyond endurance. Still I met him head on, stroke for stroke, with the heart of a lion. I slammed against him with each powerful thrust.

Suddenly his body went rigid. He nearly pulled out of me, then drove himself back into me, pinning me to the floor. Unable to move underneath him, I held him as he spurted inside of me. The growl started in his belly and moved into my ears.

The sound I heard had come from my own voice as my orgasm shook my body. I hugged my damp pillow to myself. In my mind I held him as tightly as I could, wanting to pull him inside me, my Highwayman.

The vividness of that fantasy distressed me. It had seemed so real, I had totally lost myself in it. The morning after, I realized I had been alone too bloody long. It frightened me to think I could lose myself so completely inside my imagination. I needed a serious reality check, or perhaps I needed to check in with reality.

Both my schedule and my budget allowed me the freedom to get out of my imagination and have some jollies, something fun to shake up my isolated routine. So I decided my lifelong fascination with horses would finally become real. I would take riding lessons.

I knew my friend Gwen dated a fellow who owned a local stable. She claimed he had the best stud service around Shaftesbury, perhaps even in the whole of Dorset. When she told me that, I laughed. Of course, I had to ask if she knew that firsthand. She smiled and simply said he was the dog's bollocks. The color in her cheeks told me she probably did know his stud service firsthand.

I really needed to do something immediately to convince myself I still had a grip on reality. I rang up Gwen to find out if I might be able to get riding lessons there. She told me that if I wanted to learn about horses, her friend Steve could help me. Horses had been in his family for generations. She said she would speak to Steve to make sure he did right by me. So I gave Gwen a little time to ring him before I did.

When I spoke to Steve I told him I wanted to learn how to ride but hadn't really been around horses. Growing up in London I never had the opportunity to learn. I wanted someone who could teach me to ride and also teach me about horses. I asked him for an instructor who had patience and a lot of "horse sense," one who didn't mind answering silly questions from a novice. Steve told me he had the right teacher for me and that I could sign up for lessons that afternoon.

My stomach had butterflies as I drove to the stable. I met Steve at his house and took care of the paperwork. He agreed to let me pay lesson by lesson until I knew for sure that I wanted to continue. Then he asked me when I wanted to start. I told him right away, if possible. I had made up my mind to do this, and dash it all, I would do it now!

Steve took me into the stable to meet my new teacher. When I saw him, I almost forgot why I came. As I watched, he lifted a bale of hay and carried it into an empty stall. He took a knife out of his pocket to cut the twine and then spread the hay around the floor. I knew he had to be more than six feet tall, with long, dark hair pulled back into a ponytail. He had a mustache that curved in a thin line around his mouth, filling out into a goatee at his chin. When he bent over to cut the twine, I saw the tightest bum and the longest legs in recent memory.

Somewhere behind me I heard Steve yell in his direction, "Hey, Ivan. Come over here. I have a new student for you." I noted his pronunciation, i-VAHN, with the second syllable accented. I thought his name suited him. Ivan turned around, obviously startled that we had come in. He regained his composure easily. His T-shirt, damp with sweat and covered with straw, stuck to him. Some delicious tingles fluttered inside me as he came out of the stall, brushing bits of hay from his chest as he walked.

Pulling off a crusty glove, he shook my hand and said, "So you want to learn how to ride? We'll have to see what we can do about that." My attraction to him was undeniable and I felt myself blush.

My summer job in a stable takes me as far away from a classroom as I can get. Even though I love teaching, I need a break from academia. When my eyes start to feel like piss holes in the snow while grading spring finals, I know I have to come up for air or burn out real damn fast.

My best friend inherited his father's horse farm near Shaftesbury. Every summer I travel from Northamptonshire, where I live and teach, to stay at the farm and work. All I take is room and board. I grew up working there. Going back feels like going home.

Even though Steve's father hired me as a horse groom, Steve never treated me like hired help. Since neither of us had siblings, we grew up like brothers. His father taught us how to ride together. We got hammered on ale Steve pilfered from his father's stash. And, of course, we shared learning about women.

Steve assumed I would stay on at the farm and help him run it. But I decided to go to university on scholarship instead. Once my parents passed, Steve's family was the only family I had to invite when I graduated. They all came, too. By the time I got my doctorate, only Steve came. His father had died and his mum had moved to London. That left Steve to run the farm alone.

After becoming a professor, I bought myself a house and some property near Thrapston, Kettering. My colleagues thought me daft for buying a house so far from Northampton, but I wanted a place where one day I might have a few horses of my own.

When I realized I actually had a growing bank account without the summer term, I figured, what the hell! I asked Steve if I might stay with him again over the summers. I knew he might not take to the idea, since he felt like I did him dirty not staying at the farm after we graduated. But, to my surprise, he welcomed me back.

When I arrived this summer, Steve made it clear he needed me to teach more. He hadn't yet replaced an instructor who recently left. I reluctantly agreed to take on a few students if the need arose.

When he called me over to meet my first student of the season, I rather expected so see a gangly teenager waiting. Instead, there stood a short, shapely redhead, about my age, looking very apprehensive. Steve introduced her as "Pash," a name I had never heard before. I hadn't enjoyed a female liaison in some time. I smiled to myself, thinking, *This could be an unexpected pleasure.*

Steve asked Ivan if he could spare an hour now to get me started with a few basics. Ivan hesitated. Steve took him aside and spoke to him. When they came back, Ivan smiled and said, "Of course I can jump-start you today. Let's set about it." That began what may be the most embarrassing hour of my life.

Everything started well enough. He asked me, "Have you ever ridden before?"

"Only once. I rode a pony at Battersea Park Children's Zoo in London. But I have read books and watched documentaries!" Realizing how utterly lame that sounded, I added, "I daresay I don't know too much."

Since he realized I knew absolutely naught about riding, he started from scratch. He took me around the stable, showing me a few horses. Then he opened a stall and led out a horse. "This horse, Nutmeg, has started more than a few riders on their way."

I thought she seemed awfully big for me. He patted her neck. "She's gentle as a lamb. I've put children on her and she's absolutely fine."

As I imagined myself trying to get on this monster, I started to walk around her. She snorted just as I stepped in front of her and it startled me. I jumped off to the side, thinking she was going to charge or something.

I tripped on God knows what and fell right into a big puddle filled with slimy mud and straw. Both knees sunk into the muck. I did manage to catch myself on my hands before I went completely down. Nevertheless, I made an unmitigated mess of myself.

Ivan helped me up, saying as he lifted me, "I am terribly

sorry. Before Steve came in with you, I had been cleaning the horses. I should have warned you to mind the gap." His apology barely hid his amusement.

"I've made a dog's dinner of myself!" He didn't seem to notice that he had mud all over himself from picking me up.

I assured him I had not hurt myself. With his arm still around my waist, Ivan dragged his boot through the puddle. "There is a drain here, but I think it is blocked with hay."

"You are nearly as mucked up as I am. I'm terribly sorry about that." He still held me very tightly against himself. With all the mud, we were practically sliding against each other.

"That's quite all right, I don't mind." He cleared the drain with his foot. "Now let me clean you off." He picked up the hose and turned on the water. There I stood, muddy straw all over me, with the sexiest man I had ever seen looking me over and offering to hose me down. I just wanted to disappear.

Steve caught me totally unaware when he asked if I could spare the time to start Pash's lessons right away. I wasn't prepared to be teaching a new student at that moment, even if I did find her tempting. I hadn't finished hosing the horses and cleaning their stalls, not to mention I really needed a shower.

On the pretense of asking me some inane question, Steve took me aside and said, "C'mon, guv—Pash rhymes with cash. Don't make me look bad in front of a new student!" So I agreed. I needed to find out straight away what she knew about horses, to figure out where to start. Turns out she rode a pony once upon a time. That summed up her total direct exposure.

I knew I had my work cut out for me, but reminded myself that she could be that gangly teenager coming at me with the same story. Perhaps this totty might be inclined to ride more than a horse!

To see how she responded to the animals, I walked her around the stable. She seemed a little jumpy, but I supposed that would pass soon enough. I picked Nutmeg to get her started. Nutmeg has the disposition of a kitten, quietest damn mare I've ever seen. She is on the large side, being a retired farm horse. Steve keeps her around because she is gentle and even-tempered with children.

She is a good old girl. I like to make sure she is seen earning her keep. When I took Nutmeg out of the stall, I noticed the color drain from Pash's face. I tried to reassure her. "Don't worry, my dear, Nutmeg is a sweetheart. She won't give you any grief."

Before I could finish my pep talk, Pash stepped right in front of the horse. Nutmeg must have thought Pash had a treat for her, because she raised her head, blew some air out of her nose and opened her mouth. The next thing I knew, Pash jumped a couple meters off to the side, stumbled on an uneven part of the floor and fell right on the spot where I had just hosed off a horse.

Christ, I looked down and saw the new student Steve wanted to impress kneeling in water thick with mud. That's not all I saw. She had her arse in the air, down on all fours. Bloody hell, she looked like she wanted a good seeing-to!

"Please, allow me." Bending over her to help her up, I fought the urge to join her in the mud and have it doggy fashion.

I put my arm around her to help her stand up, brushing her breasts as I did so. To prolong keeping hold of her, I asked, "Are you all right? You didn't hurt yourself, did you?"

"I'm quite all right, thank you. I just need a bath."

"Well, that's better that a slap in the face with a wet kipper," I said, trying to make her laugh. She barely managed a feeble smile.

It felt damn good having a woman against me again. I didn't want to let her go. So, I continued holding her while scraping the drain with my boot to clear it. "I should have seen to this clog earlier. It never occurred to me I would have company in here today."

Then I held her at arm's length to survey the damage. "You are a mucky pup, all right." She had mud, hay and horse hair covering her legs. Somehow I had to clean her up.

The only thing I could think to do was to hose her off, the way I did the horses. She had on jeans and sneakers, so it wouldn't hurt anything. "Now let me clean you off." I picked up the hose. "You will be wet, but at least you will be clean."

"I suppose I have to. I can't get in my car like this." Seeing as how she didn't have much choice, she agreed.

"This won't hurt a bit, I promise." Turning the hose to a gentler spray than I used for the horses, I washed her off. Straight away, I got myself a hard-on. When she fell, her tight jeans gave her a camel's hoof, clearly outlining her privy parts. I made sure I hosed her thoroughly. "Spread your feet apart so I can clean your legs properly." What better way to get a good long look at her bits!

I finished my lesson soaking wet from the waist down. How absolutely humiliating! After Ivan hosed the mud off me, he turned the hose on himself to wash off his own legs. I couldn't help noticing he had quite a package, which seemed to have grown since I arrived. When he brushed some hay from my shirt, his hand grazed my breasts. My nipples turned into pebbles.

Once he made sure he had properly cleaned me up, Ivan wanted me to get right on Nutmeg, saying, "It is best to get comfortable mounting during the first lesson."

My nerve completely left me. "Couldn't we wait for a bit? I've never been around horses before and would like to get used to them first." It's the only excuse I could think of for not mounting as he asked.

Ivan seemed a little perplexed. He took a quick look around the stable before he said, "All right, then, let's go over the gear first." I made a halfhearted attempt to listen when he explained the parts of a saddle as he put it on Nutmeg's back.

"Always from the left side," he said. "Our horses are trained to be handled from the left."

Then he showed me how to bridle a horse. I cringed when he put the bit in Nutmeg's mouth, wondering how the horse could stand that chunk of metal across its tongue. "This is an eggbutt snaffle. It doesn't hurt her at all." I didn't believe it!

After he had Nutmeg ready, he demonstrated the proper way to mount a horse by climbing on her himself. "See how easy it is! There's nothing to it." He looked magnificent sitting on that big horse, like I had always imagined my Highwayman would look.

I could see the outline of his thigh through his wet jeans. My eyes followed his leg up to his crotch. Realizing how utterly unseemly staring at his bulge would appear, I made myself look away.

He dismounted and again encouraged me to try it. "Why don't you give it a go? I'll help you up."

I politely declined. "No, thank you. I think I've had enough for one day."

"Well, next time we'll practice mounting."

I wondered why in heaven's name I had wanted to do this in the first place.

Chapter Two

After the debacle of my first lesson, I nearly decided to abandon this horse insanity and cancel my lessons. I humbly realized I might have romanticized the whole riding business. The reality seemed to fall far short of what I imagined. But I could not stop thinking about Ivan, about how he moved hefting that hay into the stall or how he looked sitting on Nutmeg or how patient he had been with my pratfall.

Then, a few days before my next appointment, something happened that guaranteed I would not change my mind. I dreamed about Ivan, an erotic dream—a real humdinger, too. I decided to return for the second lesson only because I wanted to see him again. I really didn't think I had it in me to learn to ride, but because I knew no other way to see him, I thought I would try.

In the dream, I came into the stable like I did the first day. Ivan had his shirt off as he lifted bales of hay. I watched him take the hay into an empty stall, marveling at the exquisite masculine beauty of his body. The sweat made his skin shine, the muscles in his arms and back bulging with the weight of the bales.

I had the impulse to touch myself while I watched him, but he turned around before I could stroke myself. When he saw me, he simply said, "It's time to start your lesson." He didn't leave the empty stall, but motioned for me to join him there.

Walking into the stall, I tripped. I fell into the mud, except this time I fell on my arse instead of my knees. He picked up the hose and sprayed me, the water pulsing between my legs. As the water sprayed harder and harder, my knees became weak. He caught me, pressing his chest up against my breasts as he held me. Suddenly I felt very confused. I couldn't remember why I had come there or why I felt so aroused. I asked him, "I don't know you. Are you my Highwayman?"

"You don't need your Highwayman anymore. You have me."

"Who are you?" I felt afraid. The fear only seemed to feed my arousal. My need to touch him threatened to consume me.

"I am your teacher. I will show you what you came here to learn." He took a blanket and spread it over some hay in the empty stall. He said, "Come, lay beside me." I went to him and lay down on the blanket beside him.

He opened his jeans. Taking hold of my hand, he said, "You want to touch me, I know you do. You want to touch me like this." He slid my hand up and down his erection. "Oh, yes, touch me just like that. It's fucking good."

I could feel the heat of his breath on my neck as he nuzzled me. He lifted my shirt and fondled my breasts as he pushed himself into my hand. Then he wedged his hard leg between my thighs. The slight rocking motion of his body as he moved in my hand sent ripples of pleasure into me.

I laid my head on his chest so I could hear his heartbeat. He smelled like hay and sweat. "Please, I need to come." I moaned the words into his chest as I pressed harder against his leg. He held me as I rubbed against him. I closed my eyes and lost myself in the sensation.

I still had my hand on him, stroking him as he had shown me. "I'm close, rub harder." I wanked him harder. He started to spasm, spilling himself into my hand. His cum burned my palm. Before I could tell him that, he dipped his fingers into his scalding semen and rubbed it on my nipples. My breasts ignited with heat, which set my body on fire.

He held me as I pressed myself against his leg with increasing force. "Ivan . . ." I felt my body tense as waves of sensation moved through me. My skin tingled like a thousand fireflies had nested on me. I bolted awake with the feeling of him all through me, breathless from my own climax.

I couldn't get back to sleep after that. The heat would not go away. After rubbing off again thinking about him, I picked up my journal to write about him.

I told Steve about Pash's mishap, since I thought perhaps after her first lesson, she might not come back. I actually expected that to be the case. He had a good laugh and shrugged it off with an easy-come, easy-go attitude. I asked my old friend if he knew if she was married. He grinned and said, "Why? You interested or something?"

"I might be."

"I thought the redhead might be fuckable, but I'm surprised you're on the pull. I thought you like 'em younger."

I flipped him the bird. "Sod off, mate. Just tell me what you know."

"Gwen rang this morning to tell me her friend Pash wanted lessons and asked me to help out with it. I told her to pop out today and I'd show her around." That explained the unexpected student. Steve always jumps at the chance to sign on someone new.

"While she filled out the registration form, we had a little chat. I found out straight away that she wasn't married, just in case things don't work out with Gwenny."

I ignored that crack, wanting to get more information out of him. "Do you know what she does for a living?"

"I'm not sure exactly. I think she writes or something."

"Writes what?"

"Books, you twit! What do you think?"

Not wanting to let him have the last word, I gave him something to think about. "Thanks, old man. And I must say, Gwen would probably be quite interested to know you are considering hitting on her friend." I patted him on the back and went back to the stable.

Steve getting on my case about sleeping with younger women had been going on for some time. He had told me more than once to get my finger out of my arse and grow up. I couldn't seem to stop, even though bedding the hormonal bits of fluff I taught had actually become damned tiresome.

This new lady pumped my nads. I figured I would wait and see if she came back for lesson number two. If she didn't show, I would call her. My attraction to her surprised me. But I couldn't deny it. My cock wouldn't let me deny it.

Her tumble in the mud gave me an eyeful. The wedgie from her jeans clearly opened her. Hosing her down made her jeans cling to her labia even more, not to mention the peanuts she smuggled under her shirt when I brushed her tits. That whole bit of business made a deposit in my wank bank. Every time I thought of it, my cock stirred.

For a few days I tried to push the picture out of my head. What a wasted effort! The more I tried not to think about her, the stiffer I got. Finally I gave in to my blue balls. I had stashed a few porn mags under my mattress. Every now and again I had the urge to have one off the wrist. The ladies in my mags kept me company.

Since those ladies were the only ones available to shag, I retrieved my stash and had a look. Leafing through them, I found one with red hair. She seemed a fine bird to help me take care of business.

Skimming off my clothes, I retrieved a tube of lubricant I kept in my bedside table. Tossing it on the bed, I settled in with the magazine. The redhead's tits caught my eye first. Her nipples looked like someone had just licked them, shiny and moist.

Running my finger down the page, I thought of Pash. Her tits probably looked like this. My arm pressed against her bubbies when I helped her to stand up. She had a nice set, not too big, but firm and full. Christ, how much I wanted to squeeze them and pinch those ripe nipples.

My eyes drifted farther down the page. I saw Pash there, naked and open. She had red hair covering her snatch. I knew she would. Her legs were spread wide, waiting for me. Squirting a dollop of lube on my hands, I slicked myself up. A drop of pre-cum dripped off my tip and ran down my groin. She had me going, all right. This was what I needed, to really sink myself into her.

Wanting my hand to feel like her pussy, I started to bang one out. A good ride with me would make her so wet. Oh, yeah, I wanted to do her. Pulling down those wet jeans and spreading her legs, burying my cock in her. Fuck, yes, flat on her back under me.

I grabbed the tube and smeared on more lube. The veins on my organ bulged, purple and angry. Wet pussy, I wanted her wet pussy around me. The more I thought of riding her, the harder I pumped. She had to be hot, with all that red hair.

The heat from my organ scorched my hand. I wanted her. I needed to push myself into her. I wanted to hold back, but I couldn't. She sent this picture to me, this picture of herself waiting for me, her red bush burning for me, her legs wide open, wanting my cock inside of her.

My muscles tensed and locked, the paralysis of arousal consumed me. Her pussy gripped my granite organ as I drove myself into my own hand. Sliding in and out of her, drilling her with everything I had, my nuts boiled over. My entire body shook as I creamed.

I had to have her, but how the frigging hell could I manage it?

Ivan said I would be on a horse this time. I told myself to calm down the whole drive out to the stable. My heart pounded, mostly because I was about to see him again, but also out of fear.

I kept remembering Nutmeg and then imagining me on Nutmeg. Somehow I just couldn't bring the two images together. When I walked into the stable, there he stood, brushing that big old horse. I nearly turned around and left.

Before I could pivot on my heels and leave, he saw me. He said, "Hello!" and gave me a welcoming smile. Then he asked me, "Are you ready for your first ride?" I involuntarily shivered.

I spent the next several days waiting for the cancellation call to come in. It didn't. I must have been living right, because, much to my surprise, about five minutes before the second lesson was slated to begin, she walked into the stable.

We got right down to business. These classes were the easiest way to keep seeing Pash on a regular basis, but I had to get her comfortable on a horse or she would stop coming. I tried to get her to loosen up by having her help me saddle and bridle Nutmeg. That also gave me a reason to stay close to her, which once again made me hard.

"Come here and help me cinch up the saddle." She hunkered down beside me and I showed her the buckles. "It's just like fastening this belt." I pointed to the buckle of the belt I had on, wanting her to see she had an effect on me. She glanced down at my jeans. Noticeably flushing, she quickly looked away.

When helping me put the bit in Nutmeg's mouth, she pulled her hand away. "Will she bite?"

Trying not to smile at her nervousness, I explained, "No, she won't bite. Horses don't have any teeth in the lower corners of her mouth, where the bit is inserted." I opened Nutmeg's mouth to prove it.

We finished our "identify the tack" lesson. I only managed to get my arms around her once, while showing her how to adjust the stirrup. I figured it best to bide my time and not push too hard. Her anxiety about the lesson could well throw a spanner in the works.

Then the moment came to get her on the mare. I said,

"Let's see how she feels to you," and held the stirrup iron for her foot.

Ivan really expected me to get on that damn big horse! Just like that. I looked at him like he had lost his mind, which he certainly must have. At that moment I didn't care that he looked like Adonis and was hung like Priapus. I just wanted to leave.

He continued talking like he didn't notice I hadn't budged. His voice hummed in my ears as I stood there. "Grab some mane with your left hand and put your left foot in the stirrup. Hold on to the back of the saddle with your right hand. Push off with your right foot. Swing your right leg over the horse, hefting yourself into the saddle, just like this."

With one smooth motion, he hoisted himself onto Nutmeg's back. He continued, "Don't plop down hard; you could startle her. Just sit down easy and take hold of the reins. Now you try it." With that he got off her just as easily as he had got on. He held the stirrup iron for me. I still hadn't budged.

Pash stood there, frozen to the spot. I gave her my most basic demonstration of how to mount a horse and she looked like she hadn't understood a single word I said. I thought to myself, "Damn, Redhead, you're going to get on this horse if I have to lift you up there myself."

What I actually said was considerably gentler. "Let's press on, Pash, you can do it. I'll help you." Thinking I needed to ease the tension somehow, I asked, "By the way, is Pash short for something? I never heard that name before."

She blinked a couple of times, like waking up from a nap, and found her voice. "That is what most people call me. My given name is Passion." I had to stifle a surprised whistle with that one. But she still noticed my amazement. "It is odd, isn't it?"

Hoping I hadn't been too obvious with my reaction, I said,

"Well, it is unusual. I've never met anyone named Passion before."

"That's why I use Pash. People are more comfortable with it."

"Well, Passion, let's get you on this horse."

I knew I couldn't just stand there, with Ivan waiting for me to put my foot in that stirrup. I had already made a fool of myself in front of him once and made up my mind I wasn't going to do it again. So, I came over to Nutmeg.

"Just take it slow, I'll help you."

"All right, then. Show me what to do."

"Grab on here." He put my left hand on Nutmeg's mane. "Now lift your left foot and put it in the stirrup. If it's too high, I'll adjust it." I put my foot in the stirrup. Before I had a chance to say, "Now, what?" he said, "Here we go," and started lifting me off the ground.

"Hold on to the back of the saddle and straighten your left knee. Don't worry, I have you." And have me he did. I was practically sitting on his hands. "Now swing that right leg up and over; don't graze her, now."

The next thing I knew, I was sitting in the saddle. Ivan moved forward, took the reins and stroked Nutmeg's neck, murmuring something to her I couldn't quite hear. "We have to work on that landing, Pash. You could go riding sooner than you planned." I realized I must have plopped down too hard. Who knew getting onto a horse was this complicated!

Her given name is Passion! Bloody hell! Do I have good karma or what? Well, Passion, you are going to learn to ride a horse, if I have anything to say about it. And that's not all you're going to ride, if I have my way!

I got her foot positioned correctly in the stirrup. Seeing no other way to do it, I grabbed on to that shapely arse and started steadily pushing her up into the air.

Normally I would have enjoyed that moment considerably more, except that her body weight shifted midair. I reacted instinctively. Either I had to get her on that horse straight away or risk her going backward, taking me down with her. So, onto the horse she went.

Fortunately, Nutmeg isn't a quick reactor. While Nutmeg tried to decide if she should go or not, I grabbed the reins and whispered quietly to her, calming her. She settled right down. Another horse might have bolted. I promised her a few extra treats for supper.

Regaining my professional demeanor once again—which seemed to be a constant challenge with my new student—I continued the lesson. I showed her how to properly hold the reins and had her walk Nutmeg around the stable a couple of times. Actually, I walked around and Nutmeg followed me.

That ended class number two. I knew the scales did not tip in my favor when she said, "Ivan, perhaps this is too much for me. I don't believe I can do this."

"Might I ask for one more go at it? I promise the next time, things will go more smoothly." She reluctantly agreed.

I knew I didn't do so well with my second lesson. I felt my chance to impress Ivan as an excellent riding student slipping away. If anything, he must have thought me to be an absolute cock-up. Bugger all! I finally met someone I really responded to and I just couldn't seem to catch on to his world.

Most of the men that cross my path turn out to be gay or married. I have more male "friends" than I can count, and none of them want to sleep with me. Now, I accidentally meet someone who curls my toes and all I can do is prove how clumsy I am.

I spent the next week trying not to think of Ivan. I distracted myself with my work, writing into the wee hours nearly every night. No matter how late I stayed up, that damn dream kept coming back to me just as I would try to sleep. I felt like such a fool! What had I been thinking, imagining that my world and his world could intersect? So I had the hots for him; that, and a pound sterling, would buy me a cup of tea.

The night before my third lesson, I couldn't sleep. Not wanting to dwell on seeing Ivan again the next day, perhaps for the last time, I thought of my Highwayman. I snapped on the light beside my bed. Retrieving my journal from my bedside table, I started to write.

My Highwayman arrived at the inn and asked for a tray of food to be brought to his room. When I came in, he handed me a package tied with cord. I opened it to find a new red dress with a lace-up bodice.

"Since I have to look at you when I am here, I want you to wear this instead of that," he said as he gestured to the worn dress I had on. He sat down in a chair. "Put it on for me." He watched as I pulled my everyday dress over my head. I had on only a thin shift underneath. I hadn't worn my corset or my pantaloons, it being a warm summer's day. I quickly pulled the dress over my head and laced up the bodice to cover myself.

Twirling around, I made the skirt flair. When I stopped spinning, I staggered, dizzy from the excitement and the movement. As my vision cleared, I saw him sitting there, stroking himself. Flustered at the idea of him watching me like this, I smoothed my dress to dry my sweaty palms.

Taking his hand away from his organ, he said, "Look what you did to me, dancing around like a whoring wench. Here I bring you this present and you do this to me?" I could not tell from his tone if I had truly angered him. I stood, frozen to the floor, not knowing what to do to redeem myself. Finally he broke the silence. "You would leave me like this?" I approached him.

When I got close enough for him to reach me, he grabbed my hand and pulled me down onto his lap "Woman, you will pleasure me with your whoring ways." He roughly pulled at my laced-up bodice.

Fearing he would tear my new dress, I undid the bodice

that I had so carefully laced up just a few minutes before. He opened my dress and reached inside. Pulling open the drawstring on my shift, he took my breast into his hand. I knew his habits well. When he became this stirred, nothing I could say or do would stop him.

Not that I minded. Ever since the first time he lay on top of me at the inn, I welcomed his hunger for me. The feel of him inside me made me burn with desire. I lowered my dress and shift off my shoulders, giving him full sway to my bare breasts. He kneaded the soft flesh like bread dough. Sparks crackled in my chest when his callused hands brushed my nipples.

He tugged at my skirt, pulling it up around my waist. Slipping his hand between my legs, he berated me for not wearing my pantaloons. "You are a she-cat in heat, waiting for Lucifer to lift your skirt. God-fearing women cover themselves underneath!" His words inflamed me as much as the pressure of his hand. "Well, woman, Lucifer sent me to do his business. Stand up and raise your skirt. Let me see my prize."

With trembling hands, I pulled up my skirt and shift so he could see me underneath. I closed my eyes as he reached between my legs. His rough hand found its mark. He opened me and rubbed until I squealed. Knowing he watched me in my exposed state drove me nearly mad with desire. My legs would no longer support me, so he lowered me to the floor.

He positioned himself over me and undid his trousers. Supporting himself on his forearms, he roughly entered me and began rutting me. My swollen body welcomed his invasion. I clung to him, feeling his sweat mingle with mine. Again and again he violated me. Suddenly everything disappeared and only the fire in my belly existed. Wave after wave of pleasure gripped me as he continued to grind himself into me.

Still he burrowed into me. Fearing he would ruin my new dress, I reached down to his buttocks and slid my finger inside the crevice between them. He began to spasm as I thought he would. I discovered early on I could trigger his climax this way. He could rarely endure the sensation and would finish in short order.

I didn't do it often, for fear he would catch on to my trick. But if he had been drinking or I thought him too rough, I used this to get him off me. Today I did so to keep him from tearing my dress. I preferred to have him on top of me for as long as he could have managed.

As he came back to himself, I continued to stroke his buttocks. I did not want to draw attention to the single stroke which caused him to finish. When I pulled off the new dress, I folded it neatly and put it on a bench along the wall. I now knew what wearing it would do and would tuck that away to use as I needed it.

Finishing my story bit, I closed my journal. Hugging the book to my chest, I said out loud to the empty room, "What the bloody hell am I going to do?" Through the entire story, I saw Ivan as my Highwayman. His face and his body filled my mind as I wrote, without invitation and without mercy. My clitoris throbbed with need. I turned out the light and slipped my hand inside my knickers, wishing it were his hand instead.

Chapter Three

With uneasiness and considerable embarrassment, I returned for the third session, only because I told Ivan I would. I already decided that I would thank him for his time and effort and then jack in the lessons. The longer I prolonged this fantasy, the harder it would be to end it.

When I came into the stable, I saw Nutmeg standing outside her stall, but I didn't see Ivan. "Hello, is anyone about?" I certainly had no intention of being left alone with Nutmeg.

"Hello, there. I'm back here." I heard Ivan's voice coming from the tack room. "I won't be long."

He came out a few minutes later carrying a saddle much bigger than the one we used last week. I had to ask, "Why is that saddle so big?"

"Because, my dear, we are going to have a special lesson."

My heart fluttered. "Special how?" I couldn't take much more of this. I wanted to run back to my car and leave.

"You'll see." With some effort, he hoisted the saddle onto Nutmeg's back. His arms looked as though they would pop the seams of his black T-shirt. I tried not to stare, but, my word, that shirt stretched across his back like a panther's coat. His muscles visibly rippled with the exertion.

I felt a trickle of perspiration run between my breasts. Another trickle itched between my legs that had nothing to do with perspiration. "It is a bit warm today, isn't it?"

"It surely is. I could use a pint of cold ale after being in the tack room." He buckled the saddle and adjusted the length of the stirrups. "Come. Let me help you get on."

"Ivan, I am so sorry. I don't think I can do this. Perhaps I should—"

"Of course you can do it," he said before I could finish my quitting speech. "It is perfectly simple once you get onto it." He took my hand and led me over to Nutmeg.

"If you say so." Perhaps I could wait until after the lesson to quit. I put my foot into the stirrup. This time Ivan held me around my waist and helped me on.

"Slowly now, lower yourself slowly." He put his hand under my bum. "Feel my hand? Lower yourself on my hand." I felt his hand, all right. I wanted to rub against it! Ivan didn't slide his hand out from under my bum until I sat fully on the saddle.

"Now I'm going to show you how to properly ride. Slide forward a little." He pushed my bum from behind, sliding me forward in the saddle. Then, hell's bells! He got on behind me!

I had no choice but to lean against him. "So sorry about the damp shirt. We haven't used this saddle for some time. I had to unearth it." He leaned in close to my ear. "As you can tell, I did get very warm in there."

"I don't mind it, really." I could already feel his shirt soaking through mine. The very idea that he held me that close made me even more unsteady. I clutched the reins with both hands. He put his arms around me and took the reins.

"Relax, Passion. Hold on to me, I won't let you fall." He somehow got that horse to move and we rode out of the stable.

A sheet of paper couldn't have slid between us, we sat so close together. With his hands over mine, he showed me how to hold the reins. He leaned down very close to my ear again and said, "Pash, feel how I'm controlling the horse with the reins. It is just like steering a car. You just use the reins to do it." His breath on my neck gave me shivers.

As we rode along I studied his hairy forearms and followed them down to his hands. The Highwayman's hands in my story last night looked like his, big and rugged. Everything about Ivan reminded me of my Highwayman. Putting the brakes on my imagination, I tried to concentrate on the lesson.

My attempt to focus shattered when Ivan held me tightly around the waist and said, "Put your hand on my thigh. I want you to feel how I use my muscles to send directional signals to Nutmeg." I don't know if Nutmeg felt the signals, but my libido certainly did. The feel of his arm under my breasts and his leg muscles tightening under my hand made my knickers as wet as his shirt.

We spent most of my lesson together on that horse, with Ivan showing me all sorts of things about how to ride. Clearly he knew what he was doing. I really did try to pay attention. This is what I had told myself I wanted, to learn about horses.

But being so close to him for so long, how the devil could I focus on a horse? We rode across the farm and back again. My word, leaning on his chest for more than an hour and touching him as I did excited me terribly! Blooming brilliant, it was! What's more, I could feel him rubbing against my back. His privates felt like they looked—big and deliciously hard!

By the third lesson I had to do something to get to know Pash better, PDQ. If I didn't turn it around this lesson, I doubted she would be back.

Digging around the tack room before her lesson, I found an old saddle meant for two people. By double riding with her, I could put my arms around her while holding the reins.

It worked out even better than I anticipated. Two of us on that saddle made for a bloody tight fit, which pressed her up against my chest and put the top of her head at just about my chin.

Trying not to let the intoxicating smell of her hair distract me, I started the lesson. I told her to relax and allow the rhythm of the horse to dictate body posture. This makes the movement fluid and graceful. With my arms around her, it also caused the sides of her breasts to rub against my arms.

I showed her how to press her legs into the sides of the horse so that the musculature between human and animal blends. Of course, the demonstration required she put her hand on my upper thigh to feel the muscles move. After all, I told her, when the rider feels how the horse is reacting, it becomes a seamless motion to send muscle-controlled signals to the animal about how to move and when. With time, the human and the horse learn to anticipate the movements of the other.

Nutmeg sauntered along a shady dirt road that runs through the farm. We were quite alone. When she put her hand on my thigh, my cock let me know how much I needed some.

Her breasts rested on my forearm. I allowed myself to rock with the horse so the soft flesh pressed into my arm with every step. I thought about touching her up while on the horse, but didn't want to risk scaring her off.

So, I had actually managed to sound totally professional through the whole lesson, while nursing a stonker!

I had to get this bit of totty in the sack before she drove me barking mad!

By the time Ivan lifted me down off the saddle, I had steam coming out of my ears. To be so close to him for so long gave me heart palpitations. He had such control and confidence on that horse, I never wanted that ride to end. When it did, I figured that was that! I had my peek at being up close and personal with him. Now I had to leave my lessons, and my fantasy about him. I only hoped I could manage it without tears.

Just as I meant to recite my quitting speech, the impossible happened: he asked me out to dinner. I could hardly believe my ears. I heard myself say, "Yes!" then wondered if I had shouted it at him; it sounded so loud to me. I repeated my answer—"Yes, indeed, I would be delighted"—hoping I sounded more natural.

He smiled and said, "Splendid." We agreed to meet in town the next day and decide where to go. Then he offered to walk me to my car.

With the riding lesson near completion, I noted Pash seemed to have no qualms whatsoever about having me so close to her for so long. In fact, I think she rather enjoyed the extra attention.

I hadn't deliberately meant to, but I came damn close to getting off with her on that horse. It took all the control I could manage to be professional while riding with her. Everything in me wanted to slide my hand under her shirt and feel her up.

She gave me no indication one way or another about how she felt about what happened. So, hoping for a bit of luck, I took a chance.

As she gathered herself together to leave, I asked if she would like to have dinner with me. I think I startled her with my question because she jumped and blurted out, "Yes," rather like I had poked her with a pin and she meant to say, "Ouch!" Then she more calmly said, "Yes, indeed, I would be delighted." So, we set ourselves a date for the next night, agreeing to meet in town.

I walked her to her car and opened the door for her. Before she could get inside, I pulled her close and whispered in her ear, "I'm looking forward to tomorrow." Then I kissed her, a simple good-bye kiss, but enough to give her something to think about. Reluctantly, I let her get into her car and leave.

The next day I remembered I had public library books overdue. I went to return them early that afternoon. When I did, I saw Ivan sitting alone at a table in the corner. It would be difficult to miss him, considering how striking he is.

Standing there watching him, I thought about our riding together and about the way he kissed me good-bye. He had pressed himself into me as he held me, enough that I knew his arousal had not gone away. My imagination had not invented that erection!

I suddenly realized I had been staring directly at him, hugging my books to myself like a silly schoolgirl. I returned my books, paid my overdue fine and looked in his direction again. He still seemed engrossed in whatever book he had, so I decided I would take the initiative to say hello.

As I came closer to his table, I noticed he had been taking notes. I wondered what in the world he could be doing. When I saw him intently reading a book of Yeats poetry, with several other poetry books stacked in front of him, I felt more than a little bit confounded. He picked just that moment to look up, I guess sensing someone standing beside him. He gave me that *turn me into melted butter* smile and said, "Well, hello there!"

Just when I needed them, my language skills failed me. All I could get out was a thin "Hi." I felt flustered and more than a little confused. I know Ivan noticed the bewildered look on my face, because before I could say anything else, he volunteered an explanation.

"I teach English literature at University of Northampton and have to update my lesson plans for the fall semester. I come back here to work with Steve at the stable for a break during the summer." He held up one of the poetry books as he said, "But I still have to keep up with my real job. Otherwise it will get away from me and I will be swamped with work at the end of the summer."

If I had found Ivan attractive before, the meter had just shot through the roof! I could see his amusement at my reaction, but I couldn't help being surprised. He paused, waiting for me to say something. I put my hand on the back of the chair next to him to steady myself, and said the only thought that came to me. "I had no idea!"

Thankfully he asked me a question that helped me to focus

my thoughts. "What do you do when you aren't taking riding lessons?"

"I am a writer." Given my tongue-tied disposition around him, I wasn't sure he believed me. "I have been doing some research for my next book and forgot to return some materials I borrowed." At least now he knew I hadn't followed him to the library!

The way he looked at me, I thought I had lipstick on my teeth. I ran my tongue over my front teeth, just in case. Then he asked, "Do you like to dance?"

"I truly do," I told him. I knew something had changed because instead of meeting in town, he asked for my address to pick me up. We were going someplace posh. And, much to my surprise, he gave me another kiss as he left to do some errands.

The day of our date was in fact my day off. I decided to go to the library and work on lesson plans for the fall. But I also had another reason for going. I intended to do a little digging. I wanted to know what my latest student wrote.

I checked Miss Passion's registration form to get a last name. She signed it P.F. Platonov. She had two books in print under her name, *The Search: Finding Soul in the Postmodern Age,* and another called *Sagacity*.

Well, she sounded heady, but could she give good head? I almost laughed out loud at that as I looked for her books. The library had them, but they were both checked out. Seemed I took that about as far as I could. I wrote down the titles and on my way to the poetry section, I asked the librarian to reserve them for me when they came back in.

While debating about what poetry books to take out, I saw Pash come in. I smiled, thinking, *Kismet!* I waited to see if she spotted me. She returned some books and then came over to where I sat. She seemed surprised to see me and even more surprised to see the stack of poetry books sitting in front of me. I offered an unsolicited answer to her obvious question.

I couldn't help but be a bit slighted by her reaction; she was evidently amazed I could even read, let alone teach. It had been a long while since anyone had seen me as anything less than a professor. I reminded myself she could well have an inaccurate first impression, having met me in a frigging barn!

So, I asked, "What do you do when you aren't taking riding lessons?" Just to see what she would say. She told me that she earned her living writing. I winked at her and said, "It seems we have more in common than what we first knew." As I enjoyed the flustered blush I saw creeping up her neck, an idea came to me.

"Do you like to dance?"

She said, "I truly do."

"Good, because the place we are going for dinner also has dancing. Oh, yes, and dress up—it's posh."

Of course, I had just decided to up the ante, but she didn't know that. Steve had told me about a place close by, a very romantic restaurant in an inn. They offered an atmospheric candlelight dinner and dancing, with the maître d' most amenable to supplying a room key for dessert. They just added it all together on one tab. I wanted to give it to her so badly. Perhaps dinner and dancing would get me into her pants.

With that scheme in mind, I asked her, "Why don't you write down your address and phone number? I will pick you up about seven, if that is acceptable?"

"That would be lovely. Thank you."

"If you'll excuse me, I have a few errands to run if we are having ourselves a posh night out." I gathered my books. I kissed her again, this time as an appetizer for our evening. "I'll see you later."

Making sure my credit cards and mobile were in my pocket, I went outside to make the call. I wanted to make reservations, with the intention of asking about the full-service dinner plan.

I had no problem making a reservation for that night. I supposed they weren't very busy on Wednesdays. I actually did have a few errands to run, which included picking up a pair of shoes I had left to be reheeled.

As I walked toward the shoe shop, I still felt the remnants of a sting from her reaction when she realized I didn't work in a stable for a living. I thought I had finally gotten past being poor and uneducated. So why did it bother me so damn much that she took me for a farmhand?

So he wanted posh. As I looked through my cupboard, I saw professional, I saw formal, I saw casual, but I didn't see posh. I also didn't see sexy. He had only ever seen me in jeans. Cripe's sake, here I am hoping I gave him a hard-on and he has never even seen me in a dress!

Well, I had to find something in there. I didn't have time to shop for a new dress. He would be here to pick me up in a couple of hours. I still had to have a shower and do my hair.

Then I saw the edge of a garment bag tucked way back in the corner. I pulled it out, laid it on the bed and unzipped it. I gently lifted out a calf-length, red chiffon cocktail dress, being careful not to snag it on the zipper of the bag. I had only worn this dress once, to a party last summer. I kept it, thinking I would wear it somewhere, sometime. It seemed the time had come.

As I got dressed I thought about how I had turned into a bit of a recluse over the last months, and a celibate one to boot. That's when I thought to find my cervical cap, just in case.

I took one final look at myself in the mirror. I said to my reflection, "Well, this is a fine kettle of fish! What the bleeding devil have you done?" I answered my own question, "It's a proper mess! I take riding lessons and fall for a gorgeous, horse-training professor who really rings my chimes. I'm a right one, all right!"

The wall clock read ten minutes until seven. Bugger it! Now I had time to work up a sweat before Ivan picked me up. Think cool thoughts, lemonade, ice cream, Ivan bending over to cut the twine, Ivan putting the saddle on Nutmeg. Oops, those weren't cool thoughts! How could he be so good-looking and be an English professor?

The English professors I had at university, and I had more than a few, were usually short, balding and paunchy. Except for one, who did have the height, the hair and the looks, and also a reputation for being a queen extraordinaire.

Well, professor, I am ready for you tonight. I am not a dippy Judy, even though I've given you every reason to think I am. I am going to be calm, cool and chic. I glanced in the mirror again. Sweat beads glistened on my upper lip.

After showering, I shaved, clipped my whiskers and put on the best suit I brought with me. Even though they really didn't need it, I buffed my shoes again.

I hoped to slip out without Steve noticing. If he thought I really wanted Pash, he would move in on her. We'd done that to each other for years. Don't ask me why. Neither of us ever had a problem getting some action when we really wanted it.

We really got into it a few times over women, with my having bloodied his nose at least twice. He managed to knock the wind out of me on those occasions, once giving me a black eye. I had an edge on him physically and could take him. He knew it, but the crazy son of a bitch didn't care.

Lately I didn't tell him much about what I did. His sarcastic remarks about my love life didn't sit well with me. I hoped to avoid this whole business with Pash. But as I came down the stairs, I heard a catcall from below. "Going somewhere, guv'nor?" he said, blocking my path at the bottom of the staircase.

"I have an appointment," I said, hoping that would be the end of it. I should have known better.

He pushed up my sleeve. "Must be a posh one—cuff links and all." His tone irritated me more than usual. "Wouldn't happen to be with that red-haired bit of fluff, now, would it? I saw you yesterday making time with the little luv on that horse. You know my insurance doesn't allow double riding anymore."

"Sod off. She didn't fall, now, did she, mate? I had hold of her, good and tight." I knew if I didn't cut him off, I would be late. I pushed him aside. "Bloody well don't wait up for me." With that, I headed for the car.

I heard him yell after me, "The horses aren't the only ones getting their oats tonight!" I ignored the rotter as I double-checked to make sure I had condoms in my breast pocket. Then I started out to pick up Pash.

Chapter Four

Dabbing at my upper lip with a tissue, I managed to smudge my lipstick. I took a deep breath and fixed my makeup. Hoping Ivan would be on time, I sat next to my front window to watch for him, telling myself I also needed the air.

Unless he intended to drive all night, I had narrowed the possible restaurant choices to two. A fancy place with dinner and dancing meant either a private club on the edge of town, which necessitated a membership, or an inn about half an hour away.

I had never been to either place. I knew nothing about the private club, except that it catered to the upper social classes in town. Gwen had been to the inn and had raved about it. She told me she had the most romantic night of her life there. Just as I saw Ivan arrive, I remembered she had gone there with Steve. I smiled, knowing I had just narrowed my choices to one.

Pash's place wasn't hard to find, a nice little flat in the Shaftesbury. As I parked, I wondered if I had to come to the door, but she came right out when she saw my car. I still got out and opened the car door for her, taking her hand to help her inside. I noted a flush when I took her hand, which I found both endearing and promising.

She looked great, wearing a sexy, sleeveless red dress with a low neckline. I guessed the fabric to be genuine silk. The full skirt wrapped most provocatively around her legs when she walked, and the top clung to her breasts like a second skin.

Before I closed the car door, I saw her discreetly give me the once-over. After another quick look at her legs, I took to the road.

Determined to make some reasonable conversation during the drive, I asked Ivan how he knew Steve. Finally I began putting a few pieces together about him and how he could be a professor who works in a stable. Then he asked me, "How long have you lived here?"

"I moved here late last fall. I needed a quiet place to write, so I came back to Shaftesbury."

"'Back to?' Did you live here before?"

"No, but my grandmother owned a dress shop at the corner of High Street and Angel Lane. That's how I know Gwen. Her mother worked for Nana at the shop."

"I remember your grandmother's dress shop. It has been gone for several years now, hasn't it?"

"Yes. My nana died about five years ago and my family sold the shop to a bakery."

"What about your parents?"

"My parents live in London. My father is a playwright. He also works on the docks at the Port of London for extra money." I looked at Ivan just as he glanced at me. My stomach fluttered with butterflies.

We had about half an hour's drive ahead of us. I had made our reservations for eight o'clock. I needed a little cushion in case I made a wrong turn.

I handed Pash the directions. I wanted her help navigating so I wouldn't get lost. We made small talk on the way, with some deliberately chosen soft music playing in the background.

I told her how I knew Steve and how I came to be at the stable for the summer.

Then I asked when she moved here. I asked the right question because that kept her talking for several minutes. All the while she talked, I noticed there was something akin to static electricity in the car, a charge to the air I could not explain.

Having her so close once again had an effect on me. I willed myself out of a full-blown hard-on, thinking, *Down, willie, it's too early for that.* Fortunately the tape ended at that moment, creating a well-timed distraction.

The tape clicked off and I realized we should almost be there. I knew I had guessed correctly about the inn when we headed in that direction. Ivan gave me the directions and asked me to read them twice.

After taking several turns, we found the inn, a secluded spot surrounded by trees. On the pretense of checking a road sign, I turned around to see if he had anything in the backseat indicating we would be staying the night. He didn't. Well, I knew Gwen had, with Steve, no less. *So the stage is set,* I thought. *I guess we will have to wait and see.*

As I rounded the final turn and the inn came into view, I realized why it had the reputation of being a romantic hideaway. It was unlikely anyone would find this place accidentally.

Steve had told me about his few memorable nights there—in some detail, I might add. Until this evening I never had the occasion to test the waters there. It seemed odd not carrying an overnight bag into the place. I had every intention of spending the night with Pash. But since she didn't as yet know that, it would have been imprudent to have packed my shaving kit and toothbrush.

It being a weeknight, I had no trouble arranging a quiet corner table. They must receive frequent requests such as mine, because the layout of the place was geared to privacy. Large plants and tall vases of flowers had been strategically placed throughout the restaurant, partitioning off the tables from one another.

The table they gave us actually had a live tree with lights sitting beside the table that provided a sufficiently intimate setting for our dinner. A piano player sitting off to the side played music that oozed atmosphere, with dancing slated to begin at nine o'clock. It seemed I had picked a winner, both in my new lady and in my choice of places to have a romantic liaison.

Ivan came around the car and opened the door for me, helping me out. I smoothed my skirt and hoped I hadn't become too wrinkled during the ride. He took my arm and we went inside. He said to the maître d', "I have reservations for eight o'clock—the name is Kozak."

My heart jumped when the very official-looking gentleman replied, "Ah, yes, Dr. Kozak, please follow me."

They had our table ready. I took in as much as possible as we walked through the restaurant. It looked like a fairy tale, with flowers and trees everywhere. Some of the trees had small white lights on them. Our table sat behind one of those bushy trees. I understood why Gwen swooned over coming here. Sitting across the table from Ivan, I felt like Cinderella must have felt, seeing her prince at the ball.

I sat quietly while Ivan pondered the wine list. "What is your preference, Pash: red or white?"

"White, please. A glass of chardonnay will be fine." Rather than just a glass, he ordered a particularly fine bottle of chardonnay. He also ordered a cocktail for himself, which I declined. I felt light-headed already and knew the wine would be all I could handle.

The menu had no prices listed—always a sure sign that a restaurant was not for the faint of heart. I ordered salmon, hoping it would calm my jumpy stomach without being too heavy.

I watched Ivan order his steak with the same quiet confidence I felt from him on the horse; he told the waiter exactly how he wanted it prepared. He seemed just as natural here as when I had first witnessed him in the stable. Trying not to appear too starry-eyed, I couldn't help wondering what angel had led me to him.

During dinner we continued to talk. The same charge which filled the car now hovered over our table. I realized, with some amusement, that I carried the feeling inside myself. The damnedest thing was I liked Pash. I liked her very much. What an extraordinary delight to talk to her! I discovered she did have a voice and could talk a blue streak once she got going.

I interrupted her at one point, as I thought I recognized someone. "Do you see that bloke over there? He looks familiar to me. I think I've seen him in one of the shops."

"I recognized him when we walked in. He is the dispenser from the chemist's shop."

"That's right, now I remember him."

She nearly made me choke when she told me, "I asked Gwen about him once after he patted my bum and told me to give him a call anytime. Gwen told me he is married. It seems he doesn't spend much time home alone when his wife travels for her job."

"No shit, Sherlock!"

"Definitely no shit!"

I couldn't help poking at her. "So have you ever called him?"

"Heavens, no!" She looked aghast.

This redhead had a real bite to her! Christ, I really did enjoy her company!

During dinner I probably talked too much, but I couldn't seem to stop myself. Ivan didn't appear to mind, smiling or laughing out loud practically the whole time. When he asked me if I had ever called the dispenser, I nearly panicked. I thought I might have given him the wrong impression. The dispenser fellow gives me the heebie-jeebies. I didn't want Ivan to think I had anything to do with him.

Ivan had a second drink but I still preferred to stay with just the wine. I knew I could handle the wine. Anything more and I risked getting drunk and possibly making a fool of myself. I really wanted Ivan to think well of me. More than that, I wanted to attract him like he dazzled me.

I noticed his cuff links when he refilled my glass. They reflected the lights shining from the tree beside us. I also noticed the dark hair peeking out from under the cuff of his white shirt. A ripple of gooseflesh ran down my arm. Then the lights were lowered even more than they already were, and couples started to dance.

I made sure I kept her wineglass full, wanting some insurance that the night would continue as planned. I wanted her mellow, but not drunk. I had been there, done that. It isn't much fun bedding a lady who is on the verge of passing out or spewing. But mellow . . . hell, yes, mellow is good.

By the time the dance music began, she had noticeably relaxed. Softened and suggestible—that's where I wanted her when I asked her to dance. As for me, I had another vodka. She got to me, she really did. I had a semi since getting out of the car and it had gotten more difficult to keep in check. The alcohol helped keep the situation under control.

But now, as I took hold of her to dance, I knew it wouldn't be long until she felt my erection against her body. Soon I would know which way the dice fell. Snake eyes and the evening would end, but come on, baby, give me a seven.

We talked a bit longer and then he asked me to dance. I hoped my trembling legs would support me as he led me to the dance floor. The music seemed to flow right through my heart as he held me. I felt him kiss my hair and I moved a little closer to him. He held me even tighter, squeezing my waist.

I closed my eyes and lost myself in the moment, smelling him through his coat. I felt the rhythm of his breathing, the softness of his heartbeat. Then I felt his hand on my neck.

The same man who held me yesterday on the back of a horse held me again tonight. The same hand that held the reins with mine now massaged my neck.

When Ivan stroked my bottom, I practically went limp. He must have realized how strongly I reacted because he asked me if I wanted to sit down.

She had on heels, which brought her up a couple of inches, giving her just enough height to lay her head against my shoulder. That also brought her hair maddeningly close to my nose, with the fragrance making me drunker than the vodka.

I couldn't resist—I leaned over and kissed the top of her head. To my delight, she snuggled in closer, encircling my neck with both of her hands. I had my arms around her waist and reacting from her movement, tightened my hold.

The music carried us across the dance floor and back again. One of her hands had slipped down to my chest while the other rested on my shoulder. I could feel her fingers gently kneading my coat, the way a cat would a blanket. The sensation went right from my chest to my groin.

I could feel my control slipping, so I figured, it's now or never. I slid my hand up her back and under her hair. I rubbed her neck, moving my fingers through her hair. I brushed the curve of her bottom with my other hand.

I could feel her breath quicken as she pressed into me. I thought it best to at least give her the opportunity to cool off, so I leaned close to her ear and asked if she wanted to sit down. She looked up at me with eyes that burned into my heart and shook her head no.

As much as I needed to sit, I couldn't let this end yet. I was Cinderella dancing with my prince and the clock hadn't yet struck midnight. We danced, my feet no longer touching the floor. I wanted him more than I had ever wanted anyone. Everything melted away except for my awareness of his arms around me, the feel of his body pressing against mine.

We were at the inn and my Highwayman held me in his arms. I felt how much he wanted me. His cock had come to life against me. I slid my hand under his coat to caress him. His shirt stuck to his back, the heat coming off him in waves. I tried to angle my body to feel his hardened organ against me, but it wasn't enough. I wanted to love him right there on the dance floor.

So we continued to dance. One song ended and another began. It seemed we had entered a shared trance, the music creating a spell I hoped would not end with the song. Then her hand slid under my coat and her arm went around my waist. I knew she had to feel my cock. She adjusted her position to accommodate the bulge that had grown in my trousers.

Under my coat I felt her hand moving up and down my now damp shirt. Again I leaned close to her ear and whispered, "You're making me crazy, we had better sit down before I embarrass myself." I meant what I said. Much more of this and I wouldn't make it to any room. Fortunately the dimly lit dance floor and dark suit coat hid my groin from view, although anyone with a mind to look could plainly see I had a problem.

Then I heard him whisper to me that we had to sit down, that he needed to sit down. My eyes welled up—the magic was ending, the genie was going back into the lamp, my Highwayman was leaving. My eyes stung with the tears I blinked back.

I tried to locate the ladies' loo on our way back to the table, but the place was just too darn dark and my vision too blurry. *Get a grip,* I told myself. *You're a big girl, you know the score. The clock has struck midnight. It's time to take that pumpkin home and make some pie.* The silliness of that last thought brought me some relief.

I took a deep breath and prepared myself for the polite apologies that certainly would be exchanged over dessert.

* * *

We made it back to the table and I knew what I had to do. I had taken this as far as I could without being straight with her. I could hardly get her into a room for the night until I told her I wanted to spend the night with her. I walked behind her, ostensibly to hold her chair while she sat down. Instead I turned her around to face me and kissed her, holding her as close as I could.

Always the gentleman, Dr. Kozak, I thought as he followed me around the table. I dutifully stood as I waited for him to pull out my chair. Instead I felt his hands on my shoulders. I nearly gasped out loud as he turned me around. I had only a moment to look at him before I felt him up against me. Then I couldn't breathe—not because he covered my mouth with his, but because he passionately kissed me.

Hidden behind that blessed tree, with my hand behind Pash's neck, I held her head still and kissed her harder. Instead of pulling away, as I rather expected she would, she returned the pressure of my mouth against hers, opening her lips to receive my tongue.

I felt Ivan's hand on my neck again, this time with more force. He kept kissing me, only harder, rougher. Something sparked inside of me; a long-buried yearning bubbled to the surface. I grabbed on to him, clutching at his back. I took his tongue into my mouth, wanting him inside me however I could have him.

Pash embraced me, this time with both arms under my coat. I felt her nails digging into my back. I pulled my face away from hers long enough to quietly voice the only thought in my mind. "Do you want to get a room?" That's all I could get out, for everything else inside me braced for the answer. She ran the back of her hand across my whiskers and whispered back, "Let's do." Oh, yes, I definitely threw a seven!

Chapter Five

Ivan pulled away from me. I couldn't believe he had the willpower to stop now; I almost forgot we still stood in a restaurant. I heard him ask, in a barely audible voice, "Do you want to get a room?"

Looking into eyes that pierced my soul, I touched his face. With whatever voice I could muster, I answered, "Let's do."

He gave me another small kiss. "I'll be right back."

Somehow I managed to lower myself into my chair. I still had half a glass of wine left, which I sipped in an attempt to collect myself. I watched Ivan make his way across the room, nearly bumping into a couple leaving the dance floor.

So, my fairy godmother gave me a reprieve. But would the glass slipper fit? I stifled a giggle, which caused me to hiccup, as I thought of his girth when he pressed into my side. The damn thing better fit. It would be an interesting bit of business if it didn't.

Ivan listened intently to the maître d' and then said something in return. After patting the man on the back, he hurried back across the room.

Beyond caring who might notice my groin, I went in search of the maître d' and a key. This bit of business gave me a chance to catch my wind and allow the urgency of the last few minutes to subside. This seemed a mixed blessing. I knew it would give me more sustaining power for later, but it also gave Pash a chance to cool off as well.

Not wanting to give her time to change her mind, I quickly located the maître d' and asked for a room. Even though they had told me this would be no trouble when I called for a reservation, I still felt relieved when the maître d' reached for a shelf and picked up a piece of paper with a key attached. When he noted the room number from the key on the paper, I realized they had kept it with my bill, just in case.

Without my asking, he told me, "Sir, room service will be available until midnight and then again at six A.M., if you care to order dessert or breakfast."

"Very good. It would be quite fine if we could have an iced bottle of champagne and some fruit left outside the door at eleven thirty. Thank you so much for your help."

Impressed with the efficiency of this operation, I went back to the table to see Pash sipping what was left of her wine. *Mellow,* I thought. *Just stay mellow.* When she saw me, she gave me a questioning look. I walked behind her chair, put my hands on her shoulders and whispered into her ear, "Room number twenty-two is ours." Trying to sustain at least some semblance of chivalry, I added, "That is, if you are still inclined."

She stood up, picked up her bag and said softly, "I am still inclined."

Ivan put his arm around my waist as we walked toward the lobby. As we passed a sign for the ladies' loo, I realized I really had to piddle, the result of drinking so much wine. I stopped him in the hall. "Would you excuse me for a few moments? I have to spend a penny." I pointed to the sign. "I shan't be long."

"I'm sure they have one in the room."

I felt my face get warm as I told him, "I don't believe I can wait."

He smiled, saying, "Well, go on, then. Maybe I best go now,

too." He gave my bottom a pat and headed down the hall to the gents' sign.

Before making my way into the toilet, I watched him for a moment walking down the hall. He radiated confidence, wearing his strength and virility like a tailor-made suit. Yet he had such grace and poise. The need to piddle interrupted my reverie. Even in the most delicate of situations, some things can't be ignored.

Actually, this gave me a few minutes to gather myself, to check my hair and makeup and to pop in my cap. I said a small *thank you* that I had the presence of mind to bring it. Looking in the mirror, I saw my neck had blotched and, sure enough, so had my chest. The stigma of having fair skin—it is impossible to hide a flush. It is like wearing a neon sign that flashes *I'm aroused!*

Pash's well-timed detour to the loo happened while willie was being cooperative. I actually had to piss, too. I hadn't noticed it before, what with everything else going on. Once in the room, I expected he and I would be more than a little preoccupied.

I put the condoms in my trouser pocket so they would be handy when the time came. I figured now all I needed do was let nature take its course.

Knowing it always takes a woman longer in the loo, I waited in the hall for her. When she came out, she walked right up to me and slipped her arm through mine, saying, "Shall we?"

As we went up the stairs, there was none of the twittering and fawning I had grown accustomed to in this situation. She seemed quite comfortable with the fact we were about to make love. I realized for years now that I had been bedding girls. This time I had myself a real woman.

We found room twenty-two on the second floor at the end of the hall. I had done this sort of thing before in London, but I had never felt like this. It felt very natural to be standing beside Ivan, watching him unlock the door to our room. He turned on the light as he walked in. I followed him while he waited to close the door behind me. *Still with the manners,* I thought as I laid my bag on the bureau.

The room had a quaint Old English feel, with a large, four-poster bed dominating the decor. Ivan walked past me, taking off his coat as he walked. His shirt looked like it needed to be wrung out. "It seems I got a bit warm again," he said with a good-natured smile.

"Looks like you did at that," I commented as he hung his coat on the back of a chair. My word, he looked spectacular with that shirt clinging to him. I've often heard how much men enjoy wet–T-shirt contests. It seems women should start a campaign for a reciprocal wet dress-shirt contest. "Do you know something?" I asked, waiting for his response.

"What?" He delivered his line brilliantly.

"I have never seen a wet shirt look so awfully good."

I turned to see her looking at me, unabashedly admiring me. It took me a moment to recover from that one. Christ, she threw me yet again, over a damn sweaty shirt. The time had come to see if Miss Passion had been given a right proper name.

"Is that so?" I asked, pulling her up against my damp shirt.

"That is indeed so," she replied, rubbing my chest with both of her hands.

"It seems to happen often when I am around you."

"What, you don't sweat when you're alone?"

"Not like I do when I'm with you." Still holding her tightly against me, I asked, "Now you tell me something. How the hell did you come to be named Passion?" Without taking her hands from my chest, she told me.

"According to my father, I was conceived in a moment of pure Russian passion. The day my mother delivered me, he sprinkled vodka on my head and christened me Passion, proclaiming I should grow into a beautiful Russian flower and honor my passionate soul. My mother, completely gone over this crazy Russian, agreed my name would be Passion Flower."

While explaining my name, I could feel that now familiar ridge rising between us again. As he continued to hold me, I thought surely the heat from his body should be making that damp shirt steam. He spoke evenly and conversationally while he reached up and unzipped my dress. "I saw the *F* on your registration form and wondered what your middle name could possibly be. Passion Flower, huh? That is some name. Your father must be quite a character."

"He is," I said, trying to mimic his easy manner, even though I hardly felt calm. Since he had started to undo my dress, I started to loosen his tie.

"So have you honored your passionate soul?" he said, lowering the dress to my waist.

"I do my best," I answered as he kissed my shoulder.

He stepped back then, leaving me standing there with my dress half on, half off. I had no idea what he was doing. He walked behind me and finished unzipping my dress, sliding it down my legs. "The zipper got stuck and I didn't want to tear it; it's such a beautiful dress."

I stepped out of my shoes, and then the dress, with him still holding on to it. He took it to the cupboard and hung it up, saying, "We have to see to our clothes, considering we have to wear them home tomorrow." I felt very exposed, standing there in my lacy slip, and very, very warm.

The look on her face when I took her dress to the cupboard should have been captured on film. I finished undoing my tie. "Could you please hand me my coat?" I wanted to see her move in that slip; it so nicely hugged her curves.

I took the coat, dropped my cuff links in the pocket and

then put my coat in the cupboard beside her dress. I rather liked how they looked, hanging side by side. I just kept talking, being very concerned about the state of our clothes. I watched her upper arms turn as pink as her neck. I have seen women flush with excitement before, but not as rosy as she.

I wanted to let her simmer for a while, letting the anticipation build, so I busied myself finding the thermostat, to turn up the air. The room did seem a bit warm and promised to become warmer in just a few minutes. So, I did the gentlemanly thing, seeing to our comfort.

I also knew damn straight that I had regained the upper hand. She had no choice but to wait out my disrobing and the meticulous care of our clothes. I had also inadvertently begun a striptease for her. After the comment about my shirt, I suspected she might enjoy a little show.

After handing me my coat, she sat down on the edge of the bed. I stood facing her and, one slow button at a time, I undid my shirt. I left it open while I took off my shoes and socks. Then I disappeared into the toilet, taking a hanger with me. I explained through the door, "I best hang this wet shirt on the shower rod so it dries by morning."

When I came out, all I had left were my trousers and my watch. I walked over to the bedside table and took off the watch, with a quick glance to check the time. Ten fifteen. I had more than an hour before they were to deliver the champagne, plenty of time for the first round.

All right, Dr. Kozak, have it your way. I sat down on the bed and waited. I saw him reset the thermostat and felt the cool air hit my back almost immediately. *Bless you,* I thought. Then he started with the shirt.

With each successive button, I saw more. Good God, I tried not to gape. He had the most impressive chest I had ever seen and a washboard stomach, all covered with thick, dark hair. Even with all the hair, the definition looked as though a sculptor had cut his torso from marble. *Lifting all that hay,* I thought as he bent to take off his shoes. He seemed to forget about me while he took care of his shirt.

I caught sight of myself in the bureau mirror, sitting on the bed, half dressed. I shivered, not knowing if the air had chilled me or if I just felt very vulnerable. Very probably, both.

Ivan finally came toward the bed, only to walk right past me and put his watch on the bedside table. Then he reached into his trousers and casually tossed some condoms by his watch. *So, Dr. Kozak, you came prepared. Why should that surprise me? So did I.*

I wanted him. I throbbed with wanting to touch him and be touched by him. For the last three weeks I had wanted nothing else. So my feminist nature felt indignant—she could just crack a window and get over it! I could not deny I wanted him more than I had ever wanted any other man in my life.

I remembered how I desired him in my dream, how it felt to be so close to him on Nutmeg, how he kissed me in the restaurant. I wanted more of that, more of him. He sat down beside me on the bed and slowly pushed me backward.

I had her right where I wanted her. When I sat down beside her, I knew my last little gesture had not escaped her watchful eye. Yes, Passion, I did come here meaning to sleep with you. Why else would I have condoms in my pocket?

I had her smoldering, in more ways than one. I lowered her onto the bed and ran my hand between her breasts. The lace on her slip barely hid her nipples. I brushed them lightly, enjoying the feel of the hard nubs against my hand. I would finish my striptease for her directly. Right now I wanted to enjoy her, to smell her, to taste her.

I could tell she wasn't used to this. She was usually in control. Not tonight, Redhead. I had her off balance, not being able to predict what the bloody hell I would do. She didn't know how to respond or what I expected of her. I could feel the conflict inside her as I held her still.

She strained against my hold, trying to regain some leverage. Capturing her mouth with my own, I kissed her, slowly, deeply. Her fingernails raked down my back as my tongue pierced her mouth. In one moment she resisted, trying to push me off her. In the next she surrendered, violating my mouth with hers. Our tongues met, our breath merged, our mouths fused. When I released her, she gasped for air.

Her leg, wrapped in the satin slip, pressed against my cock. As I rubbed my hard-on against the smooth surface, I licked her neck. The heady scent of her skin and hair made me burn for her even more. I whispered into her ear, "You like this, don't you?"

"You son of a bitch!" She rasped out the curse as she took hold of my arm and squeezed, damn hard, almost puncturing my bicep with her nails. My cock liked that, it liked that very much.

I rubbed her breasts and pinched her nipples, actually harder than I had intended. Arching her back, she twisted her teat between my fingers and shuddered.

"Oh, God, Ivan!" she moaned as I continued to torment her pair.

"So, Redhead, you want it a little rougher? I can handle that."

Bending over, I took her nipple in my mouth right through the slip. Squeezing it between my teeth, I sucked as hard as I could. My weight pinned her to the bed. She strained against me, but I didn't let her move. I slowly ran my hand down her belly, letting it rest between her legs. "Ivan, please, I can't stand it. I can't move!"

What I couldn't manage, the slip did for me. She involuntarily tried to open her legs more to accommodate my hand. Her slip bound her legs together, sublimely so. I applied pressure to that delicious mound and released several times, while generously lavishing attention to each breast. By the time I rolled off her, she was well on her way to being delirious with desire.

* * *

How could Ivan do this to me, how could he make me feel like this? I wanted to fight him off and submit to him at the same time. I had no recourse but to submit—he ruddy well had me immobilized!

I knew I should stop resisting and enjoy it, but I couldn't just passively lie there. I wanted to move, I needed to move, but he wouldn't let me. When I tried, he wouldn't let go of my nipple. He pinched it so hard, an electric shock shot through me and jolted my clitoris.

Then my flipping slip wrapped around my legs, making me feel like a trussed hen. The sheer torture of his hand pressing into me and not being able to rub against it nearly made me scream. I begged him to let me move, to let me rub. My clit throbbed with wanting more pressure. The complete and utter bastard just kept torturing me!

He finally got off me. Before I had a chance to recover my senses, he pulled me into a sitting position. I felt like a rag doll. I gasped out, "Are you off your head, you lout?"

He peeled off my slip, saying, "What kind of language is that for someone who writes books about postmodern culture?"

As my mind tried to register that he knew about my books, he pushed me back down on the bed. I spat at him, "Bugger off, you ignorant git!"

"I don't think so, madam," he spat back as he grabbed the waistband of my hose. He pulled them off with my scanties, leaving me completely bare. "It's time to give willie a little ride!"

Pash lay there, quite obviously fuming. Had she not been naked, I think she would have up and walked out. Now the time had come to finish my striptease. I stood up to remove my trousers, taking her in as I did.

The hair between her legs shone brighter red than the hair on her head. Her very fair skin had gone beyond flushed well into crimson. Her breath came in short gasps, making her breasts rise and fall seductively. I needed relief and I wanted it from her.

I stripped to the skin in one quick movement, stepping out of both my trousers and underpants at the same time. Not taking my eyes off her, I reached down and picked up a condom, tearing it open and rolling it onto my aching cock. Pash didn't move, lying flat on her back, right where I had left her. Almost imperceptibly, I saw her legs open a little wider.

For a brief moment I calculated how I could get around Ivan and lock myself in the toilet. No one had ever treated me like that, like some sort of trollop. But I looked at him standing in front of me, now naked, and a realization swept through me.

I had never been this aroused in my whole life, not with anyone and certainly not alone. There I lay, in the raw, with the most beautiful man I had ever seen about to make love to me. I watched him put on a condom and realized I wanted to know how that astonishing organ would feel inside me.

I expected he would simply lie on top of me, but he didn't. He lay down beside me and propped himself up on his forearm. With his erection resting against my leg, he slipped his middle finger between my legs and started rubbing. I lifted my arse off the bed, trying to press harder against his hand.

When I did that, his finger slid inside me, making me yelp a little. He didn't pull it out. Instead, he let me lunge against his middle finger while he used his thumb to rub me off. I humped harder and harder still, losing sight of everything except the sensation.

I watched as Pash masturbated against my hand. Her utter abandon mesmerized me. I had never seen a woman so lost in the act, so caught up in her own arousal. She pumped against my hand with increasing strength. I tried to help her along.

When I felt the spasms beginning, I pressed hard inside her

and rubbed vigorously. She gasped and started to shake, her whole body trembling while her arse lifted off the bed. I continued to stroke her until she had quieted, her breath still coming in ragged gasps. I smiled, knowing she, too, had come prepared with some protection.

I had my eyes closed, trying to catch my breath after the most intense orgasm I had ever had. I felt Ivan move and realized he had knelt over me. I opened my eyes to see him watching me. He held his penis, checking the condom, and then lowered himself on top of me. I opened my legs wider as I felt him press into my body. He penetrated me, stretching me with his size. He didn't hurry, giving me time to adjust. Thankfully I had ample lubrication and he successfully slid in the whole way.

At first, he didn't move. He just stayed completely inside me, supporting his weight on his forearms. I found myself holding him, stroking his back and his hair. The band had come off. I had never seen his hair down, only pulled back in a ponytail. With it hanging around his shoulders and with the whiskers, he looked like he had just stepped out of another century. It seemed I had an honest-to-god Renaissance man on top of me. Ivan looked at me and whispered, "You feel so damn good."

I whispered back, "So do you."

As he started to move, I followed suit, first slowly and then building momentum. I found myself responding to him from a place beyond arousal, wanting to help him finish as he had helped me. I used my body to help him, letting him pleasure himself as he saw fit, feeling a deep satisfaction that I could do this for him. I raised my legs so that my pelvis tilted back, allowing him deeper penetration. He lifted himself up on his hands and lunged at me, burying his cock deeply into my vagina. Again and again he lunged. With my legs still up, I relaxed and rocked with his movement.

Suddenly his body stiffened and he grimaced, making a

sound that actually sounded like an animal growling. His face transformed with his climax as he bared his teeth and snarled. His pelvis slammed into mine at least four, maybe five times. Sweat dripped off his face and splashed onto my cheek, running down my neck. He had his eyes closed, suspended in the void of his orgasm.

I wiped the sweaty beads from around Ivan's eyes and waited as he slowly came back to himself. When he finally rolled over onto the bed beside me, he muttered, "Jesus H. Christ. That was good!"

Fucking hell, she gave as good as she got! She didn't just lie there and let me do my business. She let me screw the arse off her. Christ, I wasn't used to a lover keeping pace with me! I usually had to hold back, but not this time. My intensity didn't put her off, it downright spurred her on!

Chapter Six

I felt myself going flaccid and knew I had to get rid of my condom. I gave Pash a quick kiss. "I'll be right back, I have to take care of business here." Holding my flagging willie in my hand, I went to the toilet to clean things up.

A few minutes later I heard her say, "Ivan, there is someone at the door."

"What time is it?"

"Your watch says eleven thirty."

I reached for a towel, thinking, *Right on time.* I came out, wrapping the towel around myself, and told Pash, "It's all right, it's just room service." I opened the door to find a cart sitting outside with a bottle of iced champagne, fruit and a single red rose. I wheeled it into the room, stopping by the bed. She had put her slip back on, but I noticed her hose and knickers still in the crumbled heap on the floor where I had tossed them.

"Dash it all!" She had her back to me, sliding her hand over the bed.

"What's wrong, Pash?" I asked, coming over beside her.

"Oh, I lost an earring. Here's your hair band and the earring, but I can't find the back."

I helped her look, running my hand over the spot where her head had been. "Here it is," I said, feeling it under my hand. I stood up, taking the earring and my gum band out of her hand. I replaced the back on the earring. Lifting her hair, I took the other earring off and tossed the whole business onto the bedside table with my watch.

"Just want to make sure you have them both come morning." She didn't contradict me. She walked right past her lingerie, coming over to investigate what I had on the cart. It seemed we were still spending the night.

"When did you order room service?"

I took the champagne out of the bucket and dried off the bottle. "I ordered when I got the key for the room. They close up shop at midnight and I didn't want to miss getting us a little something." I could tell she still might be a little piqued.

"You're just full of surprises," she said flatly.

Now I knew she held a loaded pistol. I clearly heard the edge in her voice. I opened the champagne and poured us each a glass, waiting to see if she would fire.

"How long have you known about my books?"

Bang! I handed her a glass and told her, "Since this afternoon. Steve mentioned to me that you write, so I looked up your name at the library before I started to work." Whether or not she believed me, it was the God's honest truth. She sipped her champagne, considering what I had said.

"Did you look at them?"

"I wanted to, but someone beat me to it." I paused, wondering how much I should volunteer. I decided to push on. "They didn't have either book so I asked the librarian to hold them both for me when they come back." She went around the cart to check out the fruit. I followed her.

"If you don't want to wait, I could lend you copies. I have a few at home."

We both reached for the same strawberry, but I got there a split second before she did. "I would like that," I said as I held out the strawberry for her to take a bite. She looked at me and then at the berry. I felt her making a bigger decision than just taking a bite from my strawberry. When she leaned over and bit it in half, she smiled at me, wiping the juice from her chin. I returned her smile, popping the rest of the berry into my mouth.

There Ivan stood, chewing on a strawberry, grinning like the cat that just ate the canary. And why shouldn't he? He did just snare his bird. I picked out a piece of melon. I shushed my feminist alter ego and held up the fruit for him to bite. He was an arrogant bugger, with bollocks as big as his donger. So why the devil did I like him so much?

Of course, he did gain more than a few points by rubbing me off before he finished, and then by wanting to read my books. He would stand to gain a few more points right now if that towel would fall off. My stomach fluttered a little when I remembered we would be sharing that bed all night, probably without the towel. I wondered how much time we actually had. "When do you have to be back tomorrow?" I asked as nonchalantly as I could manage.

"I should be back by nine; I have a student scheduled. But I'll call Steve in the morning to cover for me, so we don't have to rush. We'll have time." Ivan sipped his champagne and then refilled both glasses.

The implication of *We don't have to rush. We'll have time* both excited and frightened me. I had to get away from him and gather my wits. Walking over to the bureau, I picked up my bag. "Would you excuse me for a few minutes? I need to freshen up." Having returned to his charming and well-mannered persona, he nodded agreeably. As I turned to head for the loo, he adjusted the towel around his waist, giving me a glimpse underneath. I felt myself blush yet again.

I closed the door and leaned against it. What the devil was wrong with me? I just couldn't seem to get a grip. I felt as though he had just taken me and spun me around like a top and then asked me to walk a straight line. I simply couldn't do it. I had to let the ground stop moving under me and understand what had just happened.

I've done this before, I told myself. *I may not be the most experienced woman in the world, but I have slept with enough men to know the territory.* Not that I had my tits bored off by it all! Hardly. I liked what I had tasted, in a manner of speaking.

I couldn't help smirking over my double entendre. *Still with the jokes,* I thought as I checked my cap. It hadn't come loose, in spite of the jostling it had received. I looked at the door and thought of Ivan waiting for me on the other side. None of my reactions to him felt familiar. Sweet Jesus, I still burned when I thought of him holding me in place, forcing me to just lie there.

I closed my eyes and hugged myself, rolling his words over in my mind. I felt the burn intensify when I remembered him saying to me, "You like this, don't you?" Did I really like being forced to submit to him? But he didn't force me to submit—I did so willingly and with my eyes wide open. So what was it, then?

After I relieved myself, I washed up a bit. The cold water on my face brought me around even more. Was I afraid of him? I looked in the mirror and smiled. *Don't be a nitwit,* I thought to myself. I remembered him hosing me off after falling in the mud. I felt his arms around me on Nutmeg and his patience with my inept attempt to learn to ride. I had seen him in the library, surrounded by poetry books. No, he would never hurt me. But I had seen a side of him tonight that belied that gentleness, a more forceful, controlling side.

That wasn't what scared me, though. I held on to the edge of the washbasin, steadying myself as something unsettling rose to the surface. The intensity of my reaction to him was what scared me. He saw something in me I had never seen in myself. I did like it. I did like submitting to him. *I have never felt so helpless in my life, or so powerless, and God help me, never, ever so inflamed.* He controlled everything, including my orgasm. I looked in the mirror again and hardly recognized the face staring back at me.

* * *

Pash had started to come around. I would give her some space now so she didn't feel pressured. She had to decide to stay the night with me of her own accord. We would have to settle in for the night sometime.

Even though I knew she needed some time, I started to wonder what the hell was taking so long. I had finished my champagne several minutes ago and didn't want to pour more until she returned.

I put my trousers in the cupboard with my coat. Remembering I had a couple more condoms in my breast pocket, I retrieved them and put them on the table by the bed. Then I picked up her lingerie. Hearing the water running, I knew she wasn't yet finished. So, I indulged myself.

I separated her hose from her knickers. Brushing her tights across my cheek, I picked up the faintest trace of her scent. Her knickers were damp. I brought them closer to my face and allowed her sweet perfume to fill me. Then I folded her lingerie and put them neatly on the bureau, right next to my pants.

As I considered the possibility of knocking on the door to check on her, she emerged. I asked, "Is everything all right?" She didn't answer right away. I waited.

She put her bag on the bureau and stared for a moment at our underpants lying side by side. When she turned around, she said, "Before anything else happens between us, we need to talk."

"You sound so serious," I said, hoping I hadn't completely misread the situation. "What's wrong?" Again, she didn't answer right away. I went over to her and took her by the shoulders, genuinely concerned now. "Pash, what's wrong? Talk to me."

I didn't know where to begin. How could I tell Ivan my feelings when I didn't understand them myself? I wished to God he would put some clothes on. That hairy chest so close to me . . . I started to feel dizzy again. I felt myself leaning against him. He put his arm around me to hold me up.

* * *

I thought for a moment she might faint so I grabbed on to her. "Come on over here, let's sit down." I realized the bed was the only place where we could both sit. Why the bloody hell didn't they put a sofa in these places? I led her over to the bed and we sat. "Now, sweet thing, tell me what's going on. Are you all right?"

"What just happened between us—things got a little out of hand." She seemed uncomfortable, and I didn't know why.

I started to feel uneasy, not knowing if something had happened to her while in the toilet. "Was it too rough, did I hurt you?"

"Oh, no, you didn't hurt me. I'm fine."

"That's a relief. You just seem so upset."

"I don't mean to worry you. I'm just confused."

"Confused about what?" I really didn't have the foggiest idea.

"About what just happened, about how it felt to me."

"Pash, you really have to explain. I don't understand."

"Ivan, you were right, I liked it. You held me down and wouldn't let me move and I liked it. I wanted to fight you, maybe even spit at you, but I still liked it very much. That scares me."

So that's what this was all about. She looked like she had just confessed a mortal sin. I looked into the eyes of the hottest lover ever to share my bed, determined that this would not be our first and last night together. "Pash, it's all right to like it. I liked it, too."

"What do you mean?"

"I mean, I like being in charge, directing the action." I didn't know quite how to put it without being overtly crude, so I went textbook. "I like being dominant." We were facing each other, sitting on the bed. I put my hand over hers and she looked up at me.

"Does that mean I'm a submissive?"

So she did know the words, if not the feelings. "No, it just means you like it when someone else calls the shots." I could see her struggling with herself, digesting the information. "We were just feeling like a man and a woman." I took her chin between my thumb and forefinger. "Where the hell did you come from anyway? I have never known anyone like you." Her face reddened. That blush had become damned endearing. "You know, you are living up to your name. You are one sexy lady."

She smiled and put her hand on my chest. "You're no pantywaist yourself."

"Thank you, I think. Feeling better?"

Her voice sounded steady, in spite of her embarrassment. "I think so. I'm still confused, but I guess that's okay."

"We can take it easier next time—that is, if you still want there to be a next time."

"I'm surprised you do, considering I called you a bloody git. I'm sorry about that."

"It's not the first time I've been called a bastard. Thing is, it never sounded so good before."

"Do you know how hard it is sitting here beside you in that towel?"

"As a matter of fact, I do," I said with a wink. "How about a little more champagne?"

"I could use some, thank you." Ivan helped me up, again adjusting that damn towel. What I glimpsed this time indicated he did indeed understand how "hard" it was. "You know, you could put your underpants back on."

"What fun would that be?" He tucked the corner around his waist and secured it. "The towel is more comfortable anyway—you know, more room and all." He slid his hand back and forth under the strap of my slip. "Maybe you should try it. You might like it."

"I thought I *had* tried it and *did* like it—in fact, probably too flipping much." He gave me that smile, the one that makes me weak in the knees. I looked at him, standing so very close to me. It had to be well after midnight by now and the clock still hadn't chimed. I reached up and touched his face, wondering what Cinderella felt the first time she saw her prince in a towel.

"Maybe we should save the champagne for later," he said into my ear. Then he lowered the strap of my slip down my arm.

"Maybe we should." He leaned over and kissed my neck. I felt his breath in my ear.

"We can slow down, take our time." He sucked my earlobe into his mouth and then licked my ear. "Tell me what you would like to do."

I knew the answer to that question, but did I have the nerve to actually tell him? Once, I told Gwen I liked oral sex. She said, "Of course you do, so do I." When I explained I meant giving as well as receiving, she teased that I must be quite popular. I had actually only done it a few times, and had developed a taste for it. God, again with the double entendre. Freud would love this.

He kissed my neck, harder this time, probably giving me a love bite in the process. I felt the other strap of my slip slide down my arm, revealing most of my breasts. I knew if I didn't speak up soon, I would miss my chance. I pulled away and looked at him. "There is something I like."

Pash stepped back and her slip fell below her breasts. She made no attempt to pull it back up. "We can do anything you like." I ran the back of my hand down her breast. "Tell me, my sweet Passion, what do you want to do?"

"I don't think I can tell you outright, but I can show you." She reached out, took hold of the towel around my waist and pulled it off. There I stood, a raging one between us. If she surprised me by yanking off the towel, what she did next nearly made me pissing choke.

She knelt down it front of me, shaking her arms out of her slip. Then she started to suck me off. I would have been happy as Larry to have her squeeze my nads or touch me up, let alone this. I've had to beg, borrow and steal for this, even pay a trollop or two for the pleasure. Now, sink me, I had a half-naked redhead doing me like a pro, without my even asking! Oh, yes, I must be living right.

I thought for a moment he might grab that nerve-wracking towel and put it back on, he started so when it fell. Then I knelt in front of him. I took just a moment to appreciate his virility, realizing for the first time he was intact. I had only ever been with circumcised men, never having seen one uncut before.

I licked my lips and slid him into my mouth. I heard him gasp. I waited no more than a heartbeat and then ran my tongue along his length. His foreskin slid back and I held it there, licking him like a cat drinking milk. I felt his hands in my hair and heard him moan, a soft sound, but still feral like before. He started to slowly move in and out of my mouth. I kept licking, trying to keep the suction even and steady. We continued like this for several minutes. Then he stopped me.

I held her head still and pulled myself out of her mouth. She looked up and asked, "Do you want me to stop?"

"Not yet, but I do need to lie down." As I settled on the bed, I considered the possibility that I had actually died and gone to heaven. *If there is a heaven,* I thought, *this is what I would want it to be.*

She crawled onto the bed with me. Feeling randy as hell, I asked, "Why don't you take off your slip and do me some more?" She knelt right in front of me and slowly pulled her slip over her head, practically daring me to take her. But I wasn't ready yet. "Turn around so I can touch you, too." She moved her lovely bottom around, bent over and started to tongue me. Sink me twice!

* * *

When I took off my slip, I understood what a stripper must feel when men watch her undress. Ivan actually had his hand on his cock, wanking as he looked at me. I burned all through my body, knowing he desired me. It didn't matter that I had never been this bold before or that I didn't understand how this could be happening to me. I felt like a harlot and, God forgive me, I loved it! He made me feel terribly safe, even protected.

I wanted to make Ivan burn for me the way I burned for him. As I started to bend over to taste him again, he asked me to turn around. I did so and leaned over, my arse up in the air. I knew that his view had to be deliciously indecent. I licked him just as I felt his fingers move into me. I heard myself make a bestial sound that rivaled his.

I watched her go at me like a hungry calf, all the while rubbing her off. No way in hell did I want to finish this way. We would save that for another time. I smiled with quiet certainty, now believing that there would be more to follow. I stopped her again and pulled her up beside me. I wanted to rest for a few minutes before going on. Otherwise I knew I wouldn't last worth jimmy shit. She also needed to catch her breath.

I put my arm around her and pulled her close. I could smell myself on her breath. I kissed her lightly and asked, "Are you all right with everything?"

"Don't worry so much, I'm fine."

"I want you to enjoy this as much as I am."

"I think I am."

I moved my hand to her breast and squeezed her nipple. "I want to finish inside of you, if that is all right." I squeezed a little harder. Her breath caught. I moved closer to her ear and whispered, "I want to feel you moving like you did before. It felt absolutely smashing!"

"It felt good to me, too."

She had her eyes closed, her response barely audible, but I heard it. I knew she had more admitted it to herself than said it to me. I continued to whisper as I fondled her. "It's fine to let go with me. I know you want to."

She opened her eyes and looked at me. I ran my finger across her lower lip. "Are you ready or do you need more time?" No matter what, I had no intention of pushing her. If I hoped to continue seeing her, I knew she had to trust me.

"I'm ready. Oh, God, yes, I'm ready."

I leaned over her to the bedside table and picked up another condom, rolling it on as I had before. She opened herself for me, but I did not lie on top of her. Instead, I lay down on my back beside her. Brushing my hand across the tight curls between her legs, I said, "Why don't you get on top this time?"

"Ivan, I've never done that. I'm not sure if I can manage it."

"We'll go slowly. You can take all the time you need." I wanted her to trust me, but I also wanted to look at her. When she humped my hand, I couldn't believe a woman could be so lost in it. Never before had I seen that. Now, I wanted to see it again, only this time, I wanted to see her riding my cock. "Come on now, try it, I expect you will enjoy it."

She knelt beside me and then hesitated. I waited. "Are you sure, Ivan?"

"I'm sure, Pash." With some hesitation, she straddled me. She gingerly took hold of my cock. "Don't concern yourself, sweetheart, it won't fall off."

"Since I do fancy a bit of shag, I would suppose we'll find out if it will break." I would have laughed if she hadn't chosen that very moment to grab me and position the tip at her quim. Instead, I gasped. She had control. I had given it to her.

Now I paid the price. Instead of mounting me as I expected, she slid my tip over her clit. The warm slickness of her lips made my cock throb. Everything in me wanted to have her flat on her back underneath me, but I held on. If I didn't follow through with this, she would think me a rotter.

She stroked herself a few more times, each rub bringing me closer to finishing. Clutching the sheet, I told her, "Pet, if you keep that up, you won't have your shag."

"My, my, how the mighty have fallen! Perhaps I should make you suffer the way you tormented me." With that, she took my organ and wedged it at her opening. Lowering herself with excruciating care, she slid my cock completely into her body. I twisted the sheet in my hand, trying not to shoot off as her warmth surrounded me.

"Give me a moment, Pash, just stay still. I am so goddamn close, I'm not going to last worth ruddy Nora if you keep going."

Ivan lay there, sweat trickling down his temples into his hair. He closed his eyes and took several deep breaths. What with the beauty of his chest underneath me and his hardness inside me, he fairly filled me with his masculinity. His potency overwhelmed me.

When he opened his eyes, he said in a hoarse whisper, "You feel so frigging wonderful!" He put his hands on my hips and took another deep breath. "All right, Redhead, nice and slow until I adjust to this."

I started to move as he said, slowly, deliberately. Pretending I had one of my dildos inside me instead of his cock helped me to relax. Raising and lowering myself on his length, I fucked him the same way I masturbated with my toys.

Knowing he watched me made me so flipping hot. Putting my hands on his chest, I leaned forward, pushing his cock as deeply into myself as I could. "God, Ivan, help me to come, please."

I felt his fingers separating my lips, probing, massaging. "Ride me harder, Pash, I can manage it now." Holding myself steady against his chest, I humped him harder and harder while he rubbed me off. His cock filled me up inside. Every time I rose up and slammed back down on him, my climax edged closer. I rode him wildly, with no modesty and no reservation. All I knew, all I cared about, all I wanted was to come.

When it hit, it slammed me into an orgasmic wall. "Fuck, yes, Jesus fucking Christ, yes!" My entire body convulsed violently.

"My God, Passion Flower!" It took all my strength to hold on to her! Never had I experienced a woman so lost in her own orgasm. I rolled over, taking her with me.

Allowing myself to ride the wave with her, I hammered her spasming cunt, lunging into her again and again. She stayed with me, her pelvis smacking mine, bleeding my balls dry.

Chapter Seven

Afterwards we just held one another, neither of us wanting or needing to say anything. It took several minutes to catch our breaths. Ivan managed to speak first. "I am dreadfully sorry about this, but I have to go to the loo before this becomes a proper mess. You would think they would know that a trash bin is needed by the bed to dispose of such things."

He came out of the loo, this time with no towel, and went over to the phone. "Who on earth are you calling at this hour?" I asked, looking at his watch. "It's one thirty in the morning."

"I want to leave a wake-up call at reception. It will only take a moment."

I listened as he made the call. "Hello. So terribly sorry to bother you at this hour. This is Dr. Kozak in room twenty-two. Would you be kind enough to ring us up at around seven thirty? Thanks awfully." He sounded so collected, hardly what I had witnessed only a few minutes before. Of course, the night clerk didn't know he made the call in the altogether, but I did.

Stopping at the cart, he poured us each a final glass of champagne. He handed me a glass as he sat down on the edge of the bed.

"A nightcap, dear lady?"

"Thank you. Yes, that would be lovely." I took the glass and waited for a toast.

"To us and to the love we made. May this be the first of many such nights to come."

We clinked glasses and drank. Leaving the glasses on the bedside table, he turned out the light and settled in beside me. As I cuddled next to him and drifted off to sleep, his toast lingered in my mind.

I heard the phone ring and wondered who the hell could be calling me so damn early. When I came around enough to see Pash beside me, still asleep, I remembered our night together. I picked up my watch. *They are prompt, seven thirty on the nose.* I got up to get the phone, hearing a cheerful female voice on the other end.

"Dr. Kozak, it is seven thirty. You asked for a call. If you will be taking breakfast, a buffet is available in our main dining room until nine. You may also have something brought to your room, if you like."

"Thank you, I do appreciate the call. We will decide on breakfast shortly." I wondered how the hell she could sound so lively and enthusiastic this early in the morning.

While I had the telephone, I remembered I had to call Steve. This could be interesting, since he isn't exactly a ray of sunshine in the morning. "Good morning, old man." I tried to sound chipper, hoping it would be contagious. "I have to ask a favor."

"Where the bloody hell are you, anyway? You know you have a student at nine?"

"That's what I'm calling about. You have to cover for me. I won't be back in time."

"Thanks, guv! Always knew I could depend on you."

"Look, I'm a little involved here. I'll be back in time for the afternoon appointment. I'll owe you one, mate." I wanted to leave it at that, but he wasn't finished.

"So how good is the redhead? Think she might be interested in taking on both of us? Or maybe I should just wait until you dump her. She seems a little old for you, it shouldn't take long."

My hand involuntarily rolled into a fist. I turned and glanced in her direction. Pash seemed to be still sleeping. I wanted to reach through the phone when I said to him, "You aren't fucking man enough for her, you gormless bastard. You know, you can be one ignorant son of a bitch."

"Thanks for calling. Give her a poke for me." I heard the telephone click in my ear. I stood there for a moment, squeezing the handset. When I did ring off, I turned around and saw Pash looking at me.

"That didn't sound like it went very well. Is everything all right?"

Not quite knowing how to answer that, I just said, "I'm so sorry, I thought you were still asleep."

"If we leave now, you could be back by nine, if that would be better."

I felt I owed her some sort of explanation, but for the life of me, I couldn't think of one I could tell her. "No, actually that would make things worse. Best to let it be for a time." I sat down on the edge of the bed. "Just how much of that did you hear, anyway?"

"Enough to know the two of you had words. I don't want there to be a problem with him over this."

"I can handle Steve. He is a decent bloke, has a really good heart. It's just sometimes he can be a little coarse."

"You've known him a long time, haven't you?"

"Longer than anyone else left in my life. He's really the only family I have. Maybe that's why I put up with his bullshit."

She sat listening to me, holding the sheet up around her chest. I hadn't meant to say what I said, it just came out. I saw the corner of her slip, wrapped in the blankets. "Here, you might be needing this," I said, pulling it out and tossing it at her. "We should call for some breakfast unless you want a formal one in the dining room. Considering the clothes we have, it really would be formal, too."

* * *

His easy manner and charming smile had returned, but I could tell he was still upset. More than that, I had heard what he said on the phone. Steve had evidently made some crude remark and Ivan had flared. Obviously he didn't want to talk about it, nor did he want to talk about Steve.

The remark about Steve being his only family seemed to distress him, and if I wasn't mistaken, even sadden him. I had momentarily glimpsed a very lonely man. The mask had slipped a little, but he caught it just in time.

"Are you hungry?" he asked, obviously changing the subject. "I know I am."

"I could eat." Oh, God, am I becoming queen of the double entendre? Remembering my behavior of the night before, I knew Ivan would never look at me the same way again. I hoped he hadn't caught the double meaning, but he did.

"I know you could, but actually I would like some eggs first, if you don't mind." He put his cool hand on my very warm face. Smiling, he said, "There will be time to eat later, if you are still hungry."

I saw he enjoyed teasing me. His mood improved almost immediately. That relaxed me a little, although I still felt unsettled. I woke up feeling disoriented, and then his phone call had disturbed me. I wondered what Steve had said to make Ivan so angry. It sounded like Steve had said something about me.

Ivan rang up the desk for room service. "Bacon and eggs all right with you?" I nodded yes. When he turned around to order, I pulled on my slip. Not only did he order bacon and eggs, but croissants with several kinds of jam, and more fruit. "And throw in a very large pot of tea with that and a pitcher of orange juice."

"That is enough food to feed a fleet of sailors," I said when he hung up. "You really must be hungry."

"As I expect you to be, my dear. I'm not the only one who should have worked up an appetite last night."

It suddenly registered that he stood there, totally nude, facing me. Trying to hold my eyes on his face, I said, "You should put your grundies on. You could catch a chill that way."

"Not likely, with you here."

I saw him indeed heating up again, there being no towel to hide it. I wanted him so much, but I didn't want to get in any deeper than I already had. I really cared about him and wanted to see him again. If this turned out to be a one-night stand, I didn't know if I could handle it now, let alone if I let myself become even more involved.

I reminded him that room service would be here shortly. "Do you need the loo? I want to have a shower before the food arrives."

"By all means. I'm not going anywhere."

"And do put on your underpants. You'll give the lad quite a start answering the door in the altogether. Depending on his persuasion, he might get the wrong idea." With that I took my handbag and went to shower.

I shook my head and smiled as Pash closed the door. She did have a way about her. I went over to get my underpants and noticed that she had left her lingerie on the bureau. I thought better of putting on my pants, going back to the bed to find the towel. If nothing else, it would give her something to ponder when she came out.

I needed some time by myself to clear my head. My Lord, I had never responded to a man like I did to him. Nor had I ever felt anything this intense in my entire life. It frightened me, to want him this much.

I considered the very real possibility that he only wanted the sex. After all, this inn catered to illicit affairs, being the local adulterers' hideaway. He knew that before he brought me here.

I braced myself against the washbasin as I realized my feeling for him had already gone well beyond a casual affair. I wanted to kick myself! I felt like a bloody fool for letting myself get caught up in a romantic fantasy about him. My overactive imagination would do me in yet! I had to get a grip. I caught myself as I nearly sobbed out loud.

Since I had a few minutes to myself, I considered everything that had happened between us. I certainly wanted to see her again. It occurred to me I knew nothing about her situation. Steve said she wasn't married, but for all I knew she could have other relationships.

It surprised me to feel upset by that. Most of the time I felt relieved to know my affairs had limited lives. The semester ended and they went on their way, leaving me to explore virgin territory with each new class. I usually managed to find at least one young lady, occasionally two, who would like a little "extra" help from me, or they would simply come on to me and I would buy into it.

I looked at the closed door when I heard the water running. I wanted to join her, wondering what fun we could have together sharing a shower. It's an interesting word, *fun.* It aptly described how I felt about last night with her. I needed to find out how she felt about it all. I needed to know I would see her again.

Room service arrived in short order. A young fellow wheeled in one cart and took the other one out, stopping only to wait until I got him a tip from my coat pocket. I yelled through the door, "The food is here! Don't let it get cold!" She came out directly, the slip clinging to her damp body. "Of course, cold eggs aren't so bad," I said, coming over and pulling her to me.

She pushed me back, saying, "I thought you wanted some eggs first, and where the devil are your underpants? You actually answered the door in a towel?"

"The bloke didn't seem to mind. Either he is used to it or he really is a bit of a poof."

"I suppose it is only fair to tell you I used most of the soap chip they gave us and also most of the jigger of shampoo. I prefer to know I'm staying overnight ahead of time so I can at least bring a clean set of clothes. This slip is ready to walk on its own."

"I didn't know ahead of time we would be staying," I said, wondering where the hell this attitude had suddenly come from.

"Is that so?"

So, with the new day she pushed a little harder. "Yes, that is so. You notice I don't have anything either."

"You brought condoms."

"And you, Redhead, also brought along some protection. I happen to have felt it, up close and personal. It seems we both packed a little something, thinking ahead." She walked past me to the bureau, picking up her lingerie. I followed her. "You said you prefer to know in advance if we will be staying the night. I'll remember that for the next time." She didn't respond, so I asked, "Do you want to see me again?" It wasn't how I thought this conversation would go, but the question had now been posed. "Well, do you?" I turned her around to face me and could hardly believe it when I saw tears. "Why the Gordon Bennett are you crying?"

In spite of the obvious emotion, she sounded cool. "I might ask you if you want to continue seeing me?"

"I told you last night I wanted to see you again, didn't I?"

She wiped the tears from her cheek, saying, "I can't walk out of here thinking I'll see you again and then have it never happen. I've gone down that road too many times."

"We had a wonderful night together last night. At least, I thought we did. I said before we went to sleep that I hoped for many more such nights to come."

"That was last night, now it is morning. Things change."

"Do they?"

She looked me right in the eyes when she said, "Yes, they do."

"Have they for you?"

"Does that matter? It seems I don't have much to say about what happens now."

"Where the bloody hell did you get that idea?"

"I know Steve must have told you about this place. He stayed here with Gwen. This whole thing happened because you wanted it to happen. Doesn't it follow, then, that what happens now is up to you, too?"

She stood there defiantly, challenging me to explain my behavior. "Yes, I wanted it to happen," I blurted out before I had thought it through. "Damn straight I wanted it to happen." I scrambled for the next thought. "Did I know it would? Hell, no!"

She looked at me with eyes that saw my soul. I turned away and went over to the window. Neither of us said anything for several minutes. I just stared at the grounds below. Without turning around, I said, "There's something you should know about me before any decision is made about seeing each other again." I hesitated, but something inside my belly pushed me to go on. "The last woman I slept with graduated in May. The one before that will be a senior next year. I hear the one before that married a duke. Who knows what became of the rest of them? They graduate and move on."

I paused, not knowing what the hell possessed me, and then turned to look at her. "I wouldn't bloody well blame you if you told me to go fuck myself now. Why would you want to keep seeing me, feeling like I used you? But I want you to know something. You are the first woman I have taken to bed that I really like, I mean truly enjoy being with, in, and out, of the bedroom. I would have to be a goddamn fool not to want to see you again."

I paused again, reaching out to touch her hair; her eyes were still filled with tears. "You have plenty to say about what happens now." I could have said a lot more, but all I managed was, "I think I need to have a shower before we eat breakfast," my voice cracking a little as I said it. I turned and left.

* * *

I felt my knees start to buckle. I made it to the bed and sat down, dazed by what he had told me. He had been sleeping with his female students, apparently for quite some time now. He told me straight out, with no punches pulled. What the devil did he expect me to say to that?

Everyone had a past, including me. But this—he could ruin his career if one of them decided to charge sexual misconduct. He had to be the most appealing man I'd ever met. Why in the name of God would he have to resort to his students for companionship?

Feeling nauseous, I tried to calm myself. I got up to pour a cup of tea. I sipped it and had a bite of croissant. That quieted my queasy stomach. I could still hear him saying, "I would have to be a goddamn fool not to want to see you again."

I could not deny I still wanted to keep seeing him. The idea of not seeing him again was why I became so upset. I didn't think this meant so much to him. He had actually choked up telling me I had a say in what happened now. A few minutes ago, I thought I had no voice in this. Now I realized the decision had become mine to make.

I closed my eyes, trying to focus on what I wanted to do. I had become very smitten with him. It embarrassed me to think about how often I'd thought of him over the last three weeks, and how I had fantasized about him as my Highwayman.

We just spent the night together, the most intensely romantic night of my life. My attachment to him had really started to take hold. Now, I had to reconcile my feelings for him with this raw confession about his past.

I remembered an old Russian friend of our family asking me, whenever he visited us, if anyone had come into my blood yet. He said that's how true Russians feel it. You know you have found the right one when they flow in your blood. I always laughed at his question, telling him no one had. I looked at the closed door and realized the next time he asked, I might well have a different answer for him.

Chapter Eight

"It gets warm in there, doesn't it? There's no fan." Pash noticed I looked as damp as she had coming out of the loo.

"These old inns weren't built with vents. I suppose we should be grateful they have central air." Even if I didn't feel like small talk, I could stomach this more than I could picking up the conversation where we had left it.

"I hope you don't mind, I helped myself to some tea and a bit of food to settle my stomach."

"Not at all. Are you all right now?"

"Nearly. You should eat something, too."

The very idea of food made my gut roll. "I expect everything is cold. I'm sorry about that." I saw her lingerie still lying on the bed. This situation had moved well beyond niceties. I felt no inclination to be genteel. "I thought you would be ready to leave by now. Breakfast isn't important. We can dress and I'll drive you home."

"What time is check out?"

"Noon, but I see no reason to linger here. We best be getting on." I grabbed my pants and pulled them on and then went to the cupboard to get the rest of my clothes.

"Could we sit for a bit and talk?"

"Seems we've said quite enough already. Perhaps it's best

we leave it alone." I pulled my trousers off the hanger, involuntarily grinding my teeth.

"There's something I haven't said and I need to say it to your face."

"Well, let's get down to it, then," I said, stepping into my trousers. I braced for the tongue lashing I knew I would hear.

Ivan turned and looked at me, his jaw locked. I couldn't let his defensive posture stop me. I had to speak my own truth and tell him what I felt in my heart. So, I plunged in. "If you meant what you said, about wanting to see me again, I want to see you again, too. But you have to understand what I'm feeling."

I couldn't read his reaction; his face looked like granite. I summoned my courage and pushed on. "You have to know that this is more than sex to me. If that's all this is to you, please be gentleman enough to walk away now before . . ." I had to stop. The lump in my throat had grown too large to continue.

"Before what?"

"Before I fall even more in love with you than I already have." I barely got it out before the lump took my voice completely.

"Pash, how could you possibly be in love with me?" He sounded incredulous. "You hardly know me. I've had plenty of women think they've fallen in love with me before, only to be replaced with someone else in short order. It's easy to be confused about that after sleeping together."

That sobered me just as surely as if he had thrown a glass of water in my face. A wave of anger washed through me. I found my bag and retrieved a handkerchief. "Are you talking about those girls you've been with?"

"I suppose I am."

"Well, let me tell you something, Dr. Kozak," I said as we faced off, "I am not confused about what I am feeling, although I must be addled in the head to admit it to you. I can't speak for any of those young ladies who have fed your ego, but I don't go around telling every man I sleep with that I'm falling in love with him! You are one arrogant son of a bitch! Why I should give a frigging shit about what happens to you, I can't fathom. But I do."

I stopped to blow my nose and he started to say something. I interrupted. "I'm not finished yet." He bowed in mock deference.

"If you continue what you are doing, you are headed on a downhill path to a brick wall. It is only a matter of time before one of them brings harassment charges against you. Then everything you have worked so hard for is gone, up in smoke. And for what? To get laid? You have to be balmy, completely off your nut! The way you look, with everything you have to offer, you could have any woman you wanted. Why are you risking everything by doing what you are doing? What's more, you've been playing Don Juan for so long, you wouldn't recognize the real thing if it bit you on the arse!"

I stopped, needing to catch my breath. I went over to get some juice, feeling dizzy again.

"Let me do that for you," I said, taking the pitcher from her shaking hand. I poured juice in a glass and handed it to her. "Just sip that and breathe, before you give yourself a stroke." Pash took the glass and drank, closing her eyes. She looked as though she might faint. I watched her closely, preparing to catch her if she started to go down.

Her words rang in my ears. Lord knows I wanted to believe what she had just told me, but I couldn't accept it. "Take a couple of deep breaths." She had been chalky pale when she started, and now glowed crimson. Her blood pressure had to be all over the map. I waited for a moment until she had recovered her breath and her color, and then asked, "Are you finished now?"

"At least until I think of something else," she snapped back.

"Well, then, I'll just jump in before you do. Don't you think it has occurred to me that I've had a loaded revolver pointed to my head? Why the bloody hell do you think I asked you out anyway? I haven't responded to a woman my own age in years, until you. Damn straight I wanted to get you into bed with me after getting good and hard with you on that horse!

"Not only are you the oldest woman to keep my company in years, but also the first one I won't be paying with a better grade because you've slept with me! You are absolutely right. I do have to be off my nut for doing what I've been doing. That includes being attracted to some redhead who made her grand entrance into my life by falling into a pile of muck and coating herself with crud!"

I stopped talking and looked at Pash. She had the oddest expression. She bit her lower lip until finally she couldn't contain it. She laughed.

Still smiling, she said, "That's right, and you picked me up and hosed me off. Looks like I just fell into another muck puddle, doesn't it? Are you going to hose me again?"

"You had better learn to watch your step; you could start liking it." I felt the tension break between us, but I still had one more thing to say. "You said I could have any woman I wanted. I've never put that to the test until now."

I took the glass out of her hand and set it down. I pulled her to me and said with more sincerity than I had managed in years, "Pash, I do want to see you again. I want to get to know you and I want you to get to know me. It's too soon to know for sure how we feel about one another or where this is going, but if we don't give it a go, we'll never know." I leaned over and kissed her and then said, "Why don't we have something to eat before they throw us out of here?"

"You mean food, right?" Her humor had definitely returned.

"I mean food, as in breakfast. We'll take a rain check on the other for next time. We do agree now that there will be a next time, don't we?"

"Yes, we do agree. I just hope we get a little better at working out our differences."

"We'll practice."

"What time is it anyway?"

I looked at my watch. "Ten fifteen. We've been in this room twelve hours."

"Feels like a lot longer, somehow."

"I know. What say we have some food, get dressed and check out. Steve is already pissed off at me. I don't want to be late for my afternoon student."

"Male or female student?"

"He's a young fellow, I suppose about seventeen. Just so you know, he's one of my oldest students, except for you. I draw the line at jailbait!"

"That's a relief. Is it indelicate of me to ask if you're seeing anyone else now?"

"Yes, it is indelicate, and no, I am not. Are you?"

"No, not for several months now."

"One less thing to wonder about, then."

"Ivan, may I make a request?"

"I said just food, remember?"

"Wise arse, I'm serious."

"Make your request. I can always say no."

"I want us to be honest with one another, right down to the bone. I want to feel I can ask you anything and hear the truth, no matter what it is."

"That's a tall order."

"I know. But I can't go on guessing about what is happening between us. It's killing me."

"I know. Me, too. All right, then, we will give it a go. But I do reserve the right to refuse to answer something I am not comfortable talking about. Agreed?"

"Agreed. I reserve the same right."

"Understood. Now, my first question, and I expect an honest answer; do you really think I took advantage of you last night?"

"Yes, but I better understand now why you did. Since we are being honest, it is only fair to tell you I had a wonderful time last night. More than once, I felt like Cinderella."

"I honestly didn't know if anything would happen between us, Pash. I just stacked the deck in my favor." I uncovered our eggs. "Well, they're stone cold, but they still look good. At least the tea is still warm in the thermos pot."

"You really did stack the deck. I would have had to be dead not to want to spend the night here with you." Pash piled some eggs and bacon on her plate and then picked up two croissants and some fruit. "I'm feeling hungrier than I thought I would."

"Much to my extraordinary pleasure." I winked at her and smiled, very much relieved that she seemed all right now. She stuck out her tongue at me. "You should be careful with that! Now that I know what you can do with that tongue, you may be eating more than your breakfast!"

"Not before I ask you a few questions, Dr. Kozak. It's my turn now. Have you ever been here before with anyone?"

"No. You already guessed that Steve told me about it. He didn't even begin to describe the place. I didn't expect to walk into the Garden of Eden when I asked you to come here." I drank a full glass of juice in one gulp and went for a second. "This is fresh squeezed. They go for the full monty here, don't they?"

"In more ways than one. Did you arrange this room ahead of time?"

"Not exactly. I inquired about availability, but did not reserve one until we had agreed on it. I swear that's the truth."

"I believe you. I want you to know, I don't regret what happened, not at all. I'm glad we stayed the night. It's being discarded like yesterday's bread afterward that had me so distraught. It's happened to me before and I thought it was about to happen again. It feels bloody awful to be another notch in a bedpost."

With her sitting on the edge of the bed in her slip, I couldn't imagine anyone discarding her like yesterday's bread. "How long has it been since you've been with someone, if you don't mind my asking?"

"Since October last, about nine months. That one was a definite notch. After that I swore off men for a time and just focused on my work."

"Not a good experience?"

"No, not a good experience. His self-involvement followed him into the bedroom. I hardly needed to be there at all. Oh, but he fancied himself to be a great lover, a regular Casanova. Let's just say he didn't earn himself an entry into my journal."

"Did I earn myself an entry?"

"A lengthy one, to be sure. I could do several pages on that smile of yours, let alone the rest of the night."

"I'd like to read it sometime."

"Ivan, your ego doesn't need any encouragement! I will, however, give you copies of my books to read, if you are still interested."

"Do you know you are like cheddar cheese?"

"I'm what?"

"Like cheddar cheese. You have a real bite. I'm developing a taste for it, just like I did with extra sharp cheddar."

Before she had a chance to snap back at me, I directed the conversation to her books. "And yes, I am very interested, particularly in *Sagacity*. I couldn't find out much about it at the library." My strategy worked. She took the left turn with me and told me a little about the book, just enough to whet my appetite.

Now this is what I imagined the morning after conversation could be! I lost patience with inane drivel about grades and course work some time ago. God Almighty, how delightful to have an intelligent dialogue with a woman after spending the night together! I had a real good feeling about this, and about her.

After breakfast we both finished dressing. I went over to the bedside table to gather my things. I put on my watch, pocketed the remaining condoms and pulled my hair back. Then I picked up her earrings. She had gone into the toilet to comb her hair. I followed her in. Without asking, I put her earrings on her ears, and then kissed her neck. I felt myself starting to respond and pressed into her. "You know, I could go again."

"If you keep kissing me like that, we'll be paying for another night here."

"Lifting her hair, I kissed her neck again. "We could have a quickie, right here."

"You bugger, I'm already dressed and so are you."

"No need to take off our clothes." I lifted her skirt. "Just pull down your knickers." I palmed her breast through her dress. She pushed her bum back against my now very hard cock.

"You pull them down."

I looked at her in the mirror. She had closed her eyes, her breasts rising and falling with each breath. Christ, I wanted her now! I couldn't wait until we saw each other again. "Take off your shoes." Raising her skirt, I found the elastic of her hose. Pulling her hose and knickers down to her ankles, I took them off. "We don't have much time. Are you all right with a quick shag?"

"Yes, darling, shag away."

Opening my trousers, I exposed myself and rolled on a johnny I had in my pocket. I pulled up her skirt and rubbed my cock against her bare bum. "You want this, don't you?"

"Yes, I want it. I want to feel you inside me again. Please, do it now."

"Spread your legs wide apart and lean over the washbasin." She did as I said. I positioned myself behind her and pushed. My cock slid in easily.

"Oh, yes, Ivan, that is so good!"

"Passion, I'm going to screw the arse off you." I held on to her hips and pistoned my cock into her. "You are so frigging hot, so hot and wet!" Again and again I pounded her.

"Ivan, fuck me harder. I'm almost there!"

"Oh, yeah, sweetheart, I'll give it to you harder." I held her still and slammed into her. Within seconds, she pushed back into me, stifling a scream. "That's it, sweetheart, come for me, come hard for me." Her cunt squeezed my cock as her entire body shook. Holding her tightly against me, I creamed into her.

We stood there, welded at the hips for several seconds. I finally pulled out of her, taking care not to mess my trousers. "Are you all right, Pash? I need to see to this."

"I'm fine, Ivan, just catching my breath."

I cleaned myself up without getting any jizz on my clothes. I picked up her lingerie and checked my watch. "It's eleven forty-five. I knew we could manage it."

"If you give me a moment to get myself together, we can leave."

Within five minutes Pash came out of the loo. She appeared a bit flushed, but showed no other sign that she had just had a seeing-to. As I picked up the room key to leave, Pash put her hand on my arm. "Ivan, let me pay for some of this. With dinner, the room and all the room service, this must be costing you a small fortune."

"That is already handled. And it is a bargain, considering everything. This is not negotiable. I asked you to come here and I'm picking up the tab. Understood?"

"Understood. But then I owe you one."

"I'll be sure to remind you of that at the appropriate time. Now let's check out of here." We headed downstairs to the lobby. At the desk the bubbly young lady that woke us earlier had the bill ready. I signed it and pocketed my copy. I could tell Pash wanted a look at it, but I made sure that did not happen.

Safe to say, I had never spent so much on a single night out with any woman before. I had found myself one special lady and felt damn good about treating her right.

After I turned in the room key, the clerk said cheerfully, "Thank you, Dr. Kozak. I trust we shall see you and your wife again soon." Taking Pash by the arm to leave, I found I didn't mind the clerk's faux pas.

Chapter Nine

The trip back into town seemed far shorter than the ride out the night before. I could still hardly believe we had just spent the night together. I reached over and ran the back of my hand over his whiskers. "Do you know I have second thoughts about continuing my riding lessons? I really don't think I have what it takes to learn to ride."

"You can put those thoughts on the larder shelf! You certainly will continue your lessons." He winked at me. "You just need a little special attention."

"What do you have in mind?"

"I think you should come two—make that three—times a week. You need to learn to relax around horses. I can show you everything you need to know to care for them, and also get you riding on your own."

"My budget can only handle one lesson a week. Your time isn't cheap, Dr. Kozak. And with you around, I should be coming much more than two or three times a week!"

"Well, then, we need to discuss a scholarship plan. My time is my own after six P.M. If you can manage a few evenings, I'll teach you off the clock. You'll also be coming regularly."

"You're serious, aren't you?"

"Damn straight I'm serious—about all of it, I might add." He grinned at me. "That way I'm guaranteed to see you three times a week. Then you'll have me over a couple more times for dinner. That leaves me sufficient time for laundry and lesson planning, which is about all the personal work I have to do while I'm here."

"You've covered all the angles, haven't you?"

"And all the positions, too. It's my way. I told you I like to be in charge. You'll get used to it."

I found myself shifting in the car seat, feeling some salacious tingles move through me as I considered the possibilities. Putting my hand on his thigh, I asked him, "Just how in charge do you like to be?"

"It depends. Do you have any particular situation in mind?"

I could tell he knew what I meant. The bulge forming in his trousers told me as much. But he wanted me to squirm a little more, which I did in more ways than one. "I couldn't help thinking about our conversation last night, when you said you liked to call the shots." I paused, not knowing quite how to continue.

"Yes, I'm listening." I glanced to confirm that her blush had started. It had.

"Well, I have to admit, I'm curious."

"Curious about what?" We had reached the edge of town a few minutes before and would be at her place directly. Damn, I should have driven slower.

"I'm curious about the feelings I had, the ones we talked about last night. I want to explore them with you." She said it all in one breath, her face getting pinker with each word. I stopped in front of her flat. She jumped a bit when I stopped the car. "We're here already?"

"I'm afraid so." I looked at her, knowing we were about to part company. Her face glowed red. I wanted like ruddy hell to follow her inside and continue this conversation in privacy. "May I walk you to the door?"

"You didn't answer me."

"I didn't know I had been asked a question."

"You're playing with me now."

"Isn't that the point?" I said, holding her stare for a moment. She had her hand on my thigh, my cock nearly grazing her fingertips. I picked up her hand and placed it on my hardened organ. "This should answer your question." After sliding her hand down my length, I lifted her hand to my mouth and kissed her palm.

Saying nothing else, I got out and came around to open the door for her. I thought better of trying to go inside right now. I wanted her to simmer in her own juices about all this before we had another go. I knew I might have to wank a few times until I had her again, but, damn, it promised to be good.

I helped her out and walked her to the door. I pulled her up against me and kissed her as deeply as I had last night. She responded as she had before. I held her close and said into her ear, "I have to get back, but I will call you later today. We'll talk more about it then." I kissed her again, this time barely grazing her lips. With that, I went back to the horses, and to Steve.

I watched Ivan get into his car and then went inside. I glanced at the wall clock, wondering how long it would be until he called. I reprimanded myself for being a silly twit, acting like one of those infatuated schoolgirls that followed him around. But, then, I had good reason to wonder when he would call, seeing how we had just left things.

As I changed clothes I felt him taking off my dress again. Then I felt him holding me. Fragments of our night together kept flashing in my mind like an erotic slide show. I threw everything in the laundry basket, putting the dress aside to be cleaned. I lay down on my bed, making sure I had the roller blinds drawn on the window. Touching myself up, I remembered my night with him. I closed my eyes and allowed the images to overtake me.

Remembering how it felt to be with him excited me all over again. I thought of the curve of his arms when I held on to him, and his weight on top of me. Flexing my fingers, I imagined his hair—my God, so much hair—all over his body.

And that body, hard and cut! Sweet Jesus, I wanted him inside me again. I opened my bedside table drawer. Digging through my toys, I found a rubber dildo, the most realistic one I owned. I had managed myself for a long while now. This time, I imagined him inside me.

I drove home trying to think about my afternoon rather than about her. I would call later, after dinner. Willie twitched in anticipation.

When I drove up, I passed Steve riding one of the horses. I didn't bother stopping. I went right to the house to change. I still had a little time before my student arrived, and I needed to collect myself. I also needed a few minutes before speaking to Steve. I knew he would probably still be pissed off. I didn't want to go a round with him if I could help it.

Thing is, he could get in my face like no one else. He would say anything twice—three times if he thought he could get away with it. Usually he would be funny, going right over the top and then some. Lord knows, the things he said to me weren't for mixed company. But he didn't seem to know when to draw the line. He had discovered when we were still boys how to get under my skin. He still used it.

I had learned that certain personal matters had to remain private. Steve had no sacred cows. Everything he knew could be regurgitated. He had done as much with my telling him about my affairs. I had to be careful with him about Pash. As I changed clothes, I recalled his attitude from earlier this morning. I couldn't ask for a more loyal friend. But this time there would be no game playing with her. If Steve pushed me, I knew we could well tangle again.

The phone rang and I started awake. I had no idea what time it was or how long I had been asleep. I grabbed for the phone on my bedside table, thinking it had to be Ivan. In the sexiest voice I could manage in my haze, I said, "Hello, there."

"Hi, Pash, this is Gwen. Sounds like you were expecting someone else."

I sat up on the edge of the bed as it sunk in that it wasn't him. "Oh, hello, Gwen. I'm sorry, I was asleep."

"In the middle of the day? You must be awfully tired, or maybe you're coming down with something."

"I'm not sick, just tired."

"I'm not surprised."

Her playful mood made me suspicious. "Why do you say that?"

"Steve called me this morning. Need I say more?"

"Oh." So much for keeping this private. "What did he say?"

"This and that, small talk mostly."

"Gwen!"

"Oh, go on with ya, you know he told me about Ivan."

"What about Ivan?"

"That the two of you must have had some night together, seeing as how Ivan didn't come home last night and then rang up Steve this morning to tell him that he wouldn't be back until this afternoon. Why didn't you tell me the two of you had something going?"

"Because we didn't, until yesterday."

"Go on!"

"It's the truth. He's been teaching me how to ride and asked me out to dinner last night. That's all."

"That can't be all if Ivan didn't go home last night. Luv, you're holding out on me."

"What else did Steve say?"

"You first."

"We went to that inn where Steve took you. You know the one."

"Go on!"

"You've said that twice. Now you tell me what else Steve said."

"I had already told him a little about you when I rung him

up about the lessons, but he wanted to know more. He asked how I knew you and how close we were."

"What did you tell him?"

"A little of our history and that we are good friends."

"Did he say anything about Ivan?"

"He said he knew after the first class that Ivan had his eye on you. Ivan asked him if you were married."

"He did?"

"Steve said he also saw Ivan on a horse with you the other day, getting real friendly. He said he thought Ivan had more on his mind than just teaching you how to ride. Says he figured right. I asked Steve to make sure you got a good instructor. I guess he did!"

"Ivan is a good instructor. I'm just not a very good student. He was trying to help me that day." I failed to mention to Gwen the part about him rubbing up against me.

She didn't say anything for a moment. When she did, her voice had changed. "Pash, Steve told me something else about Ivan, something you may not want to hear."

"What, Gwen?"

"He said Ivan has a long history of short relationships, mostly with younger women. Actually, most of them have been his students. Chuffin' 'ell, Pash, he's been sleeping with them! Steve asked me to tell you not to put all your eggs in his basket."

"I know. Ivan told me himself."

"He did? I'm surprised."

"So was I."

"You like him, don't you?"

"I like him very much."

"I can tell."

"I didn't know you were seeing Steve again. I thought you weren't speaking after that argument you had a couple weeks ago." I wanted to change the subject.

"It has been a little chilly lately since the row we had. But things may be heating up again. He asked me out tonight."

"Is that good?"

"Luv, it's very good, and so is he, if you get my meaning. What about Ivan?"

"Gwen, you know I can't answer that."

"Why the bloody hell not! You know they must talk about us. Steve says they're like brothers."

"It's too soon. I need time to let the dust settle after last night. And I doubt Ivan will be telling Steve anything about what happened. They had words this morning."

"Steve said as much. He said he had to cancel a nine-fifteen appointment at the bank because Ivan didn't show up. Pash, don't worry about them. I don't know Ivan at all, but Steve says they're family. Brothers fight and make up. I'm sure Steve is over it by now."

"I hope so. Look, Gwen, I don't mean to rush you off, but Ivan is supposed to ring soon. I really don't want to miss him. It's important to me."

"You really have a thing for him, don't you?"

"Maybe. I'm not sure yet."

"You know I'll keep at you until you tell me more."

"I'm sure of it. One of these days I'll be ready to tell you more about Ivan if you'll tell me more about Steve. Deal?"

"Deal. Seriously, Pash, be careful. My intuition says you're well on your way to being arse over tit for this guy. I don't want to see you get hurt."

"I don't want to be hurt, Gwen. But right now I'm willing to take that chance."

"I can tell. He must really be something."

"He is."

"We'll talk soon, promise?"

"I promise. Have a good time on your date."

"I can only hope for a time as good as yours. Later, luv."

I successfully avoided Steve most of the afternoon. After my student left I stowed the gear and stopped to check on a new colt. I had helped deliver him a few weeks before. He promised to be a beauty, all black with four white socks. Steve agreed with me that Spats had to be this little fellow's name. I had hunkered down inside the stall to give Spats a once-over when I saw Steve come into the stable.

"Hello, guv'nor. Glad to see you could make it."

"I told you I would be back this afternoon."

"So you did. You know, old chum, I had to call the bank and cancel an appointment this morning so I could cover your arse. I didn't like having to do that so you could have a bit of skirt."

"I didn't know you had an appointment."

"I'm not in the habit of telling you everything I do. Of course, seems you don't tell me everything you do either."

"I never have."

"Makes me wonder what you've done that I don't know about."

"Plenty." I stood up. "And all of it is none of your frigging business."

"I know enough and I'm about to know more."

"What the hell does that mean?" I felt myself bristling.

"I gave Gwenny a call this morning. We had a nice chat. In fact, we're seeing each other tonight. First time in a while."

I remembered how close Gwen and Pash were. "What the bloody hell are you up to?"

"I thought my little Gwenny might like to know her friend Pash had spent the night with my mate Ivan. Interesting little piece of news, now, isn't it?"

I could see he was goading me. I had to keep my head, or risk splitting his. "I expect she might be interested. What of it?" I moved closer, coming out of the stall and latching it. He stood his ground.

"I suggested she give Pash a ring this afternoon, to have a little heart-to-heart. You know how women are when they talk, comparing notes and all. Our names are bound to come up." He stepped toward me and then stopped, waiting for my reaction. I held my temper and remained silent. Then he went that one step beyond. "And I mentioned to Gwen that you like the ladies, especially the younger ones. I thought Pash might like to know you've dipped your wick into more than a few."

That did it. My inner vision went white and I had him by the shirt before he knew what had happened. "Look, you son of a bitch, if you do anything, I mean *ANYTHING*, to hurt her and I lose her, I'll break your face and then beat you into yesterday. Do you get me?" I shoved him backward and he fell flat on his arse. I didn't wait around until he got to his feet. I went back to the house.

Chapter Ten

I went straight to the cupboard in the kitchen and grabbed a bottle of vodka. I needed a drink to settle me down. I belted some back and let the warmth spread through me. The way I felt, I could really lay into the stupid bastard and hurt him. I needed to get a grip. I heard the door open, and in he walked. I turned to face him, the open bottle still in my hand. I said nothing.

"Mind if I join you, guv'nor?"

"Help yourself." I slammed the bottle down on the table and started to leave.

"Where the hell are you going? You know I don't like to drink alone."

I turned back to him, trying to read his frame of mind. I couldn't. "If I stay, one of two things will happen. Either we'll talk about this man-to-man, or we'll go back outside and I'll beat seven shades of shit out of you. Your choice, mate."

He took a drink and then handed the bottle back to me. "Go on, guv, have another." I took the bottle from him and drank some more. I hadn't eaten anything since breakfast and could feel it working already.

"I've seen you jumped up plenty of times, but you're about to blow a gasket. I'm not looking to end up in the hospital. I have a farm to run." He took back the bottle, taking another hit.

"I'm telling you again, if your stupid-assed game playing has done me in with her . . ."

"I know. You'll beat me into yesterday."

"I think I best go upstairs to pack. I'll be leaving for Northampton tonight."

"Hold on there, Kozak! What the hell has gotten into you?"

"I am goddamned sick of being around children, that's what! I'm sick of living with them and I'm sick of sleeping with them. I finally met someone who is an honest-to-God adult, a real woman, and your prank has probably screwed me over. Do you really bloody well think I could stay here after that?"

Steve looked at me with the queerest expression. "Well, I'll be damned!" He put the bottle on the table, pulled out a chair and sat down. "You really have a case on this one, don't you? No goddamned wonder you're so bloody riled. Here I thought you nailed her. Turns out, she's nailed you!"

"Doesn't frigging matter now, does it?" I took the bottle and started toward the stairs. He got up and followed me.

"Wait a fucking minute, old man. I thought you said we could talk about this."

"I changed my mind."

"Too bloody bad. We're going to talk."

I stopped at the bottom of the stairs, not starting up them, but not turning around. "So, talk."

"Look, let me call Gwen to find out what happened. At least give me a chance to smooth things over if I did upset the apple cart."

I knew this was as close to an apology as I would ever hear from him. I turned around. "I'm supposed to call Pash in a little while. I'm either calling her from here or stopping to say good-bye on my way back home. I guess that depends on you, old man." I headed upstairs.

I made myself a sandwich, not wanting to get involved in cooking before Ivan called. Just as I finished it, the phone rang. This time I picked it up and just said a quiet, "Hello."

"Hi, Pash. It's Gwen. Has Ivan called yet?"

"No, he hasn't." Before I could rush her off the phone, she interrupted.

"Good, I have something to tell you."

"Gwen, couldn't this please wait? He's going to call any minute."

"I know, but luv, you're going to want to hear this before he does."

"For Lord's sake, what are you on about?" I knew I sounded impatient, but I couldn't help it.

"Steve just called. Ivan is in a state! He had a row with Steve about you, a bad one."

"About me? What about me?"

"If you'll listen for a moment, I'll tell you. Ivan is convinced Steve mucked things up with you by calling me. Ivan is going back to Northhampton tonight, he's so pissed off!"

"Gwen, no!"

"Pash, Ivan must think my dear boy really raked him over the coals and it got back to you. Now Ivan is saying because Steve mucked things up, he's leaving."

I felt myself near tears. "Gwen, this is so ridiculous. He can't leave, he just can't."

"Easy, luv. I don't think he'll leave after he talks to you."

"Gwen, I can't wait for him to ring me. I have to call and stop him before he does something stupid."

"I know you do. Take a deep breath. I have one more thing to tell you."

"Oh, God, what?"

"Steve thinks Ivan is falling in love with you."

"Gwen, I think I'm falling in love with him, too."

"Luv, I knew that this afternoon. Everything will be all right. Just talk to him."

"You're still seeing Steve, aren't you?"

"He's picking me up shortly. Why?"

"Tell him he can't muck things up, not after last night."

"I'll tell him."

"Thanks, Gwen. I have to go now." I found Steve's number on my desk. He answered the phone. "Hello, Steve, this is Pash. Is Ivan there?"

"He's upstairs."

"Could I speak to him, please?"

"Certainly you can. Did Gwen ring you up just now?"

"Yes, that's why I'm calling."

"Pash, before you talk to him, I want to apologize if I caused a problem. I have never seen him so ticked off. He's bloody steaming! I didn't know he cared about you so much. I want to set this right."

"Steve, he told me himself about his past. I already knew before Gwen told me."

"Then why, if you'll pardon the French, did he get so frigging pissed off at me if you already knew?"

"That's what I want to find out. Steve, I won't let him leave."

"Thank you, Red, you're all right. Pardon me while I get him for you." Steve put down the phone. I heard him yell, "Hey, guv, Pash is on the line for you." I couldn't hear if Ivan said anything back to him. Steve picked up the phone again a few moments later. "He says to ring off and he'll ring you back on his mobile from upstairs. I don't have a phone up there."

"How is he now?"

"That's a tricky one. It's difficult to say. But just so you know, he did take a bottle upstairs with him. I couldn't tell you how much of it he has put away."

"Thanks for telling me that. Have fun with Gwen."

"I'm sure we will. Cheers."

I looked at the bottle, intending to take another swallow before I rang up Pash. But when I had trouble focusing on her number, I thought better of it. She probably already thought me a lout. I didn't want to add *drunk* to the list. I wondered why the hell I hadn't written her number on a bigger piece of paper. Taking my best guess, I punched in the numbers. I heard her voice on the line. I couldn't be completely soaked; I had dialed correctly.

"Hello."

"Hello." I didn't know what else to say.

"How are you doing?"

"Fair. And yourself?"

"I could be better. I hear you're thinking of leaving tonight."

"I'm thinking on it."

"Why?"

"I got into it with Steve. If I stay here I could end up really hurting the son of a bitch. So I guess I'm going home."

"I don't want you to go."

"I have to go back sometime; might as well be tonight."

"I know you have to go back sometime; you live there. But it doesn't have to be tonight."

"Remember what we said earlier, about asking questions and getting honest answers?"

"I remember."

"What did Gwen tell you this afternoon?"

"Nothing you hadn't already told me. Steve told her you have had affairs with your female students. There were no surprises."

"You're sure about that?"

"Quite sure. Why are you so upset about that call? What do you think happened?"

I hesitated, not knowing where to take this. "That bloody sod knows most every skeleton in my cupboard. He could well have put you off me with his butting in where he doesn't belong. I thought he had."

"You could have asked me what Gwen said. You decided to leave town without even asking what she told me. You must be feeling awfully guilty about something to have such a reaction."

"I'm not proud of some of the things I've done. I didn't care to hear my dirty laundry coming back at me from you."

"Just so you know, Dr. Kozak, I'm not put off you, not at all. Quite the contrary." She paused and then asked, "Have you ever killed anyone?"

"Have I what?"

"Have you ever killed anyone?"

"Not to my knowledge, at least not in this lifetime. Where the hell did that come from?"

"Because, you twit, that's what it would take to put me off you. I'm beginning to think you are a few sandwiches short of a picnic, jumping to all these wrong conclusions."

"Christ, you do have a quirky way of putting things."

"It's my way. You'll get used to it. Now let me finish." Snippy little wench! "You've made some awfully big assumptions here. No matter what you think you've done, you can't know how I'll react to it. If we are to give this a go, we've got to get this straight between us. Ask me, for Lord's sake. I'll tell you the truth."

"You want to keep seeing me?"

"Ivan, hello! Yes, I want to keep seeing you. I thought we put that issue to bed this morning."

"I haven't eaten anything since breakfast. I guess I am a little fuzzy."

"I suppose you are. That and the bottle you took to your bedroom."

"Goddamn wanker, can't keep his mouth shut if his life depended on it."

"Well, if you are still leaving, at least wait until morning. You are in no shape to drive tonight. Steve is with Gwen anyway."

"He would have a helluva time if I were to pull out now. He's shorthanded as it is. If I stay, we'll have to settle our differences. So you're saying if I kill him, that would put you off?"

"It would certainly give me pause."

"How about if I just knock some sense into his stupid arse?"

"No permanent damage?"

I felt myself smile. “I promise.”

“Some sense could be good.”

“I’ll decide in the morning. Didn’t we have other things to talk about tonight?”

“I seem to remember something we meant to talk about.”

“So do I.”

Chapter Eleven

I followed my intuition and came right to the point. I made the right choice, because Ivan's sullen mood shifted. He remembered the reason he said he would ring me this evening. "You told me you had some feelings you wanted to explore with me. Is that still the case?"

"It is still the case. I just don't know if now is a good time to discuss it."

"Why not now?"

"You're upset and also a little tight, that's why."

"No, sweetheart. You're tight, I'm pissed."

"Well, obviously you're sober enough to be waggish. Still, maybe you should eat something before we talk."

"That's a little hard to do over the phone. You know, if we keep going, we could set a double entendre world record." I couldn't help but laugh out loud. Even drunk, his wit had a salty edge. "I think now is the perfect time to talk about those feelings. Maybe talking to you is just what I need."

"Maybe it is."

"Explain to me what you were thinking in the car. Refresh my memory."

"Ivan, I don't know if I can do this—just talk to you about what I'm feeling. It's very personal."

"My Passion, might I remind you it doesn't get much more personal than last night?" My heart skipped when he said "my

Passion." "Just close your eyes and tell me what you want to explore with me."

"Ivan, I've never responded to any man the way I respond to you." I became flustered and had to stop. "I don't even know where to begin."

"Just relax and take your time. I'm stretched out here on my bed. Where are you?"

"On the sofa in my sitting room."

"Do you have a phone in your bedroom?"

"It's a portable."

"Then go into your bedroom and get comfortable, too. Seems like a good idea, considering what we want to talk about." He had taken charge. I could feel my pulse beating between my legs.

Now that I knew I still had a chance with Pash, I felt considerably better. "What did you do this afternoon?"

"I took a nap. I should have done some work, but I seemed to have other things on my mind."

"Like what?"

"You know what."

"Tell me anyway."

"Like last night."

"Are you in your bedroom now?"

"Yes. Should I undress?"

"Only if you want to undress. I haven't—yet." I saw her blushing face in my mind's eye and smiled.

"That was a joke."

"Just remember, you are the one who suggested it. Now, tell me more about what you had on your mind."

"Before I fell asleep, I thought about you, about how it felt to be with you. It felt really good."

"Did you get excited thinking about it?" I started to stroke myself, waiting for her to answer.

"I got very excited."

"Did you do anything about it?"

"Yes."

"What?"

"I thought about how you held me. I felt so helpless, so vulnerable. But it felt so good, too."

"Did you touch yourself while you thought about it?"

"Yes, I imagined you holding me." Her voice had changed into a sultry whisper.

"Did you finish while you remembered?"

"Oh, God, I brought myself off remembering how it felt when you wouldn't let me move."

"Is that what you want to explore with me, the feelings you have when I am in charge?"

"Ivan, I want more of what we did last night. I want to know how it feels to let you take over, to do what you want to with me."

Thoughts of what I wanted to do with her stirred me up even more. I opened my blue jeans and pumped harder. "Are you excited now?"

"Terribly."

"Put the phone down and take off all your clothes. I'll do the same." I heard her put down the receiver. I had already kicked off my boots. It took only a moment to pull off my shirt and lose my jeans. I flopped back on the bed, ready for more. It took her another minute or so.

"I'm back."

"Are you naked?"

"Yes."

"So am I. Now I want you to touch yourself like you did this afternoon. Are you wet?"

"I'm very wet. Are you hard?"

"Hard and throbbing. Tell me what you want to do with me. Keep touching yourself while you talk."

"I want you to make me do things, nasty things."

"What kind of things?"

"I want you to make me kneel in front of you and suck you. I want to smell you and taste you and feel your hands in my hair. I can't stop licking and kissing you until you tell me to stop." She paused. I could hear her breath through the phone. I knew she was getting close. So was I.

I spoke very softly, my voice hoarse. "Pash, I want you to do that and more. I want to watch you take off all your clothes, very slowly. Then I'll make you get down on your hands and knees. You have to stay like that until I am undressed, with your legs spread, waiting for me. When I am ready, I will kneel behind you. Before I take my pleasure from you, I want you to beg for it. Will you beg for it, Pash?"

"God, yes, please. I need to finish."

"You'll finish when I say you can and not until. I'm putting my fingers inside you, Pash, from behind. Feel it, feel my hand rubbing you, harder and harder. You spread yourself open for me. You want it bad. Tell me you want it."

"Oh, Ivan, I want it, I want you inside me."

"Tell me you want me to fuck you, Pash. You have to beg for it; you said you would beg for it."

"God, yes, I want you to fuck me. Please fuck me."

"I'm not ready yet. I want you hotter. You've been a very naughty girl, Passion Flower. Naughty girls have to be spanked. Have you ever been spanked, Pash?"

"No." She could barely speak. I knew I had her on the edge. I held back, waiting for her to go over the top.

"No man has ever bent you over his knee, pulled your knickers down so he could fondle your pussy and then spank you?" I took my time drawing that picture for her before I asked, "Do you want me to spank you like that, Pash?"

"Oh, God, yes, I want you to spank me before you fuck me." Her thick whisper nearly did me in. I couldn't help groaning into the phone, but I still managed to hold on.

"I'm going to spank you, my pretty, naughty Passion. I am going to slap that sweet arse of yours until you squeal. Before I satisfy myself inside you, I'm going to rub you and play with your pussy. Then I'm going to fuck you. I'm pushing myself into you because that's how naughty girls like it, hard and fast. I'm taking you, Pash. I'm pounding against you, not stopping until you come. I'm not stopping, I'm taking you from behind until you come. . . ." I heard her gasp and moan right into my ear. I shuddered and started to spurt, listening to her finish.

I heard him grunting on the other end as I drifted back to earth. I knew the sound of his climax now. I listened, holding the phone tight against my ear. His breathing gave me shivers. Gooseflesh rippled down my arms and legs. I waited, not knowing when I should say something. He finally said, "Are you still there?"

"I'm still here."

"Are you all right?"

"I'm fine, even wonderful."

"Bloody hell, that was good. I made a mess here, but at least it's my bed."

"I should have such a mess in my bed."

"I expect you will, in short order."

"Have you ever done this before, on the phone?"

"Not with anyone I know. I have called a few of those numbers now and again when I've had a bit of a dry spell. Let me tell you, it wasn't anything like this! Have you ever?"

"No, nor have I ever been spanked."

"Ever thought about it?"

"If I tell you that, we could start up all over again."

"Your point being?"

"Aren't you tired?"

"Hell, yes. But it wouldn't take much to give me my second wind."

"Yes, I've thought about it."

"I figured as much. We can explore that, too, if you like."

"Dr. Kozak, your libido is one for the books."

"So is yours, my dear. Seems, in that respect, we are well matched."

"Since it appears you aren't leaving, how about tomorrow evening for the personal attention you promised?"

"I said I would schedule that. Tomorrow would be fine for the riding lesson, however."

"Very funny. What a comedian."

"Thank you. I'm pleased you appreciate my humor. Now, then, tomorrow is Friday. That means you have to get in one more lesson before your regular time on Tuesday. What's it going to be?"

"Can't we decide that later?"

"Absolutely not! You have to do food shopping if you have me to dinner. So, we need to work out what we're doing when."

"You're bloody pushy, do you know that?"

"You'll get used to it. How about we plan Saturday for dinner and Sunday for the lesson? Works for me."

"Then we will have seen each other six days running. Isn't that a little much?"

"If you really want some time alone, we'll discuss it. I'm betting you won't!"

"It's very difficult to say no to you."

"I'm banking on it. Now, do we have a plan?"

"Yes, we have a plan."

"Good. Now I should clean up my bed and get me some food. Have you had dinner?"

"I had something earlier."

"Well, you make sure you see to your own meals. You have to keep up your strength."

"Are you always this forward?"

"Let me put it to you this way: I am certainly not shy. I go after what I want and I usually get it."

"Well, mister, don't expect me to always be this agreeable. I am no will-o-wisp myself."

"I know. Bodes well. Now, may I say good night, my Passion,

and pleasant dreams. I'll see you tomorrow around seven. Remember to bring your books."

"I'll remember. Good night to you, too, Ivan. You have pleasant dreams yourself. May they be delicious."

"Yours as well, Redhead. Good night."

I sat on the edge of my bed, holding the phone. Ivan had called me "my Passion" a second time. Could I even let myself think that he actually meant it?

Chapter Twelve

I tried to clean the jizz off my bedspread. Since most of it had already dried, it would have to wait until I did my laundry. Anyway, a bit of dried jizz in a man's bed shows he's holding his own.

Pulling on my pants, I went down to the kitchen. I glanced at the clock. No bloody wonder I felt peckish—it was well past eight o'clock. I made myself a hearty sandwich and heated some leftover stew. That, with a bottle of ale, served as dinner.

While I ate, I considered that only last night at this time, we were having dinner together. That seemed more like a week ago than only a day. I sure as hell couldn't get her out of my mind! Some of the things she said kept going around in my head like a hamster on a wheel, especially her rant about falling in love with me.

We'd made love four times already. I had found myself a real pistol, no doubt about that. No question she could hold her own with me, and had a sassy way of proving it! I didn't realize until last night that she could also hold her own in bed. In fact, she appeared as hungry for a good fuck as I've always been. No way in hell could she fake that kind of arousal. Her excitement juiced me up, pushing me to push her even more.

Thinking about Pash's interest in discovering new sexual

territory stirred me all over again. She actually asked me to do "nasty" things with her.

I suppose I had always wanted to initiate a woman. Over the years I had fantasized about introducing a young lady to love. One of my favorite fantasies cast me as her guardian as I taught her how to be a woman. I had spent more than one evening beating off to that one.

I realized that's what I had been looking for with the young ladies who so often shared my bed. Most of them expected me to do all the work and rarely wanted to try new things. Some of them even tried to fake it with me, which had actually been laughable. Lately I couldn't wait to get rid of them, finding their company nothing more than tedious. I had yet to find one that lived up to my fantasies.

The last day with Pash was the closest I'd ever been to realizing my fantasies. I wanted to see her again—not just for the sex, but because I fancied her. She said I wouldn't recognize the real thing if it bit me on the arse. That might have been true before, but not this time.

I put on my dressing gown, not even bothering to pick up my clothes from the floor. I wanted a cup of tea and some quiet time to think. I could feel Ivan still with me, almost like I could smell him in the room. I really didn't care that my behavior with him since last night went well beyond anything else I'd ever done. I couldn't remember a time when I felt more alive, absolutely pulsing with life.

I put on the kettle and then went to the hall cupboard. That's where I kept the extra copies of my books. I intended to loan Ivan a copy of each—that seemed less cheeky than giving him inscribed copies. But as I dug for the box, I felt differently. I wanted to give him inscribed copies with personal messages from me to him. I wanted him to know how deeply he had touched me. Maybe I even wanted him to know I didn't mind seeing him six days running!

Ivan had almost left tonight because he thought Gwen told

me something that put me off him. Steve said himself he had never seen Ivan so steaming. I got the impression he really banged heads with Steve tonight. Picturing the two of them side by side, I could see how Ivan could hurt Steve if they tangled. He had considerably more bulk than Steve and several inches on him. I smiled, thinking I would have to ask Gwen sometime about how the two of them measured up in other ways.

The thought of not seeing me again had upset Ivan terribly. It hardly seemed likely that he would be so distraught if he only wanted the sex. When Gwen told me he planned to leave tonight, I felt like someone had punched me. I knew he had to go back to Northampton in August, but I wanted the time until then. Maybe in a month we would know if we wanted it to continue. I was realistic enough to understand it might only be a summer romance, but honest enough to admit I would like it to be more.

The kettle whistled just as I opened the box. I found a copy of each book and shoved the box back into the corner. Then I made myself a spot of tea and grabbed a few biscuits. I had to find something appropriate for the inscriptions. I put my snack on the side table with my books. I pulled out some Percy Bysshe Shelley and some Shakespeare from my bookshelf, figuring I could come up with something between them.

I curled up on the sofa and started thumbing through the books. I thought of Ivan in the library surrounded by poetry books juxtaposed by the image of him standing by the bed rolling on a condom. He absolutely oozed masculinity. But I sensed much more underneath the surface than what his virility revealed. His hunger did not seem limited to sexual appetite.

When he spoke of Steve being his only family, I caught a glimpse of something he kept tucked deep inside. All his degrees and flirtations could not give him some place where he felt at home, or, more to the point, someone waiting for him to come home. He told me of no one else in his life. I wondered if he socialized at all in Northampton, with other faculty perhaps.

He had such a clever mind and a keen sense of humor. I couldn't imagine him squandering it on anyone who didn't appreciate his intelligence and wit. Some part of him needed a change. Otherwise he wouldn't be so troubled about my knowing his history. He assumed I would judge him as harshly as he judged himself.

We had a marvelous time last night over dinner, talking and getting to know one another. I remembered how much we laughed and how relaxed we both were. I also remembered how much I wanted to spend the night with him and how conflicted I felt when it actually happened. Never in my whole life had I been so taken with a man so quickly, nor had I ever been so forthcoming with my feelings.

Both those reactions went against every rule I had established for myself over the years. With every failed relationship, I made a new rule about how I would never do whatever I had done again. Now my self-imposed rulebook had gone right out the window. My mind told me I could get burned—badly. But my heart told me something else. My heart said to go for the brass ring, or perhaps, if the wind stayed at my back, a gold one.

I found a snippet of Shelley I could use. Then I moved on to the Shakespeare for the other quote. The sonnets didn't have the right feel, being a little too heavy on the *I can't live without you* point of view. I didn't want to go there.

I turned to *The Taming of the Shrew* and started to read. Dr. Kozak had a healthy shot of Petruchio in him. The headstrong arrogance felt familiar, as did the way Petruchio kept Kate off balance. Ivan would probably see a little of Kate's sharp tongue and temper in me. So, I found a suitable passage and then personalized each book.

Even with my nap, sleepiness had crept in. When I finished with the books, I turned out the light and went to ready myself for bed. I picked my clothes off the floor and had a momentary flash of horrid embarrassment when I thought about actually having had phone sex with Ivan.

But that quickly faded when I remembered how he had seduced me, his voice deep and masterful. Then I heard again the ferocity of his climax. I closed my eyes and held my clothes to my chest, burning with the memory. He had most certainly come into my blood. I dropped my clothes back on the floor and took off my dressing gown, climbing into bed with the molten heat of him all through me.

My clock woke me at six. I rolled over to turn it off and knocked it onto the floor. I got up to get it, still half asleep. I didn't want the ringing to wake Pash. I grabbed the clock from the floor and snapped it off. I turned around and saw my own empty bed. It took me a moment to shake myself awake. I must have been dreaming, because I really thought she was asleep beside me.

I flashed back to our conversation last night and remembered she would be coming to the farm at seven this evening. I must have been more soaked last night than I thought. Why the hell hadn't I gone to her place for the night?

I had hungry horses waiting and stalls to clean, so I had a shower and went down to the kitchen to get some breakfast. Steve's car wasn't around. I supposed he spent the night with Gwen. My check, your checkmate, old chum.

I made some coffee and fried up some eggs. I heard his car just as I finished eating. A couple minutes later, he came in the back door. I had calmed considerably from the night before, but still wanted to get a few things straight between us. He came into the kitchen and threw his keys on top of the refrigerator. "Well, guv, are your suitcases still packed?"

"I never packed them. Pash and I are okay."

"Gwen thought you might be. She said Pash almost started to cry when she heard you were going to leave."

"We have things straight between us." I put my dishes in the washing-up bowl and then turned to look at Steve. "But what I said last night still stands. I'm not taking any bullshit with this. If you want to stay healthy, I would mind my manners if I were you."

"You'll have to wait in line. My own little Gwenny told me if I did anything to make you leave, she would let her German shepherd use my balls as chew toys. She said Pash has been hurt before because she trusted some joker. She hasn't seen anyone in a while now because of it. Gwen says she trusts you. If she gets hurt, it will be because you dumped her, not because of anything I did."

"I'm not going to dump her."

"Tell me that six months from now and maybe I'll believe it. The first skirt who comes on to you in the fall, it will be 'Pash who?'"

My hand curled into a fist, but I spoke calmly. "She's coming out here tonight. I'm going to help her with her riding, gratis. She'll still pay for her regular Tuesday lesson, but the rest is on my own time. I expect that is okay with you?"

"Fine with me, mate."

"I have horses to feed now." I left him standing in the kitchen. I had managed that exchange without knocking him through himself. He expected me to dump Pash as soon as the semester started. I hadn't even thought that far ahead. But, then, why would I?

He wasn't unjustified in thinking I would end it when I left here. That had always been my out: the semester would end and, with it, the affair. I had never once considered extending any of these liaisons beyond a few hot nights together. Christ, the thought of being saddled with one of them for longer than that made me flinch. That's why I always made sure I had plenty of condoms around. The last thing I needed was to accidentally knock up one of them.

What would happen when I went back to Northampton? I wanted to see Pash as often as possible during the summer. Things would get a little more complicated if we wanted to see each other after that. My usual attitude was just to wait and see how it went. But this time I knew I would need to make some decisions before leaving. Right now I definitely wanted to keep seeing her.

I figured we had to see how we got on during the summer, keeping in mind that we would need an arrangement of some sort in place by the time I left. I also wanted to prove Steve wrong. I never thought of myself as a bastard, but it seems he thought otherwise these days.

What Pash said yesterday morning came back to me yet again. For perhaps the hundredth time, I heard her say, "You have to know that this is more than sex to me. If that's all this is to you, please be gentleman enough to walk away now before I fall even more in love with you than I already have."

I woke up feeling rested and ready to work. I spent most of my day at the computer, reworking a section of my manuscript that I couldn't get quite right. Today it fell into place. I don't know why I hadn't been able to get it before this. Maybe I had a slightly different take on things today. I stopped for lunch and continued to write all afternoon.

Satisfied that I had put in a solid day's work, I made some dinner. The lesson seemed secondary to seeing Ivan again, but I knew to expect a lesson. Ivan made himself quite clear about the degree of personal attention he would give me today. Perhaps tomorrow I would get a little more.

I ate, had a shower and changed. I did another just-in-case and put in my cap. I really didn't expect I would need it tonight, but better to have that security in place beforehand. I also made sure I had on pretty scanties, again, just in case. I liked knowing I might need it.

At about six thirty I did a once-over in the mirror, grabbed the bag with my books and left for the farm.

On the drive there it occurred to me that I hadn't the foggiest idea what I could make for dinner tomorrow night. I needed some ideas from him. Perhaps some seafood pasta might be good, but I had to make sure he liked fish. I didn't know much about what he liked, except sex and steak and, of course, horses. The phrase "a man's man" seemed to apply to him in spades, yet he had the wherewithal to get a doctorate in English literature and become a full professor at a prestigious university. As I drove down the lane to Steve's farm, I started to feel flushed.

Chapter Thirteen

I parked in the usual spot, this time knowing Ivan's car from Steve's. I looked in the stable and saw Ivan brushing Nutmeg. He had her already saddled, with the smaller saddle this time. I felt a little disappointed that I would most likely be on her alone tonight. He seemed to be talking to Nutmeg and didn't notice me. As I got closer, I heard him saying to her as he brushed her neck, "That's a good girl. Do you know you're a good old girl? You still have some good years left, sweetheart. We're going to make sure you live them out right."

"She's a lucky horse, having you to watch out for her."

Ivan jumped a bit, almost like he did when I pulled his towel off the other night.

"Christ, I didn't hear you come in. You could kill a fellow doing that." He gave me that smile, his wonderful smile.

"Sorry. I didn't mean to startle you. I thought you heard me come in." I knew he hadn't, but I didn't want him to think I had been listening. "I suppose I am a little early."

"That's all right. My heart is starting to slow down." He came over and kissed me in a sweet, friendly way. "So, how are you?"

"I'm doing very well, thank you. How are you?" I asked, reaching up and brushing his whiskers.

"Much better than last night, thanks to you. I'm terribly sorry if I upset you with all this Steve hullabaloo."

"Ivan, if you still feel you want to leave, we can work something out. It isn't healthy to stay if you're not happy here." As much as I didn't want him to go, I had to let him know he could.

"Thinking I had shot my wad with you was why I wanted to leave. Since I haven't, I think I'll stick around."

"But you have shot your wad with me, four times now."

"All right, Miss Double Entendre, time for your lesson." He took my hand and led me over to Nutmeg. "Are you ready to try this again?"

"No."

"Well, you are my star pupil. So you had better think about applying yourself to the task at hand."

"Blimey O'Reilly, if I'm your star pupil, the rest of them must really be pathetic!"

"You're the only one assigned extra-credit work." He reached down and gave my bottom a sound whack. "Let's get on with it then!"

"I thought this was to be a riding lesson tonight," I said, turning to face him. "You do that again and Nutmeg can fend for herself." Again, he smiled.

"My Passion, you make it fecking hard for a fellow to do his job." He reached out and pulled me to him, kissing me as he had in the restaurant. I hungrily returned his kiss, thinking I had managed to circumvent this lesson. When he pulled back, all thoughts of a literal roll in the hay popped like a bubble when he said, "Now, are you going to get on that horse yourself or do I have to lift you onto her?"

Pash obviously had things other than riding on her mind. Her reaction to both my swatting her rump and then my kiss told me plenty. As much as I wanted to give into my own urges in those directions, I thought it best to stick to my original agenda. I needed to set a precedent that I meant what I said. I proceeded with the lesson.

This time she mounted Nutmeg with minimal help. She

had begun to catch on in spite of herself. I reached up and ran my hand up and down her back, reminding her to stay relaxed. She squirmed a little in the saddle when I touched her. "Now, now, none of that. We're here for a lesson, remember?"

"It is rather difficult, sir, to remember that at this moment!" She squirmed again, obviously enjoying herself.

"Well, we're going to lead her outside now. Steve is about. I expect he could get quite an eyeful if you continue those maneuvers." She gave me a dirty look and then sat still. "Hold the reins like I showed you on Tuesday." I took hold of the rein near the bit and gave it a tug. "Come on, old girl, let's go for a walk." We went outside and I led Nutmeg into the riding ring. "All right, Sunshine, make her walk around this circle."

"You're not serious!"

"I am absolutely serious. I have shown you everything you need to know to comfortably ride this horse. So, do it!"

"Ivan, I don't think . . ."

"Passion, you are tensing. Relax, sweetheart. Think about how you felt after we made love."

"Well, at least that will distract me." She smiled weakly.

"Now use your legs to start her moving and then use the reins to guide her. Remember, be gentle, more so than you were with me." She glared at me as though she wanted to climb down and punch me. "Mind yourself. Nutmeg can sense what you're feeling."

"If that were true she would be humping the fence." I started to laugh just as she tapped Nutmeg's side with her leg. I jumped back out of her way to keep that damn big horse from stepping on my foot. I saw Pash's surprised look when the horse actually moved. I watched for a moment, not interfering. Pash instinctively pulled the reins in the correct direction to have Nutmeg turn, and her body weight shifted in the same direction.

"Remember, be gentle!" I yelled after her. "Use the reins and your legs to guide her." Nutmeg knew the drill well enough that it didn't take much to get her to walk that circle. The slightest direction got her going and she ambled along like an old professional. Pash did one complete turn around the ring.

"Keep going. Do it again. Let your back relax so the movement of the horse rocks you." She went around again, her form improving this time. "Spot on, Pash, you're doing it! You're riding on your own!" I saw her expression change from a look of determined concentration to a surprised smile.

I had her go around once more and then told her to stop. "Don't jerk the rein, just tug it gently back toward you; she knows what that means." Pash did just as I said and, by God, she stopped Nutmeg right beside me. "You're a natural!"

"Right, and you're the Queen Mum!"

"Now, I want you to take her back into the stable."

"You're pushing, Dr. Kozak."

"It's my way . . ."

"I know. I'll get used to it."

"Indeed you will. I'll open the gate. It's a straight shot from here."

"It's a straight shot until we have to make that hard left to get her in the door!"

"I promised Nutmeg a treat for this extra duty. Do I have to promise you one as well?"

"Couldn't hurt."

"Jolly good. If you get her into the stable, I'll let you cook me dinner tomorrow night."

"That's a treat?"

"Could be if you play your cards right."

"I hope you like fish. I'm planning a seafood pasta."

"Well, get this old girl back into her stall and we'll talk about it." I walked over and opened the gate. I saw that determined look again and knew the hard left wouldn't be a problem.

Ivan walked ahead of me to the stable, not even looking back to see if I needed help. When he got to the door, he just stopped there with his arms folded across his chest, waiting. I could tell Nutmeg planned to walk right past him, clear to the horizon if I let her. So I leaned to the left and tugged the reins in that direction. Thank the Lord, she started to turn.

I kept leaning until I had her walking toward Ivan, and then straightened up and slackened the reins. I tapped her side very gently with my foot, just to let her know I wanted her to keep moving. As she walked through the door, Ivan once again looked like that cat who just polished off the canary.

I let her walk to the spot where I had mounted her and tugged back on the reins. She stopped. I just sat there, obediently waiting for my next instruction. Ivan came up beside me and rested his hand on my thigh. "Bob's your uncle! You're on your way. Let me help you down." When he said that, he slid his hand up my leg to my waist. I shivered. He apparently felt it because he asked, "Are you cold?"

"No. Quite the contrary."

"Maybe I need to hose you down again."

"Depends on which hose you use, mister."

He started to laugh. "Come on, my little spitfire, get down from there."

I swung my leg across Nutmeg's back, holding on to the saddle. When I had cleared her hindquarters, Ivan took hold of my waist and lifted me to the ground. He didn't let go, pulling me against him. He pressed his groin against my bum and said into my ear, "You see, my Passion, you aren't the only one who needs to cool down. I made it through your whole lesson with this."

I wiggled my bottom, trying to wedge his hardness deeper into me. "It's nice to know I'm not the only one hot to trot."

"No, ma'am, Nutmeg trots very well. We have to take care of her now." He let me go and started to undo the saddle.

"Do you know you drive me crazy?"

"Seems to me that's a pretty short trip for you."

"You're a real cutup, Dr. Kozak."

"Thank you. It keeps life interesting." I watched him methodically take off all the tack and put it away. Then he started to brush her.

"I could get jealous. You're paying her more mind than me."

"This is a lesson. Part of a lesson is proper care of the animal. By rights, you should be doing this, not me." He handed me the brush. "Go on, brush her. It's time the two of you bonded."

I took the brush from him. "How can you stand it?"

"Stand what?"

"This." I reached out and lightly touched the front of his jeans. He took away my hand and kissed my fingers.

"I like how it feels. I can stay this way for a long time and not go any further. Unless, of course, a brazen wench pushes me where I don't want to go right now."

"You really are a controlling bugger, aren't you?"

"I told you I was. Maybe you're starting to believe me."

"Maybe I am. But I can be just as determined as you are controlling." I pulled my hand out of his and purposely caressed his length once more. Then I turned to brush Nutmeg. Ivan walked up behind me and pressed into me again, pinning me against the horse.

"You asked if I liked fish earlier. What kind of fish?" He slowly started to rub up against me.

"Shrimp and scallops. Lobster, too, if I can find any. What are you doing?"

"That sounds good. I'm rubbing off against you."

"You're what?" He had become more insistent.

"I'm rubbing off." He pulled me tighter against him. If not for the cloth of our jeans, he would have poked my bum. "You pushed the issue, sweetheart. Now I do need some relief."

"Then let me pull down my jeans. I have my cap in."

"So you came prepared again! Well, I think I prefer to finish just as we are." Nutmeg stood there like a flipping stone wall while Ivan humped my bum. The urge to fight welled up in me again, just like it had the other night. I tried to hit him with the brush and I dropped it. Ivan reached under my shirt and squeezed my breasts. With the other hand, he grabbed between my legs. I couldn't help myself. I started to slide against his fingers.

"You son of a bitch, fuck me already."

"You do have a mouth when you get hot, don't you? No, sweet Passion, this is it for tonight. Take it or leave it." He pinched my nipple, sending electric sparks all through me. I rubbed harder. "I guess that means you'll take it."

He slid his hand in a seesaw motion between my legs, roughly grinding his organ against me at the same time. I pushed back into him, partially in resistance, but more wanting that hardness inside me.

Suddenly he groaned into my ear and gripped me hard between my legs, causing the most pleasurable pain to shoot into me. I pushed into his hand even harder, intensifying the sensation. I started to spasm and grabbed on to Nutmeg for support. His hand squeezed again, more a reflex than a deliberate act. I moaned into Nutmeg's coat as another wave of electricity washed through me.

When I had my breath enough to speak, I spit at him, "You son of a bitch, why wouldn't you fuck me?"

"Because, my Passion, then it wouldn't have been my call, now, would it?" He turned me around to face him.

"I wish to God you would make up your mind! You want to fuck me and then you don't want to fuck me! What the bloody hell is it you really want?"

"I really want you to understand what it is to be with me. Either you can handle it or you can't. If you can, you will be the first." He ran his fingers through my hair and gave me a look that burned into me. "My God, Passion, a woman has never gotten to me like you do. But I can't soft-pedal myself. I will push you as far as you think you can go and then push you some more. It is how I am. So far I haven't found anyone who can handle it more than once or twice."

"I'm beginning to understand why!"

"That's exactly what I want, for you to understand." He bent down and kissed my forehead. "I wanted to fuck you, more than I can tell you. When you walked in the door tonight, I felt it. But I don't get the rush by giving in to it. I get off on it when I control it."

"You wanted me to fight you, didn't you?"

"Damn straight I did! I don't want a passive skirt mooning over me and then phoning in a performance. I want you to resist me. When you finally give in, you aren't just giving in to me, you're giving in to yourself."

"I must be properly barking! You're actually starting to make sense."

"You know what I'm talking about. You said it yourself. You're as determined as I am controlling. It is every bit an immovable object meeting an immutable force."

"Do you mean my wanting to thump you with that brush is a good thing?"

He smiled. "Exactly. Don't you think this all sends us both to places we've never been?"

"Well, I have to fess up. I've never tried to hit anyone before. If what you say is true, it does help me better understand what happens between us. How long have you known about this?"

"Honestly, about five minutes."

"Seriously, how long?"

"Pash, really, it just surfaced inside me, looking at you. Sweetheart, we have a lot to talk about. I also have a load in my pants that is mighty uncomfortable. Maybe we best call it a night and pick this up tomorrow at your flat."

"Are you bringing an overnight bag?"

"Are you inviting me to spend the night?"

"How do I answer that? If I say yes, you'll say no. If I say no, you'll say yes."

"Why don't we leave it open, then. I can always borrow your toothbrush, can't I?"

"I'm sorry, that is beyond intimate. I'll suck on your tongue, but stay the hell away from my toothbrush."

"Yes, ma'am. I'll be sure to remember, BYOTB. Speaking of bring your own, might I bring the wine, dear lady?"

"That would be a help, thank you. You're sure seafood pasta and a salad will be all right?"

"I am quite sure. A loaf of bread, a jug of wine and thou; I'll pick up the bread, too. What time?"

"Is six too early?"

"Six is fine. By the way, did you bring your books?"

"They're still in the car."

"Then let me walk you out."

"What about Nutmeg?"

"Christ almighty, I forgot about her."

"Yoo-hoo, Ivan, knock-knock—how could you forget about this enormous animal standing right next to you?"

"I had other things on my mind."

"Must have been terribly important things."

"They were. Let me just put her in the stall. Come on, girl." He patted his leg and Nutmeg turned and followed him like the family hound. I stood there watching the pied piper of horses bed down his favorite for the night. He reached into a bag hanging outside the stall, pulling out an apple. Nutmeg got her promised treat. I saw him stroke her neck and say something I couldn't hear.

When he came out, I had to ask, "What did you say to her?"

"I told her how beautiful she is and thanked her for a job well done. Then I told her good night."

"Like I said earlier, she is a lucky lady."

"Takes one to know one. Now about those books . . ."

After I had a shower and changed, I opened the small gift bag Pash had handed me before she left. She gave her books to me outright, explaining she had more copies than she thought. I opened *Sagacity* first, since that was the one that had piqued my curiosity. It surprised me to see she had written something inside. I laughed out loud when I read:

I am as peremptory as she proud-minded;
And where two raging fires meet together
They do consume the thing that feeds their fury:
Though little fire grows great with little wind,
Yet extreme gusts will blow out fire and all:
So I to her and so she yields to me;
For I am rough and woo not like a babe.

—Petruchio,
The Taming of the Shrew

Ivan,
You obviously know Petruchio very well, to my extraordinary delight.

—Pash (P.F. Platonov)

I picked up *The Search* to see what she had written in it. My eyes filled when I read the beautiful words she had chosen.

As morning dew, that in the sunbeam dies,
I am dissolved in these consuming ecstasies. . . .
Even though the sounds, its voice, that were
Between thy lips are laid to sleep
Within thy breath and on thy hair
Like odor it is lingering yet—
And from thy touch like fire doth leap:
Even while I write my burning cheeks are wet—
Such things the heart can feel and learn, but not forget!

—From "To Constantia,"
Percy Bysshe Shelley

Ivan, I won't ever forget—Pash (P.F. Platonov)

Yes, sir, I had found myself one special lady.

Chapter Fourteen

I spent the rest of the evening in my room, reading. After skimming each book, I started *Sagacity* from the beginning. Pash's voice came through on every page. When I read her discussion on living from the soul, she really hit a nerve. She said the seat of intelligence is wisdom. In order to be wise, we have to relearn how to think with heart and how to listen to our own soul. The more I read, the clearer it became that she embodied the very essence of the book.

I read until I fell asleep, waking only when the book slid off my chest and hit the floor with a thud. I picked up the book and put it on my bedside table. Before I turned off the light, I looked again at the inscription. The very idea that I had a relationship with Pash at all seemed unreal, considering what I had just read. Add to that the amazing development that we had become lovers. Christ, I hadn't just thrown a seven, I'd won the goddamned Irish Sweepstakes!

The next morning I took the book down to breakfast with me, hoping to finish it before seeing Pash for dinner. Steve had already made coffee. I heard him in the larder, swearing about something. I poked my head in. "What the hell are you doing?"

"I dropped the frigging sugar canister on the frigging floor, that's what. The ants are bloody well declaring a national holiday to mark their victory!"

He stood there pushing sugar across the floor with his foot, a totally inadequate approach to the problem. "Ever consider getting the broom?"

"Bloody sod, you could lend me a hand here."

I got the broom from the cellar way. When I came back, I found Steve on his hands and knees, scooping small piles of sugar into the sugar bowl. "Now what the hell are you doing?"

"A damned blind man could see I'm trying to save enough sugar for my coffee!"

"You scraped it up with your foot. I hope you haven't stepped in any horse shit lately." He flipped me the bird and kept scooping. I started to sweep around him. "When you move your fat arse, I'll finish cleaning this up."

"I'm finished. I filled the bowl. By all means, Jeeves."

I swatted his legs with the broom. "Will you get the hell out of the way? I'm doing you a favor here." He went back out to the kitchen and I finished sweeping up his mess. When I came out, I saw him with the book.

"Well, guv'nor, looks like you got yourself a hot one this time. 'For I am rough and woo not like a babe.' Seems she has a taste for it."

"It would do you a ruddy lot of good to read what she has to say in that book." I took it away from him and put it back on the table. "And wash your chuffing sticky fingers before you look at it."

He went to wash his hands. "I saw her last night in the ring. I have to hand it to you, old man. I never thought you'd get her that far." He grabbed the hand towel as he said, "I almost came into the stable to say hello before she left but thought I might be interrupting."

"Good choice." I knew he wanted information, but I wasn't inclined to give him any.

"I did see the two of you at the car, though. After that kiss, I expected you to crawl into the backseat with her."

"Are you becoming a voyeur in your old age? I can suggest several films if you like that sort of thing."

"Just wanted to know how things are, is all. I have to find out for myself, since you aren't talking." He walked back over and picked up the book. "So she wrote this?"

"Every word."

"Looks pretty heavy."

"It is."

"Also looks like you've read a good piece of it already. Must be good."

"It is."

"Why the hell are you being so bloody tight-lipped about this, Kozak?"

"Maybe I think it's private and maybe you should respect that. By the way, I'm going to her flat tonight and don't expect to be back until tomorrow afternoon, when I'm giving her another lesson. Is that enough notice?"

"Plenty. That kid I taught for you the other day is going to start to work here part time. He wants to learn more about the horses. I think I've also found someone to replace the trainer I lost this spring. I have to make sure my arse is covered if you decide to split."

"Glad to know you're thinking ahead. Right now I expect to be here until late August, as I told you I would. Unless, of course, you throw my arse out of here."

"Just so you don't fuck Missy Redhead in the stable when I have customers around. That's just good business, old man."

"I'll remember that." I poured myself some coffee and sat down beside him. "We're getting low on supplies. We need to work up a list to do some ordering next week." We spent the next forty-five minutes talking horses, the only common ground we seemed to have these days.

I slept later than I meant to. When I got home last night, I started to clean, wanting to get a head start on today. Once I started, I couldn't seem to stop. I had to do something to burn off the adrenaline pumping through my system. I couldn't believe he had done it to me again! I had never tried to hit anyone in my entire life, but I wanted to lambaste him with that brush. I would have, too, if I hadn't lost my grip.

Anyone witnessing that little scene would have sworn he tried to rape me, when, truth be told, he refused me! As I furiously cleaned my flat, I thought again of the intensity of my orgasm with him.

What if he was right? What if together we created a dynamic neither of us ever managed with anyone else? It seemed that the result of an immovable object meeting an immutable force was that the impact made your eyes roll back in your head.

I didn't start to wind down until nearly two this morning. I'd finished my cleaning, except for the vacuuming. I did that even before I dressed this morning. Now I needed to get a shopping list together and get that under control.

I considered making dessert, but decided to pick up something at the bakery instead. It still felt odd going in there. At first I had avoided the place, not being able to handle the memories of Nana's shop. But I heard her scolding me and telling me not to be a silly nilly, that her time in that place had passed. The marvelous smells finally lured me in. I have been a regular ever since.

I managed all my shopping in under two hours, which included a trip to the chemist's shop. I needed to pick up a box of condoms, although I suspected Ivan would bring his own. I also needed a new tube of spermicide for my cap, realizing this morning that the tube in my drawer had expired four months ago. That's what happens when celibacy exceeds shelf life.

I had to endure the discomfort of asking the horny dispenser for my supplies, since he kept them behind the counter. I think he did that on purpose, to keep track of who had an active sex life in town. Fortunately he had both my brand of spermicide and Ivan's brand of condoms, minimizing the need to discuss the purchase. I paid him and went on my way.

I made my rounds to the different shops, saving the bakery

and the fish for last. At the bakery I chose the fruit torte over the chocolate cake, since I knew he liked fruit. As an afterthought, I also bought some pastry for breakfast. If he didn't stay, I would send some home with him. At the fish market, I got everything I needed, including lobster. By the time I finished shopping, it was already two o'clock.

I didn't want to be cooking when Ivan arrived so I prepared what I could in advance. The salad would keep so I made it up and refrigerated it. I made a dish of appetizers, with some cheese, olives and artichoke hearts. I cleaned the fish so I just had to throw it in the sauce to cook once Ivan arrived.

We would need to have dinner pretty quickly. This pasta doesn't sit well. Just before I went to clean myself up, I set the table with my best dishes and found matches for the candles. I wanted everything ready so I could focus on him.

I stopped to pick up the wine and bread on my way to Pash's flat. I also stopped at the florist and bought a dozen long-stemmed red roses. I had them packed in a box, with the biggest ribbon they had on top. I picked up one of their little cards, which didn't look big enough for what I wanted to say. Then I remembered a quote from *The Taming of the Shrew* that nicely balanced her inscription, and also fit on the card.

> *Is not this well? Come, my sweet Kate:*
> *Better once than never, for never too late . . .*
> *Why, there's a wench! Come on, and kiss me, Kate.*

I put the small card in an equally small envelope. I held it for a moment, wondering if I should somehow address it.

As if moving of its own accord, the pen in my hand wrote:

Pash
With Love
Ivan

I gave the card to the florist so he could attach it to the box. Wondering if I had the balls to give that envelope to her, I pocketed a blank one. I had always practiced extreme caution with that dangerous little word. It implied a hell of a lot more than I ever wanted to communicate to someone—until now.

I turned onto her street at five minutes till six. I parked behind her car and gathered my packages from the backseat. I nearly peeled the card from the flowers, but somehow that felt dishonest, not only to her, but to myself.

I did have feelings for her. Maybe if I couldn't yet say it outright, this broke the ice and made the word a little less forbidden. So I let it stand.

I had packed a change of clothes, my shaving kit, and, of course, my toothbrush. I considered what would have the most dramatic effect on her, taking the bag in or leaving it until later. I decided to take it with me now and simply put it down without drawing attention to it. The message would be quite clear. As always, I had my condoms tucked in my inner jacket pocket, so they would be handy when needed. This promised to be a bloody interesting night!

My parcels prevented me from knocking outright, the sound being more of a thud than a knock. A minute later I heard Pash unlatching the lock. When she opened the door and saw me, she said, "I asked you to dinner—I didn't know you planned to move in tonight!"

"Good evening to you, too! Is that how you greet a stranger bearing gifts?"

"And you're getting stranger by the minute. Here, let me take some of this."

As I came in the door, she took the bread and wine from me, taking it into the kitchen. "How much wine did you get? This is heavy."

"Enough to see us through the night." I set down my bag beside the door and waited for her to come back.

"How drunk are you planning to get, Dr. Kozak? That's enough wine for a dinner party. We're only two people."

"What we don't drink will keep for next time. Here, these are for you." I handed her the box.

"The demure response is to say, 'You shouldn't have,' but to be honest, yes, you should have. Thank you, I appreciate it."

She sat down on the sofa, holding the box on her lap. I watched as she pulled off the ribbon, finding the card tucked underneath. I didn't miss the way her fingertips lingered on the front of the envelope before she turned it over to open it. When she pulled out the card and read my response to her inscription, she burst out laughing.

"That's the same reaction I had. You outdid yourself with that analogy."

"Well, there does seem to be a developing parallel, Dr. Kozak."

"Why do you call me Dr. Kozak so damn much? My name is Ivan." I sat down on the sofa beside her.

"I like how it sounds. It suits you."

"It's too bloody formal. Makes me feel like I'm in the classroom."

"You want informal?"

"Yes, and I'm not talking about any of the many names that have come out of your mouth over the last several days."

"Neither am I. I have another suggestion. My father had a friend named Ivan. His wife always called him Vanya. I picked it up and my father explained that I shouldn't use it because it was a special nickname for Ivan, an endearment. He told me only someone close should use it, that it had the same weight as 'dear' or 'darling.' If it is all right with you, I would like to sometimes use that nickname, as well as your proper name."

I didn't answer right away, being a bit dumbstruck.

"Ivan, are you all right?"

"I'm sorry, you caught me unaware. My mother is the only

one ever to call me that name. I haven't heard it since she died."

"I didn't know. If it is too close, I won't use it."

"No, actually I would like it very much if you would use it." I paused, gauging if I should tell her the whole thing.

Something—maybe my mother's memory or maybe even her hand—pushed me to continue. "She never spoke English very well. She and my father always spoke Ukrainian in the house. My earliest memory of that name is a lullaby she would sing to me in Ukrainian. I never knew what the name in the song should have been, because she always substituted 'Vanya' for it. The last time I saw her, she hummed that lullaby in my ear." I felt myself on the edge and had to stop. I pulled out my handkerchief. "So are you going to open those or let them wilt in the box?"

"I may need that when you're finished with it," she said, pointing to my handkerchief. Her eyes were glassy.

"You use it, you own it. Remember what you said about your toothbrush?"

"Then I may need your sleeve." She pulled off the top of the box and unfolded the tissue paper. "Ivan, they are beautiful. Thank you so much." She ran her hand across the petals. I tore off a piece of the tissue paper and handed it to her as the tears slid down her cheek. "Such a gentleman, offering a lady a hankie."

"We do our best," I said, stuffing my own handkerchief back into my pocket. "I hope you don't have anything cooking. If you do, we may be going out to dinner."

"Not to worry. Everything is on hold right now."

"Good. Now how about being a courteous hostess and offering me a glass of that wine?"

Chapter Fifteen

Again, Ivan regained his composure and his cockiness faster than I could blow my nose. But I still saw a few more of the undercurrents he hid from the world. "I could use some help in the kitchen. Don't you for one minute think you're going to sit here on your bum and watch me work."

"Here love; thou see'st how diligent I am, to dress thy meat myself, and bring it thee." He took the flower box from my lap and pulled me to my feet. "I am sure, sweet Kate, this kindness merits thanks." He held me close and said very softly, "Come on, and kiss me, Kate." Then he kissed me, in a different way than he had before, softly, tenderly, almost like my lips might break if he pressed too hard.

"If you dare feed my pasta to the servants or to anyone else, like Petruchio did to Kate's food, you'll find that bag you left by the door in the middle of the street and your arse thrown out right after it."

"This flat is very nice but rather small to keep live-in help. Must be right cozy in your bedroom."

"You may find out, if you are so inclined."

"All right, then! Let's get those roses in water and pop the cork on one of those bottles."

Ivan followed me to the kitchen. Finding a vase for the flowers, I arranged them in a lovely display and then put them on the table. The pasta water had come to a boil. "I have some hors d'oeuvres and salad. I still have to cook the pasta and put the fish in the sauce. You tell me how you want to do this."

"That, my dear, is a loaded question, considering I am feeling randy already."

"Well, my Vanya," I said, emphasizing the *Vanya,* "you can just keep it in your pants until after dinner. This food won't keep."

He walked behind me and put his arms around my waist. "If my dear old mum heard what you just said, she certainly rolled over in her grave!" He leaned over and kissed my neck.

"You bugger! Let me go, I have to finish dinner." I broke free of his grasp and went over to get a bottle of wine. "Here," I said, handing him the wine and a corkscrew, "open this."

"Demanding Judy, aren't you!" He took the bottle and proceeded to remove the cork.

I gave him two glasses. Then I popped an olive in his mouth. "See if you can't behave yourself until I finish this cooking."

He smiled while he chewed, giving me an *I got the world by the arse* expression. "So give me something else to do."

"You could slice the bread. Also, put the salad on the table. It's in the refrigerator."

"Will do, madam. By the way, you look very nice tonight. That dress does nice things for your bum." He playfully patted my arse on his way to the refrigerator. "You will have to direct me until I learn my way around here. Where's the bread knife?"

"There is a rack full of knives on the side of the counter by the door. You also look very sporty, with that jacket. Looks like something a professor would wear."

"Is that a fact! I didn't know professors dressed any differently than anyone else. I think we'd better move these knives."

"Come now, professor, you're wearing a herringbone tweed coat. How many of those have you seen around here? And why the devil do you want to move the knives?"

"I just noticed it's a straight shot from here to the bedroom door. I don't want you getting any ideas later. Better they're put out of harm's way!"

"Maybe you should rethink doing anything that might provoke me in those directions." Again, he gave me that smile, helping himself to more olives and some artichokes. "Could I have a piece of cheese, please?"

"Certainly." He brought me some cheese and popped it into my mouth, as I had the olive for him. "I finished *Sagacity* today."

I nearly choked on the cheese. "Already?" I said with my mouth full.

"Swallow your food, dear heart. I don't want you turning blue on me."

I chewed and swallowed and then asked, "Did you like it?"

"I liked it very much. Stir your sauce before it burns."

"You couldn't have waited until after dinner to tell me this?" I asked, stirring the sauce and turning down the pasta.

"I have other plans for after dinner. I thought this would make good dinner conversation."

Now my head spun in two directions at once. He had finished my book and he had plans for after dinner. "Ivan, slow down. I am up for whatever happens later, but right now I want to know what you thought of my book. It's important to me."

"I told you I liked it."

"That tells me nothing. I want to know your critical opinion."

"Pash, I liked it well enough to try to find a way to work it into my curriculum this fall."

"Are you serious?"

"I am quite serious. It is an exceptional piece of work. A lot like you are. Now, I think our dinner is calling."

The astonished look on Pash's face said it all. I knew I had left her speechless, a feat worth marking with a champagne toast. I walked past her to the cooker, stirred the sauce and then tasted it. "This is very good. I would be happy to drain the pasta for you. I'm actually quite hungry." I turned around to find her staring at my back. I knocked on her head. "Hello, is anyone home in there?"

"You enjoy confounding me, don't you?"

"I enjoy it very much."

"Why?"

"Because, sweet Passion, you confound so beautifully." I turned back to the cooker and turned off the sauce and then tested the pasta for doneness by scooping out a strand and throwing it at the wall. It stuck. "Bob's your uncle—perfect al dente!" Then I ate it.

"Talk about being a piece of work—you take the prize!"

"Thank you." She still looked stunned. I took her by the shoulders. "Pash, we will talk about this. Yes, I do enjoy catching you unaware, but that's not why I'm avoiding the conversation now. We have food here that by your own declaration won't sit. If we get involved in a discussion about your book right now, dinner will be ruined."

"You're absolutely right, so why the bleeding devil did you spring this on me three seconds before the food finished cooking?"

"I already told you: you confound so beautifully." I kissed her forehead. "Let's get the food on the table and we'll talk." I took our wineglasses to the dining room table and refilled them while she poured the sauce in a bowl. I came back and grabbed a couple of hot pads she had left on the cooker. I drained the pasta. "Do you have a bowl for this?"

"In the cupboard to your right, middle shelf." I found the bowl and dumped the pasta, steam billowing up into my face. I brought the bowl to the table to find her lighting the candles.

"Pash, it's lovely. What a beautiful table." I wasn't kidding. The food, the wine, the candles, the flowers—but there was something missing. "We need music."

"Music?"

"Of course, music. What's a romantic dinner without music? Where's your stereo?"

"Around the corner in the sitting room."

I went into the sitting room and found the stereo with a rack of CDs beside it. I quickly reviewed the titles and pulled out a Sinatra collection that suited the mood well. When I came back to the table, Pash had lowered the lights. The candles flickered, making dancing shadows on the tablecloth.

I came over to her chair and pulled it out for her. When she sat down, I leaned over and kissed the top of her head, drinking in the whole scene. I don't think I have ever experienced a more perfect moment in my whole life.

I went to my own chair and sat down. She reached over and ran her fingertips across my hand. "Vanya, this is even better than the restaurant the other night. I felt like Cinderella at the ball there. Tonight I feel like I brought my prince home with me."

"You should mind yourself. Those sentiments could find us in the bedroom sooner rather than later."

"Only if you want to lie down to talk about my book. Otherwise I suggest we have our dinner and talk a little before the evening progresses in that direction."

"Then, my Passion, won't you please pass the salad?" We served the food and started to eat. "I really am hungry and this sauce is terrific! I'm glad you made plenty."

"I discovered the other night you had a bit of an appetite."

"So you did. I'm pleased to see you are inclined to satisfy it." I winked at her. Even with the lights dimmed, I could see her face flush.

"So, professor, how do you think you can justify teaching my book?"

"My students need to understand what's common to the classics they study, and that's there in your book. I will use your book to illustrate the underlying connection in great writing."

"Ivan, I'm really not following this. How am I explaining what literary classics have in common?"

"Each author had a moment of extraordinary clarity and wrote it down, much like our friend Will Shakespeare going on about how to handle you women!" She gave me a pointed look with that remark, but I pushed on.

"In your book you identify the source of that kind of insight and tell how everyone can find it. All my students need to understand they have an inner world available to them, just like the literary masters they study. How many young minds, and hearts, could be inspired by the idea that they can access wisdom and clarity inside themselves if they make the effort to look for it?"

I stopped talking, realizing I had been holding a forkful of salad in midair the whole time. "Sorry, I got carried away."

"You must be brilliant in the classroom. Do you get that fired up while lecturing?"

"Sometimes. It depends on the material. Early on I didn't have as much say in what I teach. Now I teach what I care about, which also satisfies the course requirements. It keeps me from burning out on it."

"It is heartening to know you got so much from my book."

"I certainly did. I want to talk to you about some of the points you make. I also have a favor to ask."

"What?"

"I don't suppose you have another copy I could have? I want to make some notes and really don't want to mark up the one you signed."

"I think I might have another copy I could give to you. You really are considering teaching it, aren't you?"

"Damn straight I am. What's more, if I can get it approved as course material, I want you to attend the lecture and take questions afterward." I had just taken the relationship into the fall semester.

"I would tend to think you're joking, but I can see you aren't. I'm going to ask you something now and I'm invoking the honesty clause. Are you doing all this because we're sleeping together?"

"Hell, no! If Quentin Crisp had authored the book I would still want to use it. And I can guarantee I wouldn't be sleeping with him." I refilled her wineglass as she considered my proposition. "So, will you do it?"

"I'll think about it. When would you expect to teach it?"

"I would fit it into a lecture at the end of September, if it's approved. Even though I have some say now in choosing what I teach, a new book has to be approved by a departmental committee. Thing is, I can be very persuasive when I want to be."

"I know that firsthand."

"You should." I finished my first helping of pasta and held out my plate. "Could you load me up again? That sauce is damned good." She heaped another pile of pasta on my plate and covered it with sauce.

"You see, my intuition told me to make a big batch. I had this premonition you would want seconds."

"And maybe thirds. We'll see how my stamina holds out."

"We're still talking about the book. That comes later."

Christ, I enjoyed her company! She could snap it back at me like shooting a paper wad on a gum band. "You had better have a second helping, too. You need to carb up so you don't run out of fuel."

"You're trying to kill me, aren't you?"

"Hardly. I want a warm body under me, not a cold one."

"Could we get back to the book? You said you had questions for me."

"Yes, I do. But I want you to finish your dinner. We have time to discuss the book. It's only July, you know."

"Ivan, your take on my book is important to me. I want to know what interested you."

"Pash, I promise we will talk. But I don't want tonight to be just about the book, which could well happen if we don't switch gears straight away. You're so distracted, you haven't even finished your first serving of this delicious meal. Now stop talking and eat!"

I looked at my plate where my half-eaten food lay, now quite cold. I couldn't help being preoccupied by this. To have my book used as a text at a university could help my career tremendously. However, my personal involvement with Ivan made his motives suspect. I wanted to be sure before agreeing to any of this that no one could question the legitimate use of my book. "Here, let me warm that up for you." He spooned some more sauce onto my plate.

"Ivan, I have to understand more about all this before I agree to it. Of course I want you to use my book, but not if there could be any question at all about why you are using it. I have worked very hard to gain credibility in this field. The last thing I want is to have anyone think you're using my book because you slept with me."

"Your book can stand on its own legs, Passion. No one need know we have a relationship right away. I will get approval based solely on the merits of the book. Will your publisher supply the university bookstore with an adequate number of copies on short notice?"

"I'll have to find out."

"Please do. Now, if you promise to finish your dinner, I'll make you a deal."

"What?"

"If you can give me another copy to mark up, we will spend tomorrow afternoon, after your riding lesson, working. We'll talk about my questions and using your book as a text. I have a laptop back at the house. I can type up my notes as we talk. Deal?"

I looked into those eyes of his. "It figures!"

"What figures?"

"In this light your eyes are a different color."

"They are? Sometimes, sweetheart, I need a road map to follow you. What are you talking about?"

"Nothing about you is consistent or ordinary. You are a living oxymoron. Even your eye color is contradictory. You are the most complex person I have ever met."

"Keeps life interesting, don't you think? You didn't answer me before. Do we have a deal?"

"Yes, we have a deal. And you damn well better stick to the work part. Working means no fun and games."

"My Passion, the fun and games are for later this evening."

He gave me a look that curled my toes. I knew I'd better eat something more or risk fainting later. I cleaned my plate and before I could stop him, he gave me more of everything, including more wine. He helped himself to a third serving just slightly smaller than the first two. "So, you are good for three?" I said, sipping my wine. I had begun to relax. The food and the wine helped.

"Yes, I am. From what I see, you have some catching up to do. We have to see to that."

"I thought you already were," I said, indicating my plate but thinking about our recent intimacies. I continued to eat what he had given me. "This really did turn out well. This is my nana's recipe. She taught me how to make it. This is as close as I've ever come to having it taste like hers." I raised my wineglass into the air and said quietly, "Thanks, Nana."

"Do you believe she can hear you?"

"I think so. I talk to her a lot. It feels like she is my guardian angel."

"I rather feel the same way about my mum." Ivan picked up his wineglass and held it in the air as I had. He said something in Ukrainian that I didn't understand and then sipped his wine.

"What did you say?"

"I thanked my mum for watching out for me all these years." He paused and glanced down at his plate, and then looked at me again. "I also thanked her for whispering to you to call me Vanya. This might sound silly, but it feels like she is mighty happy right now."

"It doesn't sound silly at all. Maybe she's relieved she can pass the torch."

"What, are you intimating I need someone to look out for me?"

"Seems your mum must think so. Someone has certainly been covering your arse all these years."

"I suppose you're right about that. Up to now no one but my mum wanted the job."

"Your mum is a smart lady to have stayed around until she found someone capable of taking over for her."

"Now, now, be gentle with me. I know I haven't been a pillar of responsibility in my life. As our friend Petruchio said, 'Better once than never, for never too late . . .' "

"You're quite correct, Vanya, it is never too late." I cleaned my plate a second time. Ivan picked up the bowl again. "Oh, no. That's enough for me. You might have had room for three, but two filled me up. We have dessert, too!"

"I am looking forward to it." He smiled and my heart fluttered. "Let's get this cleaned up. I don't know where anything goes yet, so I'll wash up. You dry and put away." He took off his jacket and hung it on the back of the chair and proceeded to roll up his sleeves. His hairy forearms came into view and I felt myself getting warmer. Hoping he hadn't noticed me leering at him, I started to clear the table. He emptied the wine bottle into his glass. "We need to crack another one. Fortunately, we have more."

"Thanks to your foresight, we'll have more for some time to come."

"That depends on how drunk we get tonight, doesn't it?"

"If you want to be good for three, it better not be very drunk."

"Well, if I need a little extra help I know someone who gives better head than anyone else I've ever known. That should keep me operational for the duration."

I know I blushed from head to toe; my hands even turned pink. He came around the table and put his arms around my waist and pulled me close. "I didn't mean to embarrass you. But you have to know you shocked the piss out of me the other night. No one has ever done me better, and that's the truth." He kissed the top of my head and went to the kitchen to get that bottle of wine.

I uncorked the second bottle. Pash had brought the leftovers to the kitchen to put them in smaller containers. Her face still glowed pink, but she seemed steady. "There's not much left, I'm afraid. We put most of it away," I said.

"There's enough for a lunch. I use up my leftovers that way." I watched for a moment, just to make sure I hadn't rattled her too damn much. Then I refilled our glasses. I took the wine to the sitting room and dimmed the lights. After I made sure the roller blinds were drawn, I made a quick selection of more music. I chose some soft jazz to set the stage for our evening. She had already cleared the table and had everything in the kitchen by the time I returned.

"Okay, I'm ready."

"Cor blimey!" she said, swatting me with a tea towel. "There's a news flash!"

"Do you know you're a real corker? I've laughed more since I've known you than I have in a good long while. Your delivery is one to write home about."

"You're easy," she said, swatting me again.

"Well, that's true. And I'm also a good audience." That time I made her laugh! "Let's wash up these dishes. It shouldn't take long." Within ten minutes we had everything washed and put away.

"I have a fruit torte for dessert. Let's have tea with it a little later. I'm too full to eat anything else right now."

I didn't say a word. I didn't need to. She looked at me and blushed again. I took her by the hand. "Let's go into the sitting room and have a little more wine. You look like you need a drink."

Chapter Sixteen

We went into the sitting room and I handed Pash her glass. I sat down on the sofa and patted the spot next to me. "Sit down. I have something to run by you."

"Should I be getting nervous now?" She sat down, still a little flustered.

"Sip your wine and relax. I have an interesting idea for this evening."

"What, dare I ask?"

"We are getting to know one another, right?"

"Yes, I suppose we are."

"We have more than a few gaps to fill in since we have no history together at all."

"That's true."

"So what I want to do is tell each other how we lost our virginity."

"What?"

"Hear me out. By way of getting to know one another, I thought perhaps we could each tell our story, and then see where it goes from there."

"Meaning?"

"Meaning, my Passion, I would like to have been your first. What if I could know what I know now and introduce you to the art of love? If you are comfortable with a little role-playing, I would like to be your first tonight and take your virginity."

"Ivan, I have never in my whole life known anyone like you! I don't even have to ask if you are serious because I know you are! Why do you want to do this? I mean, I understand to a point the sharing of stories, but role-playing losing my virginity to you? That is a little odd, don't you think?"

"Maybe it is. I've never admitted it before, but it has been a fantasy of mine for a long time, to be the first for someone. Even the young lady who initiated me had someone before me." She sipped her wine as she mulled over what I said. I decided to plunge right in.

"My first time happened at Steve's farm with his cousin. I sometimes looked after the place when Steve's family had to leave. One of those times Steve's aunt came to visit for a couple of weeks, bringing her daughter along.

"The family went on a shopping trip, leaving me there alone. Steve's cousin found an excuse to stay behind. I was sixteen, she had just turned seventeen. I suppose she thought me older since I had nearly my full height and had filled out some.

"I had my work to do in the stable. She found me there and started a conversation. I might have been a virgin, but I recognized a come-on when I saw one. She wanted to know if I had a girlfriend and I told her no. I don't know how I came by the line, but I asked her if she wanted to volunteer for the job. She said she might. So I made a move, expecting to be slapped down. She didn't say no."

"Did she know you were a virgin?"

"Hell, no! I didn't last very long, but I did okay. I felt a little awkward trying to penetrate her. I wasn't exactly sure where to poke. But with her help, I managed all right. Thing is, I had matured in a number of ways. She never asked about my experience, being a little preoccupied with my cock. That's when I discovered size does count."

"Did you go back to the house with her?"

"No, we did it in the hayloft, on a horse blanket. She wanked me though my jeans while I felt up her tits under her shirt. When I went for the zipper on her shorts, I thought for sure she would smack me down. But she didn't. I wasn't about to stop on my own, so I tugged off her shorts and underpants. Then she pulled up her top so I could see her tits. Christ, I had only seen a woman like this in the porn mags Steve hid in the stable."

"I'm surprised you didn't shoot off right then."

"I nearly did. I wasted no time in unzipping and getting down to it."

"She could handle you?"

"She helped me find the right spot and guided me in. I managed a decent stuffing before I creamed. Afterward she showed me how to help her finish. That's how I first learned to properly diddle a woman."

"It was very decent of her to teach you that. I suppose I should thank her if we ever meet. Does Steve know you lost your virginity in his stable?"

"Oh, he knows—he just thinks it was with another girl. Some time later, we finagled a double date with a couple of girls when his parents were away. They ended up in the stable with us. We had prearranged that one of us would be in the loft and the other in an empty stall filled with hay. I supplied the condoms. We both got some that day, but he's the only one who actually lost his virginity. He'd shit himself if he knew I lost mine to his cousin." As I talked I kept the wine flowing. "Now you tell me your story."

Pash hesitated for a few moments. She sipped her wine again. Looking into her glass like she could see the memory playing out in there, she told me her story. "My father had a play in rehearsal. During rehearsals, I developed a huge crush on one of the actors. I guessed him to be about twenty-five. I was eighteen.

"One evening he asked me to stay and run some lines with him after the regular rehearsal. I couldn't believe he asked me. A few times I played a small role when my father came up short on his casting, so I knew I could help him out by reading with him. When I told my father he wanted me to run lines with him, Papa's only response was that he could use all the help he could get. So I stayed.

"One by one, the other people left, until finally we were alone. Apparently that's what he wanted because he started making suggestive remarks to me. He said he'd noticed how intently I watched him and wanted to know what I was thinking. I stammered a bit and told him I liked his work. He came up to me and kissed me and then said, 'I know you're thinking more than that. I've seen how you look at me.' He kissed me again and started to feel me up. I didn't stop him. He suggested we go back to the dressing room.

"He kissed me some more and then became more insistent. He took my hand and put it on his erection. I touched him up like I knew he wanted me to. He kept kissing me and squeezing my breasts. When he reached under my skirt and tugged at my scanties, I let him. He pulled them off. Then he opened his trousers. I really did have a thing for him and when I realized he wanted to go all the way, I said yes."

"Did you tell him you were a virgin?"

"Ivan, I had to. He would have found out soon enough anyway, considering I had never been with anyone. He told me it was okay, that he knew what to do. He had a condom in his wallet that he put on. He threw some costumes on the floor and we went at it."

"Was it painful?"

"A little. But he wasn't equipped like you are. I recovered rather quickly."

"Did you enjoy it?"

"I honestly don't remember if I did. It happened quickly and seemed to end before I had time to adjust to all the sensations. I remember I enjoyed the fooling around before, but the actual act itself didn't leave many impressions, except that it happened."

"Did he become your lover?"

"No. I never did it with him again. The play opened and I left for university at Cambridge. I don't even know what happened to him."

"Now, wouldn't you like to replay that experience and have it be memorable, not to mention pleasurable?" I moved closer, took hold of her hand. I kissed her fingertips and then her palm. "Wouldn't you have liked it to have been me?"

I looked at Ivan and dissolved into a puddle. How could I deny the truth of what he just said? "Yes, Ivan, I would have liked it to have been you."

"It can be, Pash. It can be tonight." He put his hand behind my neck, pulled me close and kissed my forehead. "Just let me show you how."

"You are showing me how, every time we are together."

"Do you want me to show you what I know?"

His fantasy swept me away. "Yes, Ivan, I do want you to show me. What do you want me to do?"

"Just relax, I promise it will be good. I'll see to it." He kept kissing me, my eyelids and face, my neck and shoulders. "Just relax, I'll show you what to do." His voice had taken on an hypnotic monotone that lulled me. I actually went limp. Any tension I had evaporated into a sensual mist. He gently pushed me backward onto the sofa. "That's right, just let go and enjoy yourself."

He didn't have to tell me twice. I closed my eyes and turned myself over to him. From a place beyond caring how it might sound, I asked him, "Tell me what you fantasized, I want to know."

"I have always wanted to take an innocent young thing and help her discover the mysteries of life." He started massaging my breasts through my dress. "I have often imagined being made a guardian to a young woman and introducing her to the pleasures of her body. I have invented all sorts of situations where that happens."

He continued his hypnotic tone as he pinched my nipples. "Sometimes she comes home terribly upset about a date gone badly and I go to her room to comfort her. Sometimes I accidentally see her in her bath. When I realize she has grown into a beautiful young woman, I follow her to her room."

His words played out in my mind like a film; I saw each situation vividly. All the while, he continued to fondle me. "My very favorite fantasy, one that I use when I am feeling particularly randy, is to catch her in a compromising situation with a young man. Her indecent behavior both angers and arouses me. Of course, she is disciplined for her lack of self-control with a bare-bottomed spanking, which quickly becomes a lesson in what such behavior does to a man. While she is bent over from the spanking, I take her from behind." As I visualized this last scene, I heard my heart beat in my ears.

I felt Ivan move off the sofa and kneel on the floor beside me, but I didn't open my eyes. "Tonight, my Passion, you are that young woman, the one who has filled my dreams on many lonely nights." I felt his hand on my leg, moving up my thigh under my skirt. "Now, just stay calm and relaxed. I am going to touch you and make you feel very good." My whole body throbbed in anticipation.

I looked at Pash lying there, eyes closed, her breathing rapid. I stroked her lightly through her knickers and she sighed. "Does that feel good?"

"It feels very good," she murmured back.

I stroked again, this time using a little more pressure. She whimpered and squirmed against my hand. I rubbed her for a few moments. Then I stopped and removed my hand from under her skirt. She opened her eyes to see why. I unbuttoned my shirt. "I'm going to show you how to pleasure a man." I took her hand and placed it on my bare chest. "Do you want to know how to please me, Pash?"

"I want very much to please you, Vanya."

Her eyes burned into me almost as much as hearing her call me Vanya. Her hand flexed in my chest hair. "Squeeze here." I moved her hand onto my pectoral, over my nipple. "Squeeze hard, Pash, squeeze very hard." She did as I said, gripping my chest and twisting the flesh. I grimaced as the sensation washed through me, making my breath catch. "Oh, yes, dear heart." She squeezed again, even harder. "God, yes!"

My teeth clenched as another electric current jolted me. "You learn very quickly. Keep doing it while I do the same to you." I put my hands over her breasts and kneaded them with my fingers, paying special attention to her very sensitive nipples. Several long, wonderful minutes later, I said, "I want to kiss your breasts, Pash. Will you let me kiss your breasts?"

"Please kiss them. I want you to kiss them."

"I have to take off your dress so I can." I pulled her into a sitting position and undid the buttons at the top of the dress. As I expected it would, her chest had turned cherry red. I slid the skirt out from under her and pulled the dress over her head.

Again she surprised me when I found her naked under the dress except for her scanties. Still on my knees, I wedged myself between her thighs and buried my face between her breasts and licked. Then I kissed her breasts and sucked her nipples. I felt her hands in my hair and heard her moan.

I took off the gum band holding my ponytail and let my hair fall around my shoulders. Her fingernails scraped my scalp as she ran her fingers through the length. Then I took off my shirt. I forced her legs even farther apart as I leaned in and kissed her on the mouth. I could taste the wine on her breath as she returned my kiss. I pulled back just far enough to be able to look in her eyes. My own arousal needed attention. "Pash, do you want to please me some more?" I asked as I caressed her.

With her fingers still threaded in my hair, Pash slid to the edge of the sofa. She quite shamelessly wedged my hand in the folds of her underpants, increasing the pressure against herself. I let her slide against my fingers, soaking in the blatant lust I felt pouring out of her. I pulled my hand away, saying again, "Do you want to please me?"

"I want to please you, Ivan. Tell me how."

"You can kiss me here." I took her hand and rubbed it against my painfully hard member. "I want you to put this in your mouth. Will you do that for me, sweetheart?"

She answered me by trying to undo my fly. I stood and helped her open my trousers. I exposed my organ and saw her lick her lips. This time I closed my eyes, hoping to God I wouldn't shoot off the minute I felt her lick me. I felt her wrap her hand around my member. The first touch of her tongue on my flesh made me groan.

I stopped her. "Pash, listen to me carefully. I want you to hold me tightly right here." I moved her hand to the base of my organ. "Squeeze me in your hand. It will help me last longer. Now, take it slow. I'm very excited. Too much will mean you will have to wait until later to feel me inside you." I cupped her chin in my hand. "Do you understand, sweetheart?"

"I understand." She did as I told her, firmly holding my member in her hand. This time she did kiss it, first the head and then down my length. She ran her tongue back to the tip and licked it just like an ice-cream cone. Then she took me in her mouth and I shuddered. The intensity of the sensation caused me to lean on her for support until I steadied myself. As I asked, she did take it easier than last time, only keeping me in her mouth for a few seconds. She stopped for a moment and looked up at me. "Vanya, may I touch myself while I suck you?"

When I saw her waiting for my answer, I realized she had genuinely asked for my permission before proceeding. She had assumed the role of innocence beautifully, with no false modesty, only openness and willingness. "Of course you may, my Passion, but only if you first take off your underpants."

She stood and quickly peeled the lacy material down her thighs. I caught her hand before she tossed them aside. "Give them to me." She did as I asked, handing me the damp material. For the first time in my life, I revealed my guilty pleasure to a partner. I held the cloth to my face and inhaled, taking in her scent. Christ, it nearly sent me over the edge. There she stood in front of me, naked in so many ways. As much as I wanted her the other night, I wanted her more right now. The blow job would have to wait until later.

I pulled her to her feet and kissed her, rubbing myself against her bare skin. I picked her up. She yelped in surprise. "Dear heart, it is time you became a woman." I carried her into the bedroom and laid her down on the bed. I kicked off my shoes and pulled off my trousers and socks. Then I remembered the condoms.

"My johnnies are in my coat. I'll be right back."

"Wait. I have some in my bedside table." She turned on the lamp next to the bed and reached for the drawer.

"I can get them," I said, pulling open the drawer myself. I found an unopened box of condoms amid a myriad of sex toys and kitchen utensils. "Well, now, what do you have in here?" I asked, rummaging quickly through the drawer.

"A virgin has to make do somehow," she said with coy seductiveness. She quietly added, "It's been a long time, Ivan."

"Well, we're going to see to it that you don't need those toys so often now." I rolled a condom onto my cock and positioned myself over her. "Now, I just want you to relax, sweetheart. We're going to take this slow and easy."

I started jabbing at the apex of her spread legs and felt the flesh give way. "That's right, nice and slow." Given my size, she did need time to stretch. I had wondered why she didn't tense as most women did when I entered them. Now I understood. I had glimpsed a rubber phallus in her drawer that approximated my size. It appeared she had been practicing for me long before we met.

I looked up into Ivan's face. He seemed completely focused on me, allowing me adjustment time. He let my body tell him when to push more. I knew I could stretch to accommodate him. I had done it many times the other night. But it seemed my body had reacted to the increased activity of the last few days by swelling.

I focused on relaxing and opening. I held on to his arms and felt the hard curves of his muscles. How I relished the feel of him on top of me. He pushed a little more of himself into me and I moaned, his size violating the swollen space. "Are you all right, Pash?" he asked with genuine concern in his voice.

"I'm fine, my Vanya. It feels good." I put my hand on his face to reassure him, but also to convince myself he wasn't a dream. Trying to stretch for him, I asked, "Your cock is so thick. Are all men as big as you are?"

"I don't know, sweetheart. But it does seem God has given me a little extra, though."

Sweat dripped off his forehead. I saw him straining to hold back. "Vanya, please, I want more."

"We have to take this slowly, Pash. I don't want to hurt you. You're very tight."

"But I want you." I couldn't wait any longer. I had become a virgin again. I wanted him to take my innocence. I wanted to give myself to him. If we didn't finish it now, I would lose the experience of having it be real for me. "Ivan, please, it's time."

"Are you sure?"

"I'm sure. Do it!" When I said that, Ivan thrust into me with all his weight, his organ hitting the back wall of my tunnel. I felt deflowered, the sensation of being invaded overwhelming me. I clutched at his back, my vaginal muscles stretching spastically to accommodate him. I felt my eyes fill with tears, not from pain, but from the power of the experience.

I heard him say, "Breathe, Passion, you're holding your breath. Inhale." Everything stopped, with him full inside me.

He remained in control. As I gasped for air, he said, "It's all right, I've got you."

I needed some time to adjust. "Vanya." That's all I could manage to say, the sensation still taking my breath. I held him tightly. He stayed still and kissed me very gently.

"Just relax," he said softly. "It will start to feel real good if you relax." He kissed me again and then murmured in my ear, "You are a woman now, my sweet Passion. I have claimed what is rightfully mine."

He had lost himself in the experience as much as I had, taking me for the virgin of his fantasy. Gradually I felt myself expand for him. My body softened as the initial tightness loosened. When he felt me relax under him, he slid out a little and pushed back in. He whispered, "Did that hurt?"

"No, I just feel very full. Try it again." He pulled out farther and pushed in again. "Oh, yes, that's good." He continued the slow in-and-out rhythm for several minutes. My body adjusted to the motion and I began to respond. The feeling of fullness inside me started to feel very good indeed.

"Vanya, please, do me harder." He picked up the pace and I matched his movement. Within a few minutes, we moved together, as in an erotic dance. "My God, you feel so good in me." I felt more tears coming, this time from my feeling for him. They slid down my cheeks.

"Are you in pain? Why are you crying?" He managed to stop again, despite the fact that he seemed to be getting close to finishing. I put my hand on his chest as he looked at me. I could feel his heart racing.

"Oh, God, no, I'm not in pain. It feels wonderful."

"Then why are you crying?"

"Because I'm feeling so much. Because I'm in love with you." He looked at me like he didn't understand what I had said, and then closed his eyes and took a deep breath. He started to thrust again, even harder than before. Within moments he pounded against me, dangerously shaking the bed.

I couldn't do much more than hang on to him, his intensity overpowering me. He rode me like a man possessed, signaling the onset of his orgasm with a groan that quickly became a growl. His whole body spasmed as he released his demons in the exorcism of his climax.

He stayed on top of me as he quieted. I stroked his hair, drinking in every line of his face. He had his eyes closed, still apparently lost in sensation. He inhaled deeply, his chest swelling with air. His exhaled breath carried the words, "I think I'm in love with you, too."

I felt myself starting to go flaccid inside her but did not want to break the spell. I had lived my fantasy and did not want to return to anything less. I opened my eyes and looked down at her, suddenly realizing I had spoken my thoughts out loud. Her eyes remained moist, traces of newly fallen tears visible on her cheeks. I couldn't take back what I had said, nor did I want to. No one had ever opened to me the way she had. She smiled self-consciously and said, "You know, you are very heavy."

"I have to get off you, don't I?"

"Well, yes, at least until I get the circulation back in my legs."

"If you insist." I rolled over onto the bed beside her.

"I think you forgot something."

I looked down at my shrinking organ and didn't see the condom. "Christ almighty, where is it?" I looked over just as she scooped it off herself.

She held up the sagging johnny. "Fertile fecker, aren't you? Talk about shooting your load!"

"Give me that," I said, snatching the condom from her hand. "Virgins shouldn't be so brassy!"

"But I'm not a virgin anymore, thanks to you."

"At least not until next time," I said, dropping the sticky pouch into the trash bin by the bed. "Did you finish?"

"No, but I'm all right. It felt wonderful when you did. What do you mean, 'not until next time'?"

"What do you think I mean?" I said as I leaned over and started looking through her bedside table drawer.

"Get out of there, mister. There are things in that drawer not meant for your eyes."

"Too damn late for that, sweetheart," I said as I turned back to her. "We'll talk about the goodies in there later, but right now, I have what I need." I had found a phallic-shaped vibrator that looked well used. "I take it the batteries are still good in this thing?" I snapped it on and it hummed in my hand. I ran it over her breasts and down her belly.

"You asked what I meant about next time." I let the little buzzing beauty rest on her pelvic bone. "I mean you impressed me so much with your performance tonight that I expect it will become a staple in our lovemaking diet." I slid the end of the vibrator between her legs. She pushed it away. "Don't you want to finish?" I asked, holding it just above her pubis.

"Yes, I want to finish. But I have to ask you something while I still have the nerve to ask." She paused and closed her eyes, as though considering how to proceed.

"What do you want to ask?"

She opened her eyes and looked square at me. "I'm invoking the honesty pact we made. I have to know. What you said after you finished—was it part of the fantasy or did you really mean it?"

I considered playing with her a little, but thought better of it, still seeing the dried tear streaks on her face. I also realized she had just given me the opportunity to turn tail and run, if I had that inclination. But I didn't. I answered her honestly and directly.

"I don't go around telling every woman I sleep with that I'm in love with her," I said, echoing her words to me at the inn. "Yes, Passion, I have fallen in love with you. Now, shall we take care of business?"

She opened her legs and allowed that quiet hum to become a symphony.

Chapter Seventeen

After Ivan rang my chimes with that vibrator, I wanted so much to lay with him and cuddle. I knew I would be sleeping beside him again tonight, which appealed to me very much at the moment. I could easily have drifted off wrapped in his arms. However, considering how things had unfolded over the course of this evening, the very thought of him opting to fall asleep soon seemed unlikely.

Maybe going to the loo would give me a chance to rouse myself after another fabulous orgasm. It amazed me that Ivan didn't seem to have any inhibitions or reservations about bringing me off. He actually took it as part of making love with me, that it wasn't over until I had finished, too. I had never known a man who considered my orgasm as important as his. If I hadn't already fallen arse over tit for him, I would after tonight.

When I came out, I caught him rummaging in my drawer again. "I hope you're enjoying yourself," I said, throwing a towel at him.

"I'm getting quite an education at least. What's this for?" he asked, holding up the towel.

"For old time's sake. Don't you want some dessert?"

He got up from the bed, leaving the towel on the pillow. He came over to me and untied the dressing gown I had put on while in the loo. He put his arms around me and pulled me to him, our naked bodies pressed tightly together. "This is dessert," he said as he reached down and rubbed my bare bottom.

"Ivan, at this moment my spirit is very willing, but the flesh is shot! Don't you ever get tired?" I asked as I felt him thickening against me.

"I have a strong constitution. I inherited Ukrainian cossack blood from my father. He told me our bloodline increases male potency tenfold." He rubbed his hardening cock against me to emphasize his words.

"Tenfold, huh?"

"That's what I've been told. But we can certainly get some food in you before we go again."

"And what if I fall asleep underneath you?" I asked, squeezing his bum.

"Not likely, Redhead." He kissed me and then rubbed his whiskers against my cheek. "I think I can keep you awake."

I broke free of his hold and retrieved the towel. "Here, I don't have a dressing gown to fit you." He took the towel and feigned indignation at having to cover himself.

"What, I can't have dessert like this?" He held his arms out wide, openly displaying his semierect organ.

"That's what I like about you, you're so reserved. Put on the bleeding towel." I left him standing in the bedroom and went to put on the kettle for tea. I heard him laughing.

"I'll be right there, I have to take a whiz first."

When he came into the kitchen, he had the towel wrapped around his waist, his bare chest still demanding my admiration. I had teacups and plates already on the table. He came over to help me take the torte out of the box, saying, "You hold the box and I'll lift it out." As he reached into the box, he smiled. "You know, I'm really starting to believe my dear old mum picked you out of the crowd and plunked you down right in front of me. She would like the way you give me a hard time."

"It's about time someone did," I said, taking a knife out of the rack. "It seems you've gotten away with bloody murder since your mum passed on."

"I can take care of myself, thank you. I don't need a knife-wielding Judy giving me the business."

"I don't usually carry a knife," I said, laying it down beside the torte on the table, "but I will always tell you what I think."

"And what a pleasure that will be!" He gave my bottom a whack when I walked past him to retrieve the whistling kettle. "I have a question for you. Now I'm invoking the honesty clause."

"What do you want to ask?"

"What the hell do you do with all the kitchen utensils in that drawer? I saw a honey dipper, a plastic ice-cream scoop, an orange-juice squeezer, clothes-pegs and several wooden spoons, one big enough to stir the witches' gruel in *Macbeth*."

"I use them."

"For what?"

"Do I have to draw you a picture?"

"I would appreciate at least a sketch."

After I poured the hot water, I sat down across from him. "I use them to masturbate."

"I figured that much. What do you do with all that stuff?"

I could feel my face getting hot, but if he wanted to know, I would tell him. "I either rub myself with them, or rub against them. Not having a lover for so long, I had to get inventive." Ivan cut us each a piece of torte as I continued.

"I don't know if you have ever shopped for any, but sex toys are expensive. I priced nipple clamps and nearly choked. Clothes-pegs work just as well, if you bend them a little to adjust the clamping pressure. The honey dipper is like a longer, thicker finger. So is the back of the ice cream scoop."

"What about the juicer and that damn big spoon?"

"I have the urge sometimes to rub against something. I lie on my belly and hump the juicer. The spoon I wedge between the mattress and box spring, then straddle it and rub. It feels wonderful."

"I also saw a dildo in there that's about my size. How often do you use it?"

"Once or twice a week, usually. I have to be careful and not use it so much around the time of my cycle." I couldn't believe I could sit here over dessert and tell him these extremely intimate details of my life. Somehow, despite my embarrassment, it felt quite natural and comfortable. He listened intently, not making jokes or anything of the sort.

"It appears you are as unconventional as I am."

"I've had to be inventive. I'm the best lover I've ever had."

"It's a damn shame you've had to resort to those things. Any man would be a lucky bastard to share your bed. I know that firsthand. The last bloke you saw must really have done a job on you to make you so gun-shy."

"He did."

"He really hurt you, didn't he?"

I looked down and stirred my tea. "I thought I had become pregnant and told him so. After he finished blaming me for not being careful, he offered to pay for an abortion. I refused his offer. I never saw him again after that night."

"Frigging son of a bitch! Were you pregnant?"

"No, that's the real pisser, I wasn't. The book tour had my timing mucked up. I got my period a week later." I sipped my tea. The warmth comforted me. "I don't want any more scares like that. One is quite enough."

"With both of us being careful, we won't have any."

"I don't want to take any chances."

"I'm sorry if I gave you grief about that. It seems as though you always show up expecting some action."

"Well, that, too."

Ivan smiled at me, but still seemed serious. "Did you love him?"

"I thought I did. But after seeing how cruel he could be, I

just felt stupid that I could have been so naive. Since then I haven't been able to work up the nerve to try again." Ivan sat there, holding his teacup, quietly listening. "That's also why I've wanted to be so careful with you. But you've made your way past all the walls I've put up."

"Well, my dear, you've done the same with me." He put his hand over mine. "Pash, I truly don't know where we're going with this. I would be lying if I said I did. But I can tell you straightaway, I've never let anyone in this deep. Christ, I've never talked about my mum to anyone, not even Steve. I've never told anyone how I lost my virginity. I sure as hell have never shared my fantasies, let alone asked to act out any of them with anybody."

He paused, playing with my fingers, intertwining them with his own. Then he looked at me and said, "I have another month or so here before I have to go back to Northampton. You know as well as I do that I have to go back—my home and my job are there." He paused again, looking pensive, and then continued. "We need to think about what happens when I leave and my real life kicks back in."

"But don't we need to see how we get on over the next month before we can decide what to do?"

"Of course we do. You might want to throw my arse the hell out."

"If I didn't do that after last night, I probably won't."

He laughed. "Well, that's one in my favor then. But if by mid-August we do still feel like we're feeling tonight, then we have some talking to do. I want you to mull something over, in the event we do decide to give it a go."

"What?"

"Coming back to Northampton with me in the fall."

"You mean moving there?"

"Right now let's just say for an extended visit. To try it out."

"But, Ivan, all my research materials are here. I have a book to finish."

"Since when do you have to be in a particular location to write? We can box up anything you need. I have a computer at my house and my laptop."

"All my files are on my computer."

"Then we can take your machine. And as for research materials, my dear Passion Flower, you would have access to an entire university full of material. I am a professor there, after all."

"Are you trying to convince me already?"

"Maybe I am. I just want you to start thinking along those lines. Any reason for not doing it has to be better than the ones you just gave me." He spoke deliberately and firmly. "If we are falling in love, and I think we are, then we owe it to ourselves to give it a go."

"If I would go back with you, that would put the screws to your bringing home any strays. Your tomcatting days would be over. If we do give it a go, you have to understand I would not tolerate the behavior you've been inclined to over the last years." I spoke just as firmly, knowing this point was not negotiable.

"If I have you to come home to, why would I want anyone else? I'll make sure word gets around that I am no longer available. I'm not asking you to decide tonight. But right now I can't imagine going back without you."

I felt like my world had just changed, possibly forever. Before I had a chance to recover my wits from the implications of what he had just proposed, Ivan said, "Now getting back to your toys . . ."

"How can you just switch gears like that? Haven't I told you enough about my habits, anyway?"

"I've said my piece about what I'm thinking. I want to get back to what we were talking about before. I want to know what you do when you're alone. Do you fantasize when you rub off?"

I couldn't help feeling amused affection for him in spite of my bewilderment. His matter-of-fact question had the tone of *Do you take lemon in your tea?* No one had ever asked me such things before. He sat across from me, still holding my hands, waiting for an answer. Mimicking his tone, I replied, "Most of the time."

"What do you think about?"

"The last few weeks I've thought about you. I've even had a couple erotic dreams about you."

"No shit!"

"Definitely, no shit."

"Well, what do you know about that!"

Christ, there Pash sat in her pink dressing gown, telling me she had fantasies and erotic dreams about me. "Did you just have the dreams?"

"No. I had one after my first class with you. It's the only reason I came back for the second class."

"Well, I'll be damned! Do you know I didn't expect you to come back at all? I had this whole speech ready about not giving up, to convince you to come back. If that hadn't worked, then I would have gone right to asking you out to dinner. What did you dream, if you don't mind my asking?"

"Ivan, how much personal information are you going to ask me tonight?"

"Enough." I cut myself another piece of torte. "This is really good, do you want another piece? It isn't too sweet."

"You are really enjoying this, aren't you?"

"Yes, I am!" I got up to get the kettle and refilled our cups. I went ahead and cut her another piece of pastry. "Eat. We're going to be up for a while yet. Now, what did you dream?"

"What is it about you? It feels like you keep taking off my clothes—first the physical ones, then the emotional ones and now the psychological ones."

"Makes you hot, doesn't it? I know it does it for me."

"For this I'm going to give up my flat?"

"Sweetheart, you'll soon be as addicted to it as I am. Now what the hell did you dream about me after that first lesson?"

"You really want to hear this?"

"I wouldn't ask you if I didn't. It isn't every day a sexy lady tells me she had an erotic dream about me. Now, tell me what you dreamed already!"

"All right, you asked for it. I dreamed I came into the stable and you were working with your shirt off. You asked me to come into an empty stall with you. Going into the stall, I tripped and fell into the mud again, except in the dream I fell on my arse instead of my knees.

"You started to hose me down, spraying the water against my arse, then coming around and spraying between my legs. You pressed your bare chest up against my breasts while you hosed me. Then you opened your jeans and asked me to wank you off. I did, and rubbed off against your leg at the same time. I had such a powerful orgasm in my sleep that I yelled out loud and woke myself up. I couldn't get back to sleep after that and ended up rubbing off again thinking about it."

"Bloody well sink me! That's one for Freud!"

"Don't I know it!" She smiled sheepishly.

"Seems you needed a little, real damn bad. I am a lucky son of a bitch to have been the one to light your fuse. Goddamn!"

"Since then that dream keeps coming back to me, usually as I'm drifting off to sleep. Except now I have embellished it with some of what we've done together or talked about doing together."

"You know, I'm one to explore such things."

"I know you are."

"Are you? I mean, to take some of those fantasies and make them real?"

Pash closed her eyes and sat still for a moment. "Before tonight I would have felt very foolish saying yes to that. And even if I felt I did, the chances of finding someone else who could manage it would seem highly improbable. But we've already done it. Vanya, it rocked me! I have never known anything like what we did tonight. And, yes, I want more."

I patted my lap. "Come here."

"Why?"

"Don't ask why, just do it!" Pash got up and walked around the table. "Sit on my lap." She sat down as I indicated and I undid the towel, exposing my throbbing boner. Before she could say a word, I untied her dressing gown and slid my hand between her legs. "You're as wet as I am hard." I took her hand and put it on my organ. "Seems we got ourselves a little stirred sitting here talking, now, doesn't it?"

"It seems we did."

"Wank me, like you did in your dream." Pash took hold of my organ and started slowly pumping me while I rubbed her. She put her free arm around my neck and her head on my shoulder. She started sucking on my neck.

"If you give me a visible love bite, you'll have to pay the price."

"I'll take that chance." She breathed the words into my ear and the hair on my arms stood up. She kept pumping me while she sucked my earlobe and licked my neck. I felt her widen her legs, giving me ample room to maneuver. I slid my finger inside her and she moaned right into my ear. "Vanya, I want you."

"Will you do what I ask of you?" I had no doubt she would.

"Tell me what."

"Stand up." She stood, wobbling a bit. I held on to her as I got up. My towel remained on the chair. I took her hand and led her into the dining room. The only light came from the kitchen, reflecting dimly on the table surface. "Lie down on the table."

"Ivan . . ."

"Passion, do as I tell you, lie down on the table." She slid back on the table, her dressing gown falling open around her. In the faint light from the kitchen she looked like a Renoir painting, her skin soft and luminescent. I pulled out a chair and sat down in front of her. "Now slide forward and put your legs over my shoulders."

"Why?"

"Sweetheart, do as I say. You will see why." She slid forward and put her legs over my shoulders. When she did so, her womanhood opened right in front of my face. I drank in the sight of her lying there, waiting for me. I slid my hands under her arse and tilted her pelvis upward, opening her even more. I could smell her sweetness. Never in my life had the scent of a woman filled me as hers did. My hunger for her overcame me and I buried my face in her ambrosial perfume. I found my prize and sucked the hardened nub into my mouth.

"Dear God, Ivan, I can't stand it!" She twisted, trying to free herself, but I held her firmly against my mouth. I slowly licked her, teasing the soft flesh with my tongue. The musky taste of her intoxicated me. Despite her straining against me, I took my time as I sucked her. I felt her fingernails clawing at my arms and heard a soft, guttural moan. "Ivan, please, I want you."

Releasing her, I kissed her inner thighs as I lowered her legs. My jacket still hung on the back of the chair. I reached into the inside pocket and pulled out a condom. Standing, I moved the chair aside and then helped her up. She clung to me, limp as a rag doll.

"Bend over the table, Passion." I pulled off her dressing gown and let it fall to the floor. I opened the condom and rolled it onto myself, and then came up behind her and started poking. "Spread your legs apart more." I took hold of her hips and repositioned myself, feeling her opening widen. I pushed again, this time sliding in. She groaned loudly. I pumped into her, my pelvis smacking against her rump. I held myself full inside her and then reached around and roughly rubbed her clitoris.

"Oh, sweet Jesus," she rasped out as she started to shudder. Her muscles gripped me as I pulled out and slammed back into her. This time I felt my own fire move. I exploded into her, grabbing her hips and grinding myself into her arse. She moaned and spasmed again, this time taking me with her.

When I regained awareness of the room, I still had her hips

tight against me. I slowly pulled out, taking care that the condom did not slip off. Without my support, her knees started to buckle. "Careful, my lady," I said, catching her before she hit the floor. I scooped her up and carried her into the bedroom.

"I'm all right, I just need to catch my breath."

"Damn straight you do, before you faint." I put her on the bed. "Now just lie there and breathe. I'll be right back." I went into the toilet and disposed of the condom. Then I wet a face cloth with cold water. I came back to the bed.

"Breathe deeper, from down here." I massaged her belly until I felt her breathe become more regular. "You're overheated." I wiped her face with the cold cloth, which brought her around even more. I folded it into a thin strip and draped it across her forehead. "We have to teach you how to breathe properly so you don't faint when we fuck."

"Is that a fact?"

"That is indeed a fact. Now you just rest here and let me take care of the things in the kitchen. I won't be but a minute." I went back to the kitchen and refrigerated the leftover pastry. I rinsed off our cups and plates and left them in the rack to dry.

I grabbed my discarded towel, did a once-over to make sure I had finished the cleanup and then went to turn off the light. It took me a moment to find the switch, which I dutifully snapped off. I picked up her dressing gown and returned to the bedroom, only to find her sound asleep, the cloth still folded across her forehead.

With Pash asleep on the bed I had an opportunity to look at her beautiful nakedness. Watching her sleep it seemed inconceivable that she could be as passionate as I knew her to be. I could still smell her on my whiskers. Her scent made her seem part of me. I wanted that, I wanted her in my life.

I walked over to her bedside table and glanced in the drawer again before closing it. She had fire, all right, and apparently smoldered with it enough to come up with some very creative ways to keep it in check. I took the cloth from her head. She didn't stir. I shifted her over a bit to give myself enough space to lie beside her. I felt knackered, but a little too tightly wound to sleep quite yet.

She had a book of poetry by the bed. I picked it up and found it to be a volume of Shelley, with the page marked from where she had found the inscription for me. I leafed through it and came upon an especially lovely poem called "Love's Philosophy." The first verse said what I felt when I looked at her, sleeping beside me. I left the book on her bedside table, opened to that page. I wanted to be sure she saw it in the morning. Then I turned out the light. As I put my arm around her, Shelley's exquisite language burned in my heart:

The fountains mingle with the river,
And the rivers with the ocean;
The winds of heaven mix forever
With a sweet emotion;
Nothing in the world is single;
All things by a law divine
In one spirit meet and mingle.
Why not I with thine?

Chapter Eighteen

I woke up the next morning to the extraordinary sensation of a hand fondling my balls and a very soft "Good morning" whispered in my ear. I rolled over and put my arm around Pash's waist. "What the hell do you think you're doing?"

"Enjoying myself." She nuzzled my neck and then put her leg over mine.

I pulled her closer. "You're acting more like a trollop than a virgin. You're supposed to be chaste and untried, remember?"

"What, you've never paid for any?" She whispered in my ear and then slid down and started licking my nipples.

"I didn't say that." She rubbed against my leg. "The way this is feeling, I may put a few quid on your pillow before I leave." She continued down my torso, licking and kissing my belly. I still had the sheet over me, which she pulled back, exposing my lower body. I closed my eyes, anticipating what would happen next. But she didn't move on down. Instead, she slid back up to my ear.

"I didn't have a chance to do you last night the way I wanted to." She licked the edge of my ear. "I want to do you now. Do we have time?"

"Oh, yes, Redhead, we have time. Even if we didn't, we would make time." She slid back down, this time going the whole way to my feet. Before I had a chance to protest, she started licking the bottom of my foot. It caught me so by surprise, I groaned and shuddered.

She licked the sole of one foot and then the other. The intensity of the feeling made me rear up, thrusting into the air. Just when I thought I couldn't stand another moment of this treatment, she started on my toes, sucking each one into her mouth. I couldn't bear it, but I never wanted it to stop. I reached down and started to wank myself. She stopped me.

"Oh, no, you don't, Dr. Kozak. You aren't taking this away from me. Pash pushed my hand away with a forcefulness that startled me." She bent over and took me in her mouth, squeezing my balls at the same time. I thrashed on the bed and thrust upward into her mouth. With the agility of a dancer, she moved with me, never letting the suction break.

My senses completely left me. I heard myself make sounds that could well have come from a lunatic, snorting and grunting in a delirious frenzy. Without warning, she shoved her index finger up my arse and rubbed my prostrate. I exploded into her mouth. She still didn't release me, swallowing with every spurt. Only after I had emptied myself did she finally move away, pulling out her finger as she sat up.

"Christ almighty, Redhead, where the hell did you learn to do that? That damn near sent me to Jupiter!"

"Jupiter? I was aiming for Uranus!"

I grabbed a pillow and swatted her. "Many more jokes like that and I'll reconsider my invitation." She laughed, quite tickled at her own crude humor.

"Actually, I have a lot of gay friends who don't mind passing along a few pointers. I've learned how to give really good head from the experts."

"I wouldn't think they let you practice on them, did they?"

"Heavens, no! That's what I'm doing with you!"

"Sink me!" I closed my eyes and silently thanked my dear old mum for taking such good care of me.

"I have to wash." I felt her crawling over me.

"I expect you do, seeing as what you just did to me." I

watched her dash to the toilet, enjoying the view as she moved. I sat up on the bed, feeling the need to relieve myself. Fortunately she didn't take long. "My turn." I made my way past her and closed the door. It took me a few minutes to take care of business.

I came out intending to make a joke about airing out the loo before we showered. But I changed my mind when I saw her sitting on the bed holding the volume of Shelley on her lap. I noticed a crumbled hankie on the bed beside her and surmised she had gotten my message. "It's a beautiful verse, isn't it?"

"Did you mean for me to see it?"

"Yes, of course I did. I read it last night before I fell asleep. It seemed to say what I felt better than I ever could."

"Are we really falling in love?" More tears filled her eyes.

"It would seem so." I sat down on the bed beside her and put my arm around her waist. "I can't say as how I expected to feel like this, but I am telling you straight out, it feels damn good!" She leaned against me and I kissed her hair. "Maybe we should have a little brekky before we have a shower." I leaned over and whispered in her ear, "You may want to crack a window in the loo for a bit."

"You bloody sod!" She picked up the hankie and wiped her nose. "You're supposed to be enticing me to move in with you. Stinking up my flat hardly constitutes a fetching motivation for sharing a bath with you."

"I've heard lovers experience true intimacy the morning after. I guess that includes bad breath, tangled hair and breaking wind."

"And if I decide I can't stand to share a bath with you, then you'll just have to add another bath to your house, Dr. Kozak."

"I don't think so! I've already got one and a half. You're welcome to the half downstairs if you don't care to share mine."

"Do I get my own bedroom, too?"

"If you want your own bedroom, why bother coming at all?" I hugged her tightly. "You might as well share mine, I'll just end up in yours anyway." She laughed and tugged my whiskers.

"What time do you have to be back at the stable?"

"Whenever I get there. I told Steve not to expect us until this afternoon."

"You're going to hold me to this lesson today, aren't you?"

"Of course I am. Eventually I want to ride with you—I mean on two horses over a distance."

"It would be more fun on one horse with you driving!"

"How about on one horse with you driving?"

"Not in this lifetime, Dr. Kozak."

"If I'm teaching you, Mrs. Kozak, you will damn straight learn how to ride!" I heard the words come out of my mouth but knew some other voice must have said it. If I could have swallowed my tongue in that moment, I would have.

"Excuse me? What did you say?"

All I could manage to say was, "I'm sorry. I guess that's putting the horse before the cart, so to speak."

"I guess so."

I couldn't believe he had called me Mrs. Kozak. "Where the devil did that come from?"

"Blame it on my mum. I think she's putting words in my mouth." He smiled and looked away. If I wasn't mistaken, I thought I saw just a hint of color in his cheeks. I could tell it had slipped out and decided not to make an issue of it.

"Well, tell your mum she has to slow down a little. I don't even know yet if I can stand to share a bath with you." Ivan laughed, I think relieved I had taken his faux pas with humor. I got up, trying to be cool even though my stomach fluttered. "I think I had better crack that window so we can have a shower. We have to eventually put on some clothes."

"I don't mind lounging around in the nude if you don't." He stood and laid his arms on top of my shoulders. "I am so damn comfortable with you. Even the desk clerk at the inn thought we were married. Who knows, maybe it's kismet." He pulled me close and kissed me. Just then the phone rang. He whispered, "Let it ring."

"Ivan, I never get calls on a Sunday morning. Maybe it's important." I slipped out of his embrace and reached for the phone on my bedside table. I picked it up, half expecting to hear about a family emergency. Instead I heard Gwen's cheerful voice greeting me.

"Good morning, Pash. It's Gwen. I hope I'm not interrupting anything." I could tell by her tone that she knew Ivan had spent the night.

"I take it you've been talking to Steve." I saw Ivan look up when he heard Steve's name. His jaw took on that hard line I had seen on Thursday morning.

"My dear boy rang me up a while ago and asked me to come out today. I guess Ivan is there with you now?"

"You guess correctly."

"Good. I am calling to ask if you two would like to have dinner with Steve and me tonight at the farm. I'll cook. Steve said you are coming out for a lesson today. I thought it might be fun." I glanced at Ivan's rigid jaw and thought that "fun" might be overstating it just a bit. I also noticed his stony expression increased the angular definition of his profile, making him even more striking than usual.

"Let me ask Ivan." I put my hand over the receiver and turned to him. "Gwen wants to know if we would like to have dinner tonight at the farm with her and Steve. She says she'll cook." I saw his jawline move a bit, probably from grinding his teeth. "Ivan, maybe if Steve sees us together he'll stop badmouthing you so much."

"Not likely."

"What do you want me to tell her? We could just stay here today if you would rather."

He folded his arms across his chest, looked at the floor and then looked back at me. "Tell her we're planning to work later today, but we'll break to have a bite to eat." I went back to the phone and repeated what Ivan had said.

"Working on what? Your riding lesson can't last that long and it seems you would have done the other deed at your place!"

"We're going to discuss my book. Ivan has some questions he wants to ask me."

"Oh, I see. Maybe I'll listen in."

"You'll be too busy cooking dinner for four, dearie."

"Okay, I get the message. I'm bloody dying to meet him. For you to be this gone over him . . ."

"Gwen, we are about to have breakfast."

"I'm sure you are. Have fun, luv. I'll see you later."

I put down the phone. "Ivan, why does this upset you so much?" He didn't say anything. I went to him and put my hand on his chest. "Talk to me, Vanya. I want to understand."

"Pash, Steve is using Gwen. I don't mean that he doesn't care for her. Actually, I think he does. But he is maneuvering, trying to get an upper hand."

"An upper hand for what?"

"To best me."

"This must be some kind of man thing, because I'm not grasping the difficulty between the two of you."

"Sweetheart, it isn't easy to explain. We have a long history of trying to outdo each other. Lately I've tried to keep our contests friendly, but he can still get damn nasty at times. It is driving him crazy that I'm not talking about what is going on with you. He is using Gwen to get to you to get to me, if that makes any bloody sense at all."

"You're saying this dinner is Steve's idea so he can get something over on you?"

"Pash, trust me, this has Steve written all over it. I wouldn't put it past him to say something really ignorant in front of you just to embarrass me. He's done shit like that before."

"I can't help wondering why you put up with it."

Ivan put his forearms on my shoulders. "He's the only family I have, Redhead. There is no one else. Steve and those horses are the only home I have to go back to. You can put up with a lot of bullshit for the sake of not being alone." He slid his hand up the back of my neck and into my hair as he said, "But there is a limit to what I will take. This isn't a game with you, Pash. I won't let him turn it into one."

"What about Gwen? She is my best friend and she is also hot for Steve. All of a sudden this whole thing has become incestuous!"

"I don't want this situation to come between you and your friend. It is bad enough that I have to contend with Steve's games. I know I shouldn't involve you in this, but you have to know, my lady, anything you tell Gwen about us can and probably will be used against me."

"Ivan, Gwen is so curious about you. She knows I care for you and is asking a lot of questions, which I have been ducking. Maybe we should just tell them both that you've asked me to come back with you in the fall."

"Let me think on that. Tell me something . . ."

"What?"

"Would Gwen tell you if Steve put her up to asking you about me?"

"Probably. Gwen is a little on the flighty side, but she is honest."

"If she should start grilling you, just have your ear to the door. If it sounds like Steve is behind it, ask her if he is. Then use your discretion about how to answer. Is that fair?"

"Admirably so, Dr. Kozak. Tonight, though, I intend to follow your lead."

"How about following my lead right now into the shower? The loo should have aired out by now."

"Are you suggesting we share a shower?"

"It is environmentally responsible, saving water and all."

"And of course all you'll want to do is have a shower."

"Maybe so. I'm mighty hungry. What's for brekky?"

"If we're lucky, sausage!" He grinned and then took my hand and pulled me in the direction of the loo.

In the shower, we lathered each other up. Pash paid particular attention to my cock. As she slid her soapy hand up and down my shaft, she murmured, "My God, Ivan, you have to be the most beautiful man I've ever seen." She found my nipple in the wet, matted hair and suckled me.

I held her head to my chest, the warm water pelting down on us. "Pash, I want to hump your arse, turn around." I stood behind her. With one hand I palmed her breast while the water flowed over her. With the other I reached around and started to rub her.

Her smooth, slippery bum provided a delicious cushion to bump against. I continued caressing her. The water poured over us, washing away everything except our awareness of each other. She slithered against me in a slow, wet dance of unadulterated lust. We moved together, both wanting and needing the sensation we shared.

When she climaxed, she gasped, "Oh, yes, Ivan, my Vanya!" I pulled her tightly against me. If I could have I would have pulled her completely into myself, the sense of wanting to bond with her overwhelming me.

I continued humping against her bottom, my own orgasm very close. "Ivan, let me suck you off again. Please."

"Sweet Jesus, yes, do." I held on to the wall to support myself. She turned around and knelt in front of me. Once again I felt her sweet mouth take my organ. Only in my dreams had anyone ever asked to blow me. As she had earlier, she drank every drop.

We dried ourselves. Pash put on her dressing gown and I wrapped my favorite towel around my waist. I had to retrieve my overnight bag in order to shave. She watched me lather up and then take out my straight razor. She came over to the washbasin to get a closer look. "That's a lethal-looking thing. You don't use a regular razor?"

"It's how I learned to shave. My father taught me with it. He brought a few of these blades with him from the old country. He told me he learned with a knife, as was the old cossack way." I started to scrape my face with it, taking care not to damage the line of my beard. "When my father passed on, his razors and the strap he used to sharpen them became mine." I continued shaving, feeling her curious stare. "You've never seen a man shave before?"

"Not like this, I haven't. Do you ever cut yourself with it?"

"No more than I would expect someone using the newer models do. In fact, I've tried the other kind and hacked myself up pretty damn good with it. I went back to this one in short order."

I rinsed the blade and took out the leather strap. "I'll show you how I sharpen it. Here, hold this end." She took hold of the strap and I ran the blade back and forth across the surface. "It works really well, keeps the edge honed." I started on the other side of my face. "You know, my father took that strap to my backside on a couple of occasions. Let me tell you, it's not something I would recommend."

"I can't imagine you ever doing anything to warrant a strapping!"

"Well, I'm not as angelic as I look."

"Obviously."

"Once he got me damn good for cussing at him. Another time he found out I had 'borrowed' a neighbor's bicycle. I had to return the bike and apologize. When I got home he laid into me but good with a life lesson about stealing." I glanced at Pash, who was listening quietly to my memories. "What the hell is it about you anyway? I've never talked about my family like this. It's taken me years to get over being ashamed of them."

"I like hearing about your family. Why on earth were you ashamed of your family, anyway?"

"My parents were immigrants and never let go of the old-country ways. I didn't want to bring my friends home because we only spoke Ukrainian there."

"I wish they were still alive. I would like to have met them."

I dried my face and took a clean shirt out of my bag. "It's funny, I wish I could introduce you to them. I think they would like you."

"Seems like your mum already knows me." Pash watched me pull my shirt over my head. "I need to get dressed, too. Now I am really hungry." She went into the bedroom to get some clothes. I gathered my belongings and followed her. I watched her mull over the things hanging in her cupboard as I pulled on my underpants and blue jeans.

She selected a rose shell top with a scoop neck and then went over and found herself a fresh pair of scanties in her bureau. She looked over at me watching her. "What, you've never seen a woman dress before?"

"I've seen plenty of women dress, but none of them interested me as much as you do." She pulled on the lingerie underneath her dressing gown and then threw the dressing gown over a chair. When she put on the top, I noticed two small overlapping hearts on the left shoulder, neatly curving onto her breast. I came over and traced the hearts with my finger. "Interesting design."

"It seems to say it, doesn't it?"

"Yes, I do believe it does, Redhead." We finished dressing and made our way to the kitchen.

"I have bangers and eggs, if you like. I also have some pastry. Place your order, Dr. Kozak."

"Let me fry us up some bangers and eggs while you set the table and make some coffee. Let's get cracking. I'm feeling a bit peckish."

"You're on." We busied ourselves and whipped up a hearty meal in short order. We sat in the kitchen to eat. As I watched Ivan spread a thick layer of marmalade on his toast, I said to him, "I think I need a little coaching."

"About what?"

"About how to act with you at the farm."

"The same as you do here."

"Vanya, I mean, physically. How affectionate can I be? For instance, would you be comfortable if I held your hand or kissed you?"

"You mean in front of Steve."

"Yes, I mean in front of Steve."

"Redhead, short of fucking, we can do whatever we damn well please no matter who is around!"

"You're sure?"

"Quite sure. The only reason I wouldn't fuck in front of him is that he'd most probably get off watching!"

"Are we going to work downstairs or in your room?"

"I plan to work in the sitting room. If there are too many distractions, we can go upstairs. Sweetheart, I am a little more than a guest in that house."

"Have you ever made love there, in the house, I mean?"

"Why? Are you planning to jump my bones tonight?" He grinned at me.

"You never know. Should I take my toothbrush?"

"I have to be out with the horses tomorrow at six A.M. If you do stay, it's going to be up by five thirty the latest—earlier if you want to have a shower with me."

"Such a romantic invitation. I don't know if I can resist."

"Once we're living together it won't be an issue, now, will it?"

"Ivan, you keep talking like it is a done deal. It isn't, not by any stretch of the imagination."

He sipped his coffee. "Okay, then, let me ask you something. If I were to tell you I had to leave this week, for whatever reason, how would you react?"

I remembered how it had felt on Thursday when he almost left. "If I am to be honest . . ."

"And I expect you to be. . . ."

"It would hurt terribly. I already had a preview on Thursday."

"I know damn straight it wouldn't feel too good to me, either. I also had a preview on Thursday. I think we need to start planning for you to come back with me."

"Ivan, this is happening so fast. We've only known each other three weeks and have only been intimate for five days."

"Sometimes that's all it takes if it's the right person."

"But we're talking about turning my life upside down in a month."

"Seems to me Shaftesbury is just a temporary stopover to write your book. You have no family here. There are only the memories of your grandmother. Your coming back to Northamptonshire with me is a step toward a permanent life together. I think we are both overdue for that."

"It scares me, Vanya, the permanent part. How do we know we can do it?"

"We won't know if we don't try it. It is only a month away, Pash. That isn't much time for planning. We need to think about what needs to be done, don't you agree?"

"For the most part, yes."

"But . . ."

"Once you are back, your other life takes over. I know you from here, from the farm and with the horses. I have yet to really meet Dr. Kozak."

"We get on famously. What makes you think our careers will cause a problem?"

I sat for a moment, unsure if I should speak my mind. I decided there was too much at stake to be timid. "There is one other thing."

"What?"

"Once you are back at the university, how do I know you'll be able to resist the temptations there?"

"You're afraid I'm going to sleep around, aren't you?"

"Ivan, I feel more than a little threatened by your past. I

can't help it. I'm not twenty anymore. I can't compete with those young girls. If you would still want to sleep with them, I simply couldn't handle it."

"Pash, I can't guarantee I won't be tempted. I might be. But I have a way to keep those urges in check, if you are amenable."

"Dare I ask how?"

"I can come home and act them out with you."

"Oh, God!"

"Well, can you think of a better way?"

"That would make me a sexual surrogate in those situations."

"You wouldn't be a surrogate, Pash. That's just it. It would be more role-playing like we did last night. I would be loving you, just inside a fantasy. I know I would find deeper pleasure with you than I ever could with those girls. Stirs me just to think on it. Thing is, I am in love with you. I've never loved any of them."

"You are unconventional, Ivan, bordering on perverted. Says a lot about me, doesn't it, that I want to live with you?"

"It says plenty. Let's get this cleaned up. You have a riding lesson waiting."

Chapter Nineteen

After I helped Pash clean up the kitchen, she disappeared into the hall cupboard. She emerged a few minutes later with more copies of her books. Without saying a word, she threw them into a paper sack and then again disappeared into the bedroom. I made myself at home in the sitting room, figuring that my presence in the bedroom could well slow things down. I looked over her bookshelves.

Her personal library included literature, philosophy, sociology, spirituality and metaphysics, with a sprinkling of sexy romance novels topping off the lot. I also found several tattered copies of her father's plays. I definitely wanted to read those.

She came out of the bedroom carrying a small overnight bag. "Going somewhere?" I asked, amused by her statement of intention.

"I'm going with you, as I understand it," she fired back.

"I'm pleased to see you are adjusting to the idea." I picked up the other bags. "We best be heading out. We have a lot to do today." After a brief discussion about taking two cars, we agreed I would drive her home.

We made it to the farm by two thirty, a little later than I'd expected. The place seemed deserted. Steve had probably gone to pick up Gwen.

We left our bags in the car and went right to the stable. I

did a quick once-over of the place and saw Steve had handled all the morning work. I had to talk to him about getting the new fellow trained before I left. The kid would also be some help, although as scrawny as he was, I doubted if he could manage much of the heavier work.

While checking out the place, I lost track of Pash. I found her cooing at Nutmeg. I came up behind her. "What's this? Girl talk?"

"Just getting to know one another a little better. I think she knows me now."

"I'm sure she does. It also helps that you're carrying my scent."

"That sounds attractive."

"It is, at least to this old girl." I opened the stall and went in. "Come here." Pash came up beside me. "This horse has a heart as big as she is. If I had a place for her, I would buy her from Steve and take her home with me, too."

"Too?"

"Both of you. I've managed to fall in love twice this summer." Pash smiled at me and squeezed my hand. "What say we get her saddled up." I led Nutmeg out of her stall and left Pash alone with the horse while I went to get the saddle.

When I came back I found her feeding Nutmeg an apple. She had come a long way in the last couple weeks. "Bribing her, I see."

"Just making friends. Have you ever thought about having a horse of your own?"

"I've certainly thought about it. I even bought a small bit of land beside my house with that in mind. So far, though, I haven't done anything about it."

"Well, maybe we should consider it."

I smiled at her unconscious pronoun. " 'We'?"

"I guess I'm getting used to the idea."

"That's what I want!" I finished cinching up the saddle. "All right, she's ready. Mount her."

"Isn't that a tad suggestive?" Pash patted my behind as she

came over to Nutmeg's left side. I recognized her concentration and focus from Friday as she put her foot in the stirrup. She grabbed on to the edge of the saddle and hefted herself straight up and then over, catching hold of Nutmeg's mane to keep from plopping down. Pash lowered herself into the saddle the way one would a hot bath.

"Sweetheart, you don't have to be quite that careful."

"Bugger off. I'm working on it."

"Indeed you are. Now take her into the ring." Pash bent over and whispered into Nutmeg's ear. "Hey, there, I don't want you two conspiring about this. What did you say to her?"

"I told her I would give her another apple if she gets me through this in one piece." With that Pash tapped Nutmeg with her foot and the old girl dutifully started ambling toward the door. I watched closely, ready to jump in if Pash had trouble. But she took Nutmeg out the door and then leaned to the right.

I waited until Nutmeg had properly navigated the turn, and then ran ahead to open the gate to the ring. What Pash didn't know, but I did, was that Nutmeg would follow me right into the ring. That old girl had a sixth sense about what I wanted her to do.

"Now, walk her around the circle a couple of times. Then, when I tell you, cut her through the middle and do a figure eight." Pash did well going around the circle, but when I told her to take Nutmeg through the center, she became confused.

"Ivan, I don't understand what you want me to do." I could see she had become flustered.

"Pash, all I'm saying is lean one way and then lean the other, tugging the reins in the direction you are leaning, like this." I walked her through it, showing her how to lean in order to have the horse turn in the proper direction. "Walk her around the circle now and try it again."

She did as I asked, this time properly cutting across the middle but turning Nutmeg back into the circle a little too soon. "Try it again." I drilled Pash on this about half a dozen times until she had the figure eight down.

I heard Steve's car coming down the lane. I had Pash stop beside me. A few minutes later a very curvaceous blonde ran over to the fence and climbed onto it. Steve followed her. "Blimey, would you look at you! Riding a horse! Well, I'll be jiggered!"

I looked up at Pash. "Want to show them what you just learned?" I noticed a shadow of indecision, quickly replaced by determination.

"Yes, you bet I do." She looked in the direction of Gwen sitting on the fence with Steve standing behind her. "Hi, Gwen. Hi, Steve. Get a look at this." With that she took Nutmeg around the circle once, and then on the second pass did a perfect figure eight. Pash brought Nutmeg up right in front of our audience and brought her to a dead stop. I had to admit, I liked her style. I walked across the ring to where she had stopped.

"I think that's enough for today, Redhead. You've done beautifully."

Pash looked at me, her eyes glowing with satisfaction. "I have a good teacher."

"You sure as hell do!" Steve's interjection surprised me. He said to Gwen, "Do you know she's never ridden before coming here?"

"I know. Pash, this is brilliant!" The blonde gave me a not-so-subtle once-over and then said, "Hi, I'm Gwen. You must be Ivan."

"Nice to make your acquaintance, Gwen. If you'll excuse us for a few minutes, I have to get these two ladies back to the stable. We'll see you up at the house." I went over to the gate and opened it. Pash steered Nutmeg right through it and headed for the stable. I saw Steve watching Pash and Gwen watching me. It promised to be an interesting night.

We got Nutmeg squared away in her stall; Pash gave her a treat this time. Before I closed the stall I glimpsed Pash putting her face against Nutmeg and saying good-bye. "You ladies seem to have worked things out."

"I think we have. We understand each other." She put her arm around my waist. "Are we ready to do this?"

"I need a few minutes before we head for the house."

"Are you all right, Vanya?"

I turned Pash around to face me. "I am now." I held her tightly and kissed her, the intensity of her response surprising me. She dug her nails into my back and bit my tongue, and then licked my teeth. "Where the hell did that come from?" I asked as I pulled away.

"I'm feeling it, is all," she said as she came back for seconds. I happily obliged.

I pulled away for a moment and glanced at my watch. "It's getting late. As much as I want to see this through right now, we best be getting up to the house. Otherwise we risk having one of them walk in on us."

"I know you're right, but God almighty, I want you."

"If we don't stop now, we won't be able to." With all the willpower I had, I let her go.

She stood there for a moment with her eyes closed and then bent over and held her knees. She took a deep breath as she stood up. "You don't ask much, do you? I'm about to boil over here."

"At least yours doesn't show." I indicated the bulge in my jeans.

"Should I hose you down with cold water?" She stared shamelessly at my hard-on, deliberately licking her lips.

"Redhead, you do that one more time and you'll be blowing me before dinner."

"Interesting appetizer, wouldn't you say?"

"Indeed! Let's get our stuff out of the car and cool down a little." I took her hand and started toward the door. "Did you bring your dressing gown along?"

"Yes, why?"

"Because there is a water closet downstairs and only one

full loo upstairs, down the hall from me, next to Steve's room. If you need to go during the night, you better damn well have your dressing gown."

We got our bags from the backseat of Ivan's car. I couldn't help poking at him a little as I watched him bend over to get the books from the other side of the seat. "You know, my car is better."

Ivan stood up, holding the bag of books. "And why, pray tell, is your car better? As I recall, it is considerably older than mine."

"Precisely, Dr. Watson!"

"Excuse me. Maybe I'm a little dense, but I don't get it."

"My car is older; therefore, the backseat is bigger. When we go parking and do it in the backseat, we'll take my car."

"My dear Passion, if you haven't noticed, my legs are somewhat longer than yours. I prefer a bed for doing it. The backseat is too damn confining."

"But that's part of the fun."

"We'll talk." He gathered up our bags while I carried the leftover torte and pastry. We made our way to the back door, which opened into the kitchen.

"Well, there you are. I thought maybe you got lost on the way." Gwen came over and took the boxes from me. "What's this? I'm making dessert."

"It's just our leftovers from last night. I thought they might get eaten here. I'll just end up throwing most of it out."

"Well, with these two living here, I expect it won't be leftover for long." Before she turned around, Gwen mouthed the words "He's gorgeous!" I know I flushed, because Ivan gave me a questioning look.

"Pash, I'm going to take our bags upstairs and grab my laptop." He turned to Gwen. "Where did Steve go?"

"He went to the basement to get a bag of potatoes. I've elected him chief peeler."

"Well, that should keep him out of trouble for a while."

He turned back to me. "I'll be right back, sweetheart. Then we'll get to work."

Gwen put the bakery boxes on the table and waited until Ivan left the kitchen. Then she grinned as she said, " 'Our bags'? 'Sweetheart'? You two certainly haven't wasted any time, have you?" She came over and gave me a hug. "Pash, I'm so happy for you. That handsome hunk of man is smitten. It's written all over him. I won't even talk about the look in your eyes. Luv, all I have to say is it's about bloody time!"

I felt myself getting teary. "Oh, Gwen, he's wonderful. I can't believe I found someone like him here, of all places." We hugged each other again, the tears stinging my eyes.

We heard Steve coming up the stairs. Gwen whispered, "Pull yourself together, luv. My dear boy will start asking more questions than I think you want to answer right now."

"You really expect me to peel all these? It's a five-frigging-pound sackful!" Steve came into the kitchen from the hallway. "Oh, hi, Pash. I'm sorry, I didn't know you had come in."

"Yes, I do expect you to peel them. If you want to eat before midnight, you had better get started."

"See how she puts me around? I don't know why I put up with it."

"I do!" Gwen said seductively. She kissed her finger. Then she touched Steve's nose.

"So do I." Ivan stepped through the doorway into the kitchen. "For the same damn reason I'm beginning to." He came over and put his arm around my shoulders. "Are you ready to tackle this?"

"Ready when you are. Where did you put my books?"

"Right here." He reached down and picked up the bag from a kitchen chair.

"What the hell are you two doing, anyway?" Steve asked, rummaging through a utensil drawer. "Kozak, have you seen the potato peeler?"

"If you haven't used it to clean your toenails, it is probably still in the dish drainer from making the stew last week."

"Now, watch yourself! There are ladies present." Steve went over to the drainer and found the peeler in the rack. "Now, what did you say you were doing?"

"I'm considering using Pash's book in my course. I want to talk to her about it and take some notes."

"No shit!" Steve tore open the bag. "Then I don't suppose you'll want to volunteer to help me with this."

"Nope."

"This is the book with that business in the front about being rough and wooing not like a babe?"

Ivan glanced at me as he answered, "That's the one. Like I told you when you looked at it yesterday, you should read it. It would do you good."

I saw the taut line of Ivan's jaw as he spoke. I slipped my arm around his waist as a discreet reassurance. I knew Steve had just goaded him.

"You're talking about *Sagacity,* right?" Gwen picked up a knife and started peeling a potato.

"Have you read it, Gwen?" Ivan still had his arm around me. I had felt his hold tighten when Steve brought up my inscription. Now I felt him relax a little. I had to remember to thank Gwen for that one.

"It took me a few days but I did read it. It's deep."

"To put it mildly. I think it would help my students to read it."

"I never thought of it like that, but I think you're right. Kids these days are taken in by too many fads. They need to know what is really important."

"That's just what I think. See if you can get him to read it." Ivan nodded toward Steve. "Now, we had better get down to it. How long before dinner?"

"At least an hour, longer if the potatoes don't get peeled soon." Gwen splashed potato water at Steve.

"Hey, I'm doing the best I can here."

"Give a yell when it's ready. We'll be in the sitting room." Ivan took my hand and led me out the door.

Chapter Twenty

Ivan put his laptop on the coffee table and plugged it in beside the sofa. Then he sat down beside me. As the computer booted, he cracked his knuckles. "Did you see what he did?"

"I saw."

"Just so you know what happened, I had the book on the kitchen table yesterday during breakfast, trying to finish it before seeing you. He picked it up and looked at it. Save for snatching it out of his hands, there wasn't a damn thing I could do about it."

"Ivan, it's all right. I don't mind that he read what I wrote to you."

"I know you don't, Redhead. But the bloody sod knows you meant that inscription to be personal. He wanted you to know he had read it."

"So now I know. It hasn't changed anything."

"No, I don't suppose it has."

"Let him give it his best shot, Ivan. Whatever he throws at you, or at me, be cool. I know what is going on. He can't do any harm unless we let him." I reached out and rubbed his back. "Have a little faith. I really do love you."

"That's something I'm still getting used to." He took hold of my free hand and kissed my palm. "Let's get to work."

"Before we do, may I ask you something?"

"Certainly, what?"

"Do you have a garage?"

"Yes, I have a garage." He poked his index finger into my side and made me jump. "Do you want to make sure the rain doesn't leak into the backseat of your pristine car?"

"No, smarty-pants! I have an idea I want to run by you."

"I don't know if I want to hear this, but what's your idea?"

"Is it big enough for Nutmeg?"

"Excuse me?" Ivan wiggled his index finger in his ear and then said, "Could you repeat that? I'm not sure I heard you correctly."

"Is it big enough for Nutmeg?"

"You're suggesting I turn my garage into a stable? What the hell do I do with my car?"

"You park it outside, like you do here." Ivan got very quiet as he digested my suggestion. "Once we have her with us, we can work on building a small stable by your house."

"You're really serious, aren't you?"

"Ivan, have some vision. Have you ever read any Joseph Campbell?"

"Some. But mythology isn't my forte."

"He said, 'We must be willing to let go of the life we have planned, so as to have the life that is waiting for us.' That's what I'm trying to do with you and I think you're trying to do with me. He also said, 'Follow your bliss.' Horses are in your heart. You owe it to yourself to follow your bliss."

I could see him taking in what I had said. "I suppose this could work."

"She could stay in the garage until we can build a proper stable."

"What's with this 'we' stuff all of a sudden? I thought it wasn't a done deal."

"I'm trying it on for size. I'm finding it feels rather good."

"You are really something! Hearing you say 'we can build a proper stable' makes it sound almost possible."

"It is possible, Ivan. What's more, I don't know if you should leave her. It is obvious she is your horse. She is the one you've singled out to care for and she won't get the individual attention once you're gone. She needs you almost as much as you need her."

"Steve truly doesn't have the time to care for her individually if she needs extra attention."

"Do horses ever get depressed?"

"I believe they can."

"Well, I think both you and Nutmeg will have a major case of separation anxiety if steps aren't taken to bring her along."

"If that could happen with this horse, think what could happen with us!"

"That's why I'm bringing it to your attention! I've thought about how I would feel watching you leave. If Nutmeg can feel such things, she will be very sad when you go."

"I would miss her, too." He stroked his beard several times, obviously considering the possibility.

"You see, with a little thought, the pieces start to come together."

"I have to admit, it is an interesting idea. Let me think about it. We should get some work done now. Dinner will be ready soon and we haven't even started."

"What's your hurry? I'm spending the night, after all." Ivan gave me that smile of his and it lit up the room.

"Is that so! You know something? I don't recall inviting you to spend the night."

"Yes, you did! You told me if I stayed, it would be an early morning. Of course, if you would rather I wouldn't . . ."

"Sweet thing, you damn well better stay! After what happened in the stable, I'm going to need some relief later tonight."

"My, my, look at the time. We'd better get busy since it has to be an early night. We'll have to get some sleep before five thirty rolls around."

"What makes you think we'll be sleeping much?" He slipped his arm around my waist and pulled me closer. Then he kissed me sweetly, gently.

"How the devil am I supposed to sit here and talk about my book when all I want to do is to touch you?"

"It's called discipline, dear heart, something I am sure you can manage." He let me go and slid to the edge of the sofa to reach the laptop. I looked at his back and noticed his shirt sticking to his skin. I slid my hand up his back and let it rest on his neck.

"Looks like you've worked up a bit of a sweat yet again."

Ivan turned around and said, "Is it any wonder, considering how much I want you?" He reached out and took hold of me again, this time kissing me forcefully. I returned his kiss with equal force. Just then, Steve's voice cut through our private moment.

"Hey, hey, none of that. Save it for the honeymoon." I felt Ivan jump, like being caught with his hand in the cookie jar. "Sorry to interrupt your 'work,' but Gwen wants to know your wine choice and how you want your steaks cooked."

"I want red and rare, how about you?" Ivan said.

"I'll have red and medium."

Ivan still had his arm around me. "By the way, Pash will be staying here with me tonight. I hope that isn't a problem."

"Not a problem for me, old boy, but it will be for you if you don't get some sleep tonight. We have a heavy day tomorrow." Steve looked straight at me. "Of course, I might ask Gwenny to stay, too. Maybe we could have ourselves a foursome."

Ivan bristled. "Dream on, chum. There's no way in hell I want to be in the same room with your naked arse!"

I chimed in with, "Anyway, Steve, I doubt if Gwen would be any more inclined to share you than I am to share Ivan. I would check with her before making such invitations."

"Just a thought." Steve winked at me. "Dinner will be ready in about half an hour, according to the chef. Don't get too involved, whatever you're doing."

* * *

Once Steve left, I had to take a deep breath to calm myself. "Pash, I'm not so sure it's a good idea to stay here tonight. We might be asking for it."

"And I think if we leave now, it would be asking for more trouble. He'll think he's getting to you and that will egg him on. If we present a united front and really show him that his needling isn't working, then perhaps he will let up."

"I doubt that."

"Well, just for tonight, let's see how it works. Thing is, you're going to have to sit on yourself and not flare every time he makes a remark."

"I hear you, Redhead. You know, we're not getting much done here."

"Vanya, we're getting a lot done. We're talking about our future and our lives. That counts for something, doesn't it?"

"That counts for plenty."

"Tell you what—after dinner why don't we ask Steve and Gwen to join our discussion, if they like?"

"Pash . . ."

"Now, hear me out. I know Gwen is interested—she already asked me if she could listen in. I think it would be a good thing for Steve to hear a little of what this is about."

"He'll be bored."

"Fine, then he can leave. But it removes the mystery. He may not be so interested in digging if you hand him the shovel and say, 'Get to work.' It also includes him. He feels left out."

"Why do you think that?"

"If he's the only family you have, the same seems to be true of him. Your having a relationship with someone threatens him, Ivan."

I realized Pash had just applied the principles in her book. "This is part of what I want to talk to you about."

"What?"

"How you sense what is going on underneath the surface. It is all through *Sagacity*."

"You're catching me unprepared for that level of question. Give me a minute." She closed her eyes and took a deep breath. "Now ask me again."

"What did you just do?"

"I quieted my mind and centered myself so I can properly answer your question. Ask me again."

"How do you sense what is going on with Steve?"

"I listen."

"Listen to what?"

"To this." She put her hand on her stomach. "Or to this." She put her hand on her chest. "Only then, do I listen to this." She put her index finger against her temple.

"You're saying you feel it?"

"Yes. It is a ripple of feeling that I translate into words."

"So you tapped into this inner knowing with Steve? What do you sense?"

"With Steve, I feel a wave of anger." Pash closed her eyes again as though reaching for something forgotten. "He resents you, Ivan."

She opened her eyes and looked at me. "He needs you a lot more than you need him. You fill a gap for him, both emotionally and with the farm. Now, he is still getting the farm part, but not the emotional part. With me in the picture, you have closed him out of yourself."

"Which is why he is so damned pissed off at me!"

"I think so."

"So he wasn't just being a lecherous SOB when he suggested a foursome. I know he can be damned ornery, but I've never known him to suggest such a thing. Always, when we've doubled, we've taken great care to have our own privacy."

"So how many opportunities have you had?"

"Enough to know he isn't inclined to such things."

"That isn't why I asked."

"I know." Pash reached up and pulled my beard. "Ouch! What was that for?"

"Just a reminder that the tomcat has given up his prowling ways."

"Indeed. The tomcat doesn't have to prowl when he has a she-cat in heat on his side of the fence." She shot me a look that made me anticipate her spending the night. "I'll prove my point a little later, but right now I need you to repeat what you said so I can type it up." She repeated what she had said. "Do you really think everyone can do this?"

She poked me with her finger. "Anyone can do it, even you."

"What, old dogs really can be taught new tricks?"

"Yes, even indiscriminate old hounds like you."

I chuckled.

"I believe every person has the capacity to perceive their own inner knowing. I've simply chosen to exercise those 'muscles' in myself, like you do physically when you lift those bales of hay."

I smiled to myself, understanding she had to have noticed me doing it to make that analogy. I started typing to cover my amusement. She continued. "At first folks get real darn impatient when you don't snap back a response at lightning speed. To actually perceive your own truth, it is necessary to quiet yourself and calm your mind. The more you do it, the better you get at it."

As I typed what she said, I asked, "Does that also hold true in the bedroom?"

"I hope so. Only time will tell."

"Damn straight we're going to find out!"

"I hope you're being selective about what you're typing there. Some of this is off the record."

"Don't worry. I won't put down anything I wouldn't want my dear old mum to read." I looked at what I had already and a dozen more questions popped into my mind. "How the devil did you get into this anyway? It seems a little off the beaten path."

"You promise you'll listen with an open mind?"

"I will do my best." I squeezed her hand. "Tell me."

"Remember my nana?"

"Not personally, but I remember what you've told me."

"Well, she could pick up things about people, sometimes quite unintentionally. And, my, oh, my, was she forgetful!" Pash smiled at the memory. "She often thought someone had told her something, when actually she had intuited the information. When I would visit, I saw her rattle more than one poor customer by blurting out something she had no way of knowing."

She quietly rubbed her nose and then took a deep breath. "Nana told me things, Ivan, things that had happened to her during her life. It is such a shame about her. She spent her life hiding these incidents because everyone, including my mother, thought her eccentric at best and a crackpot at worst. She had a gift and I inherited it." She waited for my reaction.

"Go on, I'm listening."

"She told me about herself when she realized I had inherited her ability. That's when I started to study the process. *Sagacity* is a compilation of what I have learned." She again scrutinized my reaction. "There's something else I want to tell you. . . ."

"My Passion, just tell me."

She picked up a cushion from the sofa and hugged it to herself. "Remember I said my grandfather died in an accident?"

"I remember."

"Nana saw it happen, I mean in her mind's eye. She collapsed in the store at the very moment my grandfather was killed. She knew what had happened before anyone told her anything."

"Shit!"

"There's more. I get flashes of things, too. When Nana passed on, I was in London. I heard her call my name and I involuntarily turned around. I didn't see anyone, but I felt her—oh, my Lord, I felt her so much." Pash hugged the pillow tighter. "Vanya, I knew she had left. No one had to tell me. I knew. A couple of hours later, my mother received the call."

"Did you tell anyone you knew?"

"Heavens, no! They would have thought me loony!"

"Then you're doing the same thing your grandmother did: hiding it."

Pash picked up a copy of *Sagacity* that I had put on the coffee table and handed it to me. "Did you read my dedication?"

"No, I didn't see it."

"Read it." I opened the book and found the dedication. It read:

To Nana
For your heart, For your soul, For your life.
May everyone learn what you already knew.
Godspeed

"This book—you wrote it for her, didn't you?"

"And for everyone who ever felt like a loony because they knew."

I took her hand and kissed it. "You have to know you are the sanest person I've ever met."

"Thank you. It is a comfort to know you think so. I do believe dinner should be ready soon. We had better put this aside."

"Are you sure you want to include Steve and Gwen later?"

"I'm sure. We can discuss the book and not get into my stuff."

I smiled. "But I want to know more about 'your stuff.' "

"If we do the deed and I move in with you, you'll have to live with my stuff. You'll find out plenty."

"I intend to, although you're a little more than I bargained for, on several counts."

"Want to withdraw your invitation?"

"Bloody hell, no! I'm more determined than ever to have you come back with me. It does occur to me, however, that a few generations back you could have been torched as a witch."

"We've come a long way, haven't we? Now I just have to convince everyone I'm not psychotic."

"I'm convinced."

"Well, then, I guess I'd better start packing if I'm moving in with you." She watched me closely as she stated her intention.

"We'll get some boxes this week and decide what you'll need on the first trip. We'll come back for the rest of your things later."

"Excuse me. I didn't mean to interrupt, but dinner is ready." There stood Gwen, looking at both of us. "Did I hear this or didn't I hear this?"

Pash answered her immediately, saying, "Gwen, you didn't hear it, not yet. We thought we would tell you both over dinner."

"Whatever you say, Pash." Gwen looked visibly hurt. I figured I had better step in.

"Gwen, last night I asked Pash to come back to Northampton with me in the fall. I asked her not to say anything until I had a chance to tell Steve." Just then, Steve came up behind Gwen.

"Tell me what, old man?"

"Let's go sit down and I'll explain the whole thing,"

Chapter Twenty-One

I followed Ivan into the dining room. Gwen had the round dinner table set to perfection. As I sat down between Ivan and Gwen, she said, "I'm sorry we're running behind. All the silver and dishes had to be washed up. And it also took a bit to unearth this lace tablecloth."

Steve added, "Kozak and I always eat in the kitchen. I don't think these dishes have been out of the china cupboard since Christmas."

I couldn't help but gush a little. "Gwen, it's just beautiful, everything is so lovely. You've outdone yourself. Those flowers, they're from your garden, aren't they?"

"I wanted them to be special."

"They are. So are you." I reached over and took her hand.

Ivan turned to Steve. "You had better give them some wine pretty damn fast before they start bawling all over each other."

"C'mon, girls," Steve said as he filled our glasses, "save the balling for later when we're alone."

Ivan started to laugh in spite of himself. "You bloody sod!" he muttered under his breath. Steve finished filling the glasses. "May I make a toast?"

"Go ahead, guv'nor."

Ivan stood and looked at me and then at Steve and Gwen. "Last night I asked Pash to come back to Northampton with me next month. She has agreed."

"She's not moving in with you, is she?" Steve sounded incredulous.

"Actually, yes, she is. We're going to see if we can stand to live with each other. Then we'll decide if this is going to go further. If it does, and there is a wedding in our future, we want you both to stand for us. You are our two best friends and we met because of you." Ivan raised his glass. "So, to friends, to family and to love." He held up his glass to toast, and we all did the same. "Now, let's eat!"

Steve agreed. "Damn right, the food is getting cold. Pass the potatoes."

Gwen handed me the meat platter. "This side is rare, for the boys, and this side is medium, for us." The rare steaks were twice the size of the medium ones. "When are you leaving?" Her eyes were glassy.

I glanced at Ivan as he piled mashed potatoes on his plate. He didn't answer, so I said, "In about a month. I don't know exactly yet."

"What about your flat?"

"I'm keeping it for a while until we see if this works out."

Ivan smiled at me, letting me know he had heard what I said. "You see, Gwen, Pash isn't sure she cares to share a bath with me."

"I hear that!" Steve took one of the big slabs of meat from the platter. "I buy a case of air freshener when Kozak comes to stay with me."

"Go on with ya, it can't be that bad!" Gwen giggled at the implication, lightening her mood. I knew we had blindsided her with this news. I felt badly about that.

"I got a sample this morning, Gwen. Steve is on the right track with the air freshener."

"See, I wouldn't shit you about that." Steve seemed to eat up the insulting nature of this conversation.

"In a manner of speaking," Ivan retorted. I imagined Sigmund taking notes. I glanced at Ivan and caught his eye. He winked at me, indicating he was okay. "Not that I mind taking it on the chin about my personal habits, but we're eating here!"

We finished passing around the food. Gwen had made a vegetable medley as well as a hearty salad. "Did any of these vegetables come from your garden?" I asked as I dished up a healthy serving of the medley.

"As many as I could manage. The green beans and the cucumbers weren't big enough to pick, so I bought them."

I turned to Ivan. "Vanya, you should see the garden Gwen has. You wouldn't believe how much she can grow on such a small bit of land. And all surrounded by the most beautiful flowers!"

Steve asked with his mouth full of steak, "Who the hell is Vanya?"

I answered him directly. "Vanya is a Russian nickname for Ivan."

"I didn't know that." Steve took a drink of wine, and then said to Ivan, "Vanya, huh?"

Ivan volunteered, "That's right. It means 'darling,' so if you decide to start calling me that, I'll have to call you sweetheart." He blew Steve a kiss. Gwen giggled.

"Get out of here with that poof bullshit. Take it back to that twink you work with." Then Steve turned to me. "Did Kozak tell you one of his male colleagues has a thing for him? It's not just the ladies you have to watch out for."

I saw Ivan's jaw tighten. I had to somehow diffuse this. "I expect my gay boyfriends would like to shag him, too. Since I give brilliant head, I'm not worried. All Vanya has to do is ask. Isn't that right, luv?"

Ivan didn't miss a beat. Grinning from ear to ear, he said, "Damn straight! Best I've ever had. Sweetheart, now they know why I'm taking you home with me."

"Then maybe you should give Gwen some tips." Steve gave me a challenging look across the table.

I held his stare. "I would be happy to if she's inclined. If she's not, I know several very talented fellows who would be willing to oblige. It's an acquired taste." For a moment there was complete silence around the table. I didn't look away. I waited for Steve to make his move.

"My Gwenny takes good care of me. I don't need any peter puffer licking his chops over my equipment."

"Well, if you change your mind, I have a few phone numbers I could pass along." I turned to Gwen. "Sweetie, I'm serious. If you ever want to talk about this, we can."

"Luv, you're just full of surprises today. You bet we'll talk." Gwen shot Steve a look that indicated he had better mind himself. I looked at Ivan. He smiled and shook his head, and then squeezed my hand under the table.

He said to Steve. "Old boy, if she starts telling Gwen what she does, you had better prepare yourself. There is a dent in her ceiling where I hit it this morning."

Gwen giggled again and covered her mouth with her napkin. "What the devil did you do to him?"

"I'll tell you later. I don't want to spoil the surprise." I nodded toward Steve. "It's a lot more effective if they don't know it's coming."

"Tell me about it," Ivan said emphatically as he helped himself to another serving of salad.

"No more skirts? Think you can manage that, Vanya?" Steve said his name with a mocking tone.

"Oh, I think I can, sweetheart." Ivan mimicked Steve's taunting voice. "It's not so hard when you know what you have to come home to."

"Like I told you the other day, let's see if you can manage it for six months. Then maybe I'll believe it."

"Steve!" Gwen said angrily. "Pash, I'm sorry. Sometimes he has to pry his boot out of his mouth."

"It's all right, Gwen. Ivan and I have talked about this. He knows my feelings on the subject. We have an understanding."

"Yep, we sure as hell do. If I sleep around, she leaves.

Simple, but it makes a statement." He spoke to Gwen, effectively ignoring Steve.

"Brilliant." Gwen obviously liked my stand on the issue.

"Hasn't all this happened real damn fast?" Steve had been thwarted yet again. I wondered if he had begun to mellow or was just gearing up for the next assault.

Ivan took this one, which I appreciated. I wanted to eat at least a little of my dinner. "Yes, it has. But remember that old chestnut about love at first sight? Well, Cupid did his number on both of us."

"Sounds like he's got you by the nuts." Steve refilled our glasses. I noticed him watching Ivan closely as he spoke.

"I would be miserable if I had to leave without her." He put his hand on my back.

"And I would be a mess if I had to watch him leave. So, we decided to try this."

"There is one other thing, old man." Ivan turned back to Steve. "If I could see my way clear to find a spot for her, would you consider selling me Nutmeg?"

"Are you bloody off your nut? Where the hell would you put a horse where you live?"

"I'm working on it, mate. That's why I'm asking. I need to know if you'll sell her to me if I can work it out."

"Christ almighty, I'll give her to you if you have a place for her. You know as well as I do no one wants her for anything. She's too damn old."

"I'm willing to give you a fair price, Steve. I just have to make sure I can manage a place for her."

"You've never taken any wages for what you do here. If you want her, she's yours."

"That's mighty sporting of you, old man. Thank you."

We finished our meal with no other incident. Ivan talked to Steve about the workload coming up. Gwen told me about her German shepherd chasing a neighbor's cat up a tree and what they had to do to get it down. As the eating and the conversation wound down, Gwen asked, "Do we want dessert now or later? I made strawberry shortcake."

"With your mother's biscuit recipe?"

"The very one."

"Oh, I love that shortcake."

"I'm a little full right now." Ivan patted his stomach. "That last serving of potatoes pushed me over the top. I vote for later."

"Add my vote to his." Steve said, scraping the last bit of gravy onto yet another pile of potatoes. I'm about to bust."

"Then where the devil are you putting those?" Gwen pointed to the glob of potatoes still sitting on Steve's plate.

Steve let out a very loud belch. "Right there, my little luv. I just made room."

"For crying out loud, you could at least say 'excuse me.' " Gwen started to gather the empty dishes.

"So sorry. Excuse me." Then he dug into the potatoes.

"I only hang around him because he's cute." Gwen threw her used napkin at Steve.

"That's not the only reason."

"Go on with ya." Gwen blushed, apparently agreeing with him.

"We'll help you clean up, and then Pash and I are going to go back and talk more about her book. You're both welcome to join us, if you like."

"Oh, yes, I would like to." Gwen met the suggestion with her usual enthusiasm.

Steve seemed ambivalent. "I haven't read it."

"Doesn't matter." Ivan answered him casually. "I'm just going to ask Pash some questions. She'll do most of the talking."

"Oh, my. That makes it sound dreadfully interesting, doesn't it?" I stood and walked behind Ivan's chair. Putting my arms around his neck, I leaned over and said, "You tell him that, he'll head for the stable."

My self-effacing remark had the desired effect. "I wouldn't mind listening in, as long as I'm not expected to contribute."

"Seems to me your not contributing would be a blessing." Ivan gave Steve a pointed look.

"Don't worry Pash. I'll take the dish mop along. If he opens his mouth, in it goes."

"I would like to see you try, missy." Steve got up and went over to Gwen and grabbed her around the waist. "If you want to put something in my mouth to keep me quiet, one of these will do." He pushed his arms up, slightly lifting her breasts.

"Behave yourself." Gwen pushed his arms away, and then turned around and kissed him gently. "If you're a good boy, I'll give you a treat later. But first I need to speak to Pash." Then she kissed the end of his nose.

Ivan stood and put his arm around my shoulders. "You're in trouble now. She's got that look in her eye. Old man, we may both be shot tomorrow."

"Maybe so, but it'll be worth it." Steve kissed Gwen, quite passionately, and squeezed her arse. She didn't seem to mind one bit. I felt Ivan move his arm around my waist and slide his hand up my side. He caressed my breast with his thumb as he watched them. I could tell he responded to seeing Steve getting fresh with Gwen. I looked away, slightly embarrassed that I felt something, too.

When Steve broke the kiss, he looked at Ivan. He motioned toward the sitting room. I knew something had passed between the two of them because Ivan smiled broadly. "I don't think so, old man, at least not right now." Gwen looked at me and I shrugged, I had no idea what they were doing.

"Do you remember?" Steve asked Ivan with a grin.

"Of course I remember. They were a couple hot numbers, although I doubt as hot as these two." He ran his thumb across my breast.

"You're probably right about that." Steve squeezed Gwen's arse again.

"Would someone mind telling us what the devil you're talking about?" Gwen tugged Steve's ear.

Steve gave Ivan a nod, who shook his head and said, "Up to you, mate."

Steve happily launched into the story. "Once upon a time there were two randy teenage boys needing a little action. My parents left for the weekend and we got ourselves some dates, identical twin sisters. They made some kind of dinner that we ate right here. I don't remember what they cooked."

"Spaghetti and meatballs. You don't remember? It took us a couple of hours the next day to wash up those dried dishes and scour the burned sauce off the cooker."

Steve laughed. "Christ, I forgot about that. I am getting old. Anyway, after dinner Kozak here takes the hand of the one that was supposed to be with me and starts kissing her."

"Hell, I got them mixed up. You really couldn't tell them apart."

"So I got the other one and started doing the same. As I recall, we were standing in the same places we are now."

"He's right. I had mine right here and he had his over there."

"When Ivan came up for air, I pointed toward the sitting room. He gave me his thumbs-up. What the hell did you think I meant, numb nuts?"

"I thought he wanted me and my twin to go into the sitting room. So we did."

"What I damn well meant was that I wanted the sitting room. Well, we both ended up in there with the ladies. They didn't seem to mind. They were sisters after all. But we sure as hell did."

Ivan looked at me. "So me and my date ended up in the sitting room, while my chum here took his date upstairs. Does that answer your question?"

"Yes, I think it does."

"What question is that?" Steve looked at me.

"I asked Ivan this morning if he'd ever made love in your house. He never gave me an answer."

"Well, I don't know if he's ever made love here, but he sure as hell has fucked here! Does he still growl?"

"Growl?" Gwen asked, glancing at me.

"Yes, but how would you know about that?"

"Christ, if you're in the same house, you can hear him, let alone the next room. Startled the piss out of me the first time I heard it, in the stable I think. I really thought something had happened to one of the horses."

"Pash, he really growls?"

"He really does. Steve's right, it sounds like an animal. I rather like it."

"Damn good thing, Redhead. I can't control it."

"I expect it's put the fear of God into more than one young skirt."

"That's just fine," I shot back at Steve. "That means they won't be back for more. Now they'll have to get past me."

Ivan grinned. "She means it, too. I pity the Judy who would take her on."

"When there's something worth fighting for, I can manage." I tugged his whiskers.

"I'm counting on it, sweet thing."

"C'mon, boys. You're elected for dish duty." Gwen broke free of Steve's hold. "Pash and I will put the food away and then watch the two of you work."

"I like the way you think, Gwen." I unhooked Ivan's arm from around my waist and followed Gwen to the kitchen. The two men lagged behind.

Gwen glanced behind her to make sure we were alone. Then she said quietly, "What did you do to him, Pash? I'm dying to know."

I whispered back, "I blew him until he couldn't stand it, and then I put my finger up his arse and rubbed his prostate."

"You didn't!"

"I did! He went through the roof. He about busted his bollocks he came so hard!"

"Luv, that's nasty!"

"I know. The fellows who know about such things told me how to do it. You have to do it slowly and watch your fingernails so you don't hurt him. It really worked. He loved it, too."

"So would my dear boy. Seems as different as they are, in some ways they're cut from the same cloth."

"I'm telling you! I'm relieved we made it through dinner without a fistfight."

"Me, too. Steve can have a mouth. He says Ivan has closed it for him before."

"So I understand. Between the two of us, I think we can keep them smiling tonight. At least, I hope we can."

"We'll do our best. Can I ask you something else about what you did?"

"Anything, Gwen."

"Did you swallow?"

"Every drop."

"Yuck! Steve wants me to, but isn't it gross?"

"Not if you remember you love him. Then it is like taking part of him inside of yourself. It felt to me like I drank his *élan vital.*"

"His what?"

"Sorry, that means 'life force,' the very thing that gives life."

"It is, isn't it? It's his seed. Pash, you're so deep! What is it called again?"

"It's French, *élan vital.*" Just then Ivan and Steve came into the kitchen.

"I don't see much happening out here." Steve put some dishes in the washing-up bowl. "What the hell are you two doing?"

"We're discussing your *élan vital.*"

Ivan burst out laughing and looked at me. "My what?"

"Your life force," Gwen answered proudly.

"I'll give you life force." Steve swatted Gwen's rump.

Ivan came up to me, still grinning, and said, "I would love

to know what the hell you were talking about. I don't think Gwen pulled that out of thin air. It has you written all over it."

"I'll explain later. Are you washing or drying?"

"We tossed a coin. I'm washing."

"Then you're the winner!" Gwen came over with her hands behind her back. "I found this digging for the tablecloth. It belonged to Steve's mum. The washer gets to wear it.

"Pash, you do the honors." She handed me a piece of folded cloth. I shook it out and realized I held a very bright, floral pinafore apron. I heard Steve sniggering in the background.

"Oh, no!" Ivan started to back away.

"Oh, yes!" I threw the loop over his head and ran behind him to tie it. I knotted it, knowing he couldn't untie it without help.

"I'll get you for this later, Redhead. Damn straight I will!"

"I know you will, Dr. Kozak!" I came around to face him, feeling my heart racing. "That's why I did it."

Chapter Twenty-Two

After we finished cleanup, I went back to the sitting room to type up some questions. Steve ran down to the stable to check on the horses and Pash went to the loo. Gwen followed me in. "I'll help you out of that if you like." She pointed to the apron.

"Thanks, but I would rather Pash did. I have a few choice thoughts for her when she does."

"I expect you do. You're quite sporting for keeping it on. I think Steve would have taken a pair of scissors to it."

"No doubt." I looked down at the design. "Rather reminds me of the ones my mum would wear." Gwen sat down in an overstuffed chair beside the sofa. "May I ask you something?"

"Go ahead. I promise I won't tell Pash."

"I don't mind if you do. I just wondered how the devil *élan vital* came up between the two of you."

"Oh, my, you would ask that." Gwen looked back over her shoulder before continuing. "Pash told me what she did to you that made you hit the ceiling."

I grinned. "Did she?"

"She did." Gwen glanced over her shoulder again.

"No one is there. Go on."

"Well," she leaned forward in the chair, "I had a question about what she does, 'cause you see, I've never swallowed with Steve." This talk had taken an unexpected turn. "I asked Pash what she did with you and that's when she said it was like taking your *élan vital* into herself."

"She actually said that?"

"She sure did! You know, all of a sudden it doesn't sound so yucky to me. It sounds special and quite nice."

"She has a way of doing that, doesn't she?"

"You really love her, don't you?"

"I really do. Gwen, I'm not going to hurt her, no matter what Steve says."

"Don't pay him any mind. He'll see once you're married that you mean what you say."

"You think we're going to get married?"

"Sure, I do. I've never seen two people fall in love so fast. It's meant to be, I can feel it."

"You know something, I can, too. I just have to convince her." I heard Pash coming down the stairs. She came over to sit down beside me. "Not so fast, Miss Passion. How about untrussing me?" I stood up and turned around so I was facing Gwen. I winked at her. "There will be retribution for this indignity. You do understand that." I felt her fussing with the knot.

"Oh, I know. Hold still. I can't see this darned thing."

I folded my arms across my chest. "I don't think you are hearing me, Passion. One good trussing deserves another."

I felt the knot finally give as she pulled the ties loose. I could see Gwen thoroughly enjoying this. "What the blue blazes are you talking about?" She pulled the apron over my head and untangled my arms to remove it.

"Have you ever been tied to the bed?"

"Good God, no!"

"Well, consider the probability that one day soon, you will be."

"You wouldn't!"

"By now you should know better than to question what I will or won't do." Turning around, I pulled her to me and kissed her. It stirred me to feel Gwen drinking it in. I loved every bit of it!

When I let Pash go, I heard Gwen behind me. "Mmm, luv. A real live wire, he is. You hang on to him because I'm next in line."

I laughed, saying, "Gwen, I think Steve would have a problem with that."

"Oh, I'm sure he would. Who knows, maybe we'll have a double wedding."

"Gwen! We're not even living together yet." Pash blushed.

"Mention it to Steve, Gwen. I'm sure he'll be quite taken with the idea." I now knew I had Gwen on my team.

"Troublemaker!" Pash swatted at me.

"Mind yourself, now. I'm talking to Gwen. You've already gotten yourself in pretty deep already. You're edging into blindfold territory with that trussing I promised."

"My, my, it is getting warm in here. I think I'd better open a window." Gwen got up and opened the window. "Looks like rain. I see Steve closing the car windows."

"Are you staying the night, Gwen?" Pash walked over to look out the window.

"I wasn't planning to. I didn't arrange for anyone to feed the dog. But I could always ring up my brother and ask him to feed Churchill. He doesn't mind since he lives so close by."

"Your dog's name is Churchill?" I came over to the window to see Steve walking up the path toward the house. I leaned outside and yelled, "Hey, mate, did you close mine, too?" He gave me a thumbs-up.

"He's a hero in our family. I grew up with stories from my grandfather of Churchill and Eisenhower during the war. I named my dog Churchill because I like saying his name out loud. It makes me feel like he's close by when I do."

"I like that, Gwen. Pash isn't the only one who's deep."

"Oh, go on!" Gwen cuffed my shoulder good-naturedly, clearly appreciating the compliment. I definitely wanted this lady in my court. With Steve on one side and Pash on the other, I needed Gwen's seal of approval.

Steve came in the front door, which opened into the sitting room. "Everything okay with the horses?" I asked, noticing he looked distracted.

"Oh, yeah, everything is fine." He went over to the window on the other side of the room. "Come here and look at this."

I went to the window and looked out to see dark storm clouds gathering near the horizon. "Looks like it could be a bad one, doesn't it?"

"Sure as hell does. Gwenny, you'd better stay the night here. I don't want you to leave with it looking like this. It's going to piss down rain soon."

Pash came over to the window, asking me, "Why does he sound so worried?"

Gwen answered her as she went for the phone. "We've had some real bad storms in the summer. We had hail from one last summer that dented the hood of my brother's car!"

"Are all the horses in for the night?"

"They're all in and everything's secured. There's nothing more to do but wait it out and see what happens." Going over to where she stood, Steve listened to Gwen talking to her brother. When she finished, he asked, "Everything okay?"

"It's fine. He said he heard a weather report that there's a big storm headed our way, came up all of a sudden. He will take care of Churchill for me." She turned to face Steve, putting her hands on his shoulders. "Not that I mind staying, but I do have to go to work tomorrow. I'll need a lift tomorrow morning to get me there on time."

"Not a problem, luv. Either Ivan or I will run you ladies back in the morning."

Pash came up beside me and whispered, "I don't think we're the only ones who have fallen in love." I had to admit I saw tenderness in Steve as he talked to Gwen, a willingness to open up. He didn't open up to me anymore. It pained me to know that was mostly my doing.

Gwen turned to us. "Should I get us some dessert now? We could have it in here." We all agreed some strawberry shortcake would be quite tasty. Pash and Gwen headed off to the kitchen, leaving Steve and I alone.

I came up and put my arm around his shoulders. "You know, mate, we might hit the jackpot and have the lights go out."

"That's why God made light switches, you twit." Even with the insult, he grinned.

I thought I would test the waters. I wanted to regain some of the ground we had lost recently. "Were you serious about a foursome?"

"If you think for one frigging minute you're going to touch Gwen, think again!" He claimed Gwen as his, which I thought he probably would.

"I admit, she's a looker all right, but, no, that's not why I'm asking." I waited, letting his curiosity work.

"Not that I would mind finding out what Pash could do." Now he watched for my reaction. We had done this dance many times.

"I wouldn't want you touching her any more than you want me touching Gwen."

"Then what the hell are you talking about?"

"These two ladies seem to enjoy watching each other get hit on, not that they'd ever admit it to themselves. I could tell Pash got worked up in the dining room watching you with Gwen. While you were out, Gwen seemed to get off watching me work Pash."

"No shit!"

"No shit." We hadn't planned anything together for years, but maybe it was time to turn back the clock. I knew, if we were to remain friends, we had to find some common ground again, something besides the horses. Conspiring to get a little action going seemed a good place to start.

"What do you have in mind?" I had his attention.

"Talking about those twin sisters got me thinking. We have a couple very willing ladies here again, only this time, they know the score."

"You got that right!"

"I still want to talk about the book tonight. I told Pash we would. But we'll have time to work on it later. You could get bored with it real damn fast and start making time with Gwen. Keep her in this room, even if she wants to leave. I'll do the same with Pash."

"You son of a bitch! You want us to feel them up in front of each other!"

"Damn straight I do. If it storms, that's even better. I'll turn off the lamp, so it will be pretty dark in here. There'll only be a bit of light from the hall and an occasional flash of lightning."

"Just enough for them to get an idea of what is happening to the other."

"You get the picture. Of course, they'll also be able to hear what is going on, too."

"When did you get so damn perverted?"

"It happened living with you. What do you say?"

"I'm in. But I'm taking her upstairs to do the deed."

"Like I told you earlier, I would rather not be in the room with your naked arse either. I intend to take Pash upstairs to make love, too."

"She's really moving in with you next month?"

"Yep." I looked my old friend in the eye when I said, "I really do love her, Steve. She's a special lady."

"She must be to have reeled you in. You aren't shitting her about no more skirts?"

"I honestly mean no more skirts. I don't need any more. She's hotter than ten of them put together. Goddamn, she's good!"

Steve laughed. "To put you away, she has to be."

"She is. She's also smart as a damn whip! I really think I'm going to end up marrying her."

"Sure as hell seems like you mean it."

"I do. So, what about you and Gwen. Are you two getting serious?"

"We might be. Don't know yet." He tugged his crotch. "She also gives a bloody good ride."

I smiled. Our conspiring together brought out the old Steve, the one I knew growing up here. "We may both do a couple laps around the track tonight."

"Damn, we'd better shut the hell up before they walk in and hear this." Steve patted me on the back and walked back to the window to check the sky. I could see his concern. I knew the horses and the property were on his mind.

I came up behind him. "Don't worry, we'll see to it, whatever happens."

"It's the damn wind. The rest of it is just a storm. But it's the wind that can tear the place apart." He turned toward me. "I had the radio on in the stable. They said this one might stir up a tornado."

"Well, mate, there's nothing we can do to stop it. So let's just ride it out with the ladies." I felt for him. This place held his life. If anything happened to it, he would have to start over. Hopefully what I had in mind for the evening would provide ample distraction for him until the storm passed. God willing, there would be no damage to speak of.

"Here we are, sweets for the sweet!" Gwen came in carrying a tray with four bowls heaped with strawberries and whipped cream. She set it down beside the computer. Pash came up behind her carrying another tray with four cups and a pot of tea.

Pash picked up a bowl and handed it to me. "Somewhere buried under all those strawberries is the best darned biscuit I've ever had. Wait until you taste it."

Steve helped himself to a bowl. "She's right. I don't know what the hell she puts in it, but it makes for a stonking good shortcake."

Gwen beamed. "It's a family recipe. My mother showed

me how to make it a long time ago." She handed Pash a bowl. "I'll teach you how to make it as a wedding gift." She took the last bowl from the tray and sat down on the floor.

"Gwen, really!" Pash sat down on the sofa. "Nothing is definite. You know that."

I took a bite. "It's delicious, Gwen." I also sat down on the sofa. "That seals it. I have to marry you now if it means getting this recipe."

Pash flared. "If we ever do get married, it won't be because we have to, for any reason."

"Perhaps not, sweet thing, but this biscuit surely gives me reason to consider it."

"Better one in the bowl than one in the oven, huh, Pash?" For once, Steve timed his wisecrack well. "You two thought about kids yet?"

That one even got to me. "Christ, I'm still trying to get her used to the idea of sharing my loo! We're not that far yet."

"Hell, I figured you'd already have the names picked out, the way you two are moving with this." He eyed Pash, waiting for a comeback. She didn't disappoint him.

"We've been too busy practicing. We certainly can't discuss making babies until we're sure we can get it right." She took a bite of shortcake.

"The way I see it, we'll need at least two or three years of practice before we get it down. Isn't that right?"

"At least." Then, with conversational poise worthy of high tea, she added, "If we ever do decide to try, I understand that the doggy position is particularly effective for conception."

It took Steve a moment to realize she had just pulled his plonker. Gwen however knew immediately. "I see why the two of you get along so well." She giggled. "You're both nasty."

"Works out well, don't you think?" I winked at her.

"I think it bloody well does," Gwen replied. "Don't you, Steve?"

"Seems like you got yourself a corker, all right. You need

someone like her to keep you in line." He raised his teacup to Pash. "Good luck with it all. You're going to need it."

She picked up her teacup and raised back to Steve, saying, "Thanks for the blessing, I appreciate it." Then she looked at me. "To be perfectly honest, I think I've been handpicked for the job." Her reference blew right past Steve, but not past me.

"You have been." What I saw in her eyes confirmed my sentiment. I felt my mum smiling at me, like she smiled when I would bring her home a bouquet of wild flowers. "I only wish she could meet you."

I had forgotten Steve and Gwen could hear what I said, having lost myself in that private reverie. Steve reminded me we were not alone. "You wish who could meet her?" he asked, looking puzzled.

"Oh," I said matter-of-factly, "my mum." Feeling like I had to somehow explain my musing, I added, "I feel like she sent Pash my way, to wake me up."

"About damn time someone did. You've been sleeping at the wheel for a couple of years now." After tossing that one off, Steve wandered back over to the window.

"How does it look out there?" I asked, wondering if we should check on the horses.

"It's starting to rain, and I see some lightning off in the distance. It's coming."

"Do you want to check things out one more time before it hits?"

Steve shook his head. "It's not worth the effort. There's really nothing to do except wait it out."

"Well, let's see what we can get going here to pass the time." I reached for my laptop, giving Steve a discreet nod toward Gwen. He got my message. A low rumble of thunder followed him across the room.

"You know, old man," he said, sitting on the floor next to Gwen, "I don't know if you should have that thing on during this storm. It could get fried if the lights go out. The lightning around here can get pretty wicked."

Without realizing she helped our ruse along, Gwen added, "I have a friend whose television got knocked out by lightning the last bad storm we had."

"Really!" I feigned concern, knowing damn well my battery would automatically kick in if the electricity failed. "I wouldn't want to lose this little baby. I have all my notes for next semester on it." I glanced at Pash, hoping she wouldn't think about the battery. "Maybe we should do this later?"

Before Pash could answer, Steve spoke up. "I think you should turn it off, guv. I'd hate to see it get smoked."

"You and me both, mate." I shut off the computer just as a very loud crack of thunder echoed through the house. Pash jumped and grabbed my arm.

"Easy, sweetheart," I said, putting my arm around her waist. "Don't have yourself a heart attack."

"Sorry, I'm not very good with loud noises. I think in a past life I must have been shell-shocked."

"You believe in that stuff?" Steve asked, moving closer to Gwen. She leaned forward to put their empty bowls back on the tray and he slid his hand under the back of her shirt.

"Stop that!" Gwen caught Steve's hand as he inched toward her breast. "Behave yourself!"

"What fun is that?" Steve pulled Gwen back against him, securing his grip around her waist. "That reincarnation stuff. Do you believe in it?"

"Actually, yes, I do. Don't you?"

I had to admit, he knew the game. I saw him very discreetly squeezing Gwen's waist while he talked to Pash as though it were unconscious on his part.

"Don't know if I do. Seems to make sense, but if it is so, then why can't I remember anything?" This surprised me; I never knew Steve to have any interest in the subject.

"Because it would be too much to put in your head, that's why," she answered him without hesitation. "If we could remember all our past lives, just think how confusing it would be. If I had all my other lifetimes in my head, I would be so distracted I wouldn't be able to function. Neither would you."

Just then another burst of thunder rumbled and Pash jumped again. I pulled her closer and kissed her hair. "Grab on to me when they hit. I won't mind."

"No, I don't suppose you would." She snuggled in closer.

I joined in the conversation. "So, do you think we've had any past lives together?"

She gave me an inscrutable look. "Quite possibly. It would explain a few things, now, wouldn't it?"

"Shoot, Pash," Gwen said playfully. "Your nana would tell you right off there's something going on here."

"I expect she would." Pash squeezed my hand.

"What would your nana say about us, sweetheart?" Just then a bright flash of lightning lit the room, followed by a clap of thunder. The lights flickered.

"Goddamn." Steve glanced toward the window. "Looks like we may lose the power."

"Maybe sitting here in the dark is just what we should be doing." I reached over and snapped off the lamp. The hall light made pale streaks across the ceiling, blanketing the room in shadow.

"What do you think you're doing?" Pash turned to face me.

"I'm taking advantage of a stormy night." I bent over and rubbed my whiskers against her neck. Gwen sighed from across the room. Steve hadn't wasted any time.

"You bugger!" she muttered as I pulled her tight against me. "Is there anything you won't do?"

I licked her neck and slid my hand under her shirt. "Haven't found anything yet." I heard Gwen moan softly as I pulled Pash to me and kissed her. I heard Steve whisper something to Gwen and she giggled. Then I heard a zipper opening.

I buried my face in Pash's hair, inhaling deeply. I felt her rub her face against my whiskers and then whisper in my ear, "This is indecent. We aren't alone."

"The lamp is off. No one can see." I slid my hand between her legs just as another flash of lightning brightened the room for a moment. I saw Steve clearly in the burst of light. He had Gwen flat on her back. I saw his hand under her shirt as he rubbed off against her leg. I'm quite sure he had unzipped to do so. "They're doing their own stuff," I whispered to Pash. "Neither of them are paying any attention to us."

I felt her hand over my pectoral. "Then you won't mind if I do this." She gripped my flesh hard, the way I had shown her the night before. She caught me unaware and I groaned, certainly loud enough to be heard by our friends. I responded in kind by rubbing her harder through her blue jeans. She pushed against my hand as her inhibitions began to fade.

I felt her hand move to my zipper. "Let me." I opened my trousers and exposed my hardened organ. She immediately started to wank me. I looked over at Steve and Gwen again, now only silhouettes in the dim light. He had pulled up her shirt, her breasts picking up a streak of light from the ceiling. It made me even more randy to see him begin to suckle her. Pash saw me watching them.

"So, you are a voyeur as well as an exhibitionist." She whispered in my ear as she nuzzled my neck. She continued pumping me. I felt her move to the edge of the sofa and then slide to the floor.

I reached for her, but she eluded my grip. She knelt between my legs and started to blow me, right there on the sofa. I could still see Steve and Gwen. He had opened her jeans and had his hand inside them. They were oblivious to us. Any sense of propriety left me as I watched them work each other. I moaned, feeling Pash fondle my balls as she licked me. The lightning and the thunder came only a split second apart. I saw Steve tugging off Gwen's jeans in that flash. Then the house went completely dark.

Pash stopped, startled by the sudden blackness. I pulled her back up on the sofa, next to me. "Now what?" she whispered.

"Do you have your cap in?" I asked, hearing my friend tear open a wrapper. I knew what he intended to do.

"Yes, but shouldn't we go upstairs?"

"And risk breaking our necks? I don't think so. I can't see my hand in front of my face, for Christ's sake."

Gwen moaned loudly as Steve muttered, "Oh, yeah, Gwenny, that's good."

I wanted Pash right now, while Steve had Gwen. I started unzipping her jeans. She stopped me. I leaned in very close to her ear and whispered, "Come on, sweetheart, I'm hurting here. This is no time to be shy." I took her hand and caressed myself, to emphasize my words. I went for her zipper again, prepared to get more insistent if need be. This time, however, she let me pull it down.

"That's it, sweetheart. I know you want it, too." I pushed her back on the sofa and took off her shoes and jeans. Now both our ladies were naked from the waist down. I pulled out my wallet and found the condom I kept there. I opened it and rolled it onto myself. We could hear Gwen and Steve going at it as I positioned myself over her.

"Oh, God." Pash moaned as I pushed myself into her. "Fuck me, Vanya." I don't know if she could be heard by anyone else, but her breath in my ear drove me to the edge. I pounded her. The sounds in the room heightened to an unbearable intensity.

Steve let out a moan, saying, "Christ, Gwenny, yes, Christ, yes." He moaned again and Gwen murmured, "Oh, Steve, darling, that is so good."

Just then, Pash clutched my back and started to shudder. I had become so preoccupied listening I hadn't realized she was about to finish. She spasmed underneath me and dug her nails into my back. Then she gripped my arse, sending a shockwave of sensation up my spine. I cut loose and let out my fire, filling the room with the sound of my climax. The house remained pitch black, except for the lightning, that still flashed through the window.

Chapter Twenty-Three

"Where are my clothes?" I asked Ivan as he pulled himself out of me. I felt very exposed, lying there almost naked.

"Give me a minute, I'll find them."

I sat up beside him, unable to see much of anything. I felt him dig in his pocket for his handkerchief. He used it to dispose of the condom. I heard Steve and Gwen gathering up her clothes across the room.

"Hey, guv, you together yet?" Steve asked Ivan.

"Not yet, mate. Working on it."

"Do we still have that torch on the shelf in the larder?"

"I saw it yesterday when you spilled the sugar. Unless you moved it, it's still there."

"I'm going to find it while Gwenny gets herself around. Then we'll go to the basement and bring up those kerosene lamps we have stored down there."

"Will do, mate." Ivan stood and pulled up his jeans and then started to feel around the floor for my things. "Here's a shoe." He handed me one shoe.

"What the devil do you want me to do with this? I need my clothes!"

"I think you'd be quite fetching with only your shirt and one shoe."

Gwen laughed from somewhere in the darkened room.

"Don't encourage him, Gwen. He's incorrigible enough as it is."

"I can see that. Well, actually, I can hear it. I can't see anything right now." Just then the lightning flashed again, lighting the room for a split second.

"There they are!" I felt him lurch forward and grab at the floor. "Here, sweetheart." He put my jeans in my lap. "I think your knickers are there, too. I pulled everything off at once." I felt my face get hot in the dark, knowing Gwen could hear him.

I had just put on my jeans when Steve yelled from the hallway, "Everybody decent now?"

Gwen yelled back, "We're all dressed, if that's what you're asking."

Steve came in carrying a bright torch. "C'mon, Gwen, let's go find those lanterns."

"If you need any help, old man, come get me." Ivan sat down beside me as Gwen and Steve headed for the cellar stairs.

"Quite pleased with yourself, aren't you?" I knew I sounded a little piqued. I didn't care.

"About what?"

"You know about what. You orchestrated that whole scene."

"Why the hell do you say that?"

"Ivan, remember, we promised to be honest with one another. Did you set me up again?"

"Not exactly."

"Not exactly?"

"I just took advantage of the circumstances. One thing led to another, is all."

"So, along with being an exhibitionist and a voyeur, you are also an opportunist?"

"Sounds fair." He put his arm around me. "Anyway, maybe now Steve won't feel so left out of things. We shared something very special tonight with you two ladies. That may go a long way to getting us back on track. Now, you be honest with me. Didn't you get off just a little knowing Gwen and Steve were in the room having at it, too?"

I couldn't see him looking at me, but I could still feel his stare. "If I say no, I'd be lying. If I say yes, then I am forced to see myself in a not-so-flattering light. Nothing like being caught between a rock and a hard spot, now, is there?"

"It's the immovable object meeting an immutable force. Thing is, sweetheart, this honesty business isn't just being honest with each other. It is being honest with ourselves."

"Then you have to admit you really liked watching and listening to Gwen and Steve."

"It was hot, I'll grant you that. Seems to me you thought so, too."

"I would have preferred being alone with you."

"Which is exactly what we will be when you move in with me. That is, unless you have reconsidered."

"I haven't reconsidered. I just can't help wondering what my limits are. If you keep pushing, we may both get a surprise."

"I'll keep that in mind." He pulled me tightly against him as he unexpectedly kissed me. I melted into him, losing myself in the intensity of what I felt. In my heart, I knew I had to be with him, no matter how hard he pushed.

"I know you're an ornery son of a bitch, but for Christ's sake, it's only been fifteen minutes!" Steve came in carrying a lantern as we kissed.

Ivan looked at him and grinned. "Well, you know, mate, I just can't get enough, especially now." He ran his hand up my back and into my hair, sending a shiver down my spine.

"Do me a favor. If you plan to take it out again, dip the wick." Steve pointed to the lantern, but the look that passed between them said much more. Ivan's smile confirmed the innuendo.

"You do the same, old man."

I could tell something had changed between them. As much

as it pained me to admit it, Ivan's scheming had made a difference.

Gwen had not come back with Steve. "Where is Gwen, anyway?"

"She took the torch and went to use the loo." Steve took out his handkerchief and wiped the dust off the globe. "I guess I should have washed this. I'll clean up the other one before bringing it in." He turned to go back to the kitchen.

"How about bringing back a bottle and some glasses?"

"I'll do that. Try to stay out of trouble while I'm gone."

"We'll do our best." Ivan flexed his hand in my hair. The roots pulled, but the sensation wasn't pain. It felt more like being bonded to him, like a primal assertion that he claimed me as his. I fancied that bond with him.

I turned back to Ivan as Steve disappeared around the corner. "Dip the wick?" I poked my finger in his side. "Real subtle."

"Okay, so he isn't as glib as you. For him, that was subtle, believe it or not."

"Oh, I believe it. I also believe the two of you really do care for one another, despite the fact you seem to have a rather peculiar way of expressing it." I tugged his whiskers and then let my hand rest on his shoulder. "Maybe things will be a little better now between you two."

"I hope so. I don't want to lose his friendship. I've had my head up my arse about some things lately. I'm just beginning to realize how bloody much."

"It's not too late to patch up those things. I think your little stunt tonight actually did help your cause. I don't understand it, but I can't argue with the results. It must be a man thing."

He laughed. "Oh, I think you and Gwen might have a few things to talk over, like taking my *élan vital* into yourself."

"She told you?"

"Only after I asked how that phrase came up. I found the context to be quite flattering."

"I hope you understand I've never felt that way about anyone else. But with you, it somehow seemed sacred, to be so intimate."

"Do your thoughts always run this deep?"

"It depends. On Friday night I just wanted to smack you with the horse brush."

He leaned in very close to my ear and whispered, "You make my mouth water, my passionate one. Everything about you fascinates me." He nuzzled my neck and then whispered in my ear. "As for getting smacked with a brush, it could be quite pleasurable, especially if you are lying across my lap."

"Behave yourself," I whispered back. "You're going to get us both worked up again." I could smell the sweat on his skin. I wanted to lose myself in the scent.

"Too damn late, luv." He took my hand and moved it down to his lap. I felt the consequence of his suggestive remark.

I looked at him, into those beautiful eyes. In the dim light of the lantern, I could see a half smile playing on his mouth. I ran my fingertip across his lower lip. "We can't do much about it right this moment, but I'm feeling it, too. Teach me how to be with it, like you said the other night, about not giving in to the feelings."

His half smile grew to a full one with my request. "You're serious, aren't you?"

"I am very serious. I haven't stopped burning with wanting you since that first day I saw you in the stable. I have to learn to be in that space if I am to live with you. When we are close like this, I feel like it will consume me."

"It won't, I promise. The trick is, don't make your climax the goal. Savor and enjoy the burning. Think of it as balancing on the edge of a cliff. Stay on the crest of the arousal. Be in the fire, then be the phoenix and rise from the ashes."

His eyes glowed in the flickering light as he spoke. He transported me into a bubble where nothing existed except the fever we shared. Eros had claimed me as his. "How can I contain what I feel for you? It is like molten light flowing in my blood. My very soul burns with it."

He smiled and cupped my chin in his hand. "My beautiful Passion, your soul is supposed to burn with it. That's how we know we are truly alive."

"The poem you left for me to read this morning—you really felt it, didn't you?"

"Of course I did. Shelley said what I couldn't. 'Nothing in the world is single; all things by a law divine, in one spirit meet and mingle. Why not I with thine?' "

He stopped and looked at me. I thought the light had played a trick when I noticed something glistening on the side of his face. I touched the spot, and found his cheek wet. "You're crying!"

"My lady, you're not the only one who can turn on the waterworks." He pulled out his handkerchief to blow his nose and the used condom fell out onto the sofa. We both started to laugh, the intrusion of reality into our tender moment so ridiculous. Gwen chose that instant to come back into the room.

"Sounds like you two are having a good time," she said, shining the torch right on us.

"We are." I scooped up the condom from the sofa and palmed it off to Ivan. He swiped at his nose with his hanky and then bundled the condom back in it and shoved the whole mess back into his pocket. "Steve's in the kitchen washing up the lamp. He's been out there for a while."

"Oh, criminy, he's probably having trouble with something." She turned and almost ran to the kitchen.

"Nicely handled." He squeezed my hand. "Do you happen to have a hanky in your pocket?"

"Always." I pulled out a wad and unraveled a couple. He took them and blew his nose.

"How do you do this?"

"Do what?"

"Cry so much. I'm not cut out for it." He wiped his nose

once more and then stuffed the damp paper into the same pocket with the cloth handkerchief. "Thanks for buying me a couple more minutes."

"You're welcome." I kissed his cheek. "I love you, Dr. Ivan Kozak."

"And I love you, P.F. Platonov." He kissed me again, this time very tenderly. "God willing, you will eventually be P.F. Kozak." He smiled as he said, "As you are the probable future Mrs. Kozak, I ask for your kind assistance in reminding me to clean out this pocket later." He patted the pocket holding the remnants of our evening.

His sincerity touched me, but I didn't want him to take it for granted that it was all a done deal. "You are a presumptuous sod, Dr. Kozak. I've barely agreed to live with you and you already have us married."

"Playing hard to get, sweetheart?" I felt my stomach flutter, the directness of his question being emphasized by his piercing eyes.

I wanted to look away. Holding his stare made me feel as though I didn't have enough breath to speak. But I had to stand my ground with him or be swept away.

"I am being reasonable," I told him as evenly as I could manage. "There is something to be said for a proper courtship, as unorthodox as this one may be." I took a breath, hoping to draw in enough air to finish my thought. "There is also something to be said for a proper proposal of marriage. To assume I will just marry you if we live together presupposes my answer."

"And if I ask you to marry me right now?"

"I would ask you to wait until after we have spent more time together, until after we've tested the waters. You might change your mind once you know me better."

"As may you." Surprisingly, he looked away, apparently unnerved by that thought. "All right, then." He looked at me again. "We'll take it as it comes, one day at a time. But I want you to understand something."

"What?"

"Now that you have walked into my life, I'll be damned if I'm going to sit quietly and watch you walk back out. I want to marry you and will do what I must to convince you we are meant to spend our lives together."

"I think he means it, Red." I started as Steve once again walked in on us. He set down a bottle and four glasses on the table. Gwen followed him with a bowl and a large bag of popcorn.

"How the hell long have you been standing there?" Ivan sounded ruffled that he had been overheard.

"Long enough." Steve spoke to me. "I heard him sound like that once before." He opened the bottle and poured vodka into the glasses. "I asked him to go in with me and run this place after we graduated. He told me he wanted more in this world than his father had and he needed an education to do it." He offered me a glass and then gave one to Ivan, shifting his focus as he handed him the glass. "You won that scholarship and went off to university. I stayed here."

"That's what happened, mate."

Gwen glanced at me as if to ask where this was headed. All I could do was shrug.

"It sure as hell seems like you really mean to settle your arse down and take some responsibility for your life." Steve paused, apparently waiting for Ivan to snap back. He didn't say a word. He continued. "Well, guv, I still need a business partner. You're practically one now, except you don't get paid. How about making it a real partnership?"

"How the hell can I be your partner? I can't move back here and help you run the place year-round. I have a full-time job that I worked damn hard to get and I intend to keep it."

"Maybe not. But you're here several months out of the year now and have worked your arse off the last few years for nothing." Steve sipped his drink and studied him. "You know this place like the back of your hand, almost as well as I do."

Ivan jumped in with, "What the hell do you mean, 'almost'?"

Steve gave him a pointed stare. "Like I said, almost."

Ivan raised his glass. "I concede."

Steve remained serious. "I need some help around here. It's the business end I have the most trouble keeping together. When you're here, you handle most of it. But when you leave, who the hell else can I trust with the business?"

"I'm listening."

"You can help me with the paperwork, the bills, the ordering, all that shit, without being here. Between you and Red, you can keep my books straight while I spend my time with the horses and training new handlers."

Ivan patted his laptop. "You would have to learn how to use one of these, which you have never wanted to do."

"Why the hell do I need to learn to use a computer?"

"So you aren't frigging calling me every five minutes wanting to know the account balance or wanting to know if a bill is paid. You can bloody well check it out yourself."

Gwen spoke up. "Hell's bells, I can teach him how to use one. That's what I do at work. We can get some software to do what we need to do. I can help keep everything up-to-date."

Ivan looked at me. "What do you think?"

It surprised me that he would ask me for my opinion in front of Steve. I answered as honestly as I could under the circumstances. "I think you have to do what is in your heart. You're the only one who knows what that is."

Ivan knocked back the vodka Steve had poured and held out his glass for more. Steve obliged. "Let me sleep on it, old man. I need to think through how this would all work. I also need to call and confirm my fall schedule, to make sure I could manage the time."

Steve looked at me. "Hey, Red, wouldn't you help out if he needed you to?"

"I would if he asked."

"Well, there it is. You can't use your schedule as an excuse."

"I'll think on it. That's as good as it gets tonight."

"At least you didn't say no right off the top, guv. From the looks of things, you aren't leaving tomorrow. We can talk more once you've slept on it." Steve glanced at the window. "I haven't heard it thunder for a while now." He looked back at you. "Want to go with me to check on the horses?"

Ivan stood, saying, "Lead the way, mate." Steve picked up the torch. I knew Ivan's concern about damage to the place nearly matched Steve's. The two of them really were family.

Chapter Twenty-Four

Steve took a moment once we got outside to survey the lawn. In the dim light of the torch, we could see a few small limbs had come down from the trees. We also saw some overturned lawn furniture, but nothing terribly worrisome.

He turned around to see the house. Looking up into the drizzle that still fell, he pointed to a corner of the house. "Bloody hell, look there, guv." I followed the light of the torch to see a bare spot on the roof where quite a number of shingles had come off. "I knew those damn things were coming loose. Should've seen to them in the spring. Now I'm going to have to replace a section of roof."

"Tomorrow we can go up there and see exactly how much damage we have. Then we can hire someone to fix it." I knew he had a full plate right now. Fixing storm damage would take him away from the business of running the place. I just hoped we wouldn't find any more damage at the stable.

"Better damn well take a bucket and a mop upstairs later. That patch is right over your room." His wisecrack didn't manage to cover his concern.

"Just so it isn't over the bed! I have a lady sharing it with me tonight."

"You bleeding sod, how many times can you bonk in one

night? You're going to rub her raw the way you've been going at it!"

"Haven't heard any complaints yet." Getting a little riper, I added, "She's been so damn wet, rubbing the bacon hasn't been a problem." I meant that remark as a joke, but he didn't take it as being funny.

"Does she know what an ignorant son of a bitch you are?" Before I could answer, he started down the path to the stable. I caught up with him.

"She's beginning to. Hasn't put her off yet."

"Kozak, if you really have found a woman who'll put up with your frigging arse, I'd be mighty damn careful not to throw a spanner in the works if I were you."

"You still don't believe I mean what I say about settling down, do you?" He stopped outside the stable and turned to look at me. The rain had started up again and had quickly become more than a drizzle. He didn't seem to care.

"I've sat back and watched you shitting your life away for a few years now. I figured it was your life and none of my goddamn business. But for Christ's sake, for all your education, 'Dr.' Kozak, all your brains have gone to your pecker. It seems not much means anything to you these days except getting your rocks off with some slapper with a mind for some action."

He turned and unlatched the stable door, saying, "Do I believe you?" He turned around again to look at me. "Hell, I don't know if I do or if I don't. Pash seems to be just what you need. Maybe she can do what coming here and helping me with this place has never managed." He went into the stable.

I stood in the rain for a moment. I worked hard when I came here, damn hard. But then I left in the fall. I had my own life to live. But I had never really thought about what it was like for him when I left. I followed him into the stable. He had lit a lantern we kept hanging on the wall. I found him in the stall with the colt. "Everything all right in there?"

"Looks like dear old mum here got a bit rattled by the thunder. I think she stepped on him." I looked down to see Steve pulling bits of hay out of a gash on the colt's leg. "Do me a favor and take her out of here. I don't want to get kicked if the storm starts up again and nervous Nellie gets upset."

I led the mare out of the stall while Steve tended to the colt. I quieted her and gave her some sugar. I found another torch we had in the supply cupboard and then walked around and checked out the other horses. Everything seemed all right. When I got to Nutmeg, I stopped and went into her stall. She nuzzled me, obviously glad to see me. I gave her an apple. When I went to check up on Steve, he had just finished wrapping some gauze around the colt's leg. "How is he?"

"He'll be fine. It actually looked worse than it was. Hand me the tape out of the kit." I helped him finish with the colt. "Did you check out the other horses?"

"I did. No other problems that I could see. The stable seems all right, too. It handled the storm better than the house did."

"Thank God for small favors. How's the mare?"

"Calmer, but she needs a few more minutes before putting her back in with the colt." The high-strung mare gave me an excuse to stay here and talk to him. With Pash and Gwen at the house, the stable was the best place to do it. "Old man, I think we need to talk."

"What the hell about?" He had started to walk around, checking out things for himself.

"A few minutes ago you said you thought not much meant anything to me. If that were true, why would I keep coming back here year after year? It's not like I'm getting rich mucking your stalls! This farm and these horses do mean something to me." I stopped short of telling him that he did, too. "Why do you want me to be your partner if you think I'm such a goddamn bastard?"

He squared off, looking as if he might throw a punch. I had no inclination to fight. I hoped he didn't either. "Kozak, you may be a bastard, but you're an honest son of a bitch. You also know how this place operates. You grew up with it like I did. If you can keep your pecker in your pants long enough to help me out, I know you won't steal me blind when my back is turned."

"I'm not a businessman, mate. You're asking me to run the business end knowing full well that isn't what I do for a living."

"Christ almighty, I'm not asking you to run Harrod's. I'm asking you to keep my books straight and the supplies coming in. You already take care of the ordering when you're here. You do it by phone. You could keep doing it once you leave. Why the bloody hell aren't you taking me up on this? Is it that we haven't discussed any money yet?"

"I wouldn't be here at all if I thought that, now, would I? I just don't know if I can juggle my two lives at the same time."

"Pash will help you when you aren't spreading her legs!"

"You mean just like Gwenny will when you aren't plowin' her?" I knew I had to check myself right there and then, or we were about to get into it. "I think we best leave our ladies out of this right now until we get this settled between us or we're both going to end up with a few bruises."

"Look, Kozak, I'm not going to kiss your frigging arse to get you to stay on here. Either you do or you don't. It's up to you." He went to put the mare back in with her foal. I watched him tend to her. As much as I knew about horses, Steve knew more. I respected him. I always had. I tried to do what Pash had done earlier, center myself and feel. After a couple deep breaths, I went into the stall with him. He had hunkered down to check the colt's leg one last time.

"Steve, I want you to know something." He looked up without saying a word. "The farm and the horses are damned important to me." What I needed to say to him welled up in me. "Coming back here and staying with you is the only family I have. I could no sooner turn my back on you than I could my own brother. Let me see what I can work out."

Chapter Twenty-Five

The two men going to the stable gave Gwen and me some time alone. She barely waited to hear the back door slam shut when she said, "I can't believe they did what they did, can you?"

"Oh, yes, sweetie, I can believe it. Vanya has initiated me into all sorts of new things during the last few days."

She giggled. "Pash, he does growl! I couldn't believe what I heard. Criminy, I'm glad I knew about it before it happened. It would have scared me to death had I not known. What the devil did you think when you heard it the first time?"

I thought back to Wednesday night. It seemed so long ago. "Well, without being indiscreet, let's just say it heightened the moment."

"I bet it did, luv! I heard how the two of you are together. No wonder you want to live with him."

"Gwen!"

"Pash, please, I want to talk about this. My dear boy has always been a good lover, but tonight—oh, my, he went wild! I'm telling you, I felt like he wanted to eat me up." She giggled again, realizing what she had said. "You know what I mean."

"I do know what you mean. Those two have enough testosterone between them to float a battleship."

"Lord's sake, is that the truth."

"And you know something else? Being in the same room with us, and doing the deed together, helped them somehow. I don't pretend to understand how, I just know it did."

"Steve said something like that when we went to the basement."

"What did he say?"

"He said that tonight was better than before when they doubled here. I guess it's been a long time since that happened. Steve seemed real happy that Ivan wanted to do it in this house again, with the two of us."

"I think they used to share a lot more, Gwen. From what Ivan has told me, they grew up here like brothers."

"They did. Steve said they were quite close before Ivan went to university. He really thought Ivan would stay here and help him manage the business. After Ivan left, Steve had to run the farm himself."

"That must be why Steve is so angry. He can barely be civil to Ivan anymore. Even if they were close once, all they do now is snipe at each other."

"Why can't they just say they care for each other?" Gwen sipped her drink. "Maybe they think that makes them queer!"

"Sweetie, you may be right about that. But we both know they aren't, now, don't we?" I remembered what Ivan had said, that anything I said to Gwen could well get back to Steve, so I redirected the conversation to safer ground.

"Oh, my, yes. After tonight, we really know it! I just love how it feels when he wants me. I tingle all over. How does it feel to you?"

"He makes me feel very sexy, like there is no one else he'd rather be with. I guess that makes me feel very special."

"I know he thinks you're special. He wants to marry you, for crying out loud! I mean, how do you feel, you know, sexually, when you're with him?"

So she wanted to dish. I could tell her a little without harm being done. "Gwen, he is amazing in bed." She leaned forward in the chair. She really did want to know more. "He takes charge and he knows what he is doing, too. He sends me over the moon!"

"I bet he does! Steve says he has heard stories of some of the things he's done."

I had to ask. "Has he told you any of those stories?"

"A few." Gwen giggled. "Don't be surprised if he gives you a garter belt and silk stockings soon. I understand he likes it when that's all his ladies wear under their dress."

"My, my, isn't that an interesting bit of information? That bloody bugger! I have a garter belt. Perhaps I should surprise him when he isn't expecting it! What else did Steve tell you?"

"I'm not going to spoil any more surprises. Luv, you'll have your own stories soon and I want to hear every one of them!"

"Well, how about this? He has helped me finish every time we've been together. I don't have to ask, he just does it."

Gwen fanned herself with her hand. "We have to get the boys back together, Pash. Mine needs a few lessons in that department." I had never known Gwen to be so open about her relations with someone. Maybe tonight helped us, too. I decided to ask the question I had been wondering all week.

"Okay, you want to talk about this. I have a question."

"Wait a minute." She poured us each more vodka. "Sip that. It will make this more fun. Now, ask your question."

I could tell she was already a little tipsy, and she wasn't the only one. Maybe I needed to be to ask her this. "Gwen, I don't know if you noticed, but God gave Ivan more than his fair share in the equipment department."

She didn't even let me finish the question. "Oh, I noticed all right. I saw what happened after he kissed you, talking about tying you to the bed. Like I said, no wonder you want to live with him!" I must have looked embarrassed, because she stopped. "I'm sorry, ask your question."

"I wanted to know about Steve. I mean, how does he measure up?" That sealed it. Dr. Freud had taken up residence.

"My dear boy may not be as tall as Ivan, but have you seen his feet?"

"Gwen, that business of foot size being an indication of length is an old wives' tale."

"Not for my dear boy, it's not. Trust me, he's hung like one of those stallions down in his stable."

I laughed. Gwen would not make that up. "Then they do have something in common."

"Yeah, they both want to get laid as much as possible."

"I don't mind."

"Neither do I. Have you had your period with him yet?"

"Gwen, we haven't been sleeping together that long, for Lord's sake."

"That's right. Somehow, it seems longer. Anyway, when you do, don't be surprised if he still gets fresh with you. Steve likes to hump my titties when I can't do more."

Now I knew for sure the vodka had put her away. "Gwen, I hardly have your equipment to have that happen." My dear friend had become voluptuous in her adolescence, something my genetics never delivered. "Although Ivan may well come up with something inventive."

"Like what?"

"Do you know we're probably both drunk?"

"I know we are. We're entitled. Now, what would Ivan want to do?"

"Probably make me strip to my scanties, and then watch him wank."

"You aren't serious!"

"I'm very serious. He is a kinky SOB!"

"You like that, don't you?"

"Gwen, he is, without qualification, the sexiest, hottest man I have ever known."

"I feel the same way about Steve. Pash, I think he may ask me to marry him."

"Do you know what you will say if he does?"

"When he does, I will say yes. I want to be his wife more than anything."

"But you have known him for a long time. I've only known Ivan for a month and I've agreed to live with him." I suddenly felt total panic overwhelm me at the realization that I had actually said yes to moving in with him. I started to cry. "Oh, God, Gwen, have I lost my mind?"

Gwen came over and sat down beside me on the sofa. She put her arm around me. "Luv, it's all right. I told you last week I could tell you were arse over tit for him. After what I heard tonight, there is no question the two of you belong together."

The intensity of the last week washed through me. I continued to cry; I couldn't help it. I sputtered out, "He makes me feel more alive than I've felt in my whole life. I want to share everything with him. I want to sleep beside him every night. Now that I've tasted it, I can't live without it."

"And you even swallow."

Her joke made me laugh. It helped me regain some control over myself. "You're right, I'm arse over tit for him. I didn't know I could love a man as much as I love him."

"Thing is, dearie, he's just as crazy about you. He told me so."

"He did?"

"He surely did. He said he's going to convince you you're meant to be together. He already wants to marry you."

"I know he does." I started to cry all over again.

"Here, sip some more of this." She handed me my glass of vodka.

"I'm sorry, Gwen, I don't know what's wrong with me."

"I do. You're in love."

"I feel more like I'm being swept away in a flood of something I don't understand."

"That's what love is, Pash. I don't think you've ever really felt it before."

I pulled the remaining hankies from my pocket and blew

my nose. "Gwen, maybe that's it. As many times as I thought I had fallen in love, it never felt like this." I closed my eyes, feeling Ivan in my blood. "He makes me burn inside, like my whole heart is on fire with wanting him. I feel things with him I never knew I could feel. Oh, Gwen, I do want to marry him. But I'm so afraid."

"Afraid of what, Pash?"

"I'm afraid that this is another fantasy of mine, that it isn't real. What if it is just a summer romance? What if I go back with him and he sleeps around on me?"

"Pash, listen to me. Ivan told me he wouldn't hurt you. I believe him. You can't say no to him just because you're afraid. Your nana would be furious with you if you don't listen to your heart. She told us so many times that we have to listen to our hearts because that is how God talks to us."

"You're a very smart lady, Gwen. Thank you for reminding me."

"Stuff and nonsense, Pash! I just know love when I see it. Steve and I will expect to be godparents to your babies."

Her gentle certainty calmed me. "You know, twins run in my family. Ivan doesn't know that yet. Having two at once might give him pause." I realized Ivan and Steve had been gone quite a while. "I hope everything is okay out there. Shouldn't they be back by now?"

Chapter Twenty-Six

The worst of the storm had certainly passed, but the rain still fell. We made our way back up the path to the house, soaking our clothes through. All Steve said when I told him I would try to work something out was to let him know what I decided. I could tell he still doubted my dependability. I honestly didn't blame him for not trusting his eggs in my basket. I intended to prove to him, and to myself, that I could handle the responsibility he had asked me to accept.

Our ladies heard us come in the back door and came right out to the kitchen, Gwen carrying the lantern and Pash following. Gwen went over to Steve. "Luv, we were getting worried. Is everything all right? Lord's sake, you're wet!"

"Well, it could be a lot worse. We lost some shingles on the roof. Tomorrow we'll find out just how many and what it will take to replace them. That's the only real damage we saw. There is some stuff blown around out there, but nothing that can't be picked up."

Pash put her arm around my waist and asked, "How are the horses?"

"The horses are fine, except the colt got himself a cut on the leg when his mum must have tramped on him. We'll have to watch that mare more closely. She's a little highstrung."

"Kozak's right," Steve said as he started to unbutton his

shirt. "I don't want anything to happen to that colt. He's going to grow into one hell of a horse." As he peeled off his wet shirt, he added, "By the way, Pash, those shingles came off right over Ivan's room. You may have a soggy night here."

It did not escape me that she took a quick look at his chest while he spoke.

Not to be outdone, I pulled my drenched T-shirt over my head and threw it over a chair. "Sweetheart, if it's too damn wet up there, we may be better off sleeping in the sitting room." I succeeded in pulling her attention back to me. Even in the dim light, I noticed her skin turned pink.

"There is an air mattress in the basement I use when my cousin brings her kids here. You could use that if you need it."

Pash took hold of my hand and said, "That could also double as a rubber raft under the circumstances." Without missing a beat, she asked Steve, "Is this the same cousin who used to visit with your aunt when you were teenagers?"

"Yes, it is. How do you know about her?"

I squeezed Pash's hand hard, reminding her in the only way I could that I didn't want her to go there. That didn't stop her. "Ivan mentioned your relatives would visit when your parents were still here. It's really nice she still comes back with her kids. Does she come often?" Pash dug her fingernails into my hand, telling me she had put two and two together and come up with four.

"She manages about one trip a year, usually during the kids' spring break. Says she has fond memories of the place from when we were kids. I always thought it bored her to come here." Steve sat down to take off his boots. "Kozak, you haven't seen her in a long time. Remember how thin she used to be? Well, having kids changed that! She's put on some weight."

Steve didn't seem to find it at all unusual that we were standing in his kitchen on a stormy night discussing his cousin. I had no choice but to go along with the conversation, so I turned it to my advantage.

"I guess it's been about fifteen years since I've seen her. That must have been just before she got married. I remember she was damn skinny then." Now Pash knew I hadn't slept with her since that first time.

"Not anymore. After three kids, she's starting to look like my aunt." Steve's aunt, to put it politely, was a robust woman.

"Fancy that! I'm surprised. Well, thanks to those three kids, we won't be sleeping on the floor tonight." And I wouldn't be bedding down in a chair by myself. Obviously, Pash meant to keep me honest. "We had better go upstairs to check out my room. Where is that mattress anyway?"

"I'll get it and leave it in the sitting room." Steve picked up the lantern and started toward the cellar. Gwen went with him.

Still holding Pash's hand, I picked up the torch from the table and pulled her toward the larder. "Easy, Ivan! I don't know my way around here yet. I can't see where I'm going."

"Oh, I think you know your way around pretty damn well." I stopped short of the larder door and pulled her close. "Just so you know, you're the first woman I've had in this house in many years. You don't need to go fishing for information. I'll be happy to tell you anything you want to know."

"I'll start my list in the morning. Just remember, you volunteered to answer my questions." She flexed her fingers in my chest hair. I pulled her closer, meaning to kiss her, but she pushed me back. "Your trousers are soaking wet. You need to get on some dry clothes before you catch your death."

"That's assuming anything in my room is still dry. Stay right here for a minute." I ducked into the larder and grabbed the mop and a bucket. Then I headed for the stairs, with Pash trailing right behind me.

When we got to my room, I stood just outside the door and shone the light inside. Sure enough, the light reflected on a large puddle in front of the dresser, extending under the bed. I pointed the light up to the ceiling and could see a dark line extending halfway across the room. "There's no way I can do much about any of this tonight. I can't even see what is wet."

"It looks like your dresser is pretty wet, and the stuff you have on that chair over there."

"All I have in the dresser is some shirts, socks and underpants. The chair is mostly just laundry waiting to be done. Looks like I lucked out, Redhead. The cupboard is on the dry side of the room. Most of my clothes are in there. It also missed my desk." I walked over and felt the bed. "It's not too bad, just a little damp at the bottom. Help me shift the mattress so it doesn't get any wetter overnight."

I put the torch on the desk. We moved the mattress sideways on the bed, away from the leaking roof. My wank mags fell onto the floor. Before I could kick them under the bed, Pash grabbed them.

"Well, Dr. Kozak, it seems poetry isn't the only thing you read. She held one in the beam of light from the torch and leafed through it. "My, my, don't we like them ripe!"

"Give me those!" I snatched them out of her hand. "You aren't the only one who has had a dry spell."

She laughed. "I'm surprised you haven't asked me to pose like that for you."

"Now that you mention it, perhaps I will." I swatted her with the magazines before I put them in the desk drawer.

"Where is the mop? I can't see it."

"It's over there, by the door." I pointed the torch at where I had propped it.

"Why don't you change your clothes while I mop up this water?" Pash grabbed the mop and started swabbing the floor.

I left the torch on the desk and went to the cupboard. I remembered a new pair of pajamas I had brought along but never used. I groped around on the shelf until I found the package.

"Do you have to use the loo?" I asked as I took off my shoes.

"Well, I should before we go to bed."

I started to undo my trousers. I felt myself begin to harden again as she watched me undress. "We'll go before we go back downstairs." I took everything off in one motion. I wanted her to know all I would be wearing to bed were the pajama bottoms. "What did you bring to wear to bed?"

"A nightshirt, but I think it might be wet." She pointed to her overnight bag, sitting by the bed in a puddle of water.

"Rotten bit of luck. Now, if we weren't sleeping in the sitting room, you could curl up beside me in your scanties. But, to keep you decent, why not wear this?" I held up the pajama top from the package. "The bottoms are all I need."

"How generous of you, Dr. Kozak." She came over and took the top, handing me the mop. You can finish this while I change." I didn't care that we would be sleeping on an air mattress. We would be sleeping together.

I had just finished buttoning the pajama top when I heard Steve ask, "So, how bad is it in here?" He stood in the doorway holding the lantern.

"It's a bit of a mess, but not much damage," Ivan answered, wringing the mop into the bucket.

"Seems we got off pretty easy with this one." Steve sounded relieved.

"Seems so. Tomorrow I'll clean out the dresser. I think it got the worst of it."

"Where's Pash?" Gwen poked her head in the door.

"I'm here," I said, stepping out from the corner.

"Don't you two look cute, sharing pajamas!" Her teasing embarrassed me.

"Gwen, my overnight bag is soaked. I didn't have anything to wear."

"Well, I think it's lovely the two of you worked it out. Nighty-night, don't let the bedbugs bite." Gwen started tugging Steve's arm. "I'm ready for bed if you are."

"I'm ready. Kozak, the mattress is in the sitting room. I went ahead and blew it up with the pump, so it's ready for you."

"Thanks, mate. I appreciate it."

"Remember, we have to be up and out early tomorrow. If you're not up by six, I'll throw some cold water in your face to bring you around."

"I'll be up. Good night."

With that, Gwen pulled Steve down the hall.

Ivan propped the mop against the wall and came over to me. "Let's grab some blankets and go downstairs. The rest of this will sit until tomorrow. We can use the water closet downstairs since the one up here is occupied now."

"Did he upset you again?" The dim light did not hide his tight jawline.

"He just seems to think I'm not good for much of anything these days."

"Does he think that or do you?"

"What the hell does that mean?"

"Ivan, let's go downstairs. I don't want to be overheard up here."

"Let me get some sheets and blankets. You grab the pillows. There's also a battery alarm clock on the bedside table." With our bedding in hand, we headed downstairs. We made up the mattress Steve had left on the floor, set the clock for five thirty and then went to use the loo. Ivan followed me in, holding the torch so I could see.

"Now tell me what the hell you meant."

"I think you overreacted to what Steve said upstairs. You're projecting your feelings about yourself onto other people. You've done it to me and now I think you're doing it to Steve."

"How in bloody hell have I done it to you?"

His defensive posture didn't stop me from explaining myself. "The other night, when you assumed Steve put me off you, without even asking me if he had. It seems to me you think what you've been doing is pretty bleeding awful to be ready to hightail it out of here rather than face up to it."

"I can't take back what I've done. And I'm damn tired of being reminded of it, Redhead!"

"Ivan, stop for a moment and look at your reaction." I put my hand on his chest. "What are you feeling here?"

He stood and looked at me without answering. Then he said very quietly, "It hurts."

"How does it hurt? Let yourself experience how it feels. It's all right. It's the first step to healing it."

"I can't do that," he said flatly.

I could feel him resisting what was obviously welling up inside him. I closed the door and put the torch on the shelf. "Yes, you can, Ivan. It's time you stopped running from yourself." I put both hands on his chest and asked him again, "What are you feeling inside?"

This time he closed his eyes and got quiet. I very gently rubbed his chest, trying to help him focus on what it held. He finally allowed himself to know his own truth. He whispered, "I feel ashamed, so god-awful ashamed."

I whispered back, "Ashamed of what, Ivan?"

"Ashamed of not becoming the man my father taught me to be."

"What do you think you've become?"

He opened his eyes. "Someone not good enough to be with you."

I continued to rub his chest. "That's not what I think."

"You're not seeing what is there. If you did, you wouldn't be so taken with me."

"I think I am seeing what is there, perhaps more clearly than you are."

"Is that a fact?" He wiped his eyes with the back of his hand.

"That is indeed a fact. I have second sight, remember?"

"Pash, I'm a dog." He took a breath. I could feel his heart thumping under my hands. "In fact, one young woman last year called me a pig to my face when I told her we wouldn't be seeing each other again."

"Just breathe and let it come up, Ivan. You have to—it is eating you alive."

He closed his eyes again. I could feel him taking a deep breath under my hands. "All right, then, before you find out from Steve. A year ago, a lover from the previous fall semester had a baby. I had been with her only twice, both times with protection. However, she saw me as a better catch than the boy who had really knocked her up and blamed me. I had to take a paternity test in order to prove I had not fathered the child."

"Is this what you thought got back to me last week?"

"Well, if Steve wanted to blow the whistle on me, he sure as hell knows all the details. Last summer I had to go back to Northampton a couple of times for the tests until the whole business finally ended. Do you want to know why he's so damn down on me now?"

"Why?"

"Because even after that happened, I went back and did the same frigging thing this year, taking a few more to bed. Nothing happened because of it, thankfully. I came back here for Christmas and had too much to drink one night. I told Steve I had nailed another one. Ever since then, he hasn't had a good word for me. Truth is, I couldn't stand to be with them longer than it took to fuck them."

"I know you may not want to hear this, but Steve is so angry with you because he cares about you. He thinks you should have stayed here with him all along. He may not be able to say it to you directly, but he knows you are on the brink of ruining your life."

"I suppose I know that. But, it is damn hard to live with

how he sees me. I don't know what I can do to convince him I'm not the gormless bastard he thinks I am."

"How about if you stop thinking of yourself as one first? Then deal with the rest."

"It's really warm in here. I need to open the window." He pushed the window wide open and leaned on the windowsill. "It's stopped raining. The air smells really fresh." I could see him taking deep breaths. "You should use the loo. We need to get to bed."

"Are you all right, Ivan?"

"Trying to be, Redhead." He shook his head and muttered, "Dear God, I don't know what you see in me."

I came up behind him and rubbed his back. "I see the man who has come into my blood."

"You see what?" He turned around. There were tears on his face.

"My Vanya, there is an old Russian saying that you know it is the right one when they flow in your blood. I told you earlier tonight I feel like I have molten light flowing inside me. That molten light is my feeling for you."

"How do you know all this?"

"I didn't have a choice. I either had to accept who I am and understand how it all works, or lose myself. You'll get used to it."

"Not damn likely. I feel raw inside right now."

"It will feel better once you quiet down."

"Let's go to bed. I'm damn knackered."

With Ivan standing by the window, facing me, I went right over to the toilet and did my business. When I finished, I said, "Your turn."

With the same lack of modesty, he exposed himself and took a piss, shaking it off when he finished. Tucking himself back into his pajama bottoms, he took my hand and led me back to the dark sitting room. We settled in for the night, needing only a sheet to cover us. Nuzzling in very close to my ear, he said, "I think you've come into my blood, too. Maybe this is how love really feels."

As I drifted in a hazy mist of drowsiness, I whispered back, "I hope so, Ivan. It feels wonderful." I felt his arm tighten around me as I slipped into a cloud of sleep.

Chapter Twenty-Seven

The travel alarm rang at five thirty. The first light of day cast a dim yellow glow in the room. Watching her sleep, I smiled, thinking about how she would be sleeping next to me in my own bed soon. I wanted that very much. Leaning over, I whispered softly in her ear, "Pash, wake up, sweetheart. It's time to get up." She didn't stir. Giving her a shake, I said a little louder, "Pash, wake up. It's morning." That time, she stretched, nearly clipping my jaw. "Careful, luv, I don't want a black eye."

"Sorry," she muttered sleepily. "It's morning already?"

"Yep. The sun is up. That must mean it's morning."

"Very funny. Such wit at the crack of dawn." She stretched again, this time clearing my face. "How are you today, Vanya?"

Hearing her call me Vanya like my mum used to call me still gave me a jolt. "I'm fine, sweetheart. Still knackered, but hell, I can sleep tonight, right?"

"My place or yours?" She rolled over and wrapped her leg around mine. Then she traced a line with her fingernail down my chest and cuddled in closer. Christ, it felt good! Either she had forgotten we were downstairs or simply didn't care.

"Just to remind you, we are in Steve's sitting room and he'll be down here any minute. Remember, my room is flooded?"

"You didn't answer my question, Ivan." It appeared she didn't care.

"Are you coming on to me, Redhead?"

"Yes." She dug her nails into my chest a little harder that time, intensifying the need for some privacy.

"Perhaps we should go upstairs to have a shower. We might manage a little something there." I squeezed her arse to emphasize my point. "And your place will do very nicely for tonight, to answer your question."

"Good morning, you two. Now, mind yourselves, you're not alone." Gwen's voice cut through the room like a knife.

"You awake, Kozak?" Steve had also come downstairs right behind her. So much for any time alone down here. At least at Pash's flat we wouldn't be interrupted.

"Good morning, and yes, we're awake. Are you finished in the loo?"

"It's all yours, guv. We're going to take a look outside. I want to check it out straightaway."

"We'll join you in a few." Steve and Gwen went down the hall to the kitchen and out the back door.

"So, are we still on for that shower?" Pash squeezed my arm and rubbed her thigh against my leg.

"Do you always wake up so ready and willing?" I asked, slipping my hand under her pajama top. "You did the same thing to me yesterday."

"I think it has something to do with waking up next to you. I can't seem to help myself."

"Bodes well for sharing a bed every night, now, doesn't it? Let's go upstairs."

We took the torch with us, but only needed it to get up the stairs and down the hall. Once in the loo, the window provided enough light to see. Ivan closed the door and came up behind me, pulling me up against him. I could feel the swelling inside his pajamas. "I'm not the only one who wakes up ready and willing."

"No, I often wake up with morning wood. I usually have a

wank in the shower, but I much prefer your company." He slid his hands under my top and fondled my breasts.

"As I prefer yours to my toys, Dr. Kozak."

"Will you please stop calling me Dr. Kozak?" Ivan stepped back, letting me go. He took a moment before he said, "I'm sorry, I didn't mean to snap. It's just that hearing my professional name in this situation reminds me of the others."

I could see him struggling with his memories. I put one hand behind his neck and the other in his hair. In the most seductive voice I could manage, I said, "But didn't you tell me that if you are ever tempted once we are in Northamptonshire, you would come home and act out those urges with me?" I raked my fingernails down his back, saying, "Professor, I am a very willing student."

Before he could respond, I began kissing his chest and licking his nipples. I reached for the snap on his pajama bottoms. It popped open and his pajamas fell to his ankles. "Dr. Kozak, I find you very attractive. Won't you please let me show you how I feel?" I reached between us and touched his cock.

We stood quietly for several seconds as I stroked him. His breath deepened with each caress. Smiling at me, he said, "I think we might be able to work something out, if you are so inclined." He started unbuttoning my top. "I would like it very much if you would show me how you feel."

Once he relaxed into it, he fell into the role easily and comfortably. I knew we had just put some healing balm on his open wound. He lowered my pajama top down over my shoulders. The rush of vulnerability carried me deeper into the fantasy. "I can't believe I'm here with you like this, Dr. Kozak. I've wanted to touch you for so long." The deliberate use of his formal name came quite naturally. I continued to fondle him. "And I've fantasized about what it would be like to be with you." I wanted him to accept me as one of them. What's more, I wanted to experience him in that place. I wanted to know how he responded to those girls and what he did with them. Or, perhaps more to the point, what he wanted to do with them and never actually managed.

"I've wanted to touch you, too, dear heart." He pinched my nipples. "I've wanted to touch all your secret places." He slid his hand between my legs and rubbed me, sending fiery sparks up my spine. "I've seen how you look at me and wondered if you would like to know me better. I certainly want to know you better."

He leaned over and kissed me, forcefully pushing his tongue into my mouth. Then he breathed into my ear, "You see what you do to me?" He put his hand over mine and increased the pressure on his organ.

I did indeed see what I did to him. This time I led him into the fantasy. "Dr. Kozak, tell me what you like. I want to make you feel good, like you make me feel." I looked into his eyes and saw the man I loved.

He ran his fingers through my hair. "If you really want to make me feel good, then take me in your mouth."

"But I've never done that before with anyone. I don't know how." I had become the innocent again, waiting to be taught. I continued looking at him, giving myself over to whatever he asked of me. I wanted, even needed, to submit to him.

"Of course you can. Just kneel in front me." He stepped out of his pajama bottoms. "First, kiss me. Then use your tongue and lick the tip. I would like that very much."

I knelt in front of him and did just what he said, still astonished at the incredible beauty of his masculinity. I kissed his organ down its length. Then I kissed the head. He had his hands in my hair, guiding me. "Now lick me." I did and he groaned.

When her tongue touched my cock, the intense sensation caused me to shudder and moan. Before I could recover, she licked me again. I stopped her. "Give me a moment, my dear." I had my hands in her hair, holding her head still, until I felt able to go on. Bracing myself, I gave her the next instruction. "All right, now I want you to put my cock in your mouth, as much of it as you can manage. Then suck on it, very, very hard, being careful not to knick me with your teeth. Do you understand?"

"When should I stop?" She looked up at me with beautiful brown eyes, full of innocence and willingness.

"When I tell you to stop. Just keep sucking until I tell you to stop." She shook the pajama top off her arms, leaving her in nothing but her scanties. Christ, just before she grasped the base of my cock, I saw the same determined look cross her face as when she mounted Nutmeg. I braced myself even more.

The next thing I knew, she had me full in her mouth, giving me the kind of head I had dreamed of getting so many times. I heard a voice I knew had to be mine saying, "Fuck, yes, blow me, keep blowing me." She did just that, for several minutes, until my bollocks were like to explode with wanting to cream so badly. I had to stop her.

"Don't stop me, Dr. Kozak. I want to drink your cum."

I pulled her to your feet. "My dear, a young lady with any sort of breeding does not call it 'cum'! I have to teach you to mind yourself." I took hold of her wrist and pulled her toward the vanity. "Bend over so I can teach you some manners." Before she had a chance to digest what was happening, I had her over the edge of the vanity and pulled her knickers off. Now, we were both naked. My organ throbbed with wanting satisfaction inside her. But I held on as I gave her a hearty smack on her shapely arse.

"Dr. Kozak, what the devil are you doing?"

"This is what happens to foulmouthed schoolgirls," I said, smacking her again. "They get a good spanking." I continued to spank her with the flat of my hand. "What you so disrespectfully called 'cum' is actually my *élan vital.* It carries my seed, and with it, my life energy." I could tell the reference to what she had told Gwen last night hit the mark, just as my hand continued to do. She gasped aloud.

"Oh, God, please fuck me. I need you to fuck me!"

"You want to fuck the professor? Well, dear heart, you will fuck the professor." I pushed two fingers inside her, then three. She pushed back on my hand, trying to hump my fingers. "Oh, yes, you're ready for it." I opened the bathroom cabinet and grabbed a condom from the box Steve kept there and quickly rolled it on. With that, I came up behind her and pushed my length into her.

"Oh, yes, Dr. Kozak, please fuck me, fuck me so hard!"

"You are a foulmouthed missy, aren't you?" I wanted to spank her some more, but my bollocks couldn't hold out any longer. I reached around, roughly rubbing her pubes. She groaned and started to tremble. As the wave of her climax overtook her, I pounded her from behind. I clutched her arse to my groin and let my seed spill into her spasming cunt. "Fuck, yes!" My whole body shook. I continued to thrust into her until I had emptied myself.

I did not pull out until we both had quieted. I left her for a moment, to dispose of the condom. She continued to lean over the vanity. "Are you all right, Pash?"

"Oh, yes, my Vanya, I am very fine. I just need to get my land legs back."

"Let me help you." I put my arm around her waist and stood her upright. Holding her tightly against me, I said in her ear, "I don't know where all that came from, but thank you for seeing it through with me."

"It was certainly my pleasure, Dr. Kozak."

"You're not going to stop calling me that, are you?"

"No." She gave me an inscrutable look and then said, "You've got to understand something about me if we are to make this work. I want to know you, Ivan, all of you. That includes all those things you hide from everyone, maybe even from yourself. I will always want the truth, no matter what it may be. It is who I am."

"Well, my Passion, you've got to understand something about me. It is not my way to open easily. I have spent a lifetime keeping certain things to myself. Now you come along and open me up like a can of beans. Thing is, sweetheart, you just may find yourself holding a can of worms."

"I'll take that chance. Are you willing to let me help you with some of this?"

"I have a choice?"

"No, not if we are to make a go of it."

"That's what I thought." She had just shown me how far she would go to stand toe-to-toe with me.

"Ivan, I really want to talk about what just happened here."

"So do I. But we need uninterrupted time to do so. If we dally much longer, we'll have Steve up here pounding on the door. Trust me, Pash, none of this is going anywhere. We will talk about it all, I want that as much as you do." I kissed her forehead. "By the way, that was some performance, in more ways than one."

"Thank you. Being a playwright's daughter does pay off once in a while."

"We may have to think about picking up a few costumes once we're home."

She laughed. "Costumes? Just how far are we going to take this once we're home?" Her emphasis on the word *home* pleased me.

"Don't know. As far as we can, I hope!"

"That could be pretty far."

"I know." I squeezed her still-warm bottom. "Sweetheart, we really do have to get ourselves around. Steve needs my help today." We used the loo, showered quickly and went to my room to dress. I found myself a fresh set of clothes in the cupboard. Pash had to wear the same jeans from yesterday. I loaned her a T-shirt, as her extra clothes were still in the rain-soaked overnight bag.

"I don't suppose you have an extra pair of scanties around, do you?"

"Now, wouldn't you wonder if I did?"

She dug through the wet things in her bag. "Well, they're a

little damp, but they're clean. I just can't put these back on." She held up the pair she had been wearing.

"I'll take those." I took the used ones and tossed them on my desk. "Now you'll have a spare pair here."

"How considerate of you. You will wash them up, won't you?"

"Eventually." I winked at her and that delicious blush colored her cheeks. I liked it that she didn't look away when I rattled her.

Pash walked over to my dresser and pulled open the drawers until she found my underpants. "Well, it seems you'll have a few pairs of your own to do once the electricity is back on, seeing as how they've been mildewing in the drawer all night. You can throw mine in with yours." She rummaged around until she found a pair to her liking. "I'll just take these with me then, so you have an extra pair at my place. It isn't exactly exchanging rings, but the symbolism still works."

Figuring tit for tat, I picked up the small box where I kept the ring given to me with my doctorate. At the farm I kept it in the box for safekeeping. I considered for a moment the implication of what I was about to do and knew in my heart I wanted to do it.

Taking out the ring, I said, "Pash, please accept this from me as a pledge to you that I mean what I say, that I want to be with you." I put the ring in her hand. "I know it is too big for you, but it is the symbolism we're after, is it not?" I tugged at the underpants she held in her other hand.

"Ivan, this is your doctoral ring. I can't accept this."

"Yes, you can. We'll get a chain so you can wear it around your neck. I'll take it back once I have something a little more appropriate to replace it with." I closed her hand around it. "Pash, I have never wanted to be with someone as much as I want to be with you. Please take the ring."

"Ivan, you're absolutely sure about this?"

"I am absolutely sure."

"Then I will accept it with the same spirit in which it is

given, with a commitment to you and to us." She tucked it into her jeans pocket. "But I have nothing to give to you in return."

"Yes, you do." I walked over and picked up the undies she had taken off. "I have these." I rubbed them against my cheek, catching her perfume as I did. "And I have your love."

"Someone hearing this conversation might get the impression you just proposed."

"Perhaps I did. But you have already told me you want a proper courtship, and then a bended-knee proposal. I aim to please." I kissed her forehead. "We best be getting downstairs now. It's six thirty. I need to get to the horses."

"And I need to get home. I have work to do today. Am I cooking tonight?"

"Unless you want to go out for dinner."

"I don't mind cooking if you don't mind chicken cutlets and salad."

"Throw in a baked potato and we've got ourselves a deal."

"That can be managed, if I have electricity when I get home. Ivan, how am I getting home?"

"One of us will drive you two ladies back into town."

Chapter Twenty-Eight

I threw Ivan's underpants in with my wet things and took the overnight bag downstairs. Steve and Gwen were in the kitchen. Gwen had put out the Danish I had brought yesterday, with some fruit and juice. She saw us come in before Steve did. "There you two are."

Steve turned around. "What the hell were you doing, anyway? Or do I even need to ask! I hope it was a good one."

Without missing a beat, Ivan said, "Damn straight it was a good one, even better than last night. Sure as hell cleared my sinuses!"

He poured us each a glass of orange juice. "So, how is it out there?" I admired his ability to be direct with Steve without apology and then move on.

"Not too bad. A few limbs came down. The umbrella on the picnic table broke. I forgot about the damn thing. Should've put it down when I closed the car windows. The worst of it is the roof."

"What about the power?"

"Nothing's back on yet. I turned on my car radio. They expect all electricity to be restored later this morning. Our phone is out, too. We may need your mobile to call in our supply order later."

"Not a problem, mate. I'll bring it down and leave it here on the table. Who's driving the ladies back into town?"

"I'm taking Gwenny in shortly, so Pash can come with us."

Steve had a gas cooker, so even without electricity Gwen cooked us all some brekky. As she dished up some eggs and sausage, she said, "I would love to stay here all day, but I have to check on Churchill and change clothes for work." Gwen thrived on being a homemaker. She loved cooking and working in the kitchen. Farm life would suit her very well.

I turned to Ivan. "What time should I expect you tonight?" Gwen shot me an approving look.

"Probably about six o'clock."

Steve chimed in with, "Spending the night, Kozak?"

"As a matter of fact, I am. No offense, mate, but I prefer a real mattress to that rubber one. Mine's still wet. I'll be back here in the morning." Again, Ivan good-naturedly handled Steve. "What do you want to do about the roof?"

"The hardware store opens at seven. I'm taking a shingle with me, to match it up. I'm also going to ask if anyone there can help us fix it today."

During breakfast, I noticed Gwen had a plain gold chain around her neck. "Gwen, could I ask you a really big favor?"

"Sure, luv, what?"

"Could I borrow that chain for a day or two until I can get myself one?"

"What on earth for?"

I dug in my jeans pocket. "So I can wear this." I held up Ivan's ring.

"My, my, would you look at that!" She took the ring from me and looked at it.

Steve muttered, "It must have been a good one. That's your graduation ring."

"I keep telling you I'm serious about this. Maybe you'll start believing me." The edge in Ivan's voice softened as he continued, "I wanted her to have some sort of ring from me until I can get the real thing."

Gwen jumped in, unhooking the chain from around her neck. "Well, I believe you. I think it's absolutely smashing! Here, Pash, keep it as long as you need it."

"Thank you." I threaded the chain through the ring and hooked it around my neck. "I didn't want to risk losing it by carrying it in my pocket." We finished our breakfast talking about the storm and the damage that had been reported on the radio. Ivan ran upstairs to grab his mobile. Then we headed out to Steve's car.

"I'm going on to the stable now. I'll see you tonight." He kissed me good-bye, whispering in my ear, "I love you."

I wanted to say it back to him, but my voice caught. I reached up and felt the ring. All I could say was, "I know." He squeezed my hand and started down the path to the stable.

I sat in the back while Steve and Gwen chatted in the front seat. About halfway into town, Gwen turned around and said to me, "You're awfully quiet back there, luv. Are you all right?"

"I'm fine. Just thinking."

"I would suppose you are." She smiled and turned back around. I'm glad she didn't force conversation on me. I really felt like I wanted to be quiet.

Steve dropped off Gwen first, as she needed to get herself together for work. I stayed in the backseat, not even thinking about how it might look. Steve turned around, saying, "Red, folks will think I've been hired out as a chauffeur if you stay back there."

"Sorry. You're quite right." For the first time I realized I would be alone with Steve in the car. All my alarms went off. I sat down in the front, not knowing what to expect.

"Are you sure you know what you're doing?" Well, there it is. He had gotten right down to it.

"I think I do."

"Kozak ain't easy. I know that from way back."

"I expect you do." My voice had an edge. I didn't care.

"Shit, Red, I don't want to do him dirty. I just want you to have your eyes open about this."

"Do you think I don't?"

"I don't know. If you don't, seems to me the blinders will come off once you move in with him. I give you two a month at most."

My patience with this cat and mouse game totally left me. "Just to let you know, Steve, Ivan told me about the paternity suit and all the rest of it. He knows that's why you don't have a good word for him now. Even though you're right, you're absolutely wrong!"

"What the hell are you getting at?" Steve pulled up in front of my flat and stopped.

"What I'm getting at is you're right about wanting him to stop doing what he's been doing, but you're goddamned wrong to keep punishing him for it. He doesn't deserve that from you. He breaks his bloody back for you and your farm year after year without taking a cent for it. That counts for something."

"I never said it didn't."

"Not to his face. But I've seen how you snipe at him. No wonder he wants to knock you through yourself." I opened the car door to get out.

"I've offered him a partnership in my farm. That counts for something, too."

"If you want my support in this partnership thing, you damned well better start acting like a civilized human being. I love him and I'll be damned if I'll stand back and watch him keep getting hurt by you."

"Do you frigging think he'll walk away from the farm because of you? We've been friends for more than twenty years!"

"I'll not have a lout be part of our lives, no matter what kind of history you two have together." I slammed the door and started toward my flat. Steve got out of his car and followed me.

"Hey, Red, just a goddamned minute!" he yelled, coming up behind me. "If getting accused of knocking up some skirt didn't stop him from sleeping around, what makes you think you fucking can?"

I turned to face him. "I don't know if I can. I don't know if he'll stop. But I'm not chump change here, nor am I some schoolgirl who doesn't know her way around the block. I understand I'm taking a chance by saying yes to him. But will I say no just because he might sleep around on me? I don't think so! I believe he loves me. No, that's not true—I know he loves me. And where I come from, love can beat the odds on anything."

I turned to unlock my door. The tears had started and I didn't want Steve to see it. I felt his hand on my shoulder and he turned me around. He looked startled when he saw me crying. He handed me his handkerchief.

He hesitated for a moment before he said, "You might like to know this. That ring you're wearing of his, it's the only thing he owns that never leaves him. He told me it's the only thing he has that shows he did something with his life.

"He never took it off, even at the farm, until he got horse shit on it. He sat for an hour and a half that night, digging it out of the cracks with toothpicks and polishing it. Since then he keeps it in his room to make sure nothing happens to it." He walked away and went back to his car.

I watched the car disappear down the street. I reached up again and touched the ring. The tears wouldn't stop.

I made my way inside, leaving my soggy overnight bag beside the door. I sat down on the sofa and sobbed for several minutes until the intensity of what I felt began to subside. My phone rang and I jumped. It was Gwen.

"Luv, Steve just left here. I don't know what the devil happened between the two of you, but he came back here all upset. He asked me if I thought he was a lout. I told him of course I didn't. Then he asked to borrow my copy of your book. He said he wanted to read it, of all things!"

"Did you give it to him?" I asked, involuntarily sniffing into the phone.

"Sure, I did. Pash, are you crying? What the devil happened between you two?"

"We had words."

"I gathered that much. About what?"

"About how Steve's sarcastic sniping hurts and provokes Ivan. It all started because Steve said he gives Ivan and me a month at most once I move in with him."

"He didn't say that, did he?"

"He did."

"Oh, my, I am so sorry. His mouth will do him in yet. I'll speak to him, Pash. He has to stop this."

"Gwen, let it be. I told Steve I wouldn't let a lout be part of our lives. Let him think about what I said."

"Pash, Steve really does want to run the farm with Ivan. He's talked about it to me so many times."

"I think Ivan wants to go in with him to do it. But, Gwen, it will never work if they are at each other's throats all the time. And I can't contend with someone waiting for the other shoe to drop just so he can say I told you so. It will make us all miserable. Either they have to work out their differences or go their separate ways."

"Pash, I really am so sorry he's saying the things he's saying. I want you to know he's wrong about you and Ivan. I know in my heart that you two are meant to be together. I am so happy for you. Don't let my dear boy's mouth do anything to upset you or make you change your mind about Ivan."

"Gwen, I'm okay, really. Now, sweetie, you have to go to work and I have to shop for a pair of stockings to wear tonight."

"Luv, you're not going to do the nasty in a garter belt, are you?"

"Can you think of a better way to spend the evening? Let's just hope they don't push each other off the roof today."

"Oh, go on with ya. You and Ivan have fun tonight doing whatever you do. I'll talk to you later."

So, Steve wants to read my book. I suppose that means he intends to retrench and rearm. I shook myself out of that one. Perhaps he would learn something if he really read the book. Anyway, I had to unpack my wet bag and get to work.

Even with my preoccupation with all that had happened in the last few days, I put in a solid morning's work. I even remembered to call my publisher, who assured me they could ship as many books as I needed to the campus bookstore. I had stopped for some lunch when the phone rang again. I picked it up, expecting Gwen. Instead, I heard Ivan. "Hello, sweetheart," he said cheerfully.

"Hello, Vanya. I didn't expect to hear from you until later. How are things?"

"Not too bad. Steve has a bloke out here looking at the roof. He's going to hire him to fix it, which is a load off the two of us. Now we don't have to climb up there."

I didn't know quite how to approach this, so I just plunged in. "Did Steve say anything to you about our conversation this morning?"

"No, why?" I could hear the defensive tone in Ivan's voice.

I took a deep breath. "I read him the riot act this morning."

"What the hell happened?" The defensive tone turned to anger.

"He made a comment I didn't appreciate and I let him have it. That's all."

"Pash, what did he say? I want the truth."

"He said he gives us a month, at most."

"That son of a bitch!"

"Ivan, I want you to calm down and listen. There's more to it."

"What?" I could feel the rigidness in his jaw right through the phone.

"I called him a lout and told him I didn't want him in our lives if he couldn't act civil to you. When he left here, he went back to Gwen's all upset. She called me and said he asked her for my book so he could read it."

"He did what?" He sounded like he hadn't heard me correctly.

"He wants to read my book."

"Pash, the man hasn't read a whole book since he graduated."

"Well, he has a copy of mine to take to bed with him tonight. I'm telling you what I told Gwen: let it be for now. Give him a chance to mull over what I said. He has to face the fact, Ivan, that you can walk away and not come back if he continues this surly behavior."

"You're really something, do you know that?" I heard him chuckle. "You called him a lout to his face?"

"I called him more than that, let me tell you. I nailed the son of a bitch to the wall!"

Ivan laughed full out. "He'll know better next time than to tangle with my she-cat!"

"Ivan, I've had it with his nonsense. He has his head so far up his arse, he could chew on his tonsils. He's treating me like some dim-witted bimbo and he's treating you like the Antichrist. It has to stop!"

"I agree. We'll do it your way for a bit to see if things improve. If they don't, then we may be going back to Northampton sooner rather than later."

"Ivan, this doesn't make sense. It's almost like he doesn't want us to make it."

"My best guess is that he wants something he'll never get. He wants me here with him year-round, helping him care for this place. He's feeling threatened by you."

"He didn't feel threatened by the others."

"This is different. I'm in love with you. Once you move in with me, my work and my family are in Northampton. He's afraid I'll stop coming here altogether. The partnership he's offering me ties me to the place so I'll have to keep coming back."

"Do you want to keep coming back?"

"I've thought about that, too, this morning in the stable. I honestly can't imagine never coming back. I love it here. I always have."

"Even if you are treated so badly?"

"That's just it. If every day I have to walk away from a fight or risk putting him in the hospital, I can't go on here. That seems clear."

"Well, I think we both have to settle a bit and let it ride for a few days. There is a bit of hope that he may come around. Just before he left he told me something that makes me think he knows what we have is real, even if he won't admit it yet."

"What, may I ask, could that be?"

"He told me about your ring."

"What about my ring?"

"He told me what it means to you. Ivan, he realized what it meant for you to give it to me."

"I don't give a damn if he realizes it as long as you do."

"I did before, but after what Steve told me about it, I do even more."

"Pash, I gave it to you to show you how I feel. It's the only thing I have that's worth anything."

"Correction, my Vanya—it's the only thing you have that has any real meaning for you. That's what Steve told me. That's why I know he truly does understand what we have between us. He knows you wouldn't give it to just any skirt."

"Did he say that?"

"No, I did."

"Do you believe that?"

"I don't believe. I know it. I also know I'm glad you're coming here tonight."

"I rather sensed that. I'm glad I'm coming, too. I've been thinking about this morning. We have a few things to talk about."

"I know we do. Now, I have to shop for dinner. You're lucky. The power wasn't off for very long here. I can cook tonight."

"They got everything back on out here, too. I should do up some laundry before I come to your place."

"All of it?"

"Most of it. Some of it will wait."

"You're a kinky bugger, do you know that?"

"You have your moments, too, sweetheart. I can swear to that."

"Go do your laundry. I'll see you later."

"You bet you will. So long." The phone clicked. I closed my eyes and slid my finger through the ring that belonged to him.

Chapter Twenty-Nine

Once again, Pash surprised me. She laid waste to my mate Steve. I grinned again at the idea she reamed him and told him to act civil toward me. I had myself a woman willing to defend my honor.

It felt damn good to have someone defend me for a change. It pained me to think about how much criticism I had endured in the last while, albeit not all undeserved. I liked seeing myself through her eyes. She saw integrity in me, something I didn't know I had anymore.

During my midday break I gathered my laundry, including all the wet things from the dresser. However, I left Pash's knickers on my desk. While loading up the washer in the basement, I heard Steve come into the kitchen. He must have heard the washer running because he came down the cellar stairs.

"I wondered where the hell you got to, Kozak." He sat down on the stairs, eating an apple he had brought with him. "They're going to fix the roof tomorrow."

"Glad to hear it." I didn't turn around and continued sorting my clothes.

"Have you taken lunch yet?"

"I had a ham and cheese sarnie. That will hold me until dinner."

"Right, Pash is cooking for you tonight, isn't she?"

"When I talked to her a few minutes ago she was on her way out to do the shopping."

"How is she?"

"She's splendid, why do you ask?"

"Did she tell you we had a bit of a row this morning?"

"She mentioned it."

"Are you going to turn around and talk to me?"

"I thought we had been talking." I came over to the stairs and propped up my foot on the first stair. "So you want to talk, let's talk."

"She called me a lout!"

He blurted it out like it was the worst obscenity he'd ever heard. I couldn't help myself. I started to laugh.

"What's so damn funny?"

"She's a pistol, isn't she?"

"That's all you have to say?"

"Yep."

"Are you going to marry her?"

"I intend to, if she'll have me."

"Christ, now I have to put up with both of you!" He got up and stomped upstairs. Things were looking up.

Since I had my riding student in the afternoon, I didn't see Steve again until just before I left to go to Pash's flat. I had packed a small bag to stay the night. Stopping in the kitchen to grab my car keys, I ran into him. He saw the bag. "Moving out, Kozak?"

"Not just yet, mate."

"When do you expect to go back?" The question surprised me, especially since it didn't sound sarcastic at all. I answered in the same matter-of-fact tone.

"In a few weeks, I expect."

"Is that definite?"

"As definite as it can be. Why?"

"That row I had this morning with Pash, she was spitting tacks."

"She told me."

"Well, guv, let's just say that if you do leave earlier, give me some warning so I can find some help here before you buzz off. I have someone starting in August; figured you could train him. If you leave before then, I have a problem."

"I won't leave you high and dry. I told you that last night."

"Does that mean you're accepting the partnership?"

"I haven't decided that yet. There are things involved here I have to consider."

"How much say does Pash have about this?"

"Enough to help me make up my mind. Starting now, she's sharing my life. I hope you're beginning to understand that."

"I understand she's damned pissed off at me."

"I know."

"Then why aren't you doing anything about it?"

"Because she asked me to let it be. So I am. Now, I have to go or I'll be late for dinner." Pash's book sat on the table, opened to the first chapter. I tapped it and said, "Enjoy the book, mate." With that, I left him, no doubt stewing in his own juices.

I knocked on Pash's door a few minutes after six. "Perhaps you should consider giving me a key," I said as I came in and put down my bag.

"Hello to you, too, Ivan."

"Hello, sweetheart." I took her in my arms and kissed her, holding her tightly against me.

"Now, that's more like it. A few more like that and I just may consider giving you that key."

"I thought you might. Something smells really good."

"The menu changed slightly. I'm roasting a chicken. They had a special at the market. A whole chicken cost less than two boneless cutlets. So, we're having a stuffed bird tonight."

"You know, there's a joke in there somewhere."

"Don't look too hard for it, you might get lost."

"It occurs to me that we may be having more than one stuffed bird tonight."

"That doesn't even earn you a groan, let alone some more

points toward getting that key." She playfully pushed me away. "You're on salad duty. The vegetables are on the counter waiting to be washed up."

"Cheeky chappy tonight, aren't you?" She turned to go into the kitchen. I swatted her arse. "Maybe you're ready for more."

"Not until we talk about what happened this morning," she said, turning back around to face me. "I need to understand what I'm feeling, Ivan."

"What are you feeling, Pash?" She glanced away, as though trying to summon the nerve to talk about this. "Passion, tell me, I really want to know."

Her color rose, but she looked me in the eye. "I never dreamed I could respond the way I did this morning."

"How did you respond?" I wanted to hear her tell me straight out.

"It sent me wild, Ivan. For as good as it has been with you during the past week, this morning . . ." She paused, obviously timid about telling me what she felt.

"Go on, luv, I want to know."

"Ivan, I have never had a climax like I had this morning. To be trite and say the earth moved doesn't begin to explain it. Saying my soul moved more aptly describes it." She reached up and tugged my whiskers. "We have to talk, but dinner is almost ready. If we get too involved now, you'll miss out on one fine bird!"

"Oh, I think I snared myself one fine bird," I said, patting her bottom. "Now, you didn't think I could let that one pass, did you?"

"I hoped you might." She swatted my arm and turned to go to the kitchen. I stopped her.

"I know we have to tend to dinner, but I want to tell you something first." I put my hands on her shoulders and pulled her closer. "No one has ever accepted me as you do. Thank you for that."

"It isn't hard." She reached between us and squeezed my

crotch. "At least not yet." She gave me a coy smile and then turned and went to the kitchen.

I followed her. As she bent over to open the oven, I caught her. "Not quite yet, my Passion." I pulled her to me and kissed her again, this time more forcefully. At first she resisted, reaching behind me to point to the oven door. Giving into my insistence, she dropped the oven gloves she had in her hand and eagerly returned my kiss.

I had hardened sufficiently to make my point by the time we separated. Squeezing her arse with both hands and holding her against me, I said, "Now we will both sit through dinner feeling it. I have to teach you that you don't grab at me unless you intend to see it through."

She pushed away from me. I thought I had thrown a spanner in the works, only to see her turn around and snap off the oven. She came back and started to undo my trousers. "The chicken can sit for a few minutes. I'm good for one now." She pulled down my zipper and started to reach inside.

I grabbed her hand. "My, we are feeling our oats tonight, aren't we? I thought you didn't want any more until we had a chance to talk?" We stood there, toe-to-toe, eye to eye.

"I didn't," she fired back, "until you decided to turn up the flame several notches. Now I want it."

"Why?" I still held her hand, tightly enough that she couldn't pull free.

"Because I'm throbbing."

"So am I." I pulled her close again. "Remember what I said the other night about staying on the crest of the arousal without pursuing its climax? Let's do that now and be in this place as we talk about what happened this morning."

Her body relaxed in my arms, the resistance subsiding. "I have never known anyone as bloody intoxicating as you. Being with you is like riding on a magic carpet to some faraway, exotic place where eroticism is a way of life."

"You inspire it in me, my lovely one." I leaned over and kissed her cheek. "Let's eat dinner and then talk some more."

"All right, but you have to promise me something."

"What?"

"Stay at least two meters away from me until after dinner."

"What are you talking about?" I marveled at her ability to bewilder me with so little effort.

"If you get any closer to me than arm's length and don't intend to do some serious fucking, I will have no alternative but to go to my bedroom and take care of business myself." With that she broke free of my hold, retrieved the oven gloves and went after that bird. I smiled as I considered that I would go after mine later.

I dutifully began washing up produce. I noticed her glancing at me as she took care of finishing the food. I couldn't tell if she wanted a quick ogle or wanted to keep an eye on me. Either way, I liked it.

As I cleaned a stalk of celery, she wrinkled her nose. "Only put a little of that in, please."

"Why, don't you like celery?"

"I would enjoy being fucked by that stalk more than eating it."

"I'll make a note. She likes being fucked with vegetables. We can work with that."

"I was making a point, not a request."

I picked up a cucumber and rolled it in my hands. "Too late, luv. You've planted the seed. It is sure to grow into a fine cucumber."

"Finish the salad already. The chicken is done."

"Yes, ma'am!" After tossing all the greens together in a salad bowl, I took it to the dining room, where, once again, Pash had made a beautiful table. While she lit the candles, I found some music, this time selecting some soft jazz.

Coming back into the dining room, I saw her bend over to retrieve the corkscrew, her skirt riding up her legs. I glimpsed what looked to be the top of a stocking. Willie let me know he liked what he saw, especially when I remembered having her from behind that morning.

I had to distract myself or I would have her bent over the table right now. "Let me do that." I came over and took the corkscrew from her to open the wine.

"You're even sexy when you open wine, Dr. Kozak," she said, scrutinizing me as I pulled out the cork.

"You're not going to let me off the hook with this name thing, are you?" I poured our wine.

"No. I want you to get over the association you have with it and make a new one."

"And what would that be?" I came over and pulled out her chair, and then sat down myself.

"With us and what we do together, of course," she said as she served the food.

"I think we'd best eat our meal before we go there. This could get a little involved and our food will get cold." I pointed to her plate. "So, eat."

"I fancy it when you get masterful." She stuffed in a forkful of food and started chewing.

"Considering what happened this morning, I thought that might be the case." She threw her napkin at me. "Now, now, remember what I said about young ladies with breeding. Actions such as those could be considered punishable offenses."

"Will you get on with your dinner? You're making my palms sweat." Considering how hungry I felt, she didn't have to prod me twice. We both managed a double serving of everything. The conversation remained light even while we cleaned everything up. Then we took our wine and went to the sitting room.

"Where do we begin?" I decided to let Pash start the ball rolling, as I didn't have a handle on where this would go.

"How about with my telling you what I want?"

"What do you want, my Passion?" She certainly had my attention.

She took a deep breath and said, "Those girls you've been with, I want to be one of them to you. I want to be to you what you wanted them to be."

"Starting off small, I see." Already I felt uneasy with my history being the main focus right off the top.

"Ivan, I like when we act out scenes together. I want to be one of the girls you've seduced and have you respond to me like you did to them."

"Like this morning?"

"Just like this morning,"

"Pash, I'm still trying to understand what the hell happened this morning."

"So am I. But, Ivan, one thing I'm sure of: you went to a very private place inside yourself and you took me there with you. We made love in your secret garden."

"You make it sound so pure. It isn't, Pash. The urges I feel could very well ruin me if I continue following them."

"Ivan, it isn't the urges that could ruin you. It is what you choose to do with them. Yes, if you continue as you have been, you may well trash your career. But if you can let me in there with you and we can find ways to satisfy those urges, then it's safe to be there."

"You're almost making sense here."

"I'm invoking the honesty clause now. How did it feel to you this morning, what we did?"

She deserved the truth. "Okay, then, honestly, I lost myself in the fantasy. What we did gave me a sense of peace, even completion."

"How many times have you actually been able to realize this fantasy love play?"

"Hardly ever. Lately it has been just a body under me letting me do my business."

"But you keep going after it."

"The urges have become my demons. Don't you think I know my actions speak louder than my denials about it all? I can't seem to stop myself from going after it."

"Ivan, I am asking you to tell me honestly: did you realize your fantasy this morning?"

"Yes, Passion, I did." I looked into my glass for a moment, swirling my wine, and then looked back at her. "More than any other time in my life, I realized my fantasy."

"Don't you see? You have eroticized teaching. You want to teach in the bedroom as well as in the classroom. That includes the discipline part!" She poked me in the side with her finger.

"Maybe you're right. I've thought about doing an over-the-knee many times. I've never had anyone who would go along for the ride until you fell from the sky. It bloody well popped my nuts."

"Did it feel like a demon unleashed?"

"Hardly! I might have even heard a few angels singing."

"Do you think what we did this morning could ever destroy you?"

"No, sweetheart, I do not. In fact, I feel more settled and more myself than I have in a very long time."

"Then, my Vanya, I say to you again: we made love in your secret garden this morning. It is a place where I want to be with you, discovering the treasures you've buried there."

"You're talking like I understand what all this is. Pash, I truly don't. So much of it has been unconscious on my part. All this is damned difficult to face up to, I'll tell you that much."

"Do you have any idea what it is like for me to be in this place with you?"

"I'm not sure I understand what you mean, sweetheart."

"When we are together, I become the object of your desire. I want that, Ivan. God, I want that so much. . . ." She closed her eyes and softly whispered. "I want to be your virgin, your whore, whatever you want me to be."

She opened her eyes and looked at me with such openness and love, my breath caught. "Pash, I want it, too." I took hold of her hand and kissed it. "How you can take my vices and turn them into something so beautiful is beyond me."

"I understand you."

"You are also helping me to understand myself." I pulled her closer. "Tell me more about this morning."

"I already told you how I reacted."

"Yes, but we haven't discussed how you like me to be dominant, now, have we?"

"Ivan, it wasn't all role-playing this morning. You did take me further than I have gone before, and my Lord, I have never felt so free in my entire life." She closed her eyes again and squeezed my hand. "Something circulated between us like a high-voltage current."

I leaned over next to her ear. "Tell me, my Passion, how you feel when you submit to me." I could feel her breathing change as I nuzzled her hair.

"You make me crazy." She breathed the words into the skin on my neck, giving me a wonderful tingle down my spine. "I'm like a cat rolling in catnip when you take over. When I surrender, I lose myself in you." She rubbed her cheek against my whiskers. I almost expected her to purr. "You are without a doubt the sexiest man I have ever known. I want to wrap you around myself like a warm blanket."

"Tell me why you want to be one of them with me." I nuzzled her again as I whispered the question. She visibly trembled.

"Because you want them so much, because you use them to satisfy yourself."

"Go on, I want to know it all."

"It excites me to think of you wanting them like that." In a barely audible whisper, she added, "I want to be desired by you the way you have desired them."

"Do you want me to seduce you, Passion?" I caressed her breast as I kissed her neck.

"Oh, yes, Dr. Kozak, I want to know what it is like to be with you."

Unlike this morning, this time hearing her breathe my name inflamed me. I slid my hand under her skirt. She had a surprise waiting for me. "My dear, do you always wear a garter belt without your knickers?"

"Only when I am with you."

The smooth stocking felt cool against my hand. "Did you do this to tease me, Pash?"

"I wanted it to please you." She leaned in close to my ear. "And also tease you. I hope you like it."

"Oh, yes, sweetheart, I fancy it. The next time we go out to dinner, will you dress like this for me and let me touch you?" I kissed her neck again.

"If you want me to, I will." She gasped as I grazed her bare pussy with my knuckles. "I just don't know if I could do this in a public place."

"I promise to be discreet. No one will know when I fondle you. Have you ever been fondled by an older man before, dear heart?"

"No, but I have fantasized about it."

"Tell me about your fantasy." I stroked her pussy curls very lightly.

"I couldn't. It's just too personal."

"Yes, you can. I want to know." I continued touching her, waiting for the fire to ignite. I felt her move very slightly under my hand, adjusting her position to increase the pressure. Her pussy hair dampened as she slid against my hand. "Go on, sweetheart, tell me." I waited as she continued to rub.

Speaking very softly, she shared her fantasy. "In my story, I am still a virgin. I'm eighteen and living at home. My parents go away for the day, leaving me home alone. A friend of my father's stops by to see him, a man from the docks that he knows.

"He asks to come in to use the loo. I let him in and we talk a bit. He wants to know when my parents will be home. Innocently, I tell him the truth: not until much later that night.

"Then he asks, 'Do you have a boyfriend?' When I tell him yes, he smiles and says, 'Do you ever let him touch you?' He comes a little closer. My stomach starts to flutter. I tell him sometimes I let my boyfriend touch me. 'Do you like it?' When I tell him yes, he says, 'I bet you do.' He takes my hand. Sitting down on the sofa, he pulls me onto his lap. The queasiness in my stomach hasn't left, but something else has taken over. I have tingles all through me and I like it."

Pash had a dreamy, faraway look as she told me her story. I didn't want to break the spell, but I had an idea. "Sweetheart, why don't you sit on my lap now and tell me the rest of the story." She obediently moved to my lap. I pulled up her skirt. She offered no resistance. "Now, tell me what happens next."

"He squeezes my breasts, saying, 'Aren't you a prick-teasing scrubber in this dress?' He lowers the straps of my sundress and pinches my nipples. Then he puts my hand on his cock. Oh, my, he is so hard. He tells me to unzip him. I do. He reaches in and untangles himself from his pants, exposing himself to me. He says such crude things to me."

Pash hesitated. I didn't want her to stop. "Tell me, my Passion, what does he say?" I wanted to hear her say the words men from the docks would say.

"He asks me, 'Do you like my cock?' He puts my hand on it and wants me to wank him. His prick feels alive in my hand. It pulses and twitches while I toss him off. Reaching under my skirt, he pushes his fingers inside the crotch of my scanties. He says to me, 'So, you like to be touched. Your pussy is so wet and hot, your boyfriend must cream rubbing it.' He pushes two fingers into me and kisses me at the same time. Then he finger-fucks me, saying, 'I'm going to make you come for me, doll.' I wank him harder."

I became the man in her story, my fingers connecting with her flesh. I pushed two fingers into her. Pash moaned and tightened against my hand. Her heat had infected me. My cock strained in my pants, but I couldn't take her yet. She had to finish her story. "Do you come for him, my Passion? Tell me, I want to know."

"He says, 'I can tell you haven't fucked yet. I'm not going

to pop your cherry. I just want to have a little fun.' He tells me to stand up and he pulls my dress completely off. All I have on are my scanties. Standing behind me, he pulls my scanties down and rubs against my bum. He reaches around with one hand and diddles me. With the other hand, he pinches my nipples. He says nasty things to me. 'Touching your wet cunt makes me so hard. I'm going to make you come, baby. When you are ready, you'll ask me to fuck you, maybe even ask me to give it to you up the arse.' "

Pash had lost herself in the fantasy. "Stand up, Passion." She did as I asked. I took off her dress, leaving her in only her black garter belt and stockings. Fecking Christ, seeing her in that sexy lingerie nearly made me cream.

I opened my trousers and pushed my cock against her arse. She immediately pressed back into me. "Now, tell me the rest of the story," I said as I reached around to rub her.

"He kisses my neck and humps my bum so hard he almost pokes it inside me. All of a sudden, he squeezes me very hard and groans. I feel something warm and wet hit my back and run down the crack of my bum. He shakes a few more times and then lets me go."

"Have you finished yet? Do you come for him, Pash?"

"Oh, so hard, I yell and spasm indecently. I have my eyes closed. When I finally open them, I see him pick up my scanties and put them in his pocket. He says, 'I want to keep these to remember you.' Before he leaves, he tells me to give him a call when I get a little older and we will really have some fun."

Pash's whole body had flushed. I lowered her to the floor and allowed the fantasy to consume us both.

Chapter Thirty

My whole body throbbed. Ivan's acceptance of my story gave me the freedom to immerse myself in it. When he lowered me to the floor, reality and fantasy blended in a sensual mist. He opened his trousers. Without even taking them off, he lay down on top of me. Opening my legs as wide as I could, I wanted him to fill me

When he entered me, raw sexual energy surged through me. The impact of our coming together filled the room with primal sounds, both of us vocalizing our heat with grunts and groans. My climax struck like electricity ripping though my entire body. I clung to him as the tremors seemed to go on and on. He kept going until suddenly I felt his body go rigid. The glorious sound he made with his orgasm filled me with such joy. I couldn't help myself. Once again I felt tears sliding down my cheeks.

"Passion, are you all right?" I heard the question but couldn't yet respond. "Pash, sweetheart, are you all right?"

He had not yet caught his breath, still being in his own aftermath. Our bodies were pressed together, with his organ still inside me. The concern I heard forced me back to the present moment. "I'm fine, Ivan," I whispered. "I'm just not totally back yet."

"Nor am I." Sweat from his face dripped on my cheek, mingling with my tears. "Why are you crying?"

I reached up and stroked his hair. "My beautiful Ivan, I am just so full of what I've found with you. I have never been so completely myself in my whole life." I smiled at him, feeling a little sheepish. "I don't mean to cry every time we make love. You fill me up so much. It naturally spills out my eyes."

He smiled. "Well, I'm starting to get used to it. I'm considerably bigger than you are. I'm concerned that I've hurt you when I see the tears." He kissed my forehead. "Speaking of being bigger than you are, I have to get off you." He carefully pulled out, reaching down between us. "Oh, shit, Pash, I forgot to put on a condom!"

"Not to worry, Vanya. My cap is in and my cycle is due in a couple of days." I sat up. "I'll make an appointment this week to see about going on the pill."

"Considering the way things are going between us, I would agree with that. I'm really sorry. I got caught up in what you were telling me and I didn't even think about it." He sat down beside me, looking troubled. "We haven't discussed this, but I want you to know I have been tested."

"It never even crossed my mind, Ivan."

"Considering what I've done of late, it crossed mine. Last summer, with all the blood work I had done in the paternity case, they tested me for every disease known to mankind. Everything came back normal."

"I appreciate your telling me all this." I took hold of Ivan's hand. "Once I get on the pill, I want to go au naturel. I like the idea that your *élan vital* is spilling inside me."

"How is it possible that whenever I tell you something I think is loaded, you somehow manage to diffuse it and make it all right?"

"That's how love works. You'll get used to it."

"I expect I will, eventually." He squeezed my hand and then went over to get his bag. "Here, put this on." He tossed his pajama top at me. "I brought my half and thought to bring your half, too."

I slipped on the top, only buttoning the last few buttons. I watched as he completely stripped and then stepped into the pajama bottoms he had worn last night. It felt so right and so natural to be dressing for bed with him. "I have to go wash up. With your being such a fertile bugger, I'm a bit full."

"Point well taken. Mind if I accompany you?"

"Not at all." He helped me to my feet and we went to the loo.

"That story—did something happen that set it off?"

"Not exactly. My father did have a friend from the docks that would visit us, but he never touched me. I overheard him talking to my father about a woman. He slept with her several times before they parted company. His stories about her triggered my imagination."

"Did you ever tell anyone else about him?"

"Heavens, no! You're the first person on earth I told about this. It isn't exactly conversation for afternoon tea." I used the toilet and then went to the basin to wash. Ivan also had a piss.

"The way you described it all, I thought perhaps you might have been with an older man at some point."

"No, not like I imagined it. I guess I uncovered a piece of my shadow, didn't I?"

Ivan came over beside me and leaned on the washbasin. "Pash, you just told me a story about an older man taking advantage of an eighteen-year-old. I damn near exploded in my pants. What the hell does that say about me?"

"It says you are a normal, healthy man who reacted to a highly charged, erotic fantasy. There's nothing wrong with that."

"The difference between us is I have acted on these impulses. You haven't."

"Not until now, with you. Why do you think I've invented these stories? My libido needs an outlet for this part of myself just like yours does."

"Ever thought of playing doctor? There's one we haven't

tried yet. I'll add it to the list, along with picking up some costumes."

"You bugger. Is there anything you won't try?"

"Not much. You seem to bring it out in me."

"Since you're making a list, add the Highwayman to it."

"The Highwayman? What's that?"

"Another story I'll tell you about. I can even let you read some of what I've written about him."

"Tell me who he is."

"He is a lover I invented when I didn't have anyone. I think the role will fit you perfectly."

"Is that a fact!"

"That is indeed a fact." Running my fingers through his long hair, I knew he had already become my Highwayman. "It seems I'm transferring my lusty parts to you just like you are doing to me."

"Ask me if I mind."

"Do you mind?"

"Bloody hell, no!" Ivan took my hand. "Let's go to bed."

We went into the bedroom. "We forgot to bolt the door."

"I'll do it, sweetheart. You settle in." I watched Ivan go out to the sitting room, amazed at how it already seemed like we were living together. When he came back, he had his bag.

"I'll need this in the morning. Sorry to say, it's an early one again tomorrow. I should be at the farm by six thirty."

"I'll set the clock for five." Ivan climbed into bed beside me. "It feels like we're already married, doesn't it?"

"Sure does. And it feels damn good." He turned on his side, slipping his hand under my top and rubbing my stomach. "I really do want to marry you, but I don't want you to feel trapped into anything. You'll come back to Thrapston with me and try it all on for size. God help me if you decide you don't want to stay, but if you do want out, I'll deal with it."

"Ivan, I wouldn't be too concerned about that. I want to

be with you more than I've ever wanted anything. But an honest-to-goodness proposal of marriage would be a very nice thing to look forward to."

"I'll keep that in mind. May I ask you something?"

"What?"

"How often in your life have you been truly satisfied with someone?"

"Hardly ever. I have been the most satisfied taking care of myself." I kissed my finger and touched his lips. "Until now."

"I'm pleased to hear I make you happy."

"You make me very happy."

"It does seem we are well matched."

"I think we are, in a number of ways." I kissed him good night. "We need to sleep. Tomorrow is a workday for both of us."

"Pash, I want to thank you for trusting me."

"Thank you for deserving my trust. I hope you know I also want to marry you." Reaching over him, I turned out the light.

Epilogue

"Please tell me that's the last of it!"

Ivan pushed the door shut with his foot as he deposited more boxes on top of the ones we had already unloaded. "That's it. Both cars are empty."

"Finally. Now pardon me while I collapse!" I fell onto the sofa.

"It's already dark outside. I can't show you around the property until tomorrow. If Steve hadn't cocked up getting his ledgers and bank statements together, we'd have gotten here a bloody lot sooner."

"If not for Gwen, I wager we would still be in Shaftesbury. She's the one who got it sorted so we could leave."

"Thank God she's moving in with him. The bleeding sod needs someone to look after him."

"Just like you do?"

Ivan looked at me and smiled. "Just like I do. Except Steve also has Churchill to keep an eye on him. That dog will take him down if he gets out of line." Laughing, he added, "I would pay a few quid to see it, too." He picked up several bags from the pile on the sitting room floor. "Now, sweet thing, let me put away these groceries and get us something cold to drink. I'll be right back."

I laid my head on the back of the sofa and closed my eyes. We were here, at last. August had been a flurry of activity.

Along with my writing and Ivan's work with the horses, we also had packing, appointments with the barrister and meetings at the bank. Of course, we also fucked every chance we had.

Only a few days ago, Ivan and Steve signed the final agreement and added Ivan's name to the farm accounts at the bank. Ivan now had an official partnership with Steve. They haggled over the details for several weeks before eventually coming to an understanding over a bottle of vodka. They might not share blood, but they were brothers nonetheless.

I heard ice clinking in a glass over my head and opened my eyes. "If you had fallen asleep, I would have poured this on you."

"Only if you want to sleep on the sofa your first night at home. I think I should sleep very well in your bed alone tonight."

"Trust me, my Passion, you will not be sleeping alone tonight."

"I'm rather pleased about that." I sipped the wonderfully cold sparkling water he had brought in. "Once I catch my wind, I would like a tour. Your house is larger than I expected."

"I bought it anticipating a family at some point in my life. Shall we toast to that dream?"

We clinked our glasses. "I daresay we'll have to do more than toast to get there."

"Oh, we will. I'm quite sure of that." Ivan looked thoughtful for a moment. "We'll unpack all this tomorrow. We have to think about how best to organize the house now."

"When are they bringing Nutmeg? I miss her already."

"I'll ring up Steve when I'm ready for her. I have to clean out the garage first and buy some supplies."

"How will they get her here?"

"Steve has an older horse box he's giving to me. The bloke he just hired will deliver Nutmeg here and leave the trailer. Then all we have left to do is build a stable."

"I'm gobsmacked we've gotten this far today. Please, let's

leave planning the stable for tomorrow. Right now I just want to settle in beside you and sleep."

"My dear Passion, we certainly aren't sleeping yet. We haven't consummated our first night at home together!"

"Look at me! Do you really think I have enough juice left to fuck tonight? I'm knackered!"

"I do believe I can take care of that."

My pulse quickened, knowing full well he could.

Ivan took my glass and set it beside his on the lamp stand. Sliding closer to me, he threaded his fingers through my hair until his hand rested on the back of my neck. Kneading my neck with his fingertips, he said very softly, "We're home, Passion."

He pulled me to him, close enough to feel him exhale against my mouth. He held me like that for an eternal moment before he leaned forward and his breath blended with mine. Our mouths fused in a kiss that penetrated our souls.

This closeness, this new intimacy, still shook me. I wrapped my arms around his neck and held him as he held me. His whiskers rubbed against my face as he licked my teeth. He kissed me boldly, perhaps even harshly, his tongue engaging mine as an unspoken need arced between us.

Ivan broke the kiss, and in a smooth motion across my face, his mouth found my neck. He kissed my throat, his breath scalding my skin. "Ivan. . . ." His name came in a whisper, spoken as a plea—for what I couldn't be sure.

He simply stopped, suspended in a place of desire and longing. "What do you want, my Passion? I will move away if you ask me to."

"Ivan. . . ." I said his name again, unable to tell him how much I wanted him, unable to wrap my mind around all he made me feel. I clung to him, unable to let him go. The leather band holding his hair had slipped, freeing a strand that curved around his face. I reached up and pulled off the band, allowing his hair to cascade around his shoulders. My breath caught at the incredible beauty of the man beside me. I touched his face, allowing my hand to slide along the curve of his whiskers. "Ivan, I want you."

"Then allow me to show you my bedroom." He smiled. "Pardon me, *our* bedroom. We can tour the rest of our home in the morning."

He held my hand as we made our way to the stairs. I went first and he followed. When we reached the top, he led the way to the master bedroom. In those few minutes, I had a chance to gather myself.

I knew this was what I wanted, to be with him. Our lives had irrevocably changed with this decision. Sharing a life with him would not be easy, but I knew he would give me everything he had to give.

His bedroom had the same classic beauty as the man. The dark cherry wood of the king-size bed matched the chest of drawers and the bedside table. "My God, Ivan, this furniture is stunning." I ran my hand across the base of the bed. "And the bed is so big!"

"I like plenty of room when I sleep, and when I fuck."

"You never complained about the full-size bed in my flat."

"I didn't mind it as long as you were there."

"I hope you changed the sheets before you left."

"Not to worry, dear heart. No one has shared this bed with me for many months. And yes, I did change the sheets before I left."

He kissed me then, passionately, ardently. I grabbed on to his shoulders and returned the kiss, allowing the passion surging through me to break free. He pushed me backward onto the bed, still kissing me, still holding me. I gripped his chest through his shirt and dug my nails into him.

I welcomed, even cherished, his weight on top of me. His hands moved down my body, still fully clothed. My clothing did not block the insistence of his need. He rubbed and squeezed me with increasing hunger. He tugged at my blouse, trying to open it without unbuttoning it. He stopped himself, saying,

"You will have to help me with your clothes. I may end up tearing them."

Sitting up, I undid the buttons on my blouse and took it off. Ivan stood up to undress himself. As I opened the zipper on my jeans, I stopped and watched him. He took off his shirt, revealing his perfect masculine chest, his dark hair barely hiding the six-pack on his stomach. I stared at him, mesmerized by his virile beauty. He saw me looking at him. "You like watching me strip, don't you?"

"You are magnificent. There is no other word." He unzipped his trousers and took them off. While I watched, he removed what was left of his clothing. Completely nude, he came back to the bed.

"Shall I help you?" He didn't wait for an answer. He took hold of my jeans and pulled them off, leaving me in only my scanties. His engorged cock hung heavily from his body.

"You're dangly bits are very impressive tonight."

"That's because of you." He grabbed my legs and dragged me to the edge of the bed. "Let's have a look at your bits now." He pulled off my scanties and knelt on the floor. "Lovely, absolutely lovely." He spread my labia with his fingers and buried his face between my legs.

"Oh, God almighty, Ivan!" He sucked my clitoris into his mouth and circled it with his tongue. Using his tongue like a finger, he poked and prodded the tender flesh. Then he started nibbling at my clit, with just enough pressure to drive me mad. He had his weight against my legs. I couldn't move. He had to stop, I couldn't stand it. I tried to say his name. The only sound I could make was a guttural scream. I reached down and grabbed hold of his hair. I pulled it, hard. He still didn't stop. I pushed my pelvis against his face. He broke the suction to take a breath.

I tried to get out from under him, but I couldn't. He still had my legs pinned. "Do you want to go to sleep now, my she-cat in heat? Or perhaps you would like your Highwayman to spread your legs, as Lucifer would have him do?"

"Fuck you," I spat at him. I tried to squirm out from underneath him again.

"I know what you need." With no warning, he flipped me over, my belly flat against the bed. He smacked my bum with the flat of his hand. I yelped as another sharp slap connected. "It's all right, Passion, you can squeal here. There aren't any neighbors close at hand like in Shaftesbury."

And squeal I did. He paddled me half a dozen times, maybe more. With each smack, I went higher. Pain became pleasure, each electric jolt taking me closer to the edge. But, no matter how much I tried, he wouldn't let me move. He had me twatting wild by the time he stopped.

When I rolled Pash over on her back, I didn't know what to expect. I still held her down, not knowing if she would knee me in the groin.

"Will you let me move, you bloody bastard?" She had her fire up, all right!

"And what will you do if I let you move, sweetheart? Run for your car and go back to your flat?"

"That's not a frigging bad idea! Get off me and maybe I will!"

"Wouldn't you rather have some revenge?"

"What the hell are you talking about?" She shoved at my chest with both hands. "Either fuck me or get off me. I can't stand this!"

"You want to move, I'll let you move." I rolled onto my back. "Now it's your turn."

"My turn to what?" She pushed a shock of red hair from her face as she sat up.

"It's your turn to take over. Do what you want to me. I won't object or stop you." I watched her breasts rise and fall with each breath, waiting for her to take in what I said.

"You won't stop me?"

"Nope. I give it over to you, luv. Do what you like." I put my arm under my head and waited, knowing full well I held a lit stick of dynamite in my hand.

"All right, then! Where are your neckties?"

"What are you going to do, hang me?

"Don't tempt me. Are you going to tell me where they are or not?"

"In the wardrobe over there. There's a rack inside the door." I watched as she crawled over the side of the bed and went to the cupboard. Her whole body had a pink glow, but her bottom shone bright red. To feel her heat full force in my own bed, that's how I wanted to start our life together.

She came back to the bed with a handful of neckties. "What the bloody hell are you going to do with all those?"

"Tie you up."

"What?"

"You heard me. I'm going to tie you up." She stood there holding those damn neckties, daring me to back down. Instead, I righted myself on the bed and stretched out with both hands over my head next to the bedposts.

"So do it." I expected her to loosely tie me. But she damn straight meant business. "Bloody hell, Pash, at least let a little blood through," I said as I pulled my wrist against the tightly bound cloth.

"I thought all your blood had gone to your cock, Dr. Kozak!" She ignored my complaints and went to the bottom of the bed. Jerking my foot to the side, she threaded another tie around the baseboard and bound my ankle. After she bound the other ankle, she crawled back onto the bed beside me. "So, how does it feel to be immobilized?"

I tugged at the knots she had made. She had me tied frigging tight. I could slip out of them if need be, but it would take considerable effort. "Jesus Christ, Pash, I know I said you could have revenge! But it bloody well seems you are going for some serious payback here!"

"Dr. Kozak, you may not survive the night." My cock bounced against my belly in anticipation of what she meant to do.

Putting her leg over mine, she rubbed up against me, leaving a slick trail on my thigh. Then she buried her face in my neck, underneath my hair. Licking my ear, she whispered, "I've never smelled anyone that smells as good as you do." Her breath in my ear made me shudder. "You smell like ambrosia, absolutely delicious."

She continued to nuzzle and kiss my neck as she rubbed her pussy against my leg. Then she put her ear on my chest over my heart. "I must say, Dr. Kozak, your heart is racing. You best calm yourself before you have a heart attack." She kissed her finger and touched my nose. "The night is young."

"What are you going to do to me, luv? You can't leave me tied up like this all night."

She laughed. "Stop faffing, you shufflebutt! It's only been five minutes!"

"Feels more like a flipping hour."

"You need some time to settle down. I don't want you shooting off the minute we do a bit of tea-bagging." She reached down and fondled my balls to emphasize her point.

"You are trying to kill me, aren't you? Sucking my nuts while I'm tied up? Passion, that's inhumane."

"I know. Now, I want you to think about that while I run downstairs."

"What the fuck do you think you're doing?"

"I'm going to get my box of toys. I know right where they are. I won't be a minute."

She left me there, bound hand and foot to the bed, with a rock-hard cock. There wasn't a goddamned thing I could do about it, either. So, I closed my eyes and thought about what she could possibly do to me.

Certainly, during the last few weeks, she had embraced the storytelling with me. Becoming her Highwayman stoked us both to near delirium. But she didn't seem to have a mind for stories tonight.

To be sure, tying me up certainly had not been on our list of adventures to explore. She quite obviously wanted me to get some of my own medicine. We had added a few items to her toy box during the last month. I hadn't anticipated being on the receiving end of those gifts when I bought them for her.

I glanced down at my feet and noticed a proper, feminine bow tied to the baseboard of the bed. I twisted my head and saw the same holding my wrists. Well, there it is! She gave me an escape route by not knotting the neckties. Wiggling my fingers, I could just reach the end of the tie dangling below the bow. I smiled, knowing I could easily free myself if I felt the need.

Pash came back into the bedroom with a box and a glass of ice water. "We really need a softer light, wouldn't you say?" She put everything down and reached for the lamp beside the bed. "Well, isn't this quite charming?" she said as she playfully turned the dimmer switch down and back up again. "Isn't it marvelous that you thought to install a dimmer on the lamp?"

"Remember me? The sod you left tied to the bed?"

"I remember you very well, thank you." She turned the lamp down to not much more than candlelight and set about her business. "Let's see what we have in here."

She opened the box and took out several items. I watched as she lined up on the bed a blindfold, some clothes-pegs, a feather duster, a vibrator and a black garter belt with black silk stockings. She then sipped her ice water, making sure I saw that she held an ice cube in her mouth.

"Dear heart, you're playing with fire here."

Spitting the ice into her hand, she replied, "Oh, no, Ivan, I'm playing with ice." She proceeded to kneel on the bed and grazed my nipples with the ice.

"Jesus, Pash! That's frigging cold!" The sensation raised gooseflesh on my arms.

"Settle yourself, Ivan. We're just getting started. I trust you meant what you said, that you wouldn't stop me?"

She gave me a defiant look that told me I had better mind myself or risk torture beyond endurance. "I'll settle. Just try to have some mercy on me."

"Perhaps, but not just yet." She slid the hand holding the ice cube across the tip of my cock.

"What the fuck are you doing?" I gritted my teeth to endure the surge of cold through my groin. The rigidness of my cock softened with her ice bath.

"We have to cool you down a little or you won't last worth diddly-squat." Squeezing my bollocks in her icy hand, she added, "My Vanya, perhaps you will send me packing after tonight."

"Not damn likely, Redhead. You're chalking up some major retaliation points here. There will be tit for tat. Remember that!"

"This is tit for tat, my Vanya." She picked up the garter belt and stockings. Trailing the silk down my belly and across my groin, she said, "I'm going to be kind to you, Dr. Kozak. I'm going to give you a choice. What do you want me to be tonight, your virgin or your whore?"

Struggling to allow her control, I took a deep breath. "That seems obvious, doesn't it? No virgin would be doing this, but a scrubber on the job would."

"Then whore it is." With that, she knelt on the bed and fastened the garter belt around her waist. Sitting down beside me, she propped her feet against my side. One beautiful leg at a time, she put on the black stockings. When she lifted her leg to roll the stocking up her thigh, I caught a whiff of her musky scent.

"You smell like a brothel on a hot summer's night."

"That's because I'm very wet. I'm creaming down my leg, see?" She spread her legs wide and sure enough, she had a wet streak running down her inner thigh. Seeing her in that garter belt, with her pussy open for the taking, brought my cock back to life. "Dr. Kozak, you've made my cunt ooze every day since I met you."

Pash rarely used such language. When she did, the words sent me crazy. "I like it when you talk dirty to me. Do it, sweetheart, let me hear you talk dirty."

"My Vanya, what would you like to hear? Do you want me to tell you what I'm going to do to your cock, or perhaps to your balls?"

"No, I want to hear you talk about your pussy. Tell me how wet your pussy is." My cock swelled and started to twitch. "Pose for me, like in my mags."

As she fastened the garters on her stockings, she knelt and spread her legs wide. "See, my pussy is hot and wet and slippery, all because of you. Do you want to taste me, Dr. Kozak?"

She slid her middle finger between her legs and rubbed while I watched. Then she straddled my chest and put the same finger in my mouth. "That's it, suck off my juice. Show me how hungry you are for my pussy." I lapped at her finger, wanting it to be her clit. Dragging her finger across my lower lip, she said, "That's enough for now. We have to get on with it."

"Pash, straddle my face, let me lick you." I involuntarily tugged at the restraints, trying to grab at her. She slithered off my chest and picked up the blindfold.

"My Vanya, it's time." She put the blindfold over my eyes, shutting out the light and any sense of what she meant to do.

"Passion Flower . . ."

"Hush now, don't make a fuss. If you relax into it, you may just enjoy it." Something tickled my chest. I realized she had the feather duster. "Do you remember? That's what you said to me a couple of weeks ago when you bought me the blindfold."

I thought of what I did to her that night and groaned. "Passion, it is different for a man."

"Codswallop! If you do as you told me, you might find a

whole new garden to play in." She tickled my nipples with the feather duster and then dragged it down my chest and stomach, pausing just before she reached my cock. I tensed, expecting the feathers to tickle my cock at any moment, but they didn't. She got off the bed.

"What are you doing? You're not leaving me like this, are you?" My fingers found the end of the necktie, quite ready to release myself.

"Heavens, no!" The end of the necktie left my hand. "Now, now, my Vanya, no cheating. I'll just tuck this tie out of harm's way," which she did, straightaway. Now I had no easy escape route, save, perhaps, for begging.

"Then what are you doing?" I heard the cupboard opening.

"Getting another necktie."

"For what?" She had me where she wanted me, to be sure.

"To tie up your cock, of course."

"You're pushing me, Passion. . . ."

"As you have been pushing me for weeks now, Ivan. It's time you really understand how it feels." She came back onto the bed. "Now, are you going to stop resisting so much and relax into it?"

"I have a choice? As much as I am able, I will." I heard her turn on a vibrator, Reminding myself that I did want to ride the wave, that I did want her fire, I tried to relax. "All right, Passion, do me, sweetheart."

She slid the vibrator underneath my arse and wedged it in the crack of my bum. An electrical shock went up my spine as the vibration hit my groin.

Without pausing, she wrapped my rigid cock in the necktie, swirling it around the base and wrapping it to the tip. She took it back down to the base and tied it around my nuts. "Just like a Christmas present, Ivan, with a pretty bow. Your bollocks do tie up nicely."

She scooted back up to my chest. Taking each nipple between her fingers she pinched. I reared up and fell back on the vibrator, wedging it even deeper in my crack. "Jesus Christ, I can't stand this." I hissed the words between clenched teeth and strained against the ties.

"You will stand it, Ivan, just like I have been." She clamped something on my nipple and I roared with pleasure pain.

"Jesus suffering fuck! Passion Flower!" She clamped the other nipple.

Having me damn close to panting, my prick nearly shattering like glass, she whispered in my ear, "Now, Dr. Kozak, for some tea-bagging."

Before I could manage enough air to protest, she had my nuts in her hand. One at a time, she took them in her mouth, rolling them around like a chocolate drop. I bellowed and thrashed, the ties holding strong.

She sucked my balls, so deeply I thought she might swallow them. My cock strained against the cloth she had wrapped around it. My nipples seared my chest while the vibrator violated my arse. The blindfold surrounded me in darkness. My whole body scorched with heat as sensation consumed me.

When her mouth finally lifted from my crotch, I couldn't speak. I could barely breathe. Without saying a word, she untied one of my hands. I waited for her to finish untying me. She didn't.

I lifted the mask with my free hand to see her kneeling on all fours, her arse end facing me, her legs spread. I could see the wet streaks on her legs from her creaming cunt.

I reached over and untied my other hand and then took the clothes-pegs from my excruciatingly sensitive nipples. Reaching around her, I undid my ankles. After carefully unwrapping my tortured cock, I gave her arse several solid whacks.

Kneeling behind her on the bed, I entered her with one long thrust. As I opened the garden gate, I growled, "Welcome home, Passion."

Ivan pounded himself against my arse so hard, so brilliantly hard. He vented his punishment, his power, his passion. The sound of his climax resonated through the house, its savage ferocity filling me as much as his cock. In that primordial cry, I found consummate release. The razor's edge of my orgasm cut through me. Together, we burned in the pyre of our passion. From the remaining ashes, we are reborn.

Looking for temptation, for fantasy, for sensual adventures beyond your wildest dreams? You've come to the right place, baby. The Night Kitty—the club for every desire. It's always open . . . and the business here is endless pleasure . . .

DO I KNOW YOU?

Successful literary agent Jamal James is tired of by-the-numbers booty calls. He wants something he's never had before, something that goes deep like the no-holds-barred fantasies spun by his star erotica writer, Kat Mason. The sistah's sexy stories, published in every men's magazine, have made him rich . . . and whetted his appetite for more. Someday, he hopes to meet the mystery woman—his perfect chocolate fantasy—in person and act out every one of her sizzling tales in the flesh. For now, he'll have to content himself with some time at the Night Kitty . . .

Kat can't believe she's in this club dressed to the nines in body-hugging lingerie. She may be the hotest writer on the planet, but deep down, she's as shy and straight-laced as they come. Yeah, and she's also out of material. It's time for her to do some research—hands-on research—in a place where no one knows her, where she can be anybody indulging in a night of complete carnal pleasure. And she's just set her sights on Jamal, the one man to take her there . . .

Please turn the page for an exciting sneak peek of
Renee Luke's
Making Him Want It
coming next month from Aphrodisia!

Chapter One

Jamal James sank back into his leather office chair, smoothed both palms over his clean-shaven head, then laced his fingers behind his neck. Staring at the strategic placement of the photos spread across his desk, he tried to decide if he wanted to accept the model as a client.

While his primary focus was as a literary agent, a few years back he'd started taking on models to go along with the sexy stories his headliner wrote.

The models and other authors offered him chump change compared to what his super-star brought in. Kat Mason and her skilled way with words had him living in luxury. But it wasn't only the hefty contracts with five of the largest men's magazines in the world that made him value Kat as a client.

Her humble, almost innocent demeanor over their extensive email relationship had left him baffled. Part sexy talker. Part girl-next-door. While never having met in person, thanks to her plentitude of ready excuses, their author-agent bond had progressed to a point where he felt comfortable telling her about the hard-ons he'd get reading her work.

By the twentieth of each month, he found himself checking his email hourly, so rocked-up to read what she'd sent him. Forgetting the pictures of the man posing nude on his desk, he turned toward his computer, right clicking twice on his internet connection.

Damn!

His email was filled with nothing but unsolicited submissions. Nothing from Kat. Sliding a hand from behind his head, he moved to the aroused flesh held in check beneath his expensive trousers. He adjusted himself, making room for the expanded length, and released low and hungry groan. He'd long since imagined a body and face to go with Kat's submissions and emails, a fantasy that left him breathing hard and down right horny.

"You about ready, JJ?" Kent asked, strolling into Jamal's office. He glanced at his watch, his eyes widening when he caught sight of the sprawled male model photos gracing the surface of the mahogany desk.

Knowing where this was going, Jamal willed away his erection but the blood didn't vacate as quickly as it took residence. Following Kent's eyes, he saw when his colleague dipped his gaze from the desk to his lap, where Jamal's flagpole was standing.

Kent roared with laughter.

Great! *Just what I need.* Some loudmouth over-sexed player thinking a man's photos turns me on.

"You swinging that way now, JJ? No wonder you take on men when no one else in the office does, besides Rebecca." Kent laughed harder, his mouth opening wide enough that one of his gold fillings reflected the overhead light. "Do you eat Fruit Loops and keep lube in the shower?"

"Screw you, Kent."

"You wish."

Jamal tightened his fists. Sometimes the only way to shut up punks like Kent was to smash them in the mouth, giving him a reason for gold caps on his teeth. Kent was a pompous ass who wore three-thousand dollar designer suits daily and went to the barber three times a week to keep his fade lined up. Certainly not worth losing his temper over, despite being irritated.

Sliding his chair forward, concealing his lap beneath the shadow of the desk, Jamal swept the pictures into a stack and set them aside, ignoring Kent's continued laughter and barbs.

"Come on, JJ, you get hard looking at a guy? You sure you're a man?"

"More man than you," Jamal replied, keeping his tone light despite the growing anger.

Kent lifted his arms to the side and bucked his hips suggestively. "Yeah, I got women beggin' for *this*. A different woman every night if I want. Sometimes two."

Every man's fantasy.

Every man but him. He longed for a woman he'd never seen. Forbidden flesh—his client—Kat Mason. But her passionate words on the computer screen were about as tangible as smoke. *You can feel its effects on your body, but you can't hold it, sink into it, or relieve your aching flesh when you're gasping for breath*.

"When was the last time you fucked?"

Kent's question tugged Jamal from his thoughts. It'd been a while, but there was no way in hell he was admitting it. Not to this fool.

"I get it when I want it." Jamal shrugged his shoulders. Sure, pulling in hot women had never been a problem for him, thanks to the gene pool that had made him an image duplicate of his father, "Player of the Century," as far as Jamal was concerned. His father's apartment had been like a revolving door, more women going through than turnstiles at Grand Central Station.

He'd dipped into his fair share of chicks when he was younger, but sex for sex had grown boring and despite what others might think, predictable. He just wasn't into wham-bam don't-call-again nights. He'd matured out of it.

"Come on. This club has the finest female flesh you'll ever see." Kent blew air between his teeth. "I mean hot."

Not like this punk. Jamal snickered at Kent. Some leopards can't change their spots. Getting to his feet, he tossed the stack of pictures into the reject bin. The model didn't have the goods needed to make it in the sex industry, when looks and size were everything.

"Yeah. Let's get out of here. It's hours passed shut down time." Glancing once more at his computer screen, hoping to see a new incoming message from Kat, he rolled his shoulders to ease the mounting tension. Nothing. Hopefully by Monday, she'd give him exactly what he needed.

He flicked the switch, shutting it down for the weekend. Moving toward the door, he tossed his jacket over his forearm and turned off the overhead florescent lighting. Kent tagged along at his heels.

"What's the club called?"

"Night Kitty. You'll soon see why," Kent said, rubbing a hand over his chin. "You can get more pussy there than an alley cat."

"I'm just going for a couple of beers. I'm not into picking up strangers at bars." They walked down the dimly lit deserted hallways of the office building. This late on a Friday they'd be lucky to see a janitor still about.

"You sure you're not a little fluffy? What kind of man turns down getting some when it's offered?"

"I have women I *know* where I can make a booty-call. And, I'm man enough to snatch your girl if I wanted." All these comments about his manhood were grating his last nerve. So what if it'd been a good while since he'd had sex? That didn't mean anything.

So what if he relied on emails for pleasure? It didn't make him any less of a man because he had a fantasy woman who made him jerk off his own wad after he read her work.

"What'd you say this place is called, again?" he asked, tension coiling in his gut. They walked across the parking lot now, but not even the cooler night air offered relief to his irritation.

"Night Kitty."

They entered Jamal's SUV in silence.

"Good. Let's go." He slid his Escalade into drive, anxious to get there. Last month's issues of Kat's magazines wouldn't be enough for long.

A blank screen.

For a writer this spells disaster. The screen was bare, and all Kat Mason could do was sit there staring. Chomping down on the inside of her cheek, she gulped down a deep breath as she attempted to focus her mind on past projects. Not like anything else she'd done could save her butt now.

Feeling the rise of nervous tension, she twisted her fingers, wondering what others in her profession would think of her, leader of the pack, in this frantic position. To most people a blank screen may not seem like a big deal, open and ready for whatever comes to mind, but for her it was ruin.

Prostitutes don't get paid when they don't turn tricks, just like she didn't get compensated if she didn't put out stories.

With slumping shoulders, dread pressed upon her. The tiny cursor on the top of the page flashed like a big *loser* beacon. Clamping her lids shut, she fought off a surge of frustration. Deadline loomed and at this rate she'd have to email her agent and tell him she wasn't going to make it.

Taking a squeeze of baby lotion, she rubbed it into her tired hands. *What do I know about sex?* She thought back over her disastrous past relationships. There weren't many, but they'd all sucked. She was a wallflower and good men kept their distance.

"Three years, nine months, and almost two weeks, and I'm fresh out of material." She smirked at the irony. As a favor to her momma, who'd written headlines for a men's trash magazine, Kat had taken over when arthritis ended her momma's career. She wasn't sure how she pulled it off with her limited amount of sexual experience. But somehow she did.

Articles for the single erotica magazine had blossomed into many. Now she had an agent who pimped her pieces to the mass market. Before she knew what hit her, her persona was the hottest name in the genre, garnering national attention, top sales, and more than a thousand hits a day to her website.

Her most prominent column, *Glory's Stories*, was published in five different monthly magazines that released the hottest, sexiest stuff she could imagine. Masturbation, fornication, threesomes and orgies—yeah, she'd written about those and then some. But right now, on a Friday evening, the article due Monday morning, she had a blank page.

Not even word one.

Glancing around her upstairs bedroom, Kat saw all of the toys of the trade—things she'd gathered over the years—for what she called research. Reaching across the desk, she lifted a translucent pink dildo; its weight heavier than it appeared. *Batteries*. How could she write about a vibrating dildo if she'd never felt one in her hand? She stroked down the smooth length of the plastic cock.

Bringing the shiny head to her mouth, she glided it along her lower lip, using her tongue to smooth it. It tasted faintly like her pussy, held the subtle hint of sex and caused a moistening in her cotton panties. Feeling heat lick across her skin, she tossed the dildo to the bed.

This wasn't time for self-gratification. She'd tried that too many times, written about it nearly as often. "Good brothas aren't easy to come by," Kat mumbled to herself, to justify her need for the synthetic flesh, rather than enjoying the feel of a real man. "Or *cum* by." She laughed at the oh-so-sorry truth. "Call me desperate."

With her eyes closed, she slanted her face toward the ceiling, silently willing some wondrous idea to strike her. She needed something—a spark to make her next story fresh and exciting. To make it something she'd never attempted before.

She needed brilliance that would make her agent, Jamal, eager to pursue the money she sought for hours of writing, not to mention the added bonus of knowing about the erection he got when he read her work. She only wished she had a face to match to the hours of email conversations they'd shared. Knowing what his eyes looked like when he got aroused would have been the icing on the cake.

Spinning her office chair, Kat's gaze landed on her stuffed and overflowing extra closet. Repressing the turn of her lips into a smile, she studied all she'd acquired. She had it all—none used, but all there—for when she needed to describe an outfit or get into the mood of a character. There were whips and handcuffs, some fur-lined, some cold-hard steel. Black leather boots that reached mid thigh and tipped with four–inch silver spikes as heels.

She had sexy lingerie, lacy blacks with g-string panties. Red one-piece suits open to the nipples and crotchless. She even had a few baby-doll type sets, complete with pink lace, rose-shaped ribbons and petite satin bows. None seemed to offer the inspiration she desperately required. She needed something new. Different. *Thrilling*.

Flipping the button on her computer, she sent it into sleep mode and hit the switch of the light. Kat stalked to the mirror and studied her lackluster outfit. Her usual writing garb: sweatpants, T-shirt, floppy-eared bunny slippers. Her black perm-straightened hair was secured into a loose ponytail, in need of a root touch-up.

Pressing her full lips together, she thought of adding a touch of gloss, but feeling drab, decided what she needed was a splash of color to match the caramel tone of her skin. Glancing back at her computer, Kat released a pent up breath and decided to escape her self-imposed dungeon. She needed time away from work, to freshen up and go out. Out anywhere, where there'd be people to watch and where she'd be able to draw new material.

A crushing blow of realization hit Kat square in the chest, knocking the breath from her. *She knew what she needed to do. Not just go out and watch but to participate in a night of spontaneous carnal pleasure.*

Gasping for air and keeping her wobbly knees from collapsing, she stripped out of her clothes and stepped into the shower. Then, she lathered the shea butter Olay bar across her skin.

Fear momentarily tightened her gut. In thirty-one years she'd never experienced a one-night stand, but that's exactly what she was planning. Her roommate in college had gone from one to the next like Kleenex, but she'd had youth and alcohol to attribute such behavior. Kat could only blame being horny and behind deadline.

"I have nothin' to lose, and plenty to gain." With the decision made, arousal poured through her blood like a shot of whiskey. The overhead spray of tepid water tightened her dusky colored nipples into beads, the wash of moisture like a damp mouth, hungry with need.

Stepping from the shower a while later, clean and more excited than she'd been in a while, Kat went to the closet to select the right costume to go out on the prowl. She settled on a combination of several styles, spiked high leather boots, a suede black mini, and a black lacy bra, only slightly hidden beneath a sheer rosy shirt.

A satisfying combo of sweet and sexy.

She applied a covering of make-up, including deep red lipstick and touched the hot tip of a curling iron to areas affected by the moisture of the shower. She skipped securing her hair back, allowing the dark locks to hang loose around her face. She thought it erotic to have her hair grabbed during sex.

Sex and ideas was what she was after.

Grabbing her purse and heading out the door, Kat decided to take a cab to the closest meat market since in all likelihood, she'd need a couple of drinks to follow through with what she'd planned.

Chapter Two

Twenty minutes too soon, the cab pulled up in front of the bar. Kat sat in the dim sanctuary of the car's interior, her forehead pressed against the cool glass, her cheeks on fire. It'd been easy to choose a super-thigh-high skirt and a bra-exposing shirt when she'd been in her bedroom, but now, presented with mingling with the public, she wanted to run.

"You getting out?" the cabbie asked.

Kat didn't answer, afraid she'd order him to turn around and retrace their path. But back at home she'd be faced with the same problem, an article due and no material to write it. Drawing a deep breath, she fished inside her tiny purse, then shoved a twenty toward the driver. Getting into character, she slid from the car and steadied herself upon four-inch spiky heels on the sidewalk.

Above her, the pink neon sign read The Night Kitty, though in reality all men knew that kitty meant pussy and pussy meant sex. *Come here*, the sign called, and you'll be assured pleasure. Kat squared her shoulders, lifted her chin, and sashayed to the door mustering false confidence. She slipped into the dark smoky interior.

The scent of cigarettes, alcohol, sweat, and endorphins all tuned and primed for fucking crashed around her like a sensual wave. Bass throbbed a heavy beat that blared from the surrounding speakers. A nervous slither crept down Kat's spine as she kept herself from finding the nearest exit. She hadn't been to a place like this since her early years of college, but even then she'd had girlfriends to accompany her.

She was alone now, playing a role. Creating a façade. She stepped forward, determined to see her plan unfold.

Fine-ass men littered the room. A most beautiful specimen of male flesh stood alone across the dance floor from her. Yummy enough to be a cover model. LL Cool J fine. Sex appeal of Wesley Snipes. She'd be happy with a piece of him.

Turning away, the crush of bodies hindered her slow advance to the bar.

"Give me a shot," Kat said to a young man standing behind the counter who looked too young to drink, let alone serve the stuff.

"A shot of what?" he asked.

"It doesn't matter. Just get me tipsy and fast."

"Not a prob," he replied, reaching beneath the smooth surface of the bar and withdrawing a shot glass, which he then filled with a blue liquid, fuller than the standard two fingers. "Enjoy." He slid the glass in her direction.

"What is it?" *Please be strong!*

"Does it matter?" he asked, a lopsided grin spreading over his lips.

"Nope." She grabbed the glass and downed the contents in one smooth motion, not even gasping as the fiery liquid slid down her throat.

"Can I get you anything else?"

"Yeah, another," she replied, lifting her empty glass.

It was quickly refilled.

"Thanks." She downed the second serving, left the empty glass on the bar along with another twenty, and walked toward the flashing lights and couples crowded on the dance floor. Stud though he may be, the bartender was on duty and with the blue fluid already making her feel more at ease, she needed material now.

Kat inched her way around the room, watching the couples bumping and grinding on the floor, a planned seduction—foreplay—in view of everyone. Good stuff she filed away in her memory for future articles.

With groping hands, men held women to their groins, hiding the swell that undoubtedly pulsated there. With bodies rubbing, palms were tightly held to feminine hips. In the center of the dance floor the couples took it one step further, backs arched, the women allowed the men access to their necks and breasts, the steady rhythm of their dancing a mimic to fucking.

"What was in that drink?" she mumbled, suddenly aware of how her black thong rubbed against her clit as she walked. She shifted her hips, completing the tantalizing contact. Her pussy became damp, moisture pooled at her crotch and she could feel the telltale evidence of her arousal slick on her inner thighs.

Glancing back at the bar, Kat had to wonder if something had been slipped into her drink. Booze alone had never made her this horny. But she'd watched the entire time as the drink was poured into the glass right before she'd emptied it. Nothing had been added.

The blue liquid she'd swallowed quickly shed the last of her inhibitions. It was unlike anything she'd ever tasted, a heady combination mixed with her resolve to get laid that made her almost desperate for the right man to come along.

Her made-up persona offered her a newly found freedom. She shrugged off the euphoria of her sexual charge and she focused on her mission. It was made easier by the slight alcohol induced lulling of her fear.

She studied the dimly lit room, searching for a man not already coupled. For the hunk she'd seen at the beginning of the Too Short song.

"You here alone?" a husky voice asked her from behind.

Warmth spread across Kat's skin as the height and breadth of his body closed in behind her, more solid than the wall had been.

She need not bother turn around, for she'd watched the advance of the man as he'd made his way from across the room, working the border as if he could remain unnoticed. Like hell—every available female in the joint had to be primed for a piece of ass from this guy.

How'd I get so lucky? She'd wanted him from the moment she'd seen him.

Through the pump of music their words were barely audible. "Not anymore," she answered, hoping he didn't hear the tiny hitch on her voice as she struggled to keep the real Kat hidden.

He stood a good six inches taller than her, his masculine presence as heady as the drink she'd consumed. Taking a deep breath, she leaned her back toward him and was surprised to feel an impressive length of aroused cock nudge against the small of her back. She shifted her hips against the erection eliciting a grumble from the man behind her, though most definitely not a complaint.

"What's your name?"

Biting her bottom lip, Kat thought about her reply. This wasn't her. *She* was a wallflower. A self-made recluse who made a habit of avoiding the public. This was a woman she'd created, and as ballsy as she was feeling, delving into real names meant revealing a part of her she didn't want to face tomorrow. "I don't want you to call me in the morning."

For a moment only the incredible hum of drums could be heard above the steady breathing of the man. His warm breath on the back of her neck sent her nipples aching. He knew what she wanted. They both wanted the same thing. *Was he going to walk away*? Did the fact she'd turned the table on men's usual tactics make him think twice before taking their experimental material forward?

In answer to her silent questions, one of his large palms snaked across her lower stomach. With a slight tug, he brought her back flush against his chest, his seeking fingers caressing the hem of her suede ultra-miniskirt.

"Do you want to dance?" he whispered in her ear.

"No." Breathing was now difficult. The dance floor, though a good place for foreplay, was not nearly private enough for what Kat had in mind.

"What do you want then?"

"I want your cock inside of me, now."

Jamal felt like laughing. He didn't go to bars to pick up on women, but here he was now, with this little hottie tucked against his chest telling him she wanted a good bang. He'd seen her the moment she'd entered the bar, a Fly-Girl with a J-Lo booty.

He smoothed his fingers along the hem of her skirt, barely touching the silken brown skin covering thick, juicy thighs. Her legs jetted a mile to the floor. Her calves and feet were encased in tall, black leather boots, tipped with heels high enough to make any man with testosterone beg for mercy.

Dressed as she was, she could have stepped off the set of any Puff Daddy video, though none of those models were as luscious as this babe. The details of her face were obscured by the low lighting and haze of smoke enshrouding the place, but he could tell enough to know her beauty matched her exquisite body.

Jamal moved his hand lower, until he felt her tremble before him, her knees becoming jelly as he eased her legs apart with a subtle hint of pressure between her thighs. The honey whimpered slightly, lolling her head back against his chest, allowing him the pleasure of her fragrance.

She smelled sweetly exotic. Definitely enticing. It wasn't a scent procured in any store or produced by any brand name perfume. Her lingering aroma was purely her own, feminine and inviting.

Glancing around the packed dance floor, Jamal's gaze came to rest upon Kent as he gyrated his hips against some skinny broad in the center of the room. Outkast was pumping through the speakers now.

Jamal dipped his hand beneath the material of the woman's

skirt, his fingers encouraged further with each of her breathy moans. Easing aside the narrow strip of cloth covering her treasure, he parted her lips and dipped two knuckles deep into her oh-so-tight pussy.

Womanizing Kent, who had poked fun of his manhood, hadn't managed to score the way he had, still bothered by being caught with a hard-on earlier. But it wasn't merely the drive to prove himself a studly man that spurred the slow rhythm of his fingers as he moved in and out of the woman in his arms.

There was something about her that had drawn him from across the room. Maybe it was the wide-eyed stare she'd had when she'd first entered the bar, or the I'd-like-to-eat-you-for-dessert look she'd tossed him during that brief moment when she'd glanced his way. A siren call for sure, he'd been helpless against it.

In the dark room no one noticed how he pressed his fingers into her wet, accepting flesh. Using his thumb, Jamal found the bead of her clit and rubbed against it. The hottie went limp in his arms, sagging against him. He wrapped his other arm around her, holding her curvy body against his, and took the weight of a firm breast into his palm, tweaking the hard crest with his fingers.

"You want it now, huh?" he whispered, bending his head so he could nibble upon the tender skin just below her ear. She shuddered, then slanted her head for him to further explore her skin with his tongue. Nuzzling his face into her straightened locks of hair, he slowed the in and out of his fingers to long sensual movements.

His effort at seduction was rewarded.

"Please . . . please . . . please . . ." Her begging chant was driving him crazy. A little more of this and he'd cum in his pants. Jamal shook his head, finding his behavior hard to believe. Foolish. He'd never done this before, but something about her had him press on.

"In the club?" He moved his thumb to her clit and circled twice. "Reach behind you and undo my pants."

Kat couldn't have stopped her hands if she tried. They moved behind her, like steel to a magnet, finding the large bulge straining his pants. She cupped him in her palms, the damn fabric preventing her from feeling what she wanted so badly to touch.

She flicked her fingernail against the rough teeth of his zipper, the jagged edge abrasive against her skin. In the momentary sting of pain, reason penetrated Kat's lust miasma, his suggestion ringing loud and clear in her ears. Her blood roared through her veins.

She wanted sex and pretty badly, but she'd never been one for public displays of affection. She certainly wasn't brash enough to actually have sex while everyone there could watch, had they the mind to.

She stalled her hands progress, though not an easy feat. Where was the shy girl, she wondered briefly, taking on her new role so completely?

"Perhaps we ought to take this to . . ." Her voice trailed off. To where? She hadn't thought her plan through. Once decided, she'd rushed to the bar afraid if given too much thought she'd change her mind. Now she realized the error, too late, and too horny. She should've secured a hotel room nearby to ensure once she'd lured a man to her lair, she could enjoy him thoroughly. Her mind searched for answers. His car? The bathroom? The back alley?

The back alley. Surely there would be some boxes or something to offer a bit of privacy from the street front. Besides the thought of a cold brick wall against her back and the heat of his body before her sounded like an exciting turn-on.

"Come with me," she demanded, wiggling his hand free from her sex, moisture following his slow withdraw, knowing too, that given too much time to think she'd dart for the door. Alone. Shifting her hips to lower the skirt back into place, she grabbed his hand, slick with her juices, and pulled him after her.

He willingly fell into step beside her.

The bartender gave a knowing smile as she darted passed, a man in tow, then shifted his head to the door that read EXIT like he knew exactly what she'd been looking for. Kat tried to ignore the burning heat on her cheeks as she used the door.

Once shut from the thumping of the speakers, a bass vibration worked its way through the walls and filtered into her.

Mr. Gorgeous moved his hands to her back, turning her toward the wall, and urging her forward. But she stepped from his grasp. This was her game and she meant to play it as *she* chose. She set the rules. The pace.

"Not so fast, Bad Boy," she said, hitching her hip to the side and acting like she'd often written her heroines. Trying not to be Kat but the character she'd created, she smoothed her palm up his abdomen feeling each rippling contour beneath the silk of his buttoned-down shirt. He sucked a breath between his teeth that further incited her desire.

Staring at the man's handsome face, purely masculine but definitely beautiful, she saw dark eyes the color of midnight. They gleamed like a queen-size bed draped in black satin sheets, beneath a pair of thick, but well trimmed, brows. His dark brown skin reflected against the distant streetlight, showing how recently he'd shaved his head.

"Back up," she urged, using a slight push on his chest.

He complied.

"Put your hands above your head." She smoothed her hands up each of his arms, pulling his muscular biceps with her until she had his arms pushed up. His elbows bent, he intertwined his fingers behind his head, groaning as she shimmied up his body.

She leaned in close, inhaling the lingering scent of the club and the freshness of Ivory, splashed with the subtle hint of cologne. Needing to stand on tiptoes despite the extra four inches of her heels, she placed her elbows on his shoulder and framed his face with her forearms. She stroked her curious hands over his sleek head, enjoying his smooth and warm skin beneath her fingertips.

"I like your head," she commented when he pressed his full lips to the curve of her outstretched neck.

"Oh yeah? Which one?"

She laughed. This guy was in a hurry and that suited her just fine. No time to chicken out. She eased away from him, allowing her hands to slide effortlessly down his well-defined chest. Her fingers came to rest on the buckle of the black leather belt holding his slacks in place. Releasing the spike from the hole, she then found the single button at the top of his fly. Bulging and straining beneath the fine twill of his pants, she could feel his erection, solid and pulsing, eager for lack of restraint.

A smooth swish of jagged zipper teeth and he was left confined only by a pair of thin cotton boxers with an easy elastic waist. Kat touched his flat stomach and felt him quiver, heard him suck in a breath. Her nails scraped over his skin, swirling through the silken dark pubic hairs that plunged from his belly button to the base of his cock.

"So which head do I like? Well, I don't know yet do I? I haven't felt them both." Finding previously untapped courage, she slid her fingers beneath the band of elastic and bent her knees, drawing down his boxers as she crouched before him. The spikes on her heels clicked against the cement.

There, in the fake shades of neon signs and the soft glow of the distance streets overhead lighting, his dark cock sprung free. Bubbling excitement swept through Kat's body as she slid her hand down the rigid shaft, measuring all ten rock-hard inches.

"Impressive," she mumbled, because there was nothing else she could say when a dick as glorious and large as his was inches from her face and making her pussy hungry. Damn, she couldn't wait for him to ease open her lips and fuck her brains out.

"You know what they say," he replied, his voice sounding a little strained.

She laughed. Yeah, she knew black men had big cocks, but while the limited amount she'd known in the past had been well-enough endowed to please her, none had been hung like his before. "No. What do they say?"

"That it's not the size of the boat but the motion of the ocean."

She laughed again. He's funny *and* fine. Yummy! His answer was not what she'd been expecting. Winding her fingers around him, she wasn't surprised they didn't meet. Hell no, he was too damn thick for that. Famous for writing about it, she knew just what to do. Twisting in a languid pace, she slid her hand to his base, feeling the size of his balls brush against the heel of her hand. *Oh, yeah, those will feel great slapping against me.*

"Really? Is that what they say?" She didn't wait for an answer. She licked the satin tip of his plum–shaped head, tasting the ball of moisture that had formed there. His natural lubricant. She didn't need it. She was wet.